SIGNALS

SIGNALS

THIRTY STORIES
SELECTED AND EDITED BY

Alan Ross

CONSTABLE · LONDON

First published in Great Britain 1991
by Constable & Company Limited
3 The Lanchesters, 162 Fulham Palace Road
London W6 9ER

The right of the above to be
identified as the authors of their work
has been asserted by them in accordance
with the Copyright, Designs and Patents Act 1988
ISBN 0 09 470970 X
Set in Monophoto 11pt Baskerville by
Servis Filmsetting Limited, Manchester
Printed in Great Britain by
St Edmundsbury Press Limited
Bury St Edmunds, Suffolk

A CIP catalogue record for this book
is available from the British Library

CONTENTS

INTRODUCTION

All the stories in this volume would have appeared in *London Magazine* during the next two or three years. That they are appearing in this form is due to our reluctance to ask writers to wait that long. In an average year we print between fifteen and twenty stories; on average we receive about thirty stories a week, one thousand five hundred a year. There is virtually nowhere else for them to go. Out of these we accept, perhaps, thirty. Few though it is, an unmanageable backlog is soon built up.

In 1966 *London Magazine* published the first of several special short-story issues. In addition to stories by Nadine Gordimer, R. Prawer Jhabvala and Julia O'Faolain, among others, we invited such masters of the art as V.S. Pritchett, William Sansom and Francis King to say something about the situation of the writer of short stories. Pritchett, who began by remarking that the short story is 'one of the inextinguishable lost causes', went on to observe, "The fact is that the short story is above all the memorable form of writing. Readers forget novels; stories stay in their minds. And it is not because there is less to remember; the short story is perfectly fitted to the glancing, allusive, nervously decisive and summary moods of contemporary life.'

'The process', Sansom wrote, 'is nearer to the poem than the novel. The story story', he went on, 'should echo. It should spread beyond its economy: short, it should be enormous. Conceived at some inspirational heat, it must be made to billow out and furl in like a flag, giving a moving impression that is larger than it is.'

Francis King, like the other two, said he wrote stories for pleasure, the material rewards being as meagre as the opportunities. Yet the bringing off of a good story results in what Æ described as 'exquisite soliloquy between yourself and heaven'.

The short-story writer has to play for the highest stakes. 'One slip,' Francis King commented, 'pardonable in the novel, and the story or poem is ruined.' Both, far more than the novel, seem to await on some capricious impulse from without — on what Katherine Mansfield described as 'the strange silence that falls upon your heart — the same silence that comes one minute before the curtain rises'.

The stories collected in this volume come from all over the world and their authors are of all ages. Some of the writers have published novels, others doubtless will do so, if only to help to get their stories taken. But in almost every case, the short story will be closest to their heart. It is a pity that in every generation, in whatever country, so few can make a living out of what they do best.

ALAN ROSS

Hanan Al-Shaykh

THE FUN FAIR

My fiancé Farid insisted that I should go with him and his family to visit his grandmother's grave on the eve of the feast. I'd always thought this custom was for old or lonely people who felt comfortable sitting with their dead relatives. They say there's nothing like visiting a cemetery for curing depression. I hadn't been aware of my own parents visiting family graves on special days, although once when I was little I prayed fervently that somebody I didn't know in the family would die so that I could go inside one of the buildings people put up around their graves. I'd gone with our cook to her house overlooking the cemetery — an occasion which seems to have remained imprinted on my mind — and from then on I'd pictured the dead people living in those burial chambers, like us in our houses, only different, perhaps like Pharaohs. I thought they probably moved about without making any sound, or stayed in bed all the time.

In those days the tombs seemed strange to me, with their engraved cupolas the colour of sand. They stood among a few faded trees and mounds of sandy earth which were perfect for rolling down. The cats and dogs whose voices I could hear I was sure were the guardians of these tombs.

We called in at Farid's parents' house. As I made to reply to his father's greeting his mother appeared from nowhere and asked me disapprovingly why I wasn't wearing the diamond ear-rings.

'Diamonds for the cemetery?' I asked.

'Why not?' she nodded. 'Everyone's going to be there, I know, and they'll say, why did he only give her a ring when they were engaged?'

Then she vanished and returned with a brooch of precious stones and came towards me to pin it on my dress. I took a step backwards, insisting as diplomatically as I could that I didn't like brooches. Turning again towards her room she replied impatiently, 'All right.

Wear my marcasite ear-rings. But everybody will recognize them.'

I looked beseechingly at Farid and he said to her, 'I don't want her to wear any jewellery.'

Only then did she notice the bunch of white roses I was holding. She took them from me, smelling them and calling on the Prophet in her delight, then rushed to put them in a vase with some other flowers. The price of them had made me hesitate, but they'd looked to me as if they were just waiting for someone to appreciate their fragrant beauty. I justified buying them on the grounds that they weren't for me, and that anyway from now on there was no need for me to feel a pang of conscience every time I bought something expensive since I was going to marry a wealthy man. Farid told his mother that the flowers were for the grave. 'What a shame. They're lovely,' she replied, continuing to arrange them in the vase.

Farid signalled to me, and I understood that I shouldn't pursue the subject of the flowers. I looked about me in an attempt to escape from my embarrassment at her behaviour and pretended to be interested in the content of the baskets by the door: pastries for the feast day, bread in unusual shapes and old clothes and shoes.

I sat next to my fiancé in the front of the car, with his mother and father and adolescent sister in the back. The eve of the feast was like the feast itself, the crowded streets throbbing with noise and excitement and everywhere the sound of fireworks exploding. I remembered how as children we would wander the streets all day at this time of year and ride the fairground swings, rushing to empty the peach-coloured sand from our socks and shoes as soon as we reached home. Every year when the feast came round, it felt as if we were celebrating it for the first time. My mother would prepare the tray of kunafa and we would take it to the communal oven. Although we stood there for ages, our eyes fixed on the baker so that he would remember our tray, he always took it out late and the pastries would be rock-hard. All the same we ate them with noisy relish. I remembered the handbag I had especially for the feast, the socks I wore even at the height of summer, the shiny shoes, the hair ribbons. We used to visit all our relatives, including those who lived at a distance and were hardly related to us at all. We would knock on their doors and wish them well, not meaning what we said. We knew the uncle who said he had no change on him was lying and would sit for ages on his doorstep before we rushed off to the swings and the pickle-sellers, discussing the rumour that the feast was going to last a day or two longer this year for the children's benefit.

People spent the whole of this feast-day eve in the cemetery. The children wore their brightest clothes. Amplified voices recited the

Quran, and at the same time popular songs blared out from radios and cassette recorders. There were women selling dates and palm leaves. One was smoking and the others shared a joke, their tattooed chins quivering with laughter. Fool beans and falafel, fruit juice and pickles of many varieties and colours were all on sale at the entrance to the cemetery. I thought I would have a display of pickles in jars like that in my own house.

Farid's mother stopped at the first vendor she came to, a woman without a tooth in her head, and chose a large quantity of oranges, tangerines and palm leaves. She haggled with her for some time, then gave her a sum of money and walked off. 'Lady! Lady!' the woman called after her. When she tried to ease herself up off the ground, I begged Farid to pay her what she was asking: 'Poor thing, it's a shame on a day like this.'

We hurried to catch up with Farid's mother, elegant in spite of her plumpness, springing over the mud and earth and gravel like a gazelle. She carried her purchases, leaving the baskets to Farid, his father and sister, who looked increasingly morose. I found myself walking along beside her. She glanced at her watch and asked if I thought the sun would come out later, then lowering her voice she explained, 'I want to go to the club. Have a swim and lie in the sun.'

I smiled at her. The noise was deafening. There was the clatter of saucepans and the roar of Primus stoves where the women had spread themselves out to cook in the narrow alleyways and the open spaces between the tombs. The shrieks of children mingled with the voices of the Quran reciters who moved from grave to grave and in and out of the tombs. In vain they tried to raise their voices and their audience – families wanting private recitations for their dead – had to give them all their attention to catch what they were saying. Most of the working reciters were elderly, despite the fact that there were young ones about, leaning against tombstones looking bored. I watched Farid's mother darting from one to another, and all of them promising to find their way to her sooner or later, with the help of the cemetery caretaker. When one of the younger ones approached her offering his services, she pretended not to notice him. Angrily Farid asked her why she had snubbed him and she answered, 'Old men have more merit in the eyes of the Lord.'

Perhaps she meant because the young faces didn't bear the marks of grief and suffering as the old ones did.

We went into a courtyard with a little garden round it where there were graves with pink and white ornamental headstones. Farid said they belonged to his father's grandfather and the grandfather's two brothers who had asked to be buried in this garden, which looked green and moist as if someone had recently watered it. Then we crossed the courtyard into the main family tomb and found it crammed with members of the family, a Quran reciter and dishes of dates and cucumbers and tangerines. The grave itself was festooned with palm leaves. 'Why are we sitting in here, right next to the grave?' I wondered.

I saw disappointment, then anger on the face of my fiancé's mother, which she was unable to conceal. 'You must have spent the night here,' was her first comment to the assembled company. Nobody answered her, but to my amazement they stood up and greeted us, disregarding the recitation of the Quran: Farid's three paternal aunts, his grandfather, the husbands of two of the aunts and their children. They made room for us on wooden chairs, disfigured by time and neglect, and we all sat down except for Farid's mother who began spreading more palm leaves over the grave until it had almost vanished from sight. Then she took out pastries, bread, dates, cucumbers, tangerines and glasses for tea. She put some pastries and dates in a bag and went up to the Quran reciter, thrusting the bag into his hands. He stopped in the middle of his recitation to mumble his thanks and handed the bag to a boy who was sitting at his feet counting out notes and coins before putting them in his pocket.

Farid's mother asked him all of a sudden how much he took from each family. 'Depends how much time they want,' the boy answered slyly.

'How much?' she insisted. 'Last year, for example?'

'Last year was last year,' he replied. Then, peering into the bag, he named an amount which made Farid's mother gasp. 'That's the same as a check-up at the doctor's,' she remarked. I met my fiancé's eyes and we almost laughed aloud.

There was uproar outside, then the caretaker appeared, accompanied by a sheikh. When they heard the recitation in progress, the sheikh tried to retreat, but Farid's mother grabbed his hand and pulled him in. In spite of the family's obvious disapproval she led him over to where her daughter was sitting, while he murmured, 'I mustn't poach from someone else.'

Impatiently she answered him, 'Just relax. He'll get his share and you'll get yours.'

The sheikh obeyed and sat listening to his colleague, nodding his head with feeling, while the aunts' faces registered annoyance, one of them sighed and another turned her face away. Farid's mother declared, 'It's not a feast every day, and we want to be sure our dead go to heaven.'

Then she approached the caretaker, wishing him well, and counted out some money into his hand, enunciating the amount in an audible voice. 'I hope this place isn't opened up again as soon as our backs are turned?' she enquired sharply.

'What do I carry a weapon for?' countered the caretaker.

'No. You know what I mean,' she said. 'We heard that the previous caretaker used to let our tomb as if it was a hotel.'

'That's why he's the previous caretaker. You know I don't even let kids come through here.'

I thought that relief was at hand when from outside the smell of kebab and meatballs wafted in, making my nostrils twitch. The blind reciter rose to his feet and was led away by the boy, while the newcomer began chanting prayers. I looked around the room, at the faces, especially the aunts'. They shifted their gaze from me to Farid's mother, to his sister and back again. When our eyes met we exchanged smiles, as if they knew what I was thinking and agreed: 'It doesn't matter that Farid's mother's difficult, and I don't have any sort of a relationship with her. Farid's family all love him, even though he does exactly what she says.'

The reciter paused to clear his throat and immediately one of the aunts turned to me and said she hadn't expected me to be so pretty in spite of the descriptions she'd heard, and only an illness had kept her away from my engagement party. Another asked if we'd found a flat and what area we were thinking of. I answered these questions in all innocence at first, but from their expressions and the way Farid kept trying to catch my eye, I felt that I must be on sensitive ground as far as his mother was concerned. Sure enough, she interrupted and said there was no urgency about renting a place, her house had big rooms and was Farid's as much as it was hers.

When I replied to the aunts that we were planning a simple wedding, just the family, Farid's mother announced, as if she hadn't heard a word I'd said, that we'd be holding it in one of the big hotels. When I told them that my wedding dress was second-hand, and had been worn first in the Twenties, she was quite unable to hide her alarm. It was then I realized a state of war existed between Farid's mother and the aunts and regretted ever opening my mouth. From their loaded questions and the way they looked at one another after each of my replies, I could tell that they were using me to attack her in her most vulnerable spot. She protested, almost in a scream, 'God forbid! You're wearing a dress that someone else has worn, to your wedding? That's out of the question!'

'Is it white?' enquired one of the aunts, provoking Farid's mother to still greater anguish.

'White, black, what's the difference?' she shouted. 'It's out of the question. Marisa has to make it. I promised her. She'll be upset.'

'Upset!' remarked one of them laughing. 'She's got more work than she can handle. She'll be delighted.'

'I know you're jealous because Marisa is going to make it,' screamed back Farid's mother.

For a moment I forgot where I was. The walls were grey and the visitors' chairs blocked out the tombstone and the palm leaves. We could have been in somebody's sitting-room. Farid's father and the third aunt's husband interrupted the argument, coming to stand behind their wives' chairs. 'The clothes. Aren't you going to give them to the caretaker?' asked Farid's father, changing the subject.

His wife sighed, annoyed with herself. 'I forgot all about them,' she replied. 'Let's hope death forgets me!' Then she whispered something in his ear. When he didn't make any comment, she said, 'Who'd like some tea?' She went over into a corner where there was a Primus stove I hadn't noticed before. As she pumped it, she asked, 'What do you think about building on to the tomb? Another room, a little kitchen, a bathroom?'

Nobody answered. They were all absorbed in their own private conversations. She repeated, 'We need to extend the tomb. Farid's father agrees. What do you say?'

'Extend it!' scoffed one of the aunts. 'To hear you talking anyone would think a tomb was just like a flat or a house!'

'What I meant,' Farid's mother corrected herself, 'is that we should buy an old abandoned tomb.'

Another aunt seized on her words: 'And have our dead mixed up with other people's? That's madness!'

'I mean we should buy a plot of ground, even if it's a little way off.'

The voices rose and fell. Farid's cousins and sister whispered scornfully to each other. Farid brought me a glass of tea. Meanwhile, his mother continued to ask querulously, at intervals, 'What do you say?'

'What do we say?' answered one of the aunts at last. 'Nobody's in a position to lay out money on tombs and suchlike, that's what we say.'

Farid's mother drew a triumphant breath: 'Farid's got a marvellous job, thank God, and ...'

I looked with embarrassment at Farid, who was shaking his head like someone who wanted help. He said sheepishly, 'Why do you need to mention that?'

His mother must have felt from this response that he was siding with his aunts against her, but she went on, 'I mean God's made you rich enough to pay for the new tomb.'

She seemed to gain strength from his silence, and had the look of a cat when the mouse is finally cornered. But the spiteful looks of the other women snatched victory from her grasp. 'We know your stories,' they seemed to say. 'You want to tell your friends that you've got a big new tomb. A villa! A three-storey villa with marble stairs and wrought-iron gates!'

'Have you ever heard of anyone visiting the family tomb and sitting almost on top of the graves?' shouted Farid's mother. 'We must have a separate room to sit in.'

'We used to be able to use the one you gave the caretaker,' interrupted one of the aunts.

'At least there's only him and his wife,' persisted Farid's mother. 'Surely that's better than having a family taking it over, with children clambering over our tombstones like apes, and then not being able to get rid of them?'

'And what's wrong with being buried in the garden?' continued the aunt in a superior tone. 'You don't have to be inside the room.'

'Your father's grandfather liked the idea of being buried in the garden – that's his business,' yelled Farid's mother. 'I and my family want to be buried inside.'

In a whisper, as if divulging a secret, Farid's father said, 'Listen to me. Land prices are going to soar. People are going to start living in these buildings on a regular basis. And anyway what's wrong with our family having the very best?'

'I know,' answered his sister. 'But is it reasonable to expect you to pay while we stand with our arms folded? You know, the children are at university and there are the monthly payments to keep up with and all our other commitments ...'

'I'm ready to fall in with anything,' said her husband.

His intervention seemed to irritate Farid's mother and she snapped back at him, 'In any case, your wife won't be buried here. She'll go with your family.'

His wife ignored her and said, 'Look. Just look around. This tomb's big. You couldn't call this a small area.'

But Farid's mother came back at her with a reply which unnerved me like a physical 'blow. All along I hadn't believed that the family's scheming and arguing over the peaceful grave in its midst could be serious. I told myself it must be a family joke, and anyway it had nothing to do with me, even Farid's helping to pay.

Standing in the middle of the room, Farid's mother declared, 'No. It's not as big as you imagine. There's me, there's my husband, and now Farid's about to become two, and then there'll be his children.'

Her words frightened me. Death wasn't as distant as it had been. I didn't think of it, like a child, as something that wouldn't happen to me. Trying to make a joke, I said, 'Should we be planning for our afterlife when we're not yet married?'

'We're saying prices are going to soar,' intervened Farid's father, seizing on the same pretext as before.

I knew that all eyes were on me, especially the aunts', begging me to save them from Farid's mother's claws. But I lacked the strength even to save myself and abandoned myself to the terrifying thought that one day I'd be here in this room underneath a tombstone like that, with one for Farid and each of my children. We'd all end up here and our children's children would sit like us now, sipping tea, arguing, eating dates.

The raised voices of the men, joining in with the women now, brought me back to the present. Farid came to my rescue, taking my hand in his soothingly, and I mumbled, 'It's crazy to think about it now.'

I don't know how Farid's mother heard what I said; I hardly heard it myself, but she remarked smugly, 'Our lives are in God's hands.'

This angered me and, unconscious of what I was saying, like a child who wanted to contradict for the sake of contradicting, I replied, 'I don't want to be buried here.'

'You don't have any choice,' she said. 'When you become part of the family, that's what you have to do. Even your own family wouldn't agree to bury you with them.'

I felt as though she was already shovelling earth down on top of me. 'No!' I screamed. 'No!' I jumped up and rushed to the door. Farid's mother paid no attention even when Farid took hold of me and said reprovingly to her, 'Are you happy now?'

'She has to understand, my dear,' she said to him, 'that whoever lives with us must die with us.'

I broke free and ran. He came after me. Outside in the cemetery's main square I caught my breath and leant against a tombstone while I fastened my sandal. Children were playing with a ball there, disregarding the comments of their mothers and the older women who sat resting from the labours of their cooking. 'The dead must be trembling with anxiety down there,' remarked one.

I composed myself at last, perhaps at this spectacle of everyday life, or the glimpse of a bird abandoning itself to space, beautiful and oblivious to what was happening below. We stopped beside the car. I knew we would have to wait for his family. I felt I wanted to be free of his hand holding tightly on to mine. I turned my face away, contemplating the washing spread out to dry, the empty bowl resting against one grave, the cooking pot sitting on another, as if it was a table, and the owners of these objects going about their business   victims of the housing crisis, who had squatted in abandoned tombs, rented at the going rate, or simply occupied family tombs prematurely, and adapted them to suit their lives. I saw television and radio aerials in place; and yet Farid's mother wanted a bigger space to house her graves.

When I saw Farid's mother, father and sister appearing in the distance, I felt the breath being knocked out of me. So we were one family, living together, dying together?

Farid's father must have told his wife to keep quiet, as she hadn't uttered a word from the moment she entered the car. His sister tried to make peace with me, and told me about a friend of hers who was a social scientist and was doing a study of the people who lived alongside the dead. She said how the women would be trilling for joy at the birth of a baby, and would fall silent suddenly if they noticed a funeral procession approaching. Their noises of rejoicing would turn to keening, while the men rushed to find which tomb the music was coming from, or the news broadcast, so they could silence it. As soon as the funeral was over, life would return to normal.

But I remained silent. Surrounded by their loud voices, I felt like the ant I'd noticed on the floor of the tomb. It had moved uncertainly along, not knowing that any moment it could be trodden on and crushed to death. I realized I'd changed my mind about marriage, and I wanted to get out of the car straightaway before I was suffocated by Farid's mother. I had a vision of the aunts like three witches preparing to serve us all up to the Devil.

I thought I would tell Farid that the reason I'd changed my mind about marrying him wasn't to do with the tomb or where I would be buried. On the contrary, I'd loved all the commotion, and the cemetery itself was like a fun-fair. Anyway, I didn't like being alone even while I was alive.

Then I decided against this last sentence. I was haunted by the scene of the family in the tomb, and their voices were still ringing in my ears. I resolved to try and like being alone, alive or dead.

Translated by Catherine Cobham

Melvin Burgess
GOING OUT

Outside the house there was only one direction. All around, the city beat and moved in darkness, but the route to the local shops ran like a bright thread through everything that was mysterious. She had been that way and only that way every week of her life, ever since her mother first wheeled her to the chemist for creams and nappies. All around were the backs of houses, streets that began in the open but then vanished rapidly into thuggery and ignorance in unknown quarters. These streets hung in the air . . . she could not imagine a brick and asphalt reality that she had not seen. They lived in her mind, a pallor, a trace of smoke in the dirty air. The city itself clamoured like great wings, beating through a dark, filthy night, rushing forward with no direction, unfamiliar, filled with voices but with no voice of its own.

Janey was always fierce with adventure when she carried her torn wicker basket up the road. The landmarks of the way were familiar like the bones under her flesh . . . the yellow-and-black painted house, the crook in the road by a blind alleyway, the post-box in the old wall, the patterns of cracks on the paving stones between the baker, the greengrocer, the grubby supermarket. Her father impressed on her the need for silence. Once, he tried to demand she go only to the supermarket where it was unnecessary to talk at all. But she remembered her mother's imperative when she learned this, her only craft, as a small girl; that supermarket bread was factory bread, that supermarket greens 'had never known the soil'. Therefore, proud with initiative, she insisted on her right as surrogate wife. She held herself mute and tight, squeezing her orders from between her lips, plunging the items into the wicker bag, like a thief in public.

Food won thus was presented in the proper way. On a checkered plate, the bread; the butter with the knife laid at this angle to it, the salad in a blue dish at her left hand, the main dish by her father. The ways of doing things made the past live, made her, Janey, live. When she dropped the checkered plate for bread one day, she was horrified. She tried to glue the pieces together, but it set badly and there were chips missing. Her father did not understand her upset. 'It's only a plate,' he said, and threw it out. Janey felt that one more link had been destroyed. Reality was in the past, where her father lived. Now, time was dismantling it. Its forms shook and rippled the present which became fainter with every new day.

In the small paved garden at the back of the house her father kept Kojak the dog. Kojak was treated with authority and contempt, but unlike Janey he was not allowed out of the house at all. He had been bought shortly after her mother died to protect Janey when she was left alone while her father worked, and he was the only thing Janey loved that belonged to the present. The alsatian had long, black shaggy hair and spent his days pacing and circling round the yard. On sunny days Janey sat out with him with her sewing basket, or preparing vegetables. Then he would run between her and the edges of the tiny garden, sometimes resting his head on her lap or letting her bury her fingers into the rich, sweet-smelling hair of his shoulders. This was against orders, as he was a guard dog and her father was afraid that the neighbours might think Kojak was soft. It was clear to Janey that the dog was suffering. Although he was only an animal and gave no sign of affection other than allowing her hand to rest on his shoulders, she felt some communication was possible between them.

Although outside was the province of fear, and inside she was ruled by her father, Janey had her place. When her mother died, the dominion she had held over the housework passed to Janey's shoulders. She kept her mother alive with polish on the glassy surface of the good table, with the washing-up, with pressing the creases on her father's trousers. These were the rituals that described her. Her father protested, pointing to the smears of polish on the wood, the gang of creases that fled up and down his legs, the jells and crusts of food on the washed plates. He tried to do the jobs himself but Janey flew into a violent rage; this was an attack more intimate than anything else he could do to her. He did not recognize this emotion. His wife had been a placid woman, and now he avoided a conflict. Leaving for work each day he wore a long coat and kept an iron in his janitor's cubby-hole, among the brooms and mops. After every Janey ironing he redid the job himself. She never noticed.

Her father was an intense man who rarely spoke, who looked ill at ease with his slack, heavy body in its over-neat clothes. When his wife died he ordered his home life as nearly as possible as if nothing had happened, merely moving Janey into all her roles. At work, too, her death made no difference; his workmates did not even know. Every day, dressed in a perfect white shirt and a good suit he brushed and swept and polished, cleaning his brooms and mops after every use before he went home. Only the iron in the cupboard bore witness to his bereavement.

In his scrupulous cleanliness, it pained him that things became drab and messy at home, and he encouraged his daughter from time to time to inspect the plates carefully for old food, and once in a while took her around the house to give her lessons, soon forgotten, on housework. Janey followed sulkily; for a few days her work improved. But before long egg yolk presented itself once more on the teaspoons, a line yellowed and grew hard in the milk jug, ridges of polish gathered muck on the chairs, and Janey's father would have to have his suit dry-cleaned again.

Janey remembered her mother in two ways. One mother she knew from memory. This person moved heavily about the house, performed her tasks at a pace that seemed preordained and eyed her father carefully, as if doubting his presence, as he ate his meals, or put on his shirt. She sat in her armchair in the evenings and stared, at the wall, at the magazines she kept in a stack on the shelf behind her. Occasionally when they went shopping she bought a new one and then she'd hurry home, curl up with her feet under her on the chair with a cup of coffee and flick through the pages. At this moment she became bright and quick, like a bird. Then she'd yawn and gaze about her, and end up looking mildly at her daughter playing with her doll in the corner. Sometimes now, Janey took down the magazines and looked at them, curled up in the same armchair. She could not read, but sometimes she caught an intimation of her mother's presence in the pages, and that gave her great pleasure.

Her other mother lived a life of appalling secrecy with her father. Janey herself shared a secret of unthinkable destructive power with her father. For a long time she considered her mother holy and safe, protected in her placid strength against all corruption. Only when she died did it begin to dawn on her that she and her mother, unknown to each other, shared the same dark secret, that they had never dared tell each other and which she knew could never be let out.

Her father came to her room more and more often after her mother died, and one night he demanded that she come with him into their bedroom. Janey was disgusted; this was unnatural, this was her mother's place ... the secret wife-place by her father's side that made even him holy. Could it be that this was the bond of marriage ... not clean and pure, but unholy and seeped in filth? Was this the secret of the hymns and churches, where marriages were made ... the thing that made men and women belong to each other? Janey understood that between man and wife it must be somehow different. 'Now you are like her to me,' her father said, and Janey knew then that she was no more and that her mother, whose presence was no longer with them, was to be kept from extinction by being Janey.

Next door, her dolls and soft toys, her pretty mats cut from paper. The following morning, she knew they were no longer hers. She locked her old room and put the key in a drawer, hidden, a place only she knew. Her father never went near the room. From time to time, she'd open it and enter, standing in the dusty wreckage, and look at her small bed, her occupations of childhood still unfinished.

One evening, Janey frowned at her father over the dinner table. He looked carefully at her.

'You have to take me out,' she said.

'Out?' He was puzzled.

'You took her out. She put on her coat ... Remember?'

He shrugged and pulled a face. But Janey had found her mother's best green coat in the wardrobe. She remembered, she had tried on make-up, looked in the drawers for dresses and shoes. She had descended to all the places her mother was, now she had to have this.

'It's right that you have to take me out,' she said, determined.

Now she was strong. 'On Friday,' he told her.

Over the next few days, Janey remembered. She scoured her memory of how things were, so as to be sure it was all done right. In the wardrobe hung the green coat and other clothes. Stockings, bra, dress, perfume, high heels: she laid it all out in readiness.

When her father came back she served him his tea, which he ate in silence, then cleared her throat and said with difficulty, 'I'm going upstairs to change.' He frowned but nodded. These were the correct words, the rails that led to the secret outdoors at night. Upstairs she put on make-up, lipstick, rouge, clumsily applied. She pulled on the stockings that hung baggy around her legs, the bra, a shapeless totem on her chest. Over everything went the green coat and the perfume, and she was ready. She went down to be inspected. When he saw her, her father was perturbed and excited.

'Not like that ... You must clean your face.' He tried to convince her. 'It suited her, but not you. You're prettier with a clean face.' She nodded and did as she was bid. He followed her upstairs and told her she must take the coat off, too, as it was not good for people to see her looking like that. Janey understood. Now she began to remove all her mother's clothes, but he stopped her.

'You can keep those on,' he said gruffly. 'But wear your own coat on top.' He became excited and wanted to take her to the bed, but she was angry. First they had to go out. He must go to the bathroom and shave, put on his best suit, she would take his arm and together they would leave through the front door.

When the door closed behind them her father set off in the other direction from the shops. Within twenty paces, Janey was beyond her knowledge. Arm in arm they walked the streets, he with his heavy head hung forward, she with her hunched back in her mother's clothes, feeling the stockings strange on her legs as if they were about to fall down. There was a drizzle and they huddled together under an umbrella, stinking of too much perfume, scurrying past other walkers, hurrying along the dark little streets, across the mouths of roads, away from the busy streets and big houses, into the living city. They became part of the city's breath, its power, its blood, tiny and vital in it. Neither spoke. In the dark, everything was strange. Once, they passed the top of the road with the shops in and Janey had a strange feeling as she saw the baker's shop from this new angle, as if to tell her that it knew the world from many sides and that she was just a tiny speck in its wide life. They passed a park and climbed up a steep hill that opened suddenly on to the city below. Janey stopped, resisted his pulling arm and stared. It was a revelation . . . the lights, the spread-open city that lived all around her like a great animal, ignorant and disgusting; but now she knew also wonderful and accessible, something that had only to be entered to be revealed.

Then on, quickly through the streets, hurrying past people and windows and puddles gathering in dips in the pavement. Suddenly the strange street became familiar and they were home again.

Her father shook out the umbrella in the hall and led her upstairs. He told her she should leave the stockings on and laughed at her when he saw she had done the catches up wrong. He straightened them for her. He was pleased and told her she should dress up more often and wear her mother's clothes.

These outings became a weekly event. Every Friday Janey dressed up and hid herself under her coat, and they walked out hurriedly between the houses. Janey understood these journeys: they were flashes of the great world. They made her excited, drunk with pleasure. She looked forward all week to going out, and even to the coming home, when her father hurried her upstairs and took her on the covers across her mother's wide bed.

These outings became so vivid for Janey that her memory began to play her tricks. Had not her mother taken her out for the air from time to time? She was sure she remmembered ... But despite everything she was not her mother, she was only her mother's shade and lacked the courage to tread alone where she was unsure. But there was Kojak. He was a thing of new times. He always pressed at the edges of the garden, he too wanted to go out. The dog brought specifically to protect her. Why, then, should she not take him out to the park, where she knew other people took their dogs to run, and still be safe?

She wound thick string around his collar, and again several times round her wrist to keep her guardian secured to her. She dressed herself in the uniform of going out ... her mother's dress, and stockings, her own old coat. And this time she allowed herself to colour her lips and eyes, ill-painted like a child's drawing on her own wan, small face.

Outside was a grey and still day. Janey quickly found her way to the park but before going in dragged Kojak, choking at the collar, up the hill to admire the view at the top. There she paused. Inside the park a man bent down and let his dog off the lead. The animal jumped up to lick his face. Instinctively, Janey bent down to release the string on Kojak's neck. At once he was off; like a released arrow he fled down the hill without a backward glance and disappeared around the corner. He was gone in moments. Janey stood alone. She glanced at the man in the park but he was playing with his dog and paid her no attention. She began to walk home.

Janey was not afraid, she was alone. She began to walk in no particular direction, passively recognizing where she was but making no effort to stay within memory. She became lost and found herself again, but it did not matter. At last she was on a busy road she knew well. A light rain had begun to fall and a few women hung about, waiting in doorways or on corners. They were poorly dressed for this cold weather but Janey felt at home here and began to walk up and down the road. The rain came on harder. People on the street thinned out. The water soaked through her hair, but she still lingered, waiting for something to happen. At last she was approached by a man. She smiled at him.

'Do you have anywhere to go?' he asked. Janey said yes. He nodded to her. 'OK.' She was confused and walked away. He followed at a distance. Still unafraid, she began to enjoy her attractive power and drew him on, glancing back to make sure he was with her, towards her home.

Inside, he asked, 'Where?'

Janey recognized what was happening and felt triumphant, as if she had won a prize. She led him upstairs to the bedroom where, as she anticipated, he undressed her.

Afterwards he told her he liked the bra and the make-up but not the stockings. 'Are those yours?' He gestured towards her own childish clothes on the floor. She nodded. 'Those are better, wear those next time.' He smiled. 'Every week, I'll be on the street. You be there, too.'

He got up to leave. 'How much?' he wanted to know. Janey said nothing. 'I'll make you a present, then,' he smiled. Jahey smiled back. She enjoyed him talking to her and his kindness, so different from her father's busy silence. He left some banknotes on the dressing table. 'Remember . . . same time next week . . . and no stockings, remember? Like a little girl, OK?' Janey nodded and he left.

Janey was left alone in the house with no dog, but the banknotes on the dressing table, symbols of the adult world she would never attain. She waited, half frightened, half eager, for her father to return. She had no idea of hiding what had happened. Her heart banged when she heard his key in the door. He called her name, puzzled that she was not below waiting for him. She said nothing in reply and in a moment his step was on the stair, and he came into the room. He saw the make-up still on her face and frowned. Janey glanced at the money. He turned, found it, picked it up, looked at her with a question.

'A man came here,' said Janey. 'He followed me.'

'You went out?'

'To the park with Kojak. He ran away.'

'I told you not to go out.' But he was not angry. He stroked the notes with his podgy fingers. 'You and he . . .?'

'He was like you,' she said. 'But he didn't like Mummy's stockings.'

He nodded understandingly.

'He said he'd come again next week,' she said.

Her father put the notes into his pocket and cleared his throat.

'Do what he wants you to do,' he said. He went to the door, but paused. 'It'll be good for you to get out,' he told her. 'But only when I'm at work, understand?'

Janey nodded and followed him downstairs to lay the table for tea.

D.A. Callard
READING THE SIGNALS

The long crawl across the surface of Anatolia took most of the day, and only a faint glimmer of light remained as the train slid into the city. He had wisely travelled first class this time, avoiding the huddled peasantry, their live chickens and possessions in bags marked. *A Gift from the People of America: Not for Sale.* Half-way through the journey he had run out of cigarettes, but had been kept in supply by a constant turnover of passengers eager to practise their few phrases of English. The last of these took him to a cheap hotel near the centre, where a pound bought a roach-free room equipped with a wash-basin and even a room-service telephone. He slept through his excitement, awaking at dawn to the sound of a muezzin calling outside the window.

It all happened some years ago, when everyone and his brother seemed engaged in some tortuous spiritual quest. Hard-bitten cynics of his acquaintance threw up jobs and fell at the feet of some Indian adolescent with The Knowledge, or, if they got to India, came back with either religion or hepatitis. It came to a point at which he was almost the sole surviving hedonist among the brown-rice eaters and dhoti-toters with their soft, sibilant voices, maddening in-talk of satsangs and blissed-outness, and their nauseating air of superiority. For how long could he remain immune? After a Christmas of unusual over-indulgence, he decided to see in New Year at a retreat in the Cotswolds, expecting a Spartan regime of bare boards and simple salads. In fact, New Year came, after a pheasant dinner and limitless wine, with a chorus of 'Auld Lang Syne' in the company of several faded rock stars who, five years earlier, might have been names to conjure with. The white eminence behind this was a Turk called Cengiz, who carried no greater aura of spiritual gravity than he might have done as a jewellery salesman: the occupation he followed before becoming the organ of transmission in the West for the teachings of a dervish sect which

25

flourished, semi-underground, in Eastern Anatolia.

When the retreat was over he decided to visit the source of the teaching himself. A week's hitch-hiking took him to Istanbul; after a few weeks there he had taken the train to the city.

He washed, dressed, and stepped into the morning sunlight. Something was afoot, for the streets were thronged with people seemingly headed in one direction. Grateful that he'had brought a shawl he covered his head and noticed, not for the first time, that in spite of his Western apparel, the looks of curiosity ceased. He flowed with the crowd to the great green-domed mosque, shrine of one of the pillars of Islam, which rose above the town centre. When he removed his shoes and washed his feet, a tingle travelled his spine as if, at any moment, he might be seized and unmasked as an infidel. But, curtained beneath the shawl, no one gave him a second glance as he joined the faithful in circumambulation of the tomb, moving his hands up and down before his face, as they did, and muttering the only Muslim prayer he knew, '*La illa'he illa Allah*', over and over.

Outside he felt a buzz of excitement at carrying off the exercise without detection. So it must have been, he thought, for Sir Richard Burton entering Mecca in disguise, not knowing if his mask might be exposed, the knife of vengeance fall. Unknowing luck had brought him here on the holy man's day and the pious, having fulfilled their annual obligations, were already dispersing to the surrounding villages. He ate at the corner restaurant, and watched their slow procession homeward.

The following day he sat, drinking coffee in the square, wondering at how little interest he aroused. In Istanbul he would have had to fend off a succession of hustlers selling souvenirs, fake antiques, rugs, dope, their sisters and, in the last resort, themselves. Here life ignored him almost to the extent of denying his existence. An old man came and sat at his table, though there were many free, muttered furiously for several minutes then left without acknowledging his presence. He felt blessed with a sense of freedom: he need no longer be on guard.

'Hello, sir'.

He looked up at a smiling beatific face which seemed to fill his vision, almost obscuring a dark, worried visage which hovered behind.

'I saw you yesterday. You were praying at the shrine of Mevlana. You are Engliss? Americain?'

'English. Welsh, actually.'

'What is Welss?'

'It is a place on the left-hand side of England.'

'My name is Sa'adi. This is my friend, Bedri.'

He stood up and shook hands. 'My name is David.'

Sa'adi puckered. 'David,' he repeated, stressing the last syllable. 'It is a Jewish name?'

'It is the name ... of the Great Mevlana of Wales. Many Welsh are called David,' he replied, also stressing the last syllable, 'just as many Muslims are called Mohammed.'

'You are Muslim? Your people are Muslim?'

'No.'

'But you were praying.'

'Yes, I was praying. There is, after all, only one God.'

Sa'adi beamed. He had evidently given the right answer. For emphasis, he repeated it in Arabic.

'*La illa'he illa Allah, Mohammed rasullah*', repeated Sa'adi. 'But, never mind. I think perhaps you will become Muslim. A voice tells me this. Would you like coffee?'

Both men sat down and the conversation took a less exalted plane. They were air force officers on leave: he told them that he was a teacher of English, a harmless guise under which he usually travelled. Bedri remained silent throughout most of the conversation, nervously rubbing his palms and smiling at fixed intervals. His English seemed poor. When Sa'adi asked what had brought him to the city, he told them of the Cotswold retreat, and its connection with the sect which operated in secret around them, even as they talked.

'But you say you are not Muslim,' Sa'adi interjected.

'There is only one God,' David repeated.

Sa'adi nodded. 'Would you like to meet one of the Brotherhood?' he asked. 'I have a cousin ... a very very important man ... very high. I will take you to him if you like.'

It was as the Teaching held. You did not seek the Teaching, nor was it broadcast on street corners. You continued through life, kept yourself open, and, when you needed it, the Teaching would find you.

'I would like that very much. It is what I came here for.'

'Good. But not now. He is a very busy man. Very important. Perhaps you can meet him this evening. Do you know the café on the hill?'

'Yes.'

Then we will meet there this evening. But now, we must go to make a visit.'

They stood, bowed slightly and walked away. As they left the area of the café, Sa'adi took Bedri's hand and they crossed the square linked like a pair of lovers, as many young men did in this town.

That evening as David waited for his new friends to arrive, he felt a glow of satisfaction radiate from his solar plexus. For him there had been no searching, no waiting: he had come to the source and the magic

27

door had opened. The green dome of the mosque glistened below him, its spotlights being the only electricity functioning in the town that night. The hill on which he sat was an artificial construction built by early conquerors of the region to signify their dominance. Recent conquerors had added the café surrounding a pool with an intermittently working fountain, upon which swam a solitary, ridiculous duck.

'Good evening, Mr David.'

He greeted his friends and ordered tea. Sa'adi talked, Bedri nodded, smiling occasionally. The solitary duck swam, first clockwise, then anticlockwise. Around them families sat, in tiers of three or four generations, talking intently about whatever happened in this town where nothing happened but work and prayer.

'Will your friend come tonight, Mr Sa'adi?'

Sa'adi smiled. 'I thought he might come tonight after . . . the meeting. Perhaps tomorrow night.'

The conversation meandered on, contentless. Finally David bowed and left, saying that he would meet them there on the following night. Sa'adi wanted to meet in the afternoon, but David said he would be leaving the following day.

Sa'adi started. 'Leaving? So soon?'

David explained that he was going to spend the day in the catacombs of an underground city, some fifty kilometres distant. He would be back by early evening. They walked him back to his hotel, Sa'adi taking his hand, which made him feel very odd, but then, it was the custom there.

As planned he spent the next day in the underground city. Foolishly he took no food or drink with him, and there turned out to be no refreshment available. Finally, in desperation, he drank water from an irrigation tap. It was tepid, but seemed pure: he had drunk worse. On the journey back a growing nausea overcame him. Heat, or bad water? He put it down to heat since he still felt hungry and, when the bus pulled in, made for the nearest restaurant and ordered kebab.

Even by the standards to which he was now accustomed, hygiene in this establishment seemed at a discount. Myriad flies buzzed, leaving trails through the viscosity of the air, which seemed saturated with grease: the same grease which made a patina on the tables, cutlery and glass. From time to time the chef would break off work to hawk up phlegm into a pile of sawdust in the corner. Had he not been so hungry he would have made an excuse and left: as it was, he bolted down the greyish meat ravenously.

The next thing he remembered clearly was waking in his hotel room, his arms and legs flailing like a capsized beetle. The crack on the ceiling opened, and from it marched a line of beetles, moving, re-forming now to form the head of one great beetle whose mandibles reached out, clutching his abdomen . . .

He struggled to the sink and disgorged the kebab. Then the remains of earlier meals came up in chronological succession so, on the final retchings, he swore he could taste a melon eaten on the train three days earlier. After that there was nothing but mucous, a lot of it; after that, nothing but air. He raised his head. It was dark outside. He crawled to bed and slept.

David awoke next day to a blissful sense of emptiness. Though he was weak, his body and mind seemed weightless; he felt as if, at any moment, he might detach himself from the floor and float around the room. The cloacal slime half-filling the sink held no horrors, and he plunged his hand in it without flinching, removing the drain sieve and letting it flow away down the waste pipe. He drank nothing but fruit juice that morning, and in the afternoon walked to one of the outlying villages, eating only a yoghurt as the sun set. He resolved to make good use of his purgation by fasting, a practice highly recommended in the Teachings and sure to be doubly effective now that his system was purged utterly. There was one note of regret: he had failed to meet his friends the night before, and last night, surely, the man from the Brotherhood would have come. Or, perhaps not. *Insh'allah*, he thought. *Mektoub*; it is written, and somehow in his lightheadedness he knew that his moment would come.

He was walking down the road leading to the Great Mosque when he heard his name being called. It was Sa'adi and Bedri. 'My friend, my friend, where were you last night? We have just come from your hotel looking for you.'

David explained the events of the previous day in grisly detail. 'It was the meat,' he ended.

Sa'adi shook his head. 'Did you know that the underground city was built by Christians?' he enquired.

Yes, David had known that and, since Sa'adi did not elaborate further, guessed that he implied that some curse hung over the excavations of infidels. Sa'adi had taken his hand solicitiously by now and, as they passed one of the carpet shops, stopped.

'This is my cousin's shop. Come and look. Come. You do not have to buy.'

David smiled thinly. He had gone through this many times: had drunk countless cups of tea in souvinir shops, bazaar stalls, carpet factories in company of a tout, then made an excuse and left. Sa'adi of course was not a tout, but he did not want to buy a carpet and saw no reason to waste his, or the owner's, time. He walked on, almost dragging

Sa'adi behind him.

'Come on, let's go for coffee on the hill. Your friend may be there.'

'I don't think he will come tonight,' said Sa'adi, sulkily.

At the foot of the hill was a small shrine, one of many scattered throughout the city where minor holy men had been buried and, as they passed, Sa'adi announced that he wanted to stop and pray. The trio entered. Sa'adi stood before the sarcophagus, praying silently and moving his hands before his face in a cleansing action. As the prayer reached a climax he threw out his arms in an attitude of surrender, tossed back his head and exhaled. David stood rooted: the face before him was transfigured in orgasmic release as, momentarily, a glow of light illuminated Sa'adi's whole body which dissolved, coalesced in a microsecond before his arms dropped, his mouth uttered the final, audible syllable, *ullah*, his eyes opened and looked on the world as if for the first time. David said nothing. As Sa'adi took his hand he felt the tremor of an electrical charge. He said nothing: they mounted the hill in silence. Bedri ordered coffee.

Sa'adi's talk that night was of the Brotherhood, of the ease with which they stepped beyond physical reality, of cures effected solely by faith, holy men who ate and drank nothing, surviving on spiritual sustenance, of *baraka*, the mysterious blessing which, he said, he felt in David. 'I *know* you will become Muslim,' he repeated, clutching his hand and, yes, David thought, stranger things had happened. Bedri sat in silence, though David, in some momentary lapse in conversation, asked him why he had not prayed at the shrine also. Bedri gave a weak, nervous smile. 'I seek religion. I have not found it, yet.'

Sa'adi's cousin did not appear, but he was becoming almost superfluous, a convenient myth serving to keep the trinity together. Perhaps I will become Muslim, David thought that night before sleep took him. Stranger things had happened.

Sa'adi and Bedri were away for the weekend, which David spent drifting around the streets of the city, visiting the Great Mosque where he prayed surreptitiously, sunbathing on the roof of the hotel, eating only yoghurt as some strange energy swelled within. On Tuesday morning he would take a bus to Izmir where a friend had promised him a job in an English school. As it was his last day, Sa'adi and Bedri were to spend the whole of Monday with him.

At ten he was awakened by the hotel boy. He dressed quickly, marvelling at the lightness of his body, which now scarcely felt hunger. His friends were waiting in the lobby. Sa'adi embraced him and kissed him on the cheek: intimacies which once would have made him shrink seemed natural now. For the first time he took Sa'adi's hand himself, and together the walked into the main street, Bedri tagging behind.

'Because this is your last day, we will do something special,' Sa'adi said. 'But first, please, come and look at my cousin's shop. He has beautiful rugs. This city is famous for them. You do not have to buy.'

David groaned inwardly, shook his head and walked on, pulling Sa'adi past the shop. He did not want to spend his last day playing cat and mouse with the proprietor.

'Please,' Sa'adi persisted. 'He is my cousin. Your refusal . . . hurts me.'

It occurred to David that perhaps he was transgressing some peculiar local tradition of hospitality. There could be no harm in visiting the shop this evening, thus cutting the time of negotiations to a minimum.

'This evening, Sa'adi. The sun is shining, and we have a whole day before us.' Almost involuntarily he squeezed his hand, but it did not seem to shake him out of his sulk. The 'something special' planned for the day did not materialize, and they spent most of the afternoon eating water-melons in the garden of another 'cousin'. Sa'adi's conversation took a historical turn, and David found himself personally blamed for the foreign policy of Lord Curzon, Lord Byron's siding with the Greeks, the assault on Gallipoli, the activities of the British Mandate in Palestine and current policy in Cyprus.

'What are your politics, Mr David?'

This was a question always to be avoided though, with the country entering a third year of martial law, it was rarely asked.

'I have no politics.'

'Every man has his politics,' Sa'adi replied, implying that a man was less than a man if he had none.

No politics. No wife and children either. Dear. Well, if in doubt, turn to religion.

'Hadrat Isa said,' he quoted, using the Turkish name, '"Render unto Caesar that which is Caesar's and render unto God that which is God's."'

'Meaning what?' Sa'adi spat.

'Meaning that you must choose . . . between God and politics.' It meant nothing of the sort, and David prayed he would overlook this. He phrased the unmentionable.

'What are your politics, Mr Sa'adi?'

Sa'adi stood, and seemed about to beat his chest. 'I am a Turkish patriot. I would give my life for my country and my faith. I am a follower of Mustapha Kemal Ataturk.' He sat down. The face, once fluorescent with religious ecstasy, burned now with something like a blush. 'Do you know of the Grey Wolves?' he asked.

David knew of the Grey Wolves. So did all the world, since the attempt on the Pope's life. He knew that they were neo-Fascist, strong in the military, dedicated to reviving Ottoman glories, virulently anti-Semitic ('David. It's a Jewish name?') and generally to be avoided. He dimly remembered that Ataturk had been responsible for suppressing the Brotherhood, but decided to pass over this in silence. Doubtless Sa'adi could reconcile the apparent contradiction. In fact, it was time for a change of subject, and he was just struggling to think of one when Sa'adi obliged.

'My cousin is coming tonight.'

'Your cousin from the Brotherhood?'

'Yes.'

They spent the rest of the afternoon playing backgammon and, as evening drew on, the unpleasant effect of Sa'adi's outburst receded. He began to talk, apparently knowledgeably, about carpet design, and of how certain patterns produced different spiritual resonances. So what if his politics were suspect, David thought. And who was he, a mere transient, to pass judgement?

Just as the light faded, and Sa'adi became bored with winning, he stood and folded the board decisively. Singly, hardly talking, they walked to the carpet shop.

The owner greeted Sa'adi elaborately, briefly acknowledging Bedri before turning to David. 'Hello, my friend,' David muttered inwardly a few seconds before the owner. When trapped in these situations he would often amuse himself anticipating phrase by phrase the patter learned, presumably, at some Harvard School of Bazaar Vendors, so common was it to all: 'only the finest quality', 'customers all over the world', 'for you, because you are my friend, special price, not tourist price'. He sat on a pile of carpets and accepted coffee, as the man hauled out carpets vast enough for the Great Mosque at Cairo, worth the lifetime salary of an English teacher. Reluctantly the seller scaled down to prayer rugs. Most were around the ninety-pound mark, and David began to entertain the faint possibility of buying one. He fingered each, with the assumed air of a connoisseur. One, which he particularly liked, was only sixty pounds, and he weighed its purchase against three days' teaching in Izmir. When the man came to the end of the pile, he asked to see it again, scrutinizing it closely while Sa'adi and the vendor spoke rapidly in Turkish. Finally the man turned to David and assumed a pained expression.

'Because you are a friend of my friend, Mr Sa'adi,' (no mention of cousin, David remembered with hindsight) 'for you I make special price. Forty pounds.'

Two days' teaching in Izmir. 'I will take it.' The carpet seller allowed himself the ghost of a smile as Sa'adi leaped to his feet and gripped David by the shoulder. 'You will keep this always,' he exulted. 'And you will pray on it ... when you become Muslim.'

Stranger things had happened. 'One moment please,' David advised the vendor who was already wrapping his purchase. 'I don't have the money now. I will have to change some traveller's cheques before I leave tomorrow. Are you open at ten?'

The man nodded.

'Then I'll bring you the money tomorrow morning.' The man handed David the wrapped rug, which he refused, saying he would take it on payment.

The trio left and walked to the café on the hill. 'For when you become Muslim,' Sa'adi repeated, 'for when you become Muslim.'

They had been sitting for some time: the table was filled with empty cups and the ashtray overflowing with sunflower seed husks. David suddenly became aware that he had been talking for a long time about something and that Sa'adi was no longer listening. His eyes shone, fixed at a distance on the other side of the pool: a few seconds later he rose to embrace a stranger, a mustaschioed figure dressed in a Western suit.

'Mr David, this is my cousin Mr Ali. Of the Brotherhood,' he added, conspiratorially. David rose and shook his hand. With a gesture of perfect economy the man signalled that the party should sit, then spoke at length in clear, unaccented English.

Quite what he said, David could hardly remember. At the time it had struck him with the force of a revelation, though later recollection called up only a series of aphorisms which would have been unremarkable on the back of a matchbox. The man held his dignity, spoke, then, as suddenly as he had appeared, was gone. David stared in silence at the solitary, absurd duck wending its way clockwise, anticlockwise. Perhaps he would become Muslim, he thought.

Sa'adi drew himself up. 'So you have met my cousin from the Brotherhood, Mr David. I hope you are happy now. He is a very busy man.' David looked up. The lack of solid food was doing something to him. Bedri was also standing now.

'Shall we go?' Sa'adi took David's hand and they walked, Bedri trailing, past the pool, the solitary absurd duck, past the carpet shop, past the Great Mosque, past the filthy restaurant by the bus station, to his hotel. They entered and came up to his room. David telephoned for coffee, brought at this hour by the same boy who brought his morning *chai*. Bedri sat in the one chair, David and Sa'adi sat on his bed. They spoke of his future plans. 'You will come back?' – 'Yes', meaning 'No'; 'You will write to us?' – 'Yes', meaning 'Perhaps'; 'You will remember us?' – 'Yes', meaning 'Yes'. The impact of numerous coffees on an empty stomach suddenly hit David's bladder and he begged to be excused.

He emerged from the toilet at the end of the corridor to encounter Bedri, his nervous face, the silent witness of the past week, contorted as if by a tic. He grasped David's shoulder.

'Mr David ... as I am your friend ... do not buy this carpet.'

The words came like a slap on the face to a drunken hysteric. He knew, had always known; the hand-holdings, the master-dog relations between Sa'adi and Bedri, the constant entreaties to visit his 'cousin's' shop. It had always been clear but somehow outshone by the flash of light illuminating the man in prayer, the piety and talk of miracles.

'It's a fake, isn't it?'

Bedri's face contorted further. 'I cannot ... my English is not good ... Mr David, do not buy this carpet. Please.' With an effort he pulled himself together, the wan smile returned. 'Now I must go. I see you tomorrow at the bus station. Ten thirty.' His small hunched body trickled down the stairs and was gone.

David closed his eyes momentarily, gave a deep breath and walked slowly to his room. Did he detect a quiver of anticipation in Sa'adi as he entered? Though Bedri's seat was empty he sat next to Sa'adi on the bed: there seemed little point in prevarication. The inevitable came almost instantly, a flurry of hands, wet lips on his cheek, a breath tainted by some unidentifiable herbal fragrance, whispered Turkish endearments.

He could barely remember how he extricated himself. Some attitude of spurious moral outrage was thrown, a speech given indicating that these things were not done in his country. The Bible was quoted inaccurately several times. Sa'adi threw a sulk, then, stiffly, wished him goodbye.

'But you are coming to the bus station tomorrow?'

'Yes. Yes. *Insh'allah* we will meet tomorrow.' They shook hands as if meeting for the first time. The door closed. David gave a deep breath once more. As brush-offs went, it had been simple enough.

Early next morning he left the hotel, taking the back streets to avoid the carpet shop. Bedri's nervous face stared through the pitted glass of the filthy restaurant. David thought that he could chance a coffee there.

'Sa'adi is coming?' Bedri asked.

David shrugged, then wondered if a shrug meant the same thing here. 'I don't know. *Insh'allah.*'

'Then he did not ... did not ...'

'Stay,' David filled in. 'No, he did not stay.'

Bedri's face broke into something approaching a grin. They talked, exhausting his limited vocabulary several times over while the bus loaded its passengers and their bags. David rose, and shook Bedri's hand.

'You will write to me, Mr David?'

'Yes,' he replied, meaning 'No.'

Bedri pumped his hand further. 'I hope you are happy future. I hope you are happy future.' For a moment he leaned forward as if to kiss him, then fell back. His face puckered into a forced smile. David repossessed his hand, took his bag and walked to the bus.

Twenty minutes later the bus drew out of the station. As the bus swung around the corner, David saw that Bedri had waited for him; saw his hand waving frantically; raised his own to wave back, but too late – he and the city were lost in a cloud of dust and exhaust.

Reaching the outskirts the bus began a headlong dash for Izmir: nine hours if the schedules were right. Sa'adi, Bedri, the carpet seller, the man from the Brotherhood fell back into a past so remote as to be analysed dispassionately. Why had Sa'adi tried to sell him a fake carpet? Surely not for the minimal amount of commission. Had Bedri lied? Had the events of last night been a transient eruption of lust or had he been all the while the subject of a seduction so subtle that he had failed to read the signals: had he indeed, by some unknowing signal of his own, given assent? And how to square this with the piety, the lightning-crossed face of adoration in prayer, the constant entreaties to conversion? In brief, had he wanted his body, his money or his soul? Perhaps, by some compartmentalizing David could never grasp, he has wanted all three. Well, it was some satisfaction that he had got none.

The heat in the bus ascended toward midday. The man next to David, a young peasant with thick stubble, fell into a sleep approaching coma, his mouth lolling open, his head sagging on David's shoulder all the way to Izmir so that at fifteen-minutes intervals he was forced to push it away, only to have it returned by a jolt of the speeding bus. This country could get you down after a while, he thought.

That thought, and a craving for a cigarette on the no-smoking bus, occupied the last hours of the journey. The bus station at Izmir was full of young Americans, spoilt children of the West from the NATO base under whose aegis he was to teach. The city was a world away now. A special bus took them all to the camp, where the signals were clear once more.

Francis Downes
'*YOU HAVE TO* ·
THINK ABOUT OTHERS'

It was Father O'Mahony who suggested it. She recognized his shape through the grille, and that strong smell of pipe tobacco that he had about him. They said he smoked and drank too much, but everyone knew he was a good priest. He was the kind of priest who could listen to you.

'Don't be so silly and pious, woman. What you're telling me is no sin. Don't you think God himself would understand a wife who has trouble like yours, and blames it all on the man she married ... him being ill as well ... though that's not the issue? I'll not give you absolution for that, Mrs, but I will tell you what you should do. Come round to the house in twenty minutes and I'll talk to you then. For your penance say three Hail Marys and that's only for the other stuff.'

So Frances found herself in the company of a small dark-haired woman, swathed in a cross-over floral apron, who offered her tea and biscuits and who told her Father wouldn't be too long. Wait here, she said. Read a magazine or something. Are the family managing? And your husband? It was a surprise to Frances to find out that even this woman knew of her situation.

'I sometimes think that man has more stomach than soul,' she said, nodding to the plate, and the large mound of biscuits.

When Father O'Mahony returned, he ate four biscuits before he said anything, before he even looked at her and even then, what he said offered little ease to her curiosity. 'Mary makes wonderful shortbread,' he said.

'Father?' said Frances.

'I want you to speak to Sister Anthony, she's the Mother Superior at St Martin's Convent ... The Little Sisters of the Poor ... What you told me in the confessional was no sin, Mrs Doherty, but if you don't ease up on your work and get someone to help you, it will be. I'll get in touch with her on the telephone and she'll expect you. She'll find someone for you ... that's what they're there for.'

'Father ... ?' said Frances.

'The care of the dying, Mrs Doherty, if that's what you were going to ask. ... Now will you have some tea and shortbread?'

Sister Michael was a small pale woman whose dark eyes were framed by black plastic spectacles and whose hair and body were hidden in her grey religious clothes. Frances was all too polite at first, and there was little conversation between them until Liam, the eldest boy, who had been waiting for an opportunity, said, 'Sister, why have you been called ... Why've you got a man's name?'

There was a terrible silence for some moments, and before Frances could blurt out from her awful embarrassment some kind of apology, Sister Michael said, 'Well now, I suppose it could be because my parents thought I should have been a boy to work on the farm, or because I was a terrible menace of a girl, a real tomboy when I was a child, or because, like you, I'm a dreadful chatterbox, but it's really because God would like it better ... And isn't he the one who matters?' And that seemed to do the trick. Frances made tea, Sister played with baby Claire and chatted to the boys, and the thought of upstairs lifted from Frances' mind.

Sister Michael was to live in. That was the procedure and there was no way round it. So she took Liam's room and he moved in with the two other boys in the back room. Frances and the baby, of course, stayed with Jack in the big front bedroom that overlooked the main road.

At first, Frances spent as much time with Jack as did Sister Michael, jealous of the sick man's affection above all, but guilty at spending time away from him. So Frances would sit there anxiously while Sister Michael read Agatha Christie novels by the cartload it seemed. But whenever Jack needed attention, it was the nun who was always ready, with a damp cloth to mop his brow or some tea, or his reading spectacles. This casual confidence with her sick husband made Frances even more determined not to lose her grip on the situation.

But this would not do for Sister Michael. 'I have come here to nurse a sick man, Mrs Doherty, a man who is dying, I know. And I've come here to give you time to look after your children and to keep yourself together. I won't have you hovering around in my presence like a bleddy undertaker waiting for the corpse, God forgive me for saying so. ... It's a nice day, now, so why don't you give the children a treat and take them to the park? When you come back – come back at four, and

I'll have a dinner ready.'

Despite her initial anger, Frances did what she was told. Sister Michael was right, she shouldn't be in the room all the time, it was wrong. When they returned from Norris Green Park, the smell of roast lamb and cabbage hit them as they opened the door. But Frances was delighted to find out, though she kept it to herself for some time, that Sister Michael's roast potatoes weren't a patch on her own and her gravy was like dishwater.

Jack's brother Kevin arrived in the October, about six weeks after Sister Michael. He threw his hat over the banister post and his suitcase under the stairs. Then he went into the kitchen where Frances was preparing the tea and said, 'Well?'

'Kevin, you've come then?' said Frances, continuing to peel potatoes and turning her back. *I hope to God*, she thought. She then made him a cup of tea and placed it in front of him, with a couple of slices of bread and butter on a plate. Liam wandered into the kitchen and stared at his uncle. His mother turned to him as if to say, 'You say one thing, me laddo . . .'

'Well?' said Kevin once again.

'I don't know, Kevin, I'll have to talk to him . . . but he's sleeping now and Sister's with him anyway, so you'll have to wait. I don't know, Kevin, why didn't you . . .? It would have been better for us all, Kevin, if you'd . . . if you'd not bothered . . .'

Kevin put his teacup down and put his hand into his nephew's blond hair. Liam hated adults for doing this, but he knew that he had no choice. Perhaps this man was some kind of priest or doctor, in his dark ill-fitting suit, his white shirt and tie, his polished black shoes.

'Say hello to your uncle Kevin, Liam.'

'Hello,' said Liam, smiling when he felt the crisp note slide into his hand. 'Mum . . .?' he said, showing the five-pound note to her.

'Yes, but that's not just for you. It's for the others as well. Give it to me and I'll keep it for Christmas . . .' Liam ran out of the kitchen, slamming the door in anger at the way his mother had cheated him.

'You shouldn't have, you know. They get more than enough.'

'A few shillin's never hurt any child.'

'I don't want any trouble, Kevin. Not now,' she said.

'For God's sake, he's my brother, my own brother,' said Kevin.

'And that's why you shouldn't have come. That's why I didn't reply to the letter . . .'

Two weeks before, Frances had received a letter from Kevin, postmarked London. She knew that he was in England, but she didn't know exactly where, and she hoped that it would remain that way. But in her heart of hearts she knew that the family could not keep Kevin out in the dark, when Jack was so ill. Despite what had come between them, he had to be told of Jack's situation. So it was no great surprise to receive his letter, but when he said he would be making the trip up to Liverpool, Frances threw it into the fire where it flamed away for some moments, as she sat staring unhappily at the blackening paper. Perhaps he would forget, she thought.

In the year before her marriage, Frances met all her future in-laws at a great party in the kitchen at the family farm over in Clare. Jack's mother had killed a goose and there was ham as well. There were enormous floury potatoes, boiled in their jackets, cabbage and carrots and turnip, and to follow it all was a beautiful sherry trifle. For the men there were bottles of beer and for the women, glasses of lemonade. It was a tremendous occasion, said Jack's mother.

Then Kevin turned up, drunk to the eyeballs, and reeking of cheap scent.

'Were you with her?' said Mrs Doherty.

'Isn't that my business, sure,' said Kevin, 'and haven't I come to see the blushing English rose . . .? Couldn't you find yourself a decent Irish girl at all, Jack, for Jaysus' sake?'

And there was a dreadful silence, then, that Frances knew was maintained for her benefit, but which nevertheless made her feel like fleeing off into the empty Clare night. They all did the best to forget the whole business, and tried to laugh and dance for the guest, but the half-eaten food that remained next day was testimony to the soured feast.

And that was Frances' eternal memory of the man who was now standing in her kitchen, but it was not the only reason for her dread at his visit.

She knew that the Doherty family had had some money, there was no question about that. You only had to tally up the land they had, and the houses they owned. The children had been denied nothing, and when Kevin talked about going away to be a priest, there was no expense spared. Jack later talked about thousands being spent, only to be lost for ever when he withdrew from the seminary just two years away from final vows. A priest in the family was a mother's greatest joy, a failed priest eternal shame. And perhaps it was this shame that eventually led Kevin into a dissipated life across in Dublin.

Although, at first, the whole family were behind him. And it was Jack, being the eldest male in the family after the death of his father, who came up with the plan in the first place. Kevin would use family money to set himself up in business. The subsequent frittering away of the money on the Dublin 'crack' put a rift between Jack and Kevin that had never healed. Frances was ignorant of this when Kevin barged into the farm that first time. She never knew the full reason for the embarrassment, nor the silent bitterness between the two brothers.

And now Kevin wanted her to negotiate for him, so he could fulfil a duty.

When she went into the room she found her husband awake, reading the paper, his reading glasses at the end of his nose. Sister Michael nodded at Frances then went back to her own book.

'You know, Frances, there's a great opportunity here. Someone's wanting to sell a cobbler's business ... There's not a soul who doesn't need shoes repairing. And don't mind the joke ... We should think of something like that ...'

'Yes, I know,' said Frances. Jack's own scrap metal business was a solid earner, but it was heavy physical work, and she had always felt it was the exertions in setting it up that had ruined Jack's health.

'Or we could go into the grocery business ... but I can't see myself scrabbling round like an auld woman in a white coat all day talking about cheese and tea ...'

'I'll leave you two,' said Sister Michael. Frances watched her leave and waited until she heard the voices from the kitchen. She knew she would be charmed by Kevin. Even a sixty-year-old nun from Kerry would find him dashing. As they all used to say in Jack's family, he had a look of Errol Flynn.

'Jack,' said Frances, 'I've got something to tell you ... Your brother ... Your brother Kevin is here ...'

'Does that mean I'm dying, or is he that desperate for cash he'd break a twelve years' silence? ... Give him a plate of bacon and cabbage and send him on his way. I don't want ...' Then he started coughing before he could finish. Frances watched her husband as he struggled for breath.

'He wants to speak to you ... He wrote a letter to me a few weeks ago saying he was going to drop in. But I didn't want to upset you. To tell you the truth, Jack, I didn't think he'd come ...'

'I won't speak to him. Now now I won't. It's been too long.'

'Jack, why won't you talk to him? Surely money can't be that important?'

'It wasn't the money at all,' said Jack. 'He made a bloody fool out of me. I trusted him and he made a bloody fool out of me ... I won't have anyone doing that to me or mine. He feckin' nearly ruined the family ...'

'Jack!' said Francis, angry at her husband's loss of control, but when she looked at him, he'd fallen asleep. The last thing she wanted now for Jack was upset of this sort.

But when she got downstairs she didn't know what to think. She found her brother-in-law in tears, his head on Sister Michael's shoulder, while Liam and Sean were grinning like Cheshire cats at seeing a grown man cry. Then Kevin stopped, lifted his head and turned to Frances.

'I'm not going to leave this house until he speaks to me,' he said.

The next morning, Frances woke to find Kevin already digging away at the garden, a mound of grassy sods behind him as he worked. It was looking better already. These houses had huge gardens and since Jack's illness nothing had been done, so the grass had gone to riot. It was great fun for the children, but dangerous, with stones and bits of glass amongst the soil, so she was grateful for Kevin for putting his back into it like this.

'Will you have tea?' said Frances.

'I will indeed. There's nothing like a spot of hard work to give a feller a thirst ...'

'I have bacon and egg ...'

'Thank you, Frances,' he said, without stopping.

In fact he worked all day and only took the one break, for a cigarette after a spot of lunch. By two o'clock, when there was a strong October sun in the sky, he was down to shirt-sleeves. It was Sister Michael who said it first. She put her mouth to Frances' ear and said, 'My God, that's a fine-looking man out there. If it wasn't for my age I'd be thinking of giving up my vocation.'

Frances laughed, but she knew there was something in what the nun said. Why on earth, she wondered, had he never married? There had been women all right. All over Ireland, they used to say. That was where the family thought the money had gone, because he wasn't a wild drinker like some others that could be mentioned although he liked a pint with the lads. There had been a girl in Carrigaholt — the baker's girl - but that all passed by without anything coming of it. And there was Mrs O'Driscoll. That had been a scandal all right. The whole of the county knew what he was up to with her when her husband was away. But he had never found himself a girl to settle down with and now he must have been forty-two or forty-three.

'It'll take another day to dig it all up and then we think about levelling it out. I'll leave a bit of a patch at the bottom. You can fling a few auld praties in there after ...'

After he had finished the garden, he said, 'I think that front sitting-room of yours can do with fixing. The paper's falling off the walls. I'll see if I can't find something to put up there.' He took Liam with him, after he'd returned from school, and the two of them came back a couple of hours later with eight rolls of paper and a tin of paint.

And meal times became lively affairs. Kevin had a way with the children that you couldn't criticize. He even managed to get something out of Pat, the youngest boy, who was normally rather taciturn and gloomy. Then when the children had gone to bed, and Sister Michael was upstairs with Jack, Kevin would tell some awful stories to Frances. Stories about the building sites of London and the gangs of men just over from Ireland. Terrible stories that brought a blush to her face, but she couldn't stop herself laughing, he had the gift all right.

'Now listen to this one, Frances,' he would say, lighting up a Senior Service and leaning back into the armchair, 'though I can't guarantee the truth of it seeing as it was told me by an auld liar, Georgie Roche, and he was one to talk anyway. Concerns a feller called Martin, Patrick Martin that was, of Milltown Malbay, County Clare ...'

Later in the evening, before Kevin went off to bed himself in the front sitting-room that he'd taken over for the purpose, Frances would get the kettle on and do her last round of duties. Tea for Sister Michael and Jack, though he wouldn't always drink it, sandwiches and biscuits for Kevin. In a sense, it was as it had always been, the only difference being that the man sitting opposite her as she sat down for ten minutes before going to bed was not her husband.

Then one night she got a terrible shock. She woke in the early hours of the morning, her heart thumping in her chest and a terrible flush on her face as she remembered the dream that she had just experienced. She was a young girl, working in Littlewoods Pools, as she had really done over twenty years before. They were all there, all her old friends – Annie and Maisie and Florrie – and there they were, all girls again, laughing amongst themselves. Then she was on a bus with them all. It was some kind of summer outing. She wore a light frock under her jersey wool cardigan and she could remember feeling the warm breeze on her legs. And Kevin was there, just as he had been those few days ago when he'd been doing the garden, in his shirt-sleeves, the broad leather belt around his trousers. Then he started to sing and they all joined in. It was one of those folk songs that they used to sing years ago. Suddenly, quite suddenly, they were on a beach, a long sandy beach with huge dunes, · like Formby or Ainsdale, the sea whispering in the distance, a soft breeze blowing on her legs, lifting her skirt. Then Kevin was with her and holding her, his mouth on hers, his hand forcing its way over her body. The pleasure was so strong that she couldn't stop, and she gave herself in a gasp that woke her out of sleep and into flushed embarrassment.

She couldn't believe that she had dreamt such things about any man, let alone her brother-in-law, nor could she stifle the memory of the pleasure that she thought had passed from her life. That her body could have responded with such appalling appetite was the deepest condemnation of her own weakness. She lay there wondering whether the dream was sinful, whether the pleasure was something that she wanted and therefore an aspect of her culpability. Because she was to blame in not speaking to Kevin, in not asking him to leave them all alone. It was her fault that Kevin had become such a part of the family that the children barely thought about their own father.

And surely that was the ultimate wickedness. Forgetting about her own husband at a time like this was as near to mortal sin as she could get.

'Jack,' she said the following morning, 'you'll have to speak to him. He won't leave now and I've no idea what to be doing ... He won't leave, he said, until he's spoken to you ...'

'I won't talk to him. He'd take the last penny from a starving child, that feller would ... He's rotten through, and I'll not talk to him. That's the last of it. If that's all you have to say to me, you might as well leave me to sleep. If you mention his name again, Frances, I'll give you a bloody clout, weak as I am!' And he seemed to Frances, at that point, to be lifting himself out of bed in anger.

'Jesus!' said Frances, in exasperation and tiredness. She had lain awake nearly all night, ashamed and bewildered by her hidden desire, and now her husband was the one who was leaving her with the dilemma. Wasn't it his refusal to talk that was keeping Kevin there all the time? How in the name of the living God could she be expected to throw her own brother-in-law out of the house? And it wasn't as if he was making a nuisance of himself. He'd done more jobs in three weeks than Jack had in nearly ten years. He gave her money for his keep, and he kept the children happy where Jack had only growled at them.

'He's a damn sight more considerate to the kids than you ever were!' she said, slamming the door behind her.

Nevertheless, nothing changed. Kevin had moved on from having decorated the sitting-room to putting up shelves in the kitchen, in the unused space 'above the Creda. Now Frances could put the soap-powder and the bleach safely away from the children and she felt it was great to have a real man around the house for once. And things seemed to settle themselves even more when Kevin returned one evening to say he had found work with one of the Irish gangs working on road repairs over on the East Lancs. "'Tis only four or five weeks or so, then I suppose it's back to square one, but it's great to have a real wage dropping into the pocket on a Friday. I'll give you a decent few shillings for my keep ...'

'I don't know how long, Kevin ... I mean, Jack is as stubborn as an old donkey.'

'I'll have to wait on, then, Frances,' he said.

And though the only real problem was the fact that Jack would hve nothing to do with his own brother in his own house, Frances began to feel strangely that a new life was taking shape under her own eyes. The children adored their uncle, there was no question of that. He had them in stitches at the best of times, and silently passive at others. So really, it was no surprise to find themselves on the train one Sunday shortly before Christmas, making their way to Ainsdale and a walk along the beach.

Of course, the beach brought memories of the dream back to her, a nocturnal passion that shamed her into walking some five or ten yards ahead of Kevin and the children. But then he caught up to her and sent the children off on a race.

'It's not just Jack,' said Kevin. 'I've grown attached to the lot of you. It's the first taste of a family I've ever had ... Spent too much of my time fooling with the girls and forgetting about the future. There's nothing I'd like more now than to settle down, y'know, Frances ... with a family. I'd like to settle down with a good woman, I would. I mean, it's too late for me now to find a young girl who'd start to bring children into the world for me, isn't that so? I'm forty-three years of age now. Wouldn't it be great to find myself a rich little widow, though?' And then he laughed to himself.

Frances said nothing, but the breeze, which was warm for that time of the year, blew across her legs and lifted her skirt, embarrassing her into silence with the memory of the dream that it brought along.

'But isn't that terrible?' said Sister Michael. 'I had no idea that that was what the fuss was all about. I thought he was staying to help out ... I thought you'd asked him to come.'

'God, no. You see, I don't want Jack to ... You know, when it happens ... What I mean is when he dies, no point shying away from it ... I wouldn't like to think he was going with a grievance in his heart, that's what I mean.'

'I can understand that, sure enough. It must put you under pressure, with him around all the time as well ... I had no idea, Mrs Doherty. I'll have to do something about it. This situation can't be allowed to remain, and I don't think prayer will be enough. It's crying out in the

Lord's name for something to be done. You know, Mrs Doherty, these families from the country, sure, they have some terrible secrets to them. When I was a girl there was a man ... a rich auld feller he was but he was meaner than Judas. And he went off to Lisdoonvarna there and found himself a beautiful girl of about twenty years of age. A young girl from beyond Castlebar. And then he took her out to his bleak aul' farmhouse and he started working the poor girl like a horse. It was the scandal of the area. Then she got pregnant shortly after. He still had her working though, oh, Michael Davitt wouldn't get help in when he had his wife there. But there were complications with the pregnancy and the poor girl died on her childbed. And not a soul would ever speak to Michael Davitt again because they knew that he was too mean to call a doctor out to his wife, for the few shillin's it would cost, I mean this was in the days of having to pay ... Would you credit that now?'

'Jack isn't that bad, Sister, thank God,' said Frances.

'But it's what lies in the heart and the soul, that's what God will be concerned with. Can you imagine what He must have thought about Michael Davitt, a sinner like that? And you never know how things will fall out. You don't want people taking advantage of you because of circumstances. Your brother-in-law ... I like the chap, he's a good hard-working man, but I'm beginning to wonder who is the man around the place, would that be a fair comment to make? And what would your husband make of that?'

'You're not trying to say that ...?'

'If I said anything, the tongue would blister in my mouth. All I'm saying is that something has to be done.'

Frances hadn't told Sister of her dream. How could she? The last person who you'd expect to share those kind of feelings would be a sixty-year-old nun, a woman who'd not known the need for a man. But when Kevin came in from work that evening, Frances could have sworn she saw some kind of recognition on her face. Had she somehow given away the real fear in her own heart, when she decided to tell Sister of the dilemma in which she found herself? Did Sister have any notion that underneath it all was an attraction that was becoming more trouble-some each day?

Perhaps Kevin had sensed something about Frances, a reticence or resistance to his charms, since that day on the beach at Ainsdale. When he returned from work he had handed her a cold fleshy parcel that she later found to be a two-pound cut of fresh salmon which he wanted poached, for the whole family, with boiled potatoes and peas. He had bought apples and pears and oranges, and chocolate for the children. It was as though there was something to celebrate, as though the family were to acknowledge something over a formal meal.

And there was a coolness about the meal. Kevin's appetite for once didn't match the great plateful of food that Frances had placed in front of him. He picked at the salmon, that was all, and ate only two of the potatoes, while the rest of them behaved as though they had been deprived of luxury for months at a time. The children had never known such an unexpected feast. Christmas and Easter had reasons behind their festivities, but this Friday night had only a pay packet under it.

But then he came round to it. He gave the children a chocolate bar each and told them to leave their mother and himself alone. Popeye was on the television, anyway; the children didn't need an excuse.

'Frances, I've been wanting to ask you ... for a week or so now. It's not as though we don't get on, isn't that right? And of course, there's no accounting for what might happen in the future, if you know what I mean. With four children there you might have a job on your hands ... You know, I love kids. It's only now I'm beginning to understand it. Ah, you've probably heard the stories about myself, how I had more girls than I had hot dinners ... Well, there's a bit of truth in it, all right. I did have girls. I'm not hiding from the truth, why should I? At least I know how to make a woman happy, I know that for a fact. Yes, the girls led me a right old dance, but I wouldn't have changed a second of it, not one bit of it ... And there's girls still over there that would take me now, would marry me right off if I just so much as gave them the nod ... And that's where the money all went, Jack was right about that. After the seminary the family got me a little bookshop there in Dublin, not a bad little business. But the debts I ran up ... When I have a girl to think about, the money flies out of my pocket like a bloody helicopter. So you can ... perhaps you can understand when I say I'd love to be ... to ... have a family of my own ...'

'Kevin, what is it you're saying to me? What is it? said Frances. *My God, you couldn't be*, she thought.

'And I know you like me, Frances, I know that. I'm not the kind of chap ... I mean, it needn't go any further, that's what I'm saying, not if you don't want it to ...'

Frances' hands had gone as moist as the uncooked salmon had been earlier. And her heart raced as she looked at Kevin, saw in his presence the man who had so pleased her and yet terrified her in that dream. *Please don't say any more, please don't.*

'It boils down to, the boss has offered me permanent work as a ganger, I could be on a good wage ... And it's permanent work, you see. There's a whole new stretch of road opening up around St Helen's there and they need the men. And the boss is from my part of the world, over

Kilkee way there, and it's true what they say about Clare fellers sticking together ... Is the position I'm in, don't you see? And you'd have nothing to worry about ... If you needed to see a priest, it's not as though the Church frowns on this kind of thing. After all, it can't have been all easy with Jack so much older than you, we must be the same age nearly, and his sickness? It must have been terrible at times ...'

Then the door opened and Sister Michael entered. *God in Heaven, she was outside and she heard him,* thought Frances. 'Er ... will you have, will you have a taste of salmon, Sister, there's plenty left? Look, the children hardly, they didn't eat much. Why don't you ...?' said Frances.

'Thank you, Mrs Doherty, I will. I haven't had fresh salmon since the last time I was over. It has such a delicate flavour to it, a ... not fishy at all ... a clean taste ...'

'Well, I'll be getting the dishes done while you're eating, and you can talk to Kevin,' said Frances, making a great fuss over the plates and cutlery, to hide the desperate uncomfortable flush that was now surging across her face.

'Sit yourself down, Mrs Doherty, I've only come down to ask Kevin to go up and speak to your husband. He asked me, you see, Mrs Doherty, he asked me to speak to Kevin ... He said he wants to talk to him. Would you go up, he wants to talk ...' said Sister Michael, looking across at Kevin. As he stood up, it looked for a moment to Frances as if he was going to say something, as if he was going to finish what he had been saying earlier, but he lowered his eyes and left the room.

They heard his heavy tread ascend the stairs. Frances said, 'What did you say to him? I didn't think Jack would ever talk to him ... You're ...' but the nun put her finger over her mouth and then pointed to the room above them. There was a silence for a few minutes. Then the two women could hear a man's voice, and then, after some time, another. Then there was a definite laugh and more talk. Sister Michael smiled across at Frances.

'I told him he should think about other people, I said you have to think about other people. You have to think about your wife and children. That's what I told him. I told him that he had to think of you and the children, that you couldn't bear to think of him dying without having patched up all that business with Kevin. And I reminded him of what a sinner he would be if he let things go on ... Because the sin would be leaving somebody helpless. I told him he had no right to do that. He had no right to leave you like that ... I told him that it would be you then that would have to repay the debt, the guilt, to Kevin. And I said he had no right to do that. I said you have to think of others, that's what I told him.'

Then Sister Michael took Frances by the hand and led her, into the sitting-room that had become Kevin's bedroom. She opened the big suitcase and the two women flung whatever they could find into its open mouth.

Ciarán Folan

CITIES BENEATH THE SEA

The summer of the year I am to be sent away to boarding-school. My mother switches on the television on a particular afternoon and a dimly lit landscape fills the corner of the room. The secrets of the moon pour into our lives. My mother says a boundary has been crossed. She says now there are no limits beyond which Man cannot go. My father lights a cigarette. He pokes it at the screen. He says, 'Anything the Yanks do, the Communists can't be far behind.' My mother gazes at the screen – the slow-bouncing shadow of Neil Armstrong reflected in her eyes.

For years my mother has made predictions – the end of wars, cities beneath the sea, a universal language, pills for food, a bridge across the Atlantic, a man on Mars. Some of these are already coming to pass before our very eyes, she says. And who can doubt her? My father reads somewhere that it is all a million-dollar NASA stunt. Everything was set up in a studio in the desert. They never even left the ground, he tells my mother.

'Oh Tom,' she says, 'why do they print such nonsense?'

She looks out at the sky and, for a moment, a faint doubt floats across her mind.

Australia is my father's country, it seems. He talks about the bush and the territories, the great open spaces and the outback with an ease suggesting familiarity. During the winter he says they're scorching now on Bondi Beach. He checks the temperatures in the paper every day. He talks about the flowers of the jacaranda tree.

'Petals like the tears of a goddess,' he says.

My mother laughs. Sometimes she says, 'Your father's Australia is a state of mind.'

*

My mother has work to do. She runs the village post office. In the evenings and during the holidays she gets me to help. I count change, stamp letters, sort postal orders and deal with customers when she's tired. My father takes no part in the business.

'Your father has no head for figures,' my mother says by way of explanation.

Instead, my father travels around to old farmhouses and buys antiques. That's what he calls them when he's discussing them with my mother, but with the farmers they are 'knick-knacks' and 'stuff lying about'. Mainly we visit the houses of bachelors. These houses are always up high-hedged winding lanes. They have apple trees and gooseberry bushes at the back or side. I wander around kicking windfalls while my father sits in the kitchen drinking whiskey and discussing football. Sometimes one of these men plays a tune on the fiddle. My father winks at me as I stand in the doorway.

Driving away, he tells me to have a look at what's in the box on the back seat.

'Take them out, he says. 'Take them out, for God's sake.'

I pull out a blue glazed jug, a large brown willow pattern dinner plate, an olive-shaded oil lamp, sun-bleached linen tablecloths from a long-forgotten wedding party. 'Some bloody caper,' my father shouts. He opens the window and starts to whistle. The tune is always 'Waltzing Matilda' and I always try to sing the loudest.

Every so often the car is packed with cardboard boxes full of crockery and lamps and we all take off for Dublin. We stay, three to a room, in a hotel and next day we do the rounds of the antique shops on the quays. My mother always does the dealing. Before she enters a shop she studies herself in her compact mirror. Then she looks at my father and raises an eyebrow and smiles and he gives a low clear whistle. We wait on the footpath, sitting on heavy brown sofas that bear signs reading 'Do Not Touch'. My father lights a cigarette and I eat ice-cream and we listen for the sounds of money changing hands.

If we manage to sell everything in a day they argue about whether we should stay another night. 'Money is there to be spent,' my mother says and she reaches back to squeeze my knee. She says, 'Life is short' and 'You can't take it with you when you go.'

'Yes,' says my father. 'This caper will surely land us in the poorhouse yet.'

Thunderclouds bank up behind the line of beeches at the end of the garden. My mother tries on another sunhat.

'So, what do you think?' She stands with one hand on her hip.

My father looks up from the table. He jots something in his notebook. *'Bellissima,'* he says. He is looking at my mother as if he can't remember exactly who she is.

'Indeed,' my mother says. She picks up another hat, then heedlessly drops it back in the box. 'The sun', she says, 'has deserted us for ever.'

She goes to the window. Whenever she does this she stands on the tips of her toes. But the window is large and my mother is not small. She is like a child looking at a world she has heard mention of in passing.

As his first great undertaking of the summer my father plans to build a telescope. He gets measurements from a magazine. He makes a list of materials. One Saturday he brings a length of six-inch diameter plastic piping home from town. He writes away to England for further information. He orders lenses. I study maps of the sky.

Three weeks later a wooden crate packed with straw arrives by special delivery. As my father lifts a lens from the crate it crashes to the floor.

'Australia here we come,' my mother says. My father doesn't move. My mother gets a brush and starts to sweep up.

Ever since her sister Jean brought word of it home from Chicago, my mother's summer drink is iced tea.

'Everything stops for iced tea,' my father says. He holds a jug in front of his face before pouring the clouded liquid down the sink.

My mother, in her sunhat, is sitting on a café terrace somewhere in a hot country. She idly tips her glass towards a dallying stranger. The hour is full of tinkling and a thousand shifting points of glass-refracted light.

One Friday afternoon my mother puts me in charge of the post office and goes to town. Near closing time an old man comes in. He stands in the middle of the floor and peers about. When he spots me he takes off his hat and shakes it in my direction.

'I want to speak to somebody in charge,' he says.

'I am,' I say.

'Not you,' he says. 'I want to speak to your mother. Where is she? I have questions to ask her.'

I tell him she's gone to town.

'Ask her whose money she's spending,' he says as he leaves. 'Just ask her that, sonny boy.'

After he's gone the room echoes with the smell of drink and damp turf fires.

That evening as she waltzes about the kitchen in a new pair of white sandals, stocking up the fridge with fruit and bottles of soda water, I tell my mother about the customers.

'Nobody cranky, I hope,' she says.

'No,' I say, and she smiles and hands me a cool peach.

My mother locks the sitting-room door. The voice of John McCormack escapes into the quivering afternoon. A boy, wheeling a bike, stops on the road for a moment. He looks at the sky and then at the vacant windows of our house.

My father produces a typewriter. He keeps it in the garage where our car used to be. My mother makes mugs of percolated coffee in the morning and glasses of lemonade as the day gets warm, and leaves them outside the garage door. She says he is writing a novel. She says this with pride and conviction. My father never mentions it at all. On his breaks from work he stands at the garage door in his trousers and vest. He pushes his hand through his hair and lights another cigarette. He looks like the writers I have seen in photographs in his old magazines – intense men with two-day shadows staring at some invisible point on a black and white horizon. 'What a caper,' he says to himself as he stubs out a half-smoked cigarette.

My mother takes to preparing extravagant meals.

'A writer's brain needs nourishment,' she says. She studies numerous cookbooks. She carefully notes the ingredients, the quantities and times. But somewhere along the line she loses patience with all the instructions and goes at it in her own way. She smiles at my father as she puts a new dish on the table. She watches him eat and waits for his approval. '*Buonissimo*,' he always says. He must wonder though how long his luck will hold.

On a hot afternoon in late August a man calls to the post office. He is dressed in a suit and tie, and carrying a briefcase. He tells me to fetch my mother. ('Fetch' is the word he uses.) She is sitting on the sofa in the front room, drinking iced tea, leafing through a magazine.

'Oh love,' she whispers. 'A man in a suit on a day like this.' She fingers the neck of her blouse as she watches him through the crack at the jamb of the door.

The man and my mother go into the front room. He puts his hands on the briefcase and starts to speak. My mother nods. She arranges her skirt. He takes some papers from the briefcase and hands them to my mother. She spreads them on the coffee table beside her. She glances quickly from one paper to the other and then at the man. He checks his watch and says something again. A breeze, a fickle movement of air, lifts one of the papers off the table. My mother reaches out to grasp it and knocks against a jug full of poppies. She picks up a flower and holds it to her face. The man stares at the red explosion on the carpet. Then he checks his watch again.

'Neither of us were much good at figures, as it turns out,' my mother says.

She runs a finger along the edge of the counter, checking for dust. Already everything has been scrubbed and cleared.

'Someday,' she says, 'you will remember all this and you'll want to ask questions. Listen, don't think back. Don't stop in your life just to wonder about this. Don't fill up your life with dreams of things that may be or that might have been. You mustn't be like your father and myself.'

She tears a page from the calendar block and now it is a new day. In the yard my father carries boxes of magazines from the garage and flings them on to the fire. It flares blue and red for a few seconds before burning with a low grey flame.

'That awful smell', my mother says eventually, 'will get into everything.'

I remember this now though it never happened. My mother and father are walking through the fields, which are not their fields any more. I am somewhere else. Perhaps I don't exist. My father is carrying a guitar slung over his shoulder. My mother is wearing a pale green sunhat and a blue dress with a large white flower. She is barefoot. Now she notices a moon, hanging low like a fragment of shattered crystal in the late evening sky. It reminds her of something. She turns to my father.

'We are thieves and petty criminals,' she shouts.

'Yes,' shouts my father, 'we are that.'

He unslings his guitar and starts to strum, but it is out of tune. My mother spins around once, then sashays across the field.

'Play,' she shouts. 'Play anyway.'

Jangle, jangle, jangle, the guitar goes. Jangle, jangle. My father starts to laugh. Next he's singing. Some song he wrote during all the idle garage days. My mother keeps moving far, far away until she can no longer hear my father's voice, until she can hear only those jangling notes that sound to her like the strange radio signals emitted by the unmanned stars.

Shammai Golan

ENCOUNTER

Rosenberg could tell what time it was by the patch of sun on his morning paper. The yellow light had reached the Letters to the Editor. Advice. Complaints. Appeals. He had read them all, as he did every day. Perhaps because Nimrod's letters were so few and far between. And now, it was time. He had been here on the bench since ten o-clock. The same as always, Sitting down with the same sigh of relief. The years of work at the factory. The constant ache in his back. The joints of his hands. His feet. They said the Jerusalem climate had an effect. The bench dug its screws into him. The morning news did nothing to alleviate his pain. He knew it almost by heart. The editorial. The News in Brief column. The Quotation for the Day. By the time he came to the readers' letters, his body was tense with anticipation of the boys' arrival.

He glanced at his watch. Just to be sure. The sun always made that yellow patch at this time of day. Still, one should check. Rectangular watch. Five years on his wrist without stopping even for a moment. Heavy and stable. Stainless steel strap. Always showing the correct time, the day of the week, the date. Every day. Tirelessly. It also illuminated the night with its glowing hands. A gift from the management on his retirement. They had assured him that a man who knew the exact time and date would never experience loneliness.

But the hands moved with maddening slowness. The patch of sun was still on the readers' letters. The boys never came early. Their school principal was probably strict. Probably made them work at their lessons even if one of their teachers was absent. Youngsters had to get used to thinking for themselves. Studying in depth. Reaching conclusions. That was the only way a person could really achieve his independence. His Nimrod used to recite the principal's words from memory. He was independent from a very early age. He used to come home late. Today, too, the boys would not turn up before he had finished reading the News in Brief. And the classified ads. But he had been cutting down on his reading over the last few days. His eyes were starting to betray him. Headaches. The heart suddenly raced. The boys never came early.

But they came at the regular time. First of all the voices, from above. From the park gate opposite their school. High tones blending with deeper ones. Boys whose voices were still breaking. There was nothing regular about them, other than the time of their arrival. And here they were, following their voices. Large limbs. Wild hair. Blue shirts. Jeans. Tumultuously taking possession of the park. Making themselves at home. Shoving and being shoved. Rolling their school-bags. The sound of yowling cats. Screeching girls. Barking dogs. Pogrom.

Rosenberg keeps track of them over the edge of his newspaper. Over the top of his glasses. He is quite concealed in the shade of the tall pine. Receiving the softly falling pine needles on his bald head, his shoulders. The hard seat of the bench pushes up against him. He does not move. The nail-heads. The bougainvillaea at his back. Flower thorns.

The boys are coming from above. Down the wide stone steps. Must not miss their arrival. Must not waste the moments of their coming. They have to notice him. Stop by him. Say, Hey old man! Then disperse. Leap boldly over the bushes. Over the rosebeds.

But no. They were eyeing him. Surrounding him. Their leader was sitting at the end of the bench. Casually. Putting down his school-bag. Between himself and Rosenberg. Bare arm. Downy golden hairs. Long, tanned fingers. Feet curling over the soles of his sandals. His friends stand off a little. Bunched together. Like mountains enclosing Rosenberg. Rocks on all the paths. He is on his own. Furtively observing their movements. Knowing the position of each one. The threatening murmur intensifies. He merely smiles to himself. For he knows that one of them, maybe the leader sitting so close, will call out, OK, you guys, that's enough, leave the old man alone. And they would all leave. And Rosenberg would know that he had been one of them.

But it was different today. Something had gone wrong. The leader pulled a long brown cigarette from the pocket of his jeans jacket. Thin as a nail. Someone gave him a light. A smell of incense rose on the air. Rosenberg could sense his quickening heartbeat. Here it came. The fragrant smoke encompassing him. Penetrating his nostrils. His mouth. Entering his lungs. Another boy approaches. Pushes the leader, shoves his school-bag, Move over! As if chasing the leader from the bench. But Rosenburg knows it is directed at him. The bench is for everyone! shouts the boy, winking. His eyes are black. Shooting sparks of merriment. Your school-bag's in our way! Puts out a hand, as if to move the bag. Instead, he knocks the newspaper out of Rosenberg's hands. It's hard for the old man to bend. His back. Hunching over the iron machines in the factory for thirty years. Bending twenty- and forty-millimetre iron bars, turning them on the lathe.

Nevertheless, he bent and picked up the newspaper. Again it was snatched out of his hands. Flung to the ground. Rosenberg raised his eyes. The boy was standing in front of him. One foot flicked out, close to Rosenberg's knees. Springy, balanced stance. The boy's eyes dared him. Someone in trainers came and stepped on the newspaper. Quietly. Deliberately. Without apparent anger. Rosenberg knew that silence. Was prepared for verbal abuse. A shouted insult. He had been expecting this moment all morning. Should he get away now? The newspaper was a dead loss, anyhow. They would give him another one at the grocer's. They would wrap his two rolls, his fifty grams of hard cheese and the plastic carton of yoghurt in it. He did not do any cooking since his wife Leah died. Only tea, or coffee. He sometimes found two or three poems on the wrapping paper. Short lines. Incomprehensible. A new world. Even in poems.

The boys were becoming agitated. He could sense the agitation in their muttering. They were losing patience. One of them suggested that they should move on. Trace of alarm in his voice. Afraid of what might happen. A girl's voice adds, Not worth it. Just an old guy having a rest. Nice girl. Jeans skirt. Hair tumbling around her cheeks. Nightingale voice.

Rosenberg roared. Quiet, hoodlums! Just shut up! Deep down, he hoped to stop them from going. To give them an excuse to stay. He bent to pick up the newspaper. The shreds of complaints being trampled under a shoe. Blue and white. The laces yellow. Woollen socks, too. In the middle of the heat wave, woollen socks. He almost burst out laughing. But the trainers were ominous. They stood wide, long. Size forty-four. Maybe even forty-five. Same as Nimrod. Funny boys. So young and their shoes already so big. The faintly dusty, sweaty smell. He kept his son's shoes to this very day. Mudstains on the soles. Nimrod had gone overseas to study medicine and had not come back for his shoes.

Rosenberg gave the foot a gentle nudge. As he had nudged the horse's foot in his youth. Somewhere. In the distant homeland of mother and father and goyim who spoke Polish. He whispered in Polish, *Noga*. Which means foot. The shoe lifted. The edge of it knocked his hand. Flexing his stricken hand, he gripped the ankle and pulled the pages from under the foot. He looked up, trying to encounter the boy's eyes. He smiled. But the boy winked at his friends and hopped on to the paper with his other foot.

Again Rosenberg bent down and grasped the foot. He could feel the vein beating in the ankle, under the sock. In the evenings, he used to kiss the tiny soles of Nimrod's feet. He would remove the little light-soled trainers, put on his floral pyjamas. Nimrod would laugh, kicking his little feet and shouting, Wanna sleep in them! and the whole room laughed with him. The window panes, the curtains, the carpet, the lampshade. Rosenberg would cover his son's body with kisses. Now Nimrod was a well-known doctor. In the country over the sea. Sometimes, on the rare occasions when he wrote, he would include a casual photograph of his son. Your grandson, he would write. Indeed, he resembled Nimrod. The fair shock of hair, the freckled, upturned nose.

The boy flicked his shoe again, hitting Rosenberg on the thigh, near the groin. Rosenberg, mechanically, punched the boy in the stomach.

Zap, old man! came the taunting cry. The boy's eyes darted around, seeking witnesses to his insult, the revenge he was about to take.

Leave the old man alone! called the nightingale's voice. But the others crowded closer, jostling each other. Like a train jolting its carriages in a sudden halt. The boy was standing in front of him, his hands close to the old man's chest, at throat level. Warm hands, half hesitant, half threatening. Rosenberg began imperceptibly to slide along the bench. The nail-heads hurt him as he slowly pushed himself backwards against the wood. The yellow paint flaked on to the seat of his pants. Making a big yellow patch. The insult surged in his heart, rose in a ball of fury to his throat. He stood up, grabbing the lapels of the boy's jacket in both hands. Good cloth. It held. He took pleasure in tensing his muscles. He still had power in his hands. Now he would show them who Old Rosenberg was. It seemed as if his whole life force was concentrated in his hands. All at once he lifted the boy off the ground. Saw with amazement the big helpless feet. The huge trainers dangled in the air. The impudent look in the boy's eyes gave way to fear. Rosenberg took a deep breath. He raised his eyes to heaven for a moment. Thankful for his great victory. Then he carefully lowered the boy.

So you're going to be a doctor, eh? he grinned into the boy's face. A big-time doctor!

Translated by Riva Rubin

Bryn Gunnell

DR RAO'S
EVENING OUT

It was the thunder that woke Dr Rao the first time. When he put on the light, the sly shadows skittered back into the dark corners of the big silent room and the naked bulb shone down on to the damp-bloomed almirahs and the photograph of her husband in his general's uniform that stood on the writing table. The large eyes seemed to be fixed on the intruder who was sitting up in bed, wearing only his drawers, for he had not brought his pyjamas and she had not offered any. The face had an arch look that always surprised Dr Rao when it sprang out of the darkness. One eyebrow was slightly, sardonically raised as if the general were saying, 'She'll grind you to powder, like she did me. She'll eat you raw. Oh, she may seem absent-minded, but she knows exactly what she wants, and gets it.'

Why, thought Dr Rao, was it always this room when she was not in the mood? There were twelve rooms in the rambling bungalow. She lived in one, furnished with the barest necessities; the others were hardly ever used and her servant, a stiff-necked old Brahmin who always moved soundlessly on bare feet and had a way of suddenly appearing when you least expected it, occupied a shack at the bottom of the garden. Neglect, the carpenter bees and the Himalayan rain had done their work thoroughly: the house was a wreck, as cold and cheerless as the dreariest dak bungalow.

The rain tinkled and rat-tatted on the louver overhead and there were ominous drips in several parts of the room. Then it began to crash down, snorting and gurgling in the broken gutters. Sometimes, out there in the windy dark, it sounded like cheering or the roar of distant breakers, but after a while the downpour slackened and became a silvery syncopation of drops which eventually lulled Dr Rao to sleep again.

When he woke the second time, everything was very still. He knew at once that the thing was there.

He lay in the dark for a while, bracing himself, but it was only when he switched on the light that it began – a shooshing and rustling, like heavy curtains being drawn. The rustling ceased abruptly. A cane chair creaked.

He waited, straining to pick up the sound again, and suddenly it was all round him, a low murmur that gradually rose to a sharp hiss, broken by bursts of angry whispering.

The whispering came now from this side, now from that; it flitted up into the dark pit of the ceiling and stopped for a moment, only to break out again right beside Dr Rao's ear – a terrible whisper of desperate entreaty, so clear he could almost make out individual words. He was being pelted, slashed with words, and just when the tension created by this incoherent flood became unbearable, the whispering faded until it sounded like a drizzle of voices in the next room, and then there was silence.

Why did this girl always pick on him, he wondered? It was said that the only daughter of the British colonel who had built the bungalow had hanged herself in that room after being jilted by a young lieutenant from the cantonment. He had probably come, flushed and tight-mouthed, to announce the break to the girl whom Dr Rao imagined as tall, already a little withered, with a horse face and pointed knees. The words 'I am going away' must have been like a rush of darkness to her. Dr Rao knew what it was like to be alone in a house where one never heard the patter of children's feet or squeals from the swing in the garden, and for a woman, for Miss Bartlett – he suddenly remembered her name – to sleep always alone is like sleeping on a bed of cold sand. To spend the rest of her life waiting on her irascible father, struggling to keep her dignity, having to admire other people's children; to lie old and ill and alone in the end with the light beating, beating against the shutters and the koel calling, calling out there among the trees: it was unthinkable. Miss Bartlett had somehow slung a rope on that central beam and, in her long dress, with her lank hair over her face, she had hung kicking and choking in the shaft of moted light that filtered down from the louver.

Dr Rao put out the light. He knew from experience that the whispering would not start again. He was impressed, but he was not afraid. In fact, he took a clinical interest in what he called a manifestation of thwarted sexuality and he had read too much Marx to be upset by the many stories of ghosts and ghouls that were supposed to haunt the town.

The house was quiet. The moon shone through the lattice door that opened on to the garden and, lighting up the short passage that led to it, revealed on one side a black patch of damp shaped like India and on the other a poster of a Japanese playboy in a karate pose, his muscles bulging and an expression of tigerish ferocity on his mask-like face.

Sushila had pinned it there Sushila who lay only two rooms away, her big yellow cat's eyes closed, her slender legs stretched out under the covers. 'A woman is the softness of the parrot's breast, the hardness of a diamond, the ruthlessness of the tiger, the sweetness of honey.' The old words came into Dr Rao's mind.

Sushila was at the age when a woman desperately tries to exert more power, before it is too late. 'For you know, Krishna,' she had once said to him, 'old age is close: It has already put threads of grey in my hair, and before I become all out of shape and like an old hen turkey, I want to show people that I am still here, that I have ideas of my own, so please bear with me, even if I am sometimes difficult.'

She had his life by the neck. Whatever she asked, Dr Rao did. 'Undress in the bathroom and come to me. You're spry still for a man of your age. Why, you can still manage the pillar position, though I have to steady you a little with my right leg. You are my Krishna. If only you weren't almost bald, I would call you Keshawa, He of the Long Hair!' And she would laugh, that high fresh laugh, like a girl's, for her voice had not changed over the years.

When she was in company it was always 'Oh you *must* know Dr Rao, my neighbour. Always at my elbow in time of need. Such a *nice* man! I wonder he never married. As honest as an elephant. Of course I'm much alone now, and he does me such good service.' Once a fortnight, to be exact.

To the doctor himself she said, 'We get along pretty well. There is a kindness between us and stimulating talk. I'm not thinking in terms of anything permanent, mind. I couldn't face it again. Men just want someone to prepare a tasty curry and heat up their bath water. That's not for me. Marriage tapers off so quickly, you know. A quiet relationship is all I want. My heart is no longer in a thousand pieces at the sight of a fine man. Ah, men, Krishna, men ... Embraced by a woman, a man forgets everything else. Ah, men, Kirshna, men ... Embraced by a woman, a man forgets everything else. Take care, though. You might have a mystic stroke one day; rise from a woman's arms to the Formless, the Atman, the Creator himself in tune with the Infinite!' There was always an edge to what she said, a little salt in the honey of her speech that he found irresistible. She made him feel like a small boy, and whenever she called, he came. He had nothing to complain about. In the midst of enjoyment one does not argue about its quality, but she sometimes warned him, saying 'Sugar cane is sweet, but do not bite it to the root.'

Though he never breathed a word of it to her, Dr Rao longed to grow really old, to reach the third stage, the *Vanapsathashram*, when all ties are cut off, when desire at last relaxes its hold and a man can pay homage to the creator by simply admiring a woman. 'I wonder he never married.' Dr Rao knew what she said about him. He thought 'of his epileptic brother who crouched in a dark room in their family home on the outskirts of Bangalore and of his father who had been given to fits of black depression when he would retire to his study and sit hour after hour in an armchair, breathing asthmatically and talking to his books because he had no one else to talk to, and who had always said, on the rare occasions when Krishna stood before him, 'Well, I hope you got good marks. Can you imagine what I am having to fork out for your education so that I can see you foreign-returned before I die?'

He thought of his mother with the rolls of fat hanging over her waistband and the way she paced the house, jingling her bunch of keys and making plans for him. But she was not to blame. That was how women were brought up in those days: bored stiff, grumpy and tearful; treated by their in-laws like a *banian* in the wash basket; their only outlet gossip and meddling; their only privilege that of ruling home, husband and children with an iron hand. His father was dead. He had had to stand by the riverside and see the flames rise and hear the skull explode, and now there was only his mother, his brother and some rascally servants, all to be provided for.

Dr Rao had always thought that girls should be encouraged to leave home and see something of the world. Sushila did not altogether agree. 'A woman should develop her independence of mind, I grant you, but do you want us to be like those girls in Europe with their thighs showing and their easy kissing? Or in America where it's even worse, where they'll do anything to try and remain young-looking? Hm, I've seen them at work, the fifty-year-old hags, all tarted up, who single out a Sirdarji and sweep him off to bed and then ask him if he believes in God! They drink and smoke and powder their wrinkles, and when the Sirdarji gets fed up and clears out, they scream and beat their heads against the wall. Huh, women with no class, no self-respect, no real understanding of love. You're lucky to have me, you know, and, I must admit, discerning enough to have picked out a real woman, home-made, with plenty of chili and spice!'

Dr Rao chuckled. As he lay there, quite composed now after his experience, he began to relive the party they had had that evening. Sushila had shone as usual and arranged everybody, prompting or dampening her guests as occasion required. She had worn her dark green and orange sari that looked like a sunset with bamboo outlined against it so that, when she moved, you expected to see a tiger's face peep out just above her shapely hips.

'Oh, no doubt about it, Dr Rao is the life and soul of the Paradise Clinic,' Dr Chandra was saying. A large bony woman who always seemed to have forgotten to do her hair, she had a cough like a sheep's. Sushila looked at her with something like commiseration. 'Yes, you're quite right,' she said. 'He really holds the clinic together. I always marvel at his ability to live surrounded by swabs and plastic pipes. I can't bear to set foot in the place myself – the dirt and the smell are too much, and all those old women having drugs or salt water or whatever it is pumped into them; old women with moustaches who swell and swell – yet he emerges from the place as happy as a boy out of school!'

'Oh, he may be very popular, but how many patients has he killed? He doesn't tell anybody that!' This was the voice of Mr Kalla, the Chief Forest Officer, a handsome man with calculating eyes and a jaunty manner who had come along with a young crony of his, known to everyone as Woppo, whose father, a big landowner, had for years been trying to persuade Sushila to sell him her bungalow. Woppo was a large slouching creature. He already wore a look of greasy dissipation, and Dr Rao noticed that he had black hair on the back of his hands. Mr Kalla was known to have a loft filled with teak and ivory which he sold illicitly at exorbitant prices, with Woppo's help. Both men called Sushila 'Auntieji', but in private referred to her as 'the fancy woman'. Dr Rao was always warning her against the two *badmash*, as he called them. 'Don't worry,' she would say. 'I know how to handle them: one flick of my wrist, and they are at my feet.' And it was so.

'Yes, how many people do you doctors kill?' Mr Kalla insisted. They were both laughing stupidly into their whisky.

Dr Rao had recently been invited to the wedding of Mr Kalla's daughter. He looked confused, but Sushila came to his rescue at once. 'What a ridiculous question,' she said, 'and an impertinent one. I'm surprised at you, Mr Kalla. In some cases if you have a disease, the body either conquers it or you peg out; no medicine will help.'

'Well, that's a poor comment on our profession, but I suppose it's true,' said Dr Rao. 'We have to make people believe in what we are doing so they can help themselves to get better.'

'The trouble is, you see,' Dr Chandra interposed, 'that now more people are relying on ayurvedic medicine. They seem to have lost confidence in what the West has to offer. Take our Police Chief's old father, for instance. We could easily have cured him of pleurisy, but he absolutely refused penicillin and died.'

Sushila glared at Dr Chandra. 'You may like to know,' she said, 'that I use ayurvedic remedies regularly. My guru swears by them. That Shankhapushpi syrup now – I find it very helpful.'

'Good heavens!' Dr Chandra gave a shrill laugh. '"Improves memory. Subsides distension. Beneficial for low IQ. Useful in insomnia."! Really, how can you? I hope that if you are ever seriously ill, you'll come straight to us!'

'Oh, what harm is there?' said Dr Rao, 'Whether it's an old remedy or a new one, so long as we think it does us good, that's half the battle. At one time women used to soothe a sick person with a soft hand. That was a good thing our moderns laugh at.' Sushila gave him a flashing smile.

'By the way, I hear your swamiji is a remarkable man,' said Dr Chandra.

'Remarkable? You mean he's a genius!' cried Sushila. 'Why, the very first time he came he seemed to know all about me already. "You've been unwell," he said, "and you're interested in spiritual matters."'

'Perhaps he saw your bottle of syrup on the shelf and that book of *vashanas* open beside the harmonium,' suggested Dr Rao.

Sushila bridled up at this, but there was a twinkle in her eye. Religion was a subject they always disagreed about. It had become a kind of game.

'Of course, you would want to wither everything with some rational explanation, wouldn't you?' she said.

'Now don't get me wrong, madam,' said Dr Rao. 'I just feel that someone of your intelligence should not be so easily taken in. You know these people are all humbugs. Why, he even performs in public, as at a circus! I once saw him trying to do meditation on his head, but he toppled over as soon as you could say Jack Robinson! Such a vulgar fellow, too. Someone in the audience handed up hundred rupee note as an offering, and he waved it gleefully over the heads of his adepts to show how highly he was appreciated. Disgusting.'

'Still,' said Dr Chandra, 'there is that story about his seeing off some foreign guests at Delhi airport and, lo and behold, when they got to Bombay, who should they see waiting in the hall to meet them but the swami himself! You can't explain that sort of thing.'

'Bah, some dumb-cluck dressed up as him, I dare say! And as regards the foreigners who come here craving spiritual nourishment, most of them – the girls especially – end up as the hypnotized slaves of some bogus nonentity. I've seen it time and again. I think our women go to them out of sheer boredom, but they get over it, luckily,' said Dr Rao.

'That's a very unkind thing to say,' said Sushila, pinching up her mouth. 'I mean, this man has really opened my eyes to so many things. For instance, I had always thought I was born under Cancer – you know, the gentle, yielding type – but he proved to me that I am Leo and my whole attitude has changed!'

Dr Rao burst out laughing, but made no comment. 'Anyway,' he said, 'I will say one thing for them: if you ask them what caste they belong to, they tell you they're not interested, which is refreshing, and though they're pretty sharp when it comes to money, they also know the value of doing nothing. We tend to forget that it is sometimes good just to sit and eat the air.'

'Oh, I couldn't agree more, doctor.' Mr Chandra suddenly spoke for the first time. A slight old man with a watery smile, he usually left all the talking to his wife and when he did have something to say, it nearly always began with his favourite phrase: 'Now we in India . . .' He was a retired District Collector and had given up his three-piece suit for khadi cloth and untiring attendance at temple festivals and charities. Dr Rao suspected that Mr Chandra also had an eye on Sushila's bungalow. There was even a rumour that he had obtained a rate rebate on his own spacious house for reminding the council that it was against the law for one person to occupy so large a bungalow without paying supertax.

Dr Rao waited. Mr Chandra cleared his throat. 'Now we in India', he said, 'have given the world a priceless gift, the gift of spirituality, but somehow things have gone wrong. I know Gandhi said, "Let us mismanage our own country in our own way," which is exactly what we have done, yet I fail to understand why our spiritual values have become degraded. Even our gods are not what they used to be. What happened to Brahma, Vishnu, Agni? No one ever hears about them. They just faded out. Now people only pray to Ganesh for luck and Lakshmi for wealth . . .'

'And Krishna for love,' said Sushila, shooting a glance at Dr Rao as she took a pinch of *supari* and tucked her legs under her. 'Haven't we been taught, though, that even the gods are mortal? After living through worlds as numberless as grains of sand, their garlands wither and they too have to return to nothingness.'

Mr Chandra ignored this and went doggedly on. 'As I was saying, our values have been sadly undermined. I deplore, for example, the way young people's English has gone down. How can they expect to get the right job if their English isn't up to scratch? The other day only our nephew was with us. At school they had told him to write a sentence containing the expression "by fits and starts", and do you know what he wrote? "I fits my boot and starts for the college"! How could anyone be such a dunce?'

'Oh, don't take it to heart, Mr Chandra,' said Dr Rao. 'The language of the conquerer has worn thin, that's all. And look at me – I don't know how to speak Hindi properly, but I'm sure your nephew does.'

'Yes, but you're from the South so there is some excuse.'

'Thank you. I was just going to say that my English is none too grand either, but who cares? We speak as we can. I went to the same sort of school as you, Mr Chandra, where they taught us to speak in a phoney Oxford accent – "Take a pew, old chap" and all that stuff.'

'I suppose the thing is we always go for the superficial in each other's cultures,' said Sushila with a sigh.

Dr Rao smiled. 'Quite right, madam. Foreigners see us as the only people in the world who have always been trying to prove the world doesn't exist! They don't realize what a hard, grasping lot we really are, ready to kill one another for a rupee. It's very easy to fool people with a lot of sanctimonious nonsense, and we all like to think our homes are palaces of prayer when really they are hotbeds of violence and vice. We doctors have to deal with the results every day.'

Mr Chandra had become very restive. 'But where do you stand, Dr Rao?' he squeaked. 'I mean, you seem to be against everything.'

'I don't stand anywhere. I just try to carry on with my job, and that's what most people here can't understand. They don't care what they do so long as it brings money and prestige.'

'Dr Rao is a bit of an anarchist, you know,' said Sushila placatingly.

'I can't think why. We have the same background – a pukkah Brahmin family; a decent education. I always thank my lucky stars that I went to a good school. Perhaps you were unhappy at school, Dr Rao?'

'Oh, I suppose it was no worse than any other school, but they made us do silly things which went quite against our customs, like wearing a belt with a clasp in the form of a snake. My mother almost had a fit when she saw it! Being strick Brahmins, too, we were taught to respect books of any description – if you fell over a book, you said sorry – so when it poured, the other boys, Christian or what have you, used to hold their books over their heads and get home almost dry, whereas I always turned up looking like the proverbial dying duck!'

'I sympathize, Dr Rao,' Suschila said. 'No doubt we are rather mixed up. My grandfather, who was very pro-British ...'

'He had to be. He was a High Court judge.'

'*Chup chup*, Dr Rao, if you don't mind. Well, he was summoned to Simla by the Viceroy and presented with a medal. I still have it. Solid silver, too. He went in his best bib and tucker, spats and all – a three days' journey, mind. Strange to say he died a few weeks after his return.

Perhaps it was all the excitement. I was alone in the house at the time. Some neighbours sent for the priests and do you know I almost had to fight with them to prevent them from taking the body away and then, all of a sudden, I realized that they were probably hungry so I fed the brutes and they became as meek as lambs.'

'Ha,' said Mr Chandra, 'my father always used to say, "Never trust a well-fed Muslim or a hungry Brahmin."' There was an awkward silence.

Mr Kalla and his companion had long since lost all interest in the conversation. They had drunk half a bottle of whisky and were giggling together on the settee. Dr Chandra, too, had obviously had enough. 'Well, tomorrow is another day,' she said, her usual signal for departure.

They all rose to go. Dr Rao retrieved his umbrella and, standing as straight as a ramrod, said to Sushila, 'Can I take you home, madam?'

'But I *am* at home, Dr Rao, thank you.' Dr Chandra tittered.

Goggling lasciviously, Mr Kalla and Woppo stood unsteadily in front of Auntieji, trying to hold their hands high above their heads in salute. 'Off you go now,' she said, 'and do try to drive me on the road.' Mr Kalla perfunctorily offered the Chandras a lift which they coldly refused, preferring to send the servant for a taxi. With obvious relief, the two *badmash* shuffled out and climbed into their Toyota.

As soon as the taxi arrived, Dr Rao walked the Chandras to the gate. 'Shall we drop you at your place? 'Dr Chandra enquired.

'No, no, it's only a step away. The walk will do me good.' He called a loud cheery 'Good-night' and disappeared into the darkness.

It began to pour as he climbed the hill. He reached the little row of shops and saw that a lamp was still burning inside one of the stalls. Ducking to avoid the bunches of bananas that hung above the courtier, he leaned inside and gently tapped the sleeping storekeeper on the shoulder. 'Ten Goldflake,' he said. He stood in the porch of the Sikh temple and smoked one. Inside the temple an old man with a flowing beard sat reading a great book with bronze clasps by the wavering light of a lamp. Bats squeaked under the eaves.

The rain had stopped and a star or two had rubbed through. Dr Rao looked at his watch. Twenty minutes. The coast would be clear now. He walked slowly back down the windy road to the bungalow. Her light was still on, but she was sitting in a basket chair at the dark end of the verandah. He heard the sharp click of her bangles as she turned slightly. Her hair was unbound and fanning over her shoulders.

'So there you are,' she said. 'I thought you wouldn't be long. But I can't tonight. Didn't you see the signals I was making?'

'What signals?'

'Well, I was sort of winking.'

'I didn't notice.'

'No, you were too anxious to make sure they saw you go!' She was bubbling now. 'Oh *Doctor* Rao, you do make me laugh, and that's so good; I feel like a girl again!'

'Thank you, *madam*.'

'*Doctor* Rao! *Madam*! What a show we put on!' She lay back in her chair, helpless with laughter. 'And, oh dear, how you banged them! I think you went a bit too far, though, like that time when you made such a fuss at the opening of the new Gymkhana Club.' Her eyes were dancing.

Dr Rao looked rather abashed. 'Well, there was some fellow there with ten cars and some skinny woman painter who only paints racehorses and a whole pack of bores who only talked stocks and shares while those poor devils of peons wagged red banners to scare away the kites which were trying to snatch pieces of tandoori chicken. That place overlooks our shanty town, and with those mountains of food and everyone talking big money, I felt it was indecent and I said so.'

'I know, but these people ... There's no point in making enemies.'

'Don't worry. Their skins are thick. I don't know why you have them in. I wouldn't offer them seat or water. Just a bunch of gossips and trouble-makers.'

'You take them too seriously. In fact, I think you're jealous of those two *badmash*! How can you be so stupid? What young pony would touch such withered hay? And just because you don't appreciate "the glamorous and flamboyant life-style of those who frequent the Gymkhana Club", as they said in the local paper, you don't need to fly off the handle. After all, who cares if they flash their money about and talk big? They'll only be reincarnated as scorpions!'

'Or cockroaches.'

'Exactly. And even if they managed to take this house away from me — and I know they couldn't do it legally — what then? As one grows older, one needs less and finally one needs nothing at all. You too will soon reach the last stage.'

'Another of our categories: learning, earning and – stage three rotting!'

'Not necessarily. You always exaggerate. I am seriously thinking of spending the rest of my days in the ashram. You mustn't mock those who are aspiring to something, however crazy it may seem. Remember what it says in the scriptures: "There are no blessings here, no happiness, no joys, but He himself creates blessings, happiness and joys.

There are no rivers, lakes or tanks, but He creates rivers, tanks and lakes."'

Dr Rao was silent. The wind blew through the garden. A night bird called.

'You are right,' he said after a while. 'My tongue runs away with me. But all that business about the gods, Sushila! I felt like saying, "How do you recognize a god anyway?"'

'Nothing simpler. He stands four inches above the ground and he neither blinks nor sweats! Anyway, I'm going to bed, Krishna. I've decided to do *puja* all next week and to be in good voice tomorrow I must be pure. The photographer is coming in the morning, too, to take a picture of me at the harmonium. But you can stay. The middle room is ready as usual.'

For a moment they stood like two guests waiting for the other to go; then, with an abrupt 'Good-night', she turned and walked quickly into the house.

A wisp of cool light appeared high in the sky. It was dawn.

'The fair, the bright one has come with her white children. She sets afoot the coiled sleeper. She for the sun has left a path to travel and we have arrived where men prolong existence.' The words were running through Dr Rao's head as he had a quick wash in the cold little bathroom adjoining his room. He had not slept so badly after all; felt quite refreshed, in fact.

While he was dressing, he heard the harmonium start up and Sushila's voice rising and falling. 'I am ground to flour before you. I will prepare for you betwen my breasts a palace of purple and gold.' How badly she sang – all off key – and it seemed a strange song to begin her week of abstinence. 'After the seizing of the waist, there is no going back. Mother, I am being burnt by a fire without a flame.' She sang badly, but Dr Rao liked the song and would have stayed to listen only he had to get back to the clinic.

As he opened the lattice door and stepped out into the garden, the sun broke through the clouds and touched a lychee tree into emerald. Everything glistened. Mynas cheeky-whistled from the roof. By the verandah hung a pouchy pitcher plant flower. A bee dithered towards it. Oh, if it went in there ... The bee veered away.

Dr Rao was half-way down the path when he became conscious of a little sound, like a child singing to itself, up and down, up and down. A happy sound.

At the end of one of the wet black flowerbeds, all so carefully tended, he saw a grizzled head, a bony back and one stick-like leg. The old *mali* was naked, except for a loin cloth. He was crouching down and slowly oaring himself along while, with a slender hand, he gently reached out, plucking a weed here, tucking a plant back into the soil there. He was singing to himself.

The old man heard a step, turned and smiled a toothless smile. His face was wrinkled like a pie crust, but his eyes were light and young.

Dr Rao felt he was in the presence of someone not quite of this world, someone touched by grace, and a sense of peace came over him. 'Was it you singing?' he said.

'Yes, sahib. I sing to the green things to help them grow, but gardening is work, sahib. Before you drink the milk of paradise, you have to feed the cow.' The old man was laughing silently.

'How long have you been working here?'

'Ten years, sahib. I was here before the lady's husband closed his eyes.'

'Strange. I don't remember . . . How old are you?'

'I used to be sixty, sahib.'

'Have you an children?'

'Oh plenty, and grandchildren. One of them is a post office clerk. You may have been seeing him. Khaki uniform he has and all.' As he spoke, the old man picked a small blue flower and handed it to Dr Rao. 'Blue is the colour of hope, sahib.'

Dr Rao looked at the flower. He did not know what made him suddenly stoop and touch the ground at the old man's feet before he hurried down to the gate.

When he reached the top of the hill, the monsoon sky was torn open and a great pane of blue swam through. For a moment a distant mountain peak, miles high, blazed like a white tooth, but was immediately lost in cloud.

Dr Rao stopped in the middle of the road and stood for some time looking up at that one patch of sky.

Kenneth Harvey

ORDERLY

I iron my white hospital pants on the living-room carpet. They must be creased and crisp like the bed-sheets themselves. The white T-shirt is fine as is. I stand, slip on the pants, then pull the T-shirt over my head, smooth it across my broad chest.

At fifteen minutes to eight I leave the house. It will take ten minutes to drive, four minutes to enter the building and change, and precisely one minute for the ride up the elevator.

My shift commences at eight o'clock. It could be a.m. or it could be p.m. Shifts alter but the actions remain the same. What happens happens with definite structure. Within an institution such as this – one occupied by patients of disorder – the need for routine is intrinsic.

I instil order. No matter how extreme the tactics, the preservation of order must be foremost and unquestionable.

For instance: Mrs Gallant is between medication. She asks me to see her husband. Can she call him? Can I lend her a quarter? I comply and guide her to the pay phone in the social room. She dials. The number has been disconnected. She listens to the recorded voice. It repeats itself. She listens three times then returns the receiver to its cradle.

'Something's wrong,' she says, slowly, hauntingly baffled. 'The number's out of order.'

'Perhaps it's being repaired,' I offer.

'Yes,' she says, vaguely.

'Let's go back and try later.'

'Yes.'

We walk together. She is thinking of her husband. Her husband was killed in a blaze only three months ago. A small child was trapped in the house as well. She hears it crying.

71

When they pulled out the charred, still child, she screamed, 'He's crying, give him to his mother.' The medication fades and she hears it crying. She halts now, bends her head as if listening to a distant voice. Her lips are slightly parted and her meek face begins to tighten.

The nurse sees us coming.

'Mrs Gallant,' she says. 'I have something for you.'

Mrs Gallant is startled by the voice. With complete humility, she stares at the nurse and takes the tiny plastic cup of pills. She swallows them.

'I'll call again later,' she says, handing the empty cup back to the nurse. The nurse nods. Mrs Gallant nods and steps back, across the threshold of her room as if reversing.

'Yes,' I say, closing her door, locking it.

I will not see her again for the remainder of my shift. In this institution she may believe in anything that calms her. The preservation of order means trust in lies. Patients may do as they choose, believe in the outrageous. This is order and it is something I do not deny.

Mr Elliot's face is vicious with intention. He is watching television but he is watching me through the corner of his dark eyes. He wants to say something to me, but instead he scowls at Mrs Penney.

'Cunt,' he barks.

Mrs Penney tut-tuts. 'I know,' she says. 'Tell someone who doesn't.'

'Virgin Cunt Mary.'

'Mr Elliot,' I caution. He glances sharply my way.

'Yeah,' he says. 'Nazi,' he says. 'Don't tell me who you are, Nazi.'

I lift my finger to my lips. 'Shhhh.'

'Easy,' he says, staring at Mrs Penney, watching her white legs beneath the edge of her cotton skirt.

Across the room, Mrs Martin is writing words in the air with her index finger. Her lips whisper, along with her actions, reading. She looks down at the book in her lap.

'What're you doing, Mrs Martin?' I ask, nodding to the pages.

'I'm studying French,' she says, grandly flicking back her grey-haired head.

'That's an English book,' I say.

'I'm studying French in English,' she snaps.

'I understand,' I say, and I almost do understand her. There lies the key: in that one word – almost.

Returning to the door, I stand and fold my arms. The television is playing an old romance. Black and white. They are kissing on the screen. Mr Elliot begins undoing his pants and so I move for him and quickly lead him away.

In the corridor, Nurse Dunphy looks up from her station. Her uniform is unbearably white. She smiles sweetly. I ignore her. A job is a job.

'Hello, Mr Hayter,' she says to me.

I am silent.

'Where are you taking Mr Elliot?'

'To his room.'

'He's been naughty again, eh?'

I move up the hallway, my arm around Mr Elliot's shoulder as if we are old pals. All the while he stares at me. He stares at the side of my face, his hands down his pants, thrusting violently.

'My room,' he says, smiling, smiling victoriously as he scampers into privacy.

I look down the long corridor and Nurse Dunphy is watching me. She waits, taps a pen against the side of her head, then returns to her chart.

Mr Elliot shouts, 'Holy Mary Mother Of God Pray For Us Sinners Now And At The Hour Of Our Death.' I open his door and see him drop to his knees with both hands clutching.

'Amen,' he says, gasping for mercy. 'Amen, amen ...'

Nurse Dunphy is blonde with her hair swirled up into a bun and clipped beneath her nurse's hat. She has a young thin face. It is attractive with long lashes and teeth that are a touch crooked. She is well humoured and insists on teasing.

'Get back to work,' she says as I pass her station.

'There's only Mrs Penney,' I say.

'She's enough.'

In the social room, Mrs Penney (she is not married, but it is customary to refer to the female patients as Mrs) is crying with her head in her hands. I look up to the screen and see the image fading out. 'The End' fades in along with booming music and then the tiny, hazy credits roll.

Cry, I say to myself. Cry, cry, cry. It is therapy. I know that much.

Mrs Penney lifts her eyes to me. They are tiny and pink, and she is smiling.

'How's my hair?' she asks.

'Fine,' I say, returning the smile.

'Look,' she says. She pulls down the collar of her pink sweater. I see the thick scar running down to top of her breast. I can see no further but

I know the scar continues down. She was cut as a teenager. A maniac with a knife and then later the necessity of heart surgery. The incisions scarred her insides as well, implanting obsession beneath the lifted line of scar tissue. She is engrossed with her appearance.

'Look,' she says. Reaching down into her brassiere, she pulls up her left breast. She taps the thick nipple as if sending messages in morse code. She taps it frantically.

'Understand?' she says. 'I love you. I love you.'

'Time for bed,' I say and she nods with the enthusiasm of one about to receive a gift.

'Yes.' She follows me without question.

Nurse Dunphy says, 'Tuck her in real good.' She speaks with her nurse's voice; the one that is set in a compassionate mode. It is up-tempo and soothing. Trouble-free. Breezy.

Mrs Penney takes my hands. Her fingers are small and chubby. They are wet with perspiration, or perhaps fluid of another nature.

'You understand why we'd never get along,' she says.

I nod sympathetically.

When we reach her doorway, she leans close, steps up on her tiptoes and kisses me.

'Good-night,' she says.

'Good-night,' I say.

She looks up at the ceiling as if at a brilliant moon. She senses the calm light brushing her face. She sighs.

'It's for the best,' she says. I agree and watch her step into the room. Inside, she stands close to the small square window of her door. She watches as I lock it. She hears the sound and her face suddenly changes.

'Don't look at me,' she shouts through the glass. '*Killer.*' I turn my back before I can hear the threats issue from her. I step away and move for the social room. It is quiet as I step across the tiles. The new movie concerns a mental institution. It is very old and the acting is forced, overly dramatic. I laugh at that and sit on the couch. Cross my legs. Fold my arms. Order.

In a moment Nurse Dunphy joins me. She shows me a run in her nylon, how far up it rides.

'Up to here,' she says. 'Look,' she says and I think of Mrs Penney revealing herself.

Nurse Dunphy lifts her skirt higher until I see she is not wearing underwear beneath the white nylons. She turns around to innocently show me her behind.

'See how the seem runs right up the crack of my ass?' She doesn't wait for a response. 'Isn't that the prettiest thing?'

I watch the screen. A nurse's black and white eyes are wide. Her long lashes flutter as she fills a syringe. It is a silent movie.

'We're on all night,' says Nurse Dunphy. 'Later we'll go visit Mrs Penney. Have some fun. Three of us.'

I nod and she skips merrily from the room as if all is well; all matters reduced to a carefree level of operation.

'Reports, reports,' she says on her way to her station.

Someone says to me, 'Death is perfect order.' I turn and look at the doorway, but no one is standing there. The light from the corridor is clean and reassuring. The social room is dim. The lights are off and I sense the patients stir in darkness.

It is only the pulse from the screen that gives light. The institution of television is quite appealing. People enter willingly and remain for their entire lives. A schedule set by the TV guide. Order in one form or another. Direction. We must lead each other in a calm, uneventful direction. The craving of order. Books set in rows, cars parked side by side, forms in triplicate, perfect human symmetry ... Neat, clean lines guiding us straight to death. Symmetry. Cemetery.

Up on the screen, the nurse is chasing a male patient around a table. The patient throws over the table and laughs dramatically, freezes stiff and begins to howl. The nurse moves beside him. She loves the patient. She tenderly swabs his forehead. Then, when he has calmed, she dramatically thrusts the hidden needle into his arm. Order. It is a silent movie. I cannot hear the scream. It is silent, or the sound is turned down. One or the other.

'Death is perfect order,' says the TV nurse, but I know she is not saying it at all.

Clyde Hosein

THE BOOKKEEPER'S WIFE

By two, Merle's hunger was a burning that serpentined from the pit of her stomach to her throat. She hid behind her curtains and when she saw her English neighbour fold up her garden chair and take her paperback and suntan lotion into the air-conditioned house, Merle rushed into her own yard. Her fingers closed over the calabash mango that had fallen from the Englishwoman's tree into the hibiscus hedge that separated the properties.

Back in her kitchen, Merle bit into the golden pulp. Eyes closed, she chewed. Her mind caught on the tomatoes bushing up beside the back stairs, but Langley had counted the fruit again before he sallied forth that morning to his bookkeeping at the commission agency.

The contents of the ten-cubic-foot Frigidaire — seven herrings, five slices of breadfruit, two plantains and six pickled pommecytheres – also tempted her. She swallowed, fought off her desire for salt.

She dried her hands, crossed to the living-room, sat again behind the Singer and began to sew the other leg of the floral pants-suit for Mrs de Peiza.

The machine whirred, the stitch travelled towards her; a tear fell upon the polyester at the memory of his angry veto of her request for a dress-length when they had roost-chatted about the disposition of her earnings the night before.

She was tired of the pleated V-neck she wore every Friday evening to the St Ann's Hi-Lo supermarket when she tagged along behind Langley and the shopping cart into which he, after much assessment, placed the cheapest brands and dented cans on sale.

She unlocked the top drawer, unzipped the pin cushion. Her gaze held the square of folded bills: her recent fee increase she had managed to conceal from Langley.

Abruptly, she arose, switched on the black-and-white TV set. The defiant act, she knew, could be her undoing, but she persisted in watching the school quiz long enough to realize her wish that the girl from the country town from which she hailed would win.

The complicit laughter of schoolchildren on the burning street announced that it was after three. She wet a towel, wrung it dry, placed it atop the TV set and resumed sewing. She sang as she pedalled. Her plangent notes attentuated the vigour of the Sparrow calypso: *Making love one day, with a girl they call she May-May.*

Within the hour the Taunus reverberated in the shed. Langley's jejune smile popped up over the half-door of the kitchen.

She allowed him time to count the herrings, breadfruit slices, plantains and pommecytheres. Dishes clattered. She stopped pedalling when he called her.

He had already set the table and was serving the dinner: two herrings for him, one for her; a slice of breadfruit each; the jar of pommecytheres stood between their plates.

He burdened her with the trouble he had suffered all day in coming up with the profit and loss statement. He laid on her the problems of working with a boss who had no idea of financial management.

'That ass failed his CA three times!' He rose and she stopped eating.

From the living-room he shouted, 'Merle!' She knew exactly what was coming.

She raised her arms to shield her face but the first cuff penetrated her defence.

'How-many-times-do-I-have-to-tell-you-only-*Scouting-for-Talent*.'

The slap resounded in her ear.

'I only looked at a part of a quiz,' she said.

'When you buy your own TV, you can look at quiz show.' He swung again. 'You thought you could fool me, eh? You see these hands, they always know when that TV's been on.'

As she flew out of the kitchen she heard English voices behind the hedge.

The moon breasted the hill and caught her at the very end of the yard still seated in the low fork of the Jamaica plum tree; the blue tanagers and the schoolchildren had already picked off its fruit. Drooping broad leaves caparisoned the nearby plaintain trees.

The feeling reared in her to step through the gap in the fence and lay her troubles at the feet of Giselle Newson. In that prodigal house owned by the bank, she might wrench pity from that temperate stone whose emerald eyes disdained her from a distance; she might also watch *Mission Impossible.*

But even as Merle dwelled upon the thought its appeal deserted her:

though the Englishwoman often said good morning since the day Langley had given Newson a lift to the bank in downtown Port of Spain, Merle and her neighbour inhabited different worlds.

Fresh tears arrived upon her understanding of how alone she stood ringed by hills under the waxing moon, and from the yard of candleflies and moths she was borne back to the dug earth and the lowering of her mother's coffin.

In his Peek Frean treasure trove of lockets, rings and watches held against loans of paltry sums to his co-workers, Langley kept the silver-plated cross he had twisted off the lid of the casket before the diggers swung it on long ropes into the grave. This claim of what was not his, not even rightly hers, now hurt her.

She was saying a silent prayer to the bright star on the brow of the hill when the third cock crowed and sent her feeling her way to the door.

How charitable of him, she thought when she pushed it open.

In the mid-afternoon glare, David Newson said, 'I'm glad my car broke down that day or I might never have met Langley, and you, of course.'

Among the orange blossoms and ginger lilies, Merle sipped her second scotch and soda and surveyed the bright-scarved gathering which, for ages of Saturdays, she had watched from the other side of the hedge.

'I had no idea your husband was such an authority on cricket,' Newson said, 'and has even met Everton Weekes and Hanif Mohammed.'

He introduced her to the manager of Ontario Hosiery and his wife, joined Langley in the group clustered at the bar over which the liveried African presided.

The Ontarians engaged Merle in polite chit-chat, handed her over to the grizzled wiseacre from the advertising agency who fetched her another drink and, over and over, said, 'What a great little island this Trinidad is.' Langley appeared at her side, gave her the extra glass he held and took the scotch and soda from her grasp.

She sipped. She threw the wish-wash on the grass, splashing the dirndled servant as she passed. 'I want the drink I had,' merle said.

Langley took her arm. 'Let's go.'

She planted her feet, raised her voice. 'Mr Newson, ask him if he knows anything besides cricket and bookkeeping. Ask him why he starves me and beats me when I protest.' Lifting her sleeve, she exhibited a bruise.

His grip tightened but she shook him off, turned to her amused-appalled hostess, said, 'He measures what I eat. He counts the fish, the pieces of meat, even the tomatoes I myself planted.'

She felt for a moment she was that ash-smeared ululating woman she, as a child, had seen at a cremation on the banks of the Caroni.

Now the sea of puzzled faces wavered back. 'And he never lets me watch TV,' she flung at the silence that made her hang her head and whisper, 'only *Scouting for Talent* ...'

Like one of her house plants Mrs Newson's broad-brimmed presence bowered Merle. 'There, there.'

She allowed the woman to take her hand and lead her to the gap in the hedge.

She must have been ten minutes at the Singer when she heard his steps.

He swayed in the doorway, pointed, exhaled a fusty breath. 'You're too lickerish, woman. I had my eyes on you the whole time you were eating all that good food. And since when you become this bigtime drinker, eh?'

As he sucked her into his cantankerous gaze, her hand dived into the top drawer, grasped the long cool smoothness under the ribbon pompom.

She had already released the scissors by the time he aimed himself at her. She found she could not rise.

He pulled the chair from under her. She staggered up into the full sweep of his arm.

'Whore.' His mechanical nods, like those of the decorative dog glued to the fascia of the Taunus, told her the degree of his determination. The window seemed her only chance.

As she clambered upon the sill, she saw that they had all gone from the garden behind the hibiscus. He dragged her back.

She fought him to her feet; she shouted for Mrs Newson, for Mrs de Peiza. She called every name she could muster which she associated with the silent street.

All at once an anger exploded from her depths. With surprising strength she cried, 'Give me back my mother's cross.' She elbowed her way out of his clutch, ran for the bedroom.

Seizing the Peek Frean tin from his father's highboy, she turned and brought it down upon his head.

Whether he simpered from the blow or from the alcohol she did not care. He tottered, shook his head, but stood.

He came at her again; this time she caught him with a kick where he was tender. He dropped.

His pallor, his impotent rage, his cursing caused her to resist the urge to whack him on the head again.

She licked the blood from her lips, put the cross into the top drawer and wheeled the sewing machine through the front door, on to the path and out the gate.

She avoided Mrs de Peiza's gaze as she pushed and pulled the castors from the pothole.

At the junction she looked back through a haze at her cage of thirteen years.

She steered the Singer into the road to Port of Spain.

Cars passed dangerously close. Horns sounded. A passenger in a taxi yelled at her.

She walked with all she owned and she did not know where on earth she was going.

Alma Hromic

ORA PRO NOBIS

It was exactly like the last time, except that she had not been around to hear the explosion then. Only to pick up the pieces. This time she heard the roar, and the crash of glass, and, in the peculiar human-silence as the world blew up, a single short scream. But that was in the first instant. A moment later, there was noise again, street noise, a human hubbub, cars screeching to a halt, someone crying, softly, piteously, in a voice entirely unhuman, like an abandoned puppy.

She reeled backwards in a delayed kind of shock, her mind drenched in double vision, presenting her with images that had gone before. Twenty years ago ... nearly twenty years ago. Was it possible? God, God, she ran away, she came to a different country, and now here it was again, different accents, different quarrels, the same bloody mayhem on the streets ...

Someone jostled her as he rushed past and glanced back at her, eyes blank, without apology. He was heading towards the place where the crowds were gathering vulturinely, staring at something at their feet. Somewhere in her mind there was a slow and mournful pealing of church bells, entirely appropriate; but she knew it was only in her mind.

Shall I go? Shall I run away again?

But where?

There was a man in his shirt-sleeves who came out of the throng towards her, moving in a businesslike manner. His face was the colour of his shirt. No, it wasn't. The shirt was stained at the cuffs. Red stains. Fresh. The face had no trace of red. The man looked as if he was going on autopilot, relying on memory of long years to take him where he wanted to be rather than looking for landmarks. He came past her, very close, and she stretched out a hand which trembled with its desire not to be moved.

'Excuse me,' she said, 'has anyone been hurt?'

'What?' He looked at her blankly, as at a wall.

'Has anyone ...'

'Are you a doctor by any chance?'

'No, but ...'

'Excuse me, lady. Those people need help. I have to find a phone.' His briskness, the briskness that the stain of blood at his shirt cuffs had temporarily blanched out of him but which was written into his features, was reasserting itself. He all but shook her hand off and made as if to resume his headlong rush to nowhere, searching for the phone out in the street where it had no business being, rather than inside the shopping centre with its shattered panes and paths sown with diamond-shard glass and one or two bits from the unprotected windows, which someone would unobtrusively harvest into their pockets.

'I am ...' she called after him, but he crossed the suddenly quiet street and went off along the block on the other side. 'I used to be,' she corrected herself, 'a nun.'

Once, twenty years ago in Belfast, she had turned a corner in her grey habit and come across a crowd like this. Then, someone had grabbed her hand and thrust her forward into the maw of the crowd. 'Help her,' the voices had sussurated around her, herself too baffled and taken too much by surprise to offer much resistance. She had seen the child only at the last possible instant, and the mangled bike, and the other stretched-out form that someone had covered, but not completely enough, with a black leather motor-cycling jacket. The child was lying on her back, her face grimy and bloody, her feet and legs a mangled stew of tissue and blood and white bone. She had felt her gorge rise. Someone pushed her forward. 'Help her, for God's sake.'

She fell to one knee, close to the apparition of the half-dead child more by accident than design. The eyes, closed in the blackened face, flickered open.

'Sister ...?'

'How?' gasped the nun in an agonized whisper. 'How am I to help her?' Her eyes darted up towards the crowd. Some of them had their caps in their hands. There was expectation in their eyes. *Arise, little girl, and walk.* Were they really expecting a miracle?

'Sister?' the small voice again. 'Am I going to die?'

She could not answer, her heart begging of her God the answers to the reasons behind what she was seeing. The fingers on the child's hand twitched towards her.

'Sister, will I see Jesus?'

And she had looked on the tranquil face of Jesus's youngest angel, and struggled to her feet, her hands blindly before her, staggering into the crowds which parted before her. 'No,' she heard herself say, and then carry on saying it, screaming it, 'No, *no*, NO!'

There was a cry behind her that might have been the child she was leaving behind, the child which might have taken that anguished, repeated 'no' to be in answer to her question, dying in the simple agony of a child who has seen her last and great request seemingly denied. But that child's senselessly shattered limbs burned themselves into the nun's eyes, her mind; she ran sobbing from the scene. There was a steeple of a church over it all. She had veered towards it, in search of self-vindication, but the guilt and fear showed her the steeple as a pointing finger – a woman of God, letting one of God's children die uncomforted by his presence. She turned from the church, and walked, and walked, until she sank down on the pavement next to a street lamp and sat there half in exhaustion and half in a mindless stupor which had her completely lost in her own city. A passing taxi driver had picked her up, and delivered her like a limp doll to the doors of her convent. Two weeks later she had quit the convent. The presence of the God she had betrayed was too heavy within those walls, an incense of guilt.

For twenty years she had said no prayers, not since she had left the sanctified halls in Ireland. She had struggled to make her way alone, afterward, eventually taking the ship to other shores like many ancestors must have done, her way leading her not to America but down Africa's shores and finally into Cape Town. Her family, unspeakably shocked at what they saw as her backsliding, turned their backs, in what only seemed to her one more proof of God's callousness, the God to whom she had made her marriage vows, and to whom she had kept those vows for almost ten years. Ten years she had spent with Aves and Hail Marys, and twenty years without a word exchanged between her and Him whom once she had loved. It was time to pay her debts.

She made her way slowly towards the thickening ranks of the whispering crowd. 'Excuse me,' she murmured politely, and most people, assuming she had legitimate business at the centre, obligingly twitched aside for her to pass. 'Excuse me,' and a woman would turn, and stare at her. 'Excuse me,' and a youngster would sidle out of her way. 'Excuse me.' If only she could say that to God, and be done with it.

She got to the front edge of the crowd, and someone in a blue peaked cap put out a politely restraining hand.

'I'm sorry, madam, but there is nothing ...'

'Excuse me,' she murmured. The arm dropped uncertainty.

'Can I help you?'

'I have come to help them make their peace with God,' she said. *And my own. And my own.*

Peaked Cap looked at her with misgivings. 'You? But what can you ...'

She looked down at the drab cardigan she wore, at the plain grey skirt and the sensible, unattractive shoes below thickening ankles, and smiled to herself. There were unhabited orders; she would pass.

'I am a nun,' she said.

A sceptical glance was her reward. She looked back at the policeman with steady eyes. His own gaze wavered, and he looked away for a second, probably to call in reinforcements to deal with this annoying woman. As if they didn't have enough on their plate. But she was past him, with another murmured 'Excuse me', like a mantra. Like a litany.

She made her way slowly to where someone had propped a folded jacket in lieu of a pillow under the head of a child. Another child. This one had beads of sweat on his brow, a brow that was darker by far than that which she had abandoned back in Ireland, in Belfast's street. But the eyes that were turned on her when they were opened were much the same eyes, caught in the same snare of pain and fear. She lifted her hand and wiped the sweat beads with a cool palm.

'Who are you?' asked the boy, his voice surprisingly strong but very quiet.

'Are you in pain?'

He could have been about fifteen, no more. He closed his eyes and his head, half raised to look at her, sank back into the makeshift cushion. 'Oh, God, am I going to die?'

It was twenty years ago, but the words came back to her with astonishing ease. She began a whispered Hail Mary, her eyes closed to the expression on his face.

'Are you a Catholic?' came his voice.

'I used to be ...' she said. It was where she had intended to stop, but the sentence did not seem inclined to end there. So she carried on. 'I used to be a nun in Ireland.'

He was fading fast, and perhaps he only heard part of what she said. His eyes were filmy. 'Sister ...?' he said, and shivers ran down her spine. 'Sister, pray for me ...'

Peaked Cap was coming over to remove her, accompanied by a senior officer with a bushy white moustache. They themselves couldn't put a finger afterwards on what stopped them from carrying out their intentions, but perhaps it was the smile on the dead boy's face, with his eyes turned straight up to the grimy city sky as the nearest path to Heaven. Or the tears that glistened on the cheeks of the old woman who knelt by him, whispering pure Latin words laced with sobbing English.

Perhaps it was the words themselves, which they only dimly understood.

'Pray for us. God in Heaevn, pray for us. *Dominus Deus, ora pro nobis, Ora pro nobis.*'

Mark Illis

THE WHOLE TRUTH

After the reading there was the usual pause. Some shuffling in seats, much studying of fingernails. There was always this wait, while courage was plucked up and questions were silently rehearsed. Thoughtful expressions giving way, as long seconds passed, to a certain tension, a growing embarrassment, finally an oppressive longing for the moment of consummation when someone would speak up.

It didn't bother Jill in the least. She was immune to both tension and embarrassment, having been inoculated against them by a very large number of similar occasions. How many? she wondered. After three novels and about seventy short stories, she must have been involved in at least forty readings. She was approaching, she realized with some amusement, the *grand old lady of letters* status. She looked out over her audience with unfeigned serenity, almost with indifference. She always liked to guess who, if anyone, would ask the first question. Today, she decided, it would be the young woman in the black dress, who had been listening with a particularly rapt expression, nodding now and then in a rather irritating way.

This settled, Jill asked herself how the reading had gone. Had she read loudly enough, without bellowing? Slowly enough, without droning? Expressively enough, without over-dramatizing? The answer to all three questions, of course, was 'Yes'. She had no doubts really about her confidence. Her mind turned to the remaining events of the evening. A drink with the organizers, a taxi home. She probably wouldn't phone Andrew, although he would be waiting for her call. His youthful energy and eagerness to please, which were his most attractive qualities, were not quite what she felt like tonight. All she wanted was some Marks and Spencers salmon, a good bottle of wine, some television. Fine. Just this tedious ritual to get through first.

There was a cough, and a tentatively raised hand. Was this a question? No, it was something in someone's eye.

It would be easier, Jill thought, if she asked the questions. After all, she knew exactly what to expect. From the would-be critic, hoping to impress his or her partner: 'How important to you is the influence of Joyce?' (Or Lawrence, or Hemingway, or Salinger, or someone she had never even heard of.) From the would-be writer, with something of a pleading look in his or her eye: 'Can you explain how you went about getting your first volume published?' From a fan, glaring at Jill as if she is deliberately out to disappoint: 'Why don't you write another collection like your first one?'

And always, whatever else happened, the two favourite questions recurring time after time: 'Why aren't your men and women ever really able to talk to each other? And: 'Why is there so much death in your stories?'

She quite looked forward to these two inevitable and perfectly justified questions. She always remembered her story 'Long Distance', in which a woman talks to her husband, who is on a business trip in Japan. First they have a crossed line, and it appears that he is speaking in Japanese, then a peculiar time lapse makes them keep interrupting each other, and then it sounds as if he is shouting something, or crying out, and as his voice disappears in waves of interference the woman wonders if, thousands of miles away, her husband is having a heart attack, dying.

Yes, the two predictable questions were justified. Jill practised her answers. Why don't my men talk to each other? Well, one of the great problems in society today is lack of communication between people, and between men and women in particular, so naturally I wish to dramatize this in order to ... etcetera, etcetera. Why is there so much death in my stories? She liked to smile at this question, betraying a faint sadness, and shrug slightly, suggesting that mortality is something she understands only too well. More sensitive members of the audience always recognized this as a tacit reference to her late husband who died tragically, in rather horrible circumstances, thirty years ago, when her career was just beginning to blossom. She must have loved him, because she never remarried. In the midst of life, she says, we are in death. I like, if I can, to remind the reader ... etcetera, etcetera. Out it all came, so easy, just what they expected, and wanted, to hear. All the lies.

As was her habit in front of unresponsive audiences, Jill considered more honest answers. She could for instance admit that she enjoyed writing about death. That was part of the truth. Who could not relish descriptions of falling, that most atavistic of fears, the splayed limbs helplessly flailing, the contorted face, the hard ground hurtling up to meet brittle bone and soft flesh? And what writer could fail to get a kick out of drowning? The swarming, inescapable presence, the desperate, aching pressure, the inevitable surrender, the silent scream. And even a heart attack had its potential. That word 'massive' that we link with coronary, suggesting the broad, heavy weight of oblivion, the knock-out punch.

That confession alone would be enough to shock those readers who assumed her fascination with death was associated with grief and fear. Such relish was a far cry from the poignancy and delicacy with which she treated death in her fiction, carefully disguising her glee. ('Ms Morley', said the reviewers, 'looks unflinchingly at death.')

Her second semi-truthful confession would further disillusion her, to use her publisher's phrase, *legions* of readers. She silently addressed her silent audience: Why do my men and women not talk to each other? Because they don't like each other, of course. Because I am a largely realistic writer and I describe what I see in relationships, that is, discord, deceit and downright hatred. And yes, it's more fun to write about vigorous emotions. I would simply get bored concentrating on fondness and love. They are, almost always, so wishy-washy. The real passion, I assure you, is to be found in hatred. You recall, I expect, my well-known story, 'Double Fantasy', in which a man fantasizes about his wife dying in a plane crash at the very same time that she, thousands of feet up, is imagining him dying in a car crash. Which of you can honestly say you felt no touch of recognition when you read that story? Which of you has not fantasized, in loving detail, the whole scenario? Receiving the news, the sympathy and attention of your friends, the brave face, the funeral at which you are praised for how well you are coping with the shock. Who hasn't totted up the financial, psychological and sexual benefits of freedom?

Such frank cynicism bore very little relation to the discreet, under-stated unhappiness, the inarticulate emotions and wistful failures of communication to be found in the fiction. ('Ms Morley', said the reviewers, 'explores the troubled territory of human relationships with unerring sympathy and perception.')

Sympathy and perception, that was a laugh, her husband would have enjoyed that. Why was she so interested in death and lack of communication? The half-truth was that she enjoyed writing about them, but the whole truth was infinitely more interesting, in terms of character development and narrative trust.

The whole truth. Jill had made a career out of approaching it obliquely, by indirections and distortions. She made no secret of this.

When asked – Ms Morley, can you tell us what advice you would give to apprentice writers – she propounded this approach as a philosophy, quoting various authorities, including John Donne: 'He who would approach the truth about and about must go.'

All the more reason then for her to sometimes feel an urge to change her habits and tell the whole truth, decoded and unelaborated. Because in fact it was simple enough. Unlike her fiction, the unsophisticated truth had a fairly clear beginning, middle and end. In the beginning, thirty-five years ago, she married Edward; in the middle the marriage broke down; in the end, thirty years ago, she murdered him. The murder was a clear and simple decision, a turning away from the complications and subtleties offered by patient suffering and the repression of feelings. She had no wish to live in a complicated plot which concerned itself with varieties of misery. She firmly believed that life should only be complicated in fiction.

In the years since Edward's death, while constructing blurred reflections and faint correlatives of reality in her stories and novels, Jill had, at least forty times by now, found considerable satisfaction in silently repeating the crucial scenes of the true story in front of an audience.

The beginning. A lavish party in a large house in an elegant Georgian terrace. High-ceilinged rooms the size of her whole flat. Champagne and a six-piece band, lobster claws in the buffet, with little bowls of satay sauce. She still clearly remembers the thrill she felt when she first entered this house, had a drink put in her hand, heard the music, smelt the food. The whole small story is contained in that thrill of pleasure. She felt a happy, vital epiphany of time and circumstance; this was the only place to be and here, walking towards her, was the only man to meet. Who else but the host? And what better advice for a young writer than to marry a rich spouse?

The middle. 'Do you know,' she says, 'I had no idea I could feel so strongly about anything.' He doesn't answer. 'Don't you want to know what it is I feel so strongly about?' There is nothing but the hollow crackle on the line. 'Darling?' She imagines him staring around the lobby of the hotel. She knows his expression precisely. The hard, straight line of the mouth, the contemptuous curve of the nostril, the bored eyes. 'What I feel darling, is loathing, for you.' Still nothing, just a pause, and then he puts the phone down. She sits alone in one of the large, high-ceilinged rooms and begins to plot. It is an unusual feeling for her because she has never before plotted her own life, only fantasized about it. She finds that she enjoys the novelty.

The end. Well, what else but murder? For a banal problem a melodramatic solution. How melodramatic? A glossy black spider as big as your hand with a lethal bite, sitting on your bare chest, like some horror-show prop come to life. She had joined Edward on a business trip to Sydney, where they stayed together in a friend's empty house on the North Shore. While Edward worked, Jill wandered in the garden, and discovered the home of a funnel-web spider. It was a hole only three or four inches wide, covered by a fine, sagging trapeze, a funnel, of web. The difficult part, by far the most difficult part, was catching the thing. After that, after opening up its lair with a spade and shovelling it into a large, lockable jewellery box, the next part was easy. At half-past four in the morning, in the thin grey light, she crept out of her bed and tiptoed across to Edward's. When she picked up the jewellery box she felt a stirring inside it, and when she shook it she felt a furious scuttling. Suppressing a shiver, she unlocked the box, laid it on the mattress beneath the sheet and then, standing well back, as if from an unpredictable firework, she lifted the lid. The speed of the thing was terrifying. Jill backed quickly into the doorway as she watched its shape shoot up Edward's leg and then, emerging from the lip of the sheet, run across his stomach to stop abruptly on his chest. 'Don't move, Edward,' she said, as his eyes flickered open. 'Don't try to move or even to speak. You might antagonize it. I should just listen if I were you.' So, leaning in the doorway, she chatted to him for a while. 'After all,' she said, 'I'm used to monologues.' She told him first that, if the spider bit him on the chest, he would probably be in a coma in minutes, and then she began to tell him how miserable he had made her. Whenever he opened his mouth to speak, she reminded him of the importance of not moving a muscle. What finished him in the end was a fit of trembling. She would never be quite sure whether it was fear of the spider or rage with her that caused it. She noted with a writer's attention to detail that it took in fact only slightly more than a minute for him to sink into the coma, after the creature had injected its poison.

There was a cough, and Jill's eyes refocused on her audience. She congratulated herself, because it was indeed the young woman in black whose hand was up, fingers stretching just above the level of her shoulder.

'I wonder, I may be wrong, but I've noticed that there's a lot of death in your stories. I was wondering, is this deliberate?'

Jill's smile betrayed a faint sadness. She shrugged slightly. 'In the midst of life,' she said, 'we are in death ...'

The young woman started nodding again, sympathetically now. She was blushing too, as if concerned that her suggestion might have been tactless.

Jeff Keefe

THE FREE HOUSE ·

Mary Smith was out in the pouring rain, which showed no sign of abating. There was no cross-wind and so it came straight down from the heavens. The rain fell so straight and hard that it threatened to drive her into the ground.

Mary tightened the belt of her raincoat as she ran. She felt OK. The light raincoat was deceptively warm and benevolent, and she wasn't concerned about her hair, which she allowed to grow as it pleased, just tying it in a ponytail to keep it out of the way. What concerned her was that she might slip over as she ran. She was wearing new boots, with smooth and slippery leather soles, and twice in the last hundred yards she'd skidded on the wet pavement, only managing to keep her balance and stay upright by frantically waving her arms around. Yet Mary felt it necessary that she risk life and limb by running, because she was late for work. She hated to be late. Lateness aroused in her a great deal of anxiety; more often than not it would cause her to break out in a cold sweat. And yet she had nothing, or more precisely, no one to fear by being late. Certainly not the landlord. That was a laughable suggestion. It was just that Mary hated to be late.

But for the moment she felt OK. The pouring rain gave rise to an excuse sitting indistinctly at the back of her mind (an excuse that would, as was often the case, escape articulation, so that she was unable to tell it to herself). Once again Mary skidded on the pavement, this time swaying to her right and grabbing hold of a concrete bollard that guarded one of the entrances to the estate. She paused there to compose herself. Looked up at the livid sky. Rain-water flowed down from her brow and the bridge of her nose into her eyes. She closed them slowly and it felt as though she was crying. Late again. Seemingly always late these days. She frowned.

*

Lunchtime. Only The Coopers' wasn't a lunchtime pub. Instead it relied on local trade. Consequently only four old men and a couple of lads on the dole were in attendance. Mary hadn't served anyone in fifteen minutes. She watched one spotty ginger lad toying with his last mouthful of beer, causing it to swirl around in the glass by describing quick circles with his wrist. She was fed up. Inertia. Inertia carrying Mary to her grave. She took one of the cheese sandwich quarters that the new landlord had been putting on the bar at lunchtimes. The new landlord. Compliments of the new landlord. It tasted all right. But it was a wasted effort.

The two youngsters finished their beers and left; the tall ginger lad and his barrel-chested black friend. She lifted the hatch and went over to collect their glasses. One of the old men said something about fucking sambos; the others grunted in assent. They were playing a seemingly endless game of rummy for negligible stakes. Mary went over to collect the old men's glasses; as she stacked the four pint pots inside one another an unsteady hand, pale and flabby as raw chicken, came out into the centre, dropped a card face down on the discard pile, and took the few coppers, slowly, and without reaction from the others. Then the stock and discard piles were joined, the cards shuffled, and methodically dealt. One of the men used the hiatus to roll a cigarette. She watched him. More haste less speed was his motto. Experience had taught her that they'd linger over their game for another half-hour, without buying more drinks, then move on to the betting shop. After that The Coopers' would probably be deserted for a couple of hours, until he'd come down from watching telly upstairs, put the bolts on the street doors.

Mary ate another sandwich. It tasted more insipid than the last, more like slices of lard than cheese.

She didn't feel like it today. She just didn't ... She tried to tell him. She said, Tom I don't ... and that was when Tom gagged her with his tongue.

It was raining outside; she could hear it against the windows and along the gutters. Perhaps it hadn't stopped since that morning. She listened to the rain while he ... what in Christ's name was he doing now? He'd locked up at three, like every other weekday for the past two months. Now he was tiring himself out on top of Mary in the morbid fuchsia bedroom. There were four bedrooms to choose from, four similarly tasteless environs in which to do it. That was supposed to be exciting. How thrilling, Mary said to herself.

What babe? he said breathlessly, still hard inside her, but taking a rest from his labour of love.

Nothing.

Chilly, did you say it was chilly?

A bit, yeah.

He tutted, got up. His penis was still erect but the helmet was sickly jaundiced. Tom went over to the radiator, turned it up.'She rolled over, now lying prone.

What's this? he said as he climbed back into bed.

I don't feel like it, she said with her mouth to the pillow.

What? he said.

She sighed. Her arms were at her sides and her hands rested lifelessly on the covers, palm upward.

Are you fed up with me? he said dolefully.

No, just fed up.

What's the matter then? he asked with compassion, placed his hand on her shoulder and gave it a squeeze. Come on, you can tell Uncle Tommy, he said, then frowned at his own idiotic facetiousness. He climbed out of bed and walked over to the dressing-table, the frown still on his face. Took his pipe from the dressing-table, began playing around with it, was picking at the remnants of burnt tobacco in the bowl.

Nothing, she said, quite a few seconds later.

Nothing, he mimicked. Began poking agitatedly at the burnt tobacco in the pipe bowl with a stiff index finger. What are you? he fumed. A brick wall, for Christ's sake ... Jesus ... a brick wall ... You even fuck like a brick wall.

Well, you know what you can do, she said.

Mary was peering at him over the white hemispherical blur of her shoulder. He seemed to have taken her rebuttal in his stride. Began stuffing his pipe with fresh tobacco. Now he was walking up and down, up and down. And his penis was flaccid. She felt OK.

What can I do? he finally said.

You can find some other tart, she said, then immediately tried to feel pity for him, but could find none. What she found instead was an entombing sense of responsibility toward him.

Jesus, he gasped, now turning first one way and then the other. We can't ... There's no ... Jesus ... I may as well give up. He was crying now. You ... you ... He lit the pipe with a match. Wiped his eyes first with the back of his right hand, then with the thumb and index finger of the same. He looked at her lying prone and naked on top of the bedclothes. She was a touch overweight. Little rolls of fat protruded under either cheek of her croup. Croup. Croup because she reminded him of a horse lying there: she was a big-boned broad-hipped woman, with a long thick mane of black hair spread across her back, easily covering her shoulder blades. Mary. She was peering at him from under it, this mane.

He felt a bit better. You're all I've got, he said quietly.

It's only been two months, she said.

He sniffed.

Blow your nose, she said, sitting up and patting the bed beside her.

Tom smiled. What with? he said. Your knickers?

Yeah, she said, smiled. He climbed on to the bed and cuddled up close to her. She held him around the shoulders, and he had his head first on her shoulder and then against her bosom. Tom is like a little boy, she told herself. She felt OK.

Now the smoke from his pipe was in her eyes. She told him so and he placed the still-burning pipe on the bedside table. It would go out of its own accord before long. He sat up straight against the headboard. You know you've got to help us, Mary, he said. Things are deteriorating, I can't ... He grabbed hold of his ear and screwed it up inside a fist. Shook his head from side to side.

Well, just leave, she said. Cut your losses, this place will drain you dry otherwise. I should know, Tom, I'm an expert on this place.

But a free house, he said. A fucking free house, Mary ...

People don't ...

And you said it yourself, it's only two months.

People don't care, Tom, they couldn't give a monkey's, beer's beer ... and ... and it's four months ... since you took over.

He shrugged. Four, then, four. He held up four fingers, only he was having to hold them close together, curl them over, and generally distort the effect he'd set out to achieve in order to keep his thumb tucked inside. Four's nothing, Mary, it's not time at all.

Yeah, but what about the years and years before that, Tom, before you came? McCabe ... I can assure you that McCabe ... Oh, I don't know, leave me out of it. She was going to say that McCabe had tried his heart out and he couldn't do it, old McCabe was bested by the bastard place, and he was a better landlord than you, Tom, at least he'd talk to the punters, for fuck sake. But no, that wouldn't help matters. In truth, low though it had been to start with, trade had actually fallen in those four months. This was McCabe's doing. His new tenancy, The Greyhound, was gradually siphoning off the larger part of The Coopers' goodwill trade. Soon only the sullen diehards, meaning the moribund and the bone idle, would remain. Mary could, and did, rattle off a list of those in next to no time. Blow your nose, she said.

He, too, was thinking about McCabe. That name, it set it all in motion. The machinery of his paranoia. These were the parts. He couldn't help but notice that whenever Mary mentioned McCabe, accidentally let that name slip out, she'd get all flustered then shut up. Plus, a good-looking self-confident single man, McCabe. Plus, Mary ... her clean black mane of hair spread across and easily covering her collar bones ... Plus, all those years just the two of them. Plus, the reticent desperation this place instilled in people. Plus, why if Tom could ... fucking hell, yes. And if found to be true, fuck that. It was the thought that she was part of the deal. A household appliance. A chattel. Capital. Capital! Yes I've grown rather fond of the old girl, says McCabe, I'll be sorry to see her go, damned sorry, so, er, do take good care of her for me, won't you, old man? The thought disgusted him. He hated himself for so much as entertaining such a disgusting notion. And he loved Mary all the more, loved her so forcefully in fact that he wanted to murder her. Since, however, he lacked the courage to murder Mary he fancied at such times that he might kill himself instead.

Tom was working himself up into a terrible state.

What is it? she said.

I ... I ... He felt that he was teetering on the brink of self-destruction. It was terrible, Terrible. Terrible, but there was something else. Mary, he gasped, please be my partner.

She smirked. No, Tom, there's no way, as an expert, like I told you, there's no way I would. He'd asked once before, recently, at the beginning of last week, in fact. And she'd set forth her good reasons then. She'd been impressive. But now she couldn't bring them to mind. She squirmed with irritation.

Tom didn't persist. He picked up his pipe, which had gone out. Began fiddling with it. He said quietly, as though to himself, McCabe.

She watched him staring into space, and she began to worry about him. Then Mary calmed herself down. Blow your nose, she said.

Predisposed to tragic circumstances. Hmm. A wind was whistling through some part of the building. The loft, probably. He turned again, a further twist in the hot quilt. There was a glass of water on the side. How long had it been standing there, collecting dust, stagnating? He swallowed. His mouth tasted of mucus. He felt OK, surely. Surely Tom felt OK. When he opened his eyes in the morning he would leap out of bed like a madman and set about the task with new vigour. Bob and weave, my son, bob and weave. Stick and jab. That was the stuff. He would sort everything. Bastard McCabe. Her. The partnership. He would sort it all, and tomorrow night she'd stay, as a partner. Yes, Tom. Or maybe it might sort itself. Maybe Mary. At least he would mention McCabe. That at least would set the wheels in motion. At least that. And the workmen would soon follow. The carpenters and the sign painters. The smell of sawdust. Paint. Dark green paint. The headiest kind, my son. Have you seen The Coopers'? What, The Coopers'?! I know, but just you wait and see, my son, it's a fucking revelation. Oh, spread the word, you lovely fucking people. And Mary, come here, he might say, because I love you. No Tom, no Tom, no. Unrequited love, Tom. Used goods, Tom. The love of my life, Tom. Mc . . .

He pulled the pillow down hard around the back of his head and over his ears, with his face pushed deep into the second pillow. He believed that he was trying to suffocate himself. Only no, he realized after a bitter struggle, Tom was too young to die.

I'll call you when your breakfast's ready, he'd said excitedly, then disappeared upstairs. What a fool he could be, she reflected. What a complete and utter plonker.

She laboured up the cellar stairs with a heavy crate of mixers, a hand either side and the moulded yellow plastic crate resting on and digging into the upper part of her legs, so that the crate see-sawed up the stairs as she herself ascended, one step at a time. When she was behind the bar Mary carefully lowered the crate to the floor and quickly put the mixers out on their shelves. And that was the bottling up finished. Bloody pathetic, really. She said aloud, It's bleeding obvious to those who care, and to those, like myself, who are strangely in the know, that the amount of time spent bottling up is directly proportional to the volume of trade. Mary smiled sadly. I've flipped my lid, she said, then thumped the bar spasmatically with her fist.

Mary lit a cigarette, and brought into focus this bastard thing that was troubling her. His offer of partnership. She believed that a partnership would seal her fate. Would make permanent her responsibility toward him. A partnership in which she would only give and he could only take. What a bastard contract. Mary too weak, before long, to break free even if she wanted to, and Tom never having the strength to let her go, because all that he took found no fibre to build upon. It was a bastard thing, a bastard contract. But after all, it only put into writing a commitment she'd already made. And what the fuck, didn't she enjoy this state of being buried alive? Wasn't hers a martyr's arrogance? A martyr's fear of self-love? Maybe. And then again, maybe not.

He called her from upstairs: Breakfast! Breakfaaast! Christ and God. She hated to feel superior, but what could she do? Mary climbed the stairs to the first floor and the kitchen. Every single step creaked beneath her weight, alerted Tom to her imminent arrival. Like a bell around her neck.

It suddenly occurred to her that he might make a proposal of marriage. Jesus, she said under her breath, and continued up the creaking stairs.

In the kitchen two plates of bacon, sausage and baked beans were set out on the table. There was also a white enamel teapot carefully positioned dead centre, and white porcelain cups with saucers. He was smiling complacently. Sit down, he said, tuck in. She did as he said.

The sausages were underdone. She shook her head. Any idiot knew not to underdo sausages, for Christ's sake. They could give you worms, underdone sausages. He was making a lot of irritating noises eating. Slurping. Sucking. Chewing. Swallowing. She used her knife to remove a piece of sausage from her fork, pushed it to the edge of the plate. I've already had breakfast, she said.

I'll ignore that, said Tom, that provocative smile still on his face. She made two fists under the table. Now he poured the tea, slowly and from a great height, so that a froth formed on the surface of the tea in the cup.

Don't, she said, and strongly exhaled through her nostrils.

Sorry, he said. The smile went. Though fuck knows what for, he continued. He handed her the cup and saucer.

Thanks, she said curtly.

Eat your breakfast, he said.

I've already fucking eaten breakfast, she snapped, pushed the plate away. You eat it, she said.

Next time I won't bother, he said.

All right then, don't. Fucking hell, you're so annoying, you behave just like a big fucking schoolgirl.

He didn't reply, went back to noisily eating his breakfast.

She sighed. There's something I want to say, she said.

No ... don't, he said, without looking up from his food. There's something I want to say as well, let me say mine first.

Why not, she said. After all, its your breakfast.

He put the knife and fork down on the plate and looked up at her. Well, as it goes, it's a question I want to ask you ...

I can guess what it is, Tom, she cut in.

No ...

The answer's yes, Tom ...

No, let me ask you the question.

She fuffed.

OK, then ... OK ... When you worked for McCabe for all those years ... what was it like?

She sniggered. Boring, repetitive, er ... soul-destroying, all that kind of stuff. Just like it is now, I suppose you could say.

Just like it is now ... OK, he said, OK, be truthful, promise to tell the truth.

I don't lie, Tom. At least not to you, you're too ... harmless for that.

He ignored her last remark, continued, OK then, OK, did you and McCabe ever ... Jesus, did you ever ... did you ever ... fuck?

Did me and McCabe ever fuck? she echoed incredulously.

Yes, he said, his head down, his eyes cast to the mashed orange-brown debris on the plate. I'm sorry, he said ashamedly.

You've got to be off your fucking head, she exclaimed. You've just got to be. She fuffed and shook her head. He wasn't saying anything now. His head was locked in that position of shame, with the chin tight against the chest as though it had been stapled there.

Jesus, she said.

Tom arranged his knife and fork so that they lay side by side in the middle of the plate. His lips parted tentatively. He swallowed. Then he whimpered, What was it you was going to say?

She drank some tea. Swallowed. I'm handling in my notice, she said. He didn't seem to move or make a sound, but there was a palpable tensing of his neck and shoulders, and Mary fancied his heart missed a beat. She took another mouthful of tea, got up and walked out of the kitchen.

Down in the bar-room she could make out through the thick reinforced glass the silhouette and muted clamour of someone knocking at the door. She looked at her watch; it was ten minutes after opening time. Mary went over to the door. OK, OK! she shouted, stood on tiptoes and stretched for the top bolt.

Sheridan Keith

EMERALD SELLS TIME

Emerald sells time. An ethereal product, but supremely measurable. She sells time in thirty-second portions, the time it takes to read a message of around seventy-five words.

She took the job at the radio station, left her husband, and changed her name to Emerald all in the one week. 'If I am to sell anything, I must be memorable,' she tells people. She has red hair, wears sharp clothes, and gets involved too easily with men, and alternative religions.

This week she is selling time in packages. The package has a cute name, the better to sell it by. It is called the JAMPACK, thought up by the station manager, who has risen from the days of being a copywriter. The JAMPACK gives the advertiser thirty commercials, each thirty seconds long, over three days, for $500. The name is supposed to imply that the airwaves will be jammed with the advertiser's commercials over those three days, and that they will bring home the jam.

Emerald is ringing Mr Thomas at Prestige Products Ltd. She has never met him, but knows he holds the position of Marketing Manager . from referring to a trade publication. She asks for him by name, but is put through instead to his secretary. She puts on her 'nice-to-secretaries' voice. She is careful always to identify herself fully in a confident voice.

'Hullo, I'm Emerald Boyd from XYZ station. May I speak to Mr Thomas?'

'Yes, I'll just put you through.'

That was easy. Often secretaries ask all sorts of annoying questions; some even have the audacity to say, 'Is it about advertising?' and then Emerald says, 'No, I'll ring back later, thank you.'

Emerald puts the sugar into her voice, holds the in-built laugh in reserve, and adopts a leisurely pace. 'Mr Thomas, this is Emerald Boyd from XYZ radio station. You may remember me, I spoke to you earlier in the year.'

'Yes, Emerald.' He sounds annoyed. 'I'm rather busy at the moment ...'

'Mr Thomas, the last time I spoke to you you did tell me that your budget had been allocated, but you suggested that I phone you later in the year, about now ...'

'Emerald, I'm afraid the situation is still the same, no budget I'm afraid ...'

(This is a dangerous moment, she has to keep the conversation going somehow.) 'So things are going fairly well for you in the market-place at the moment?'

'Well, I wouldn't say that exactly ...'

'Certainly most retailers I talk to say things are very depressed at the moment, and I chat to such a wide range of business people ...'

'It's certainly true, Emerald, that the market-place is pretty stagnant.'

'Yes, Mr Thomas, I know many operators hoped that the increase in the goods and services tax would generate a rush of buying, you know, before the tax came on and pushed prices up, but it just doesn't seem to have happened.'

'So that's been a general trend, has it, Emerald?' (Now he's beginning to pay attention.)

'Well, there have been some exceptions. I think big ticket items like cars, and carpet have experienced a bit of a boost, but most retailers of general merchandise haven't felt much impact. And that's why, in fact, our radio station has decided to offer retailers we feel have good radio potential something really exciting.'

'Oh yes,' he says in a bored voice.

(If you're losing him, ask him a question.) 'Are there any good reasons why people should come and buy from your shops, Mr Thomas?'

'Well, of course. We offer by far the best value for money on most of our items. It makes me so wild when I hear Jones and Serby saying they are the best value for money in town. How does he get away with it?'

(Now she's got him.) 'And are your goods cheaper than his, Mr Thomas?'

'In most cases, yes.'

'Well, are you telling everybody? Are you telling anybody? You should be telling the world!'

'But I can't afford to. Advertising is very expensive, and how do I know it's going to work?'

'Mr Thomas, just let tell you about our JAMPACK, as we call it. We jam the airwaves with your commercial for three days in a row, you get thirty commercials so you're hitting that audience over and over again ... it's what we call frequency of impact. We will write and produce your ad for you here in our studio, there's no charge for any of the production. It's all part of the package deal.'

'And how much is this JAMPACK, as you call it?'

'Well, normally on our station thirty commercials would cost you $2400. But the management have decided, just for this month, because business has been so slow for most people, to offer it at a fantastic discount. The price has been reduced to just $500, but only for July.'

'It certainly sounds like a huge discount, Emerald.'

'There's something else I should tell you. Every $500 pack gives you one chance in a draw to win a major prize. And that prize is a $10,000 free advertising campaign on this station. Just think what Prestige Products could do with $10,000 worth of airtime, Mr Thomas! You could blast Jones and Serby out of existence ...'

'It certainly would be a great prize to win, Emerald.'

'But Mr Thomas, the main thing is that the advertising itself will bring you new customers ...'

'Leave it with me, Emerald, I'll see if I can reallocate budget. Give me a ring next Friday, and I'll let you know my decision. It certainly does sound like a good deal.'

'I assure you, it is, Mr Thomas. And thank you for giving it your consideration. I'll ring you next week. Goodbye.'

Emerald hangs up the phone, makes a diary note for the following Friday, and thinks if he doesn't buy this month he certainly will next month. Some of them take years of nurturing, but once you get them interested it is as if you've started an alarm clock ticking away somewhere, and there'll come a moment when they'll buy, sure as eggs are eggs.

Frances writes commercials. She is gazing out of her window considering the azure blue of the sky, and the outline of the building next to the radio station. It used to be a pleasant old wooden house but it has been redeveloped into a neo-classical concreted façade and houses the TAB. It is outlined in a lurid purple, and it is this outline Frances is considering, though she often watches the mob of pathetic people who shuffle in and out, putting their money on the horses, when they look as if they can't even afford a meal.

She is endeavouring to write an ad for a monumental mason. Frances is given all the difficult ones. Last week it was an incontinent product, this week headstones. What are the qualities one looks for in a headstone? Obviously durability was a primary concern. Who is it who makes the buying decision in relation to headstones? Not the deceased, though instructions could be left, maybe were left, by elderly people in their wills. It is an area Frances knows little about. She decides the least she can do is phone the man up, and have a chat; however, he is away for the day.

Her mind wanders to the only famous headstone inscription she knows, that of W.B. Yeats: 'Cast a cold eye on life, on death ... horseman pass by.' She has always felt that, coming from such a hot, impassioned participant as Yeats, it lacked credibility. (The problem of credibility was ever present for Frances, so few people believed in advertising claims any more.) Frances had ambitions towards poetry herself as a young woman. But now, in middle age, she finds it difficult to imagine herself in any glamorous role. There was a time when, lit with wine at the occasional agency party, she might collar some young male account exec and talk about the art of writing a thirty-second commercial as if it were as sacred as Japanese haiku.

She would speak of the absolute discipline of the thirty-second time-frame, how the commercial must open with a bang of surprise, how it must create feelings of delicious warmth and desire, how it must end with an exhortation to action! And always the eternal quest for different ways to say larger, better, bigger, more prestigious, newer, faster, sharper, cleaner, more careful, more caring, more exciting, more impressive, of greater worth, cheaper (but without implying cheap), of greater value for money. Each word, she would say, must hang in the air like a lure, gently quivering and flashing.

But now that she has been churning out commercials for ten years she no longer feels much enthusiasm. Certainly she has a way with words, and can be expected to come up with an orderly progression. But original thought? Hardly. She writes down a few words that come into her mind in relation to headstones: durability, dignity, eternal, precious memories, solid, remembrance, focus your memories, enduring.

Her eyes wander to the blue sky again, and her mind goes tight and solid, and refuses to think about headstones or thirty-second commercials. The sky seems so achingly beautiful, so beautiful she feels like crying. It is a winter sky although the sun is shining, and now in the middle of the day it is certainly warm. The tree outside her window is bare of leaves, the naked, slender twigs just moving slightly against the blue backdrop.

Now she is thinking of images from the film she saw the night before, images of love, images in which the hand of a man moved across the naked body of a woman, his fingertip caressing his nipple, tracing the outline of her mouth, slipping inside her mouth to fondle her tongue. She goes to the pictures every Friday night with her flatmate Deirdre who is also without a lover. They call it their 'girls' night'.

Frances has had no one in her life for two years now. She is beginning to wonder if there will ever be anyone again.

Julie is the schedules girl. She punches the advertising schedules into the computer. She wears a big diamond ring and worries about her fingernails. In so doing, she often makes mistakes.

She is unaware of the delicious ironies and juxtapositions which pass before her eyes. The first commercial break for tomorrow morning contains the following messages: an invitation to have your chimney swept, a catfood ad that ends suggestively (make sure your pussy gets what it wants), then a commercial that tells the listeners not to be embarrassed if they spring a little leak (the incontinent Frances wrote last week), followed by the monumental mason's spot, which unless Frances gets an idea soon, and forgets about needing someone to hold her, will not be recorded in time.

Julie spends all her time dreaming about her fiancé. He was rich when he bought her the diamond ring, working as a client account executive for a stockbroking firm. Times have changed, and the stock market crash has happened. Now he is very poor, and is considering asking Julie if she would mind if he resold her ring . . . just for a year or so until he can get on his feet again. He is obligated to take up certain options, although he knows they are now worthless, and his only other possession, the smart sports car which endeared him to Julie in the first place, means more to him than Julie.

Penny is the accounts clerk. She chases bad debts. In the current economic climate cash flow is a problem for everyone, and unlike cars and washing machines, time cannot be repossessed. Therefore it is imperative that contracts are signed, and New Customer Account Forms are filled out religiously.

These forms ask all sorts of embarrassing questions: where your bank account is, if other firms have given or refused you credit, the address of your private home, who really owns your company, the names and addresses of all your business partners. The sales people never like getting them filled out: they can totally destroy a sale.

Penny has an exact mind, but she is married to a man who exaggerates. Together they expend an enormous amount of energy arguing about the facts. When they are out to dinner with other young couples Penny's husband tells stories embroidered with fanciful emphasis. Penny is determined to assert herself and accuracy, and is forever obliged to remove his flesh from the bare bones of their joint experiences. If Penny could only learn to tolerate creative recall perhaps her husband would feel more hesitant about spending their money, which he does in an alarmingly undisciplined way.

Penny has a lot to deal with. How would you like it if every time you phoned someone up they pretended not to be there?

Susan is the on-air host. She has everything most women could possibly desire: beauty, intelligence, and the love of a Member of Parliament. However, she believes her face to be too thin, and wishes she could put on weight. She worries that her hair-style looks dated, and indeed it is. Her blonde hair cascades down over her shoulders like a Flower-child of the Sixties, but of course her wayward, slightly disarrayed look is part of her charm. Her opinions are outdated too. She still has sympathy for street kids and believes in abortion. She listens with kindness to little old ladies who ring in with their old-fashioned remedies for aches and pains. There is no doubt that they love her.

Yesterday Susan attended the funeral of a baby. She had never been to a funeral before in which the coffin was open, inviting the mourners to look inside and to see the child in death. She can hardly bring herself to look at the small, white coffin. But it is expected of her, and as a media person used to being in the public eye, she will fulfil this expectation. She takes the shortest possible glance, but in that moment has cauterized an image into her consciousness of the rouged face of a waxen, well-formed doll with sleeping eyes, surrounded by love objects: soft woolly toys that will no longer be clutched, a cream knitted blanket no longer able to warm her, even her baby bottle, washed clean and empty.

It is a bizarre and poignant montage. Susan has no children of her own, although her husband, the MP, has two grown-up sons from his former marriage. He has persuaded Susan not to bother herself with the messy demands of a family, and her career anyway has always held her self-interest. Lately her insecurities have made her wonder if her position as talk-back host in the important morning time-slot owes more to her significant husband than to her own ability. Certainly her ratings are perilously low. Is the audience becoming tired of her sweet-girl-next-door style? There is a new rating survey due out at the end of the week. Is it possible she could lose her job?

*

Walter is the on-air guest. Sixty-five, he has recently retired, and has been invited to the radio station to talk about the high points of his career with the police force as one of the top detectives. There are plenty of things he has a mind to say, and not all of them are complimentary, especially when he thinks about his successor.

He has felt somewhat anxious about this interview all week. He keeps telling himself it could certainly never be as difficult as some of the court appearances he has had to make over the years, and the idea of listeners phoning in with questions should hardly worry him, he who has been under cross-examination from the sharpest criminal lawyers in the business.

Still, there remains a sense of foreboding. He has difficulty parking his car in the garage area under the radio station's building, and in fact he damages one of the cars parked there while attempting to back into a space. The garage area is dark and gloomy, and each parking space has a name painted on the concrete floor. He has parked over that allotted to NEWS CAR, and has collided, in a modest way, with the white Holden Gemini on the left-hand side. Aware that over the last few years his eyesight has been deteriorating, he has failed to realize just how imperfect it has become.

He waits for the lift to ascend to the first floor. Although it appears very modern with glass on two sides, and carpet on the other two, it moves extremely slowly, as if it required a great deal of thought before determining where and how to proceed. There is a difficult moment when the doors refuse to open, and he has to look closely at the various buttons to press one that says 'Doors open'. At Reception he is welcomed by a comely young woman who gives him a coffee and sits him down outside the studio, but who otherwise treats him as if he were invisible. She answers phones non-stop, feeds documents into a bank of fax machines, and types addresses on to envelopes on her electric typewriter, simultaneously.

Ten minutes pass.

Walter listens to the programme that is going out on air and wishes he could just stay there, sitting comfortably while watching the marvellous dexterity of the receptionist, and staring at the red cue light outside the studio door.

His coffee finished, he wonders what to do with the cup, and ends up by placing it by his feet. Now the red light goes off for the commercial break, and Susan comes out to introduce herself, and escort him into the glass studio, where she positions him in the fashionable chair with the microphone poised above his forehead, awaiting to accumulate his articulations and broadcast them to the listeners.

The coffee and his mental anticipation have encouraged his heart to begin an extraordinary dance.

Off air he begins to explain to Susan about his mishap in the car-park. She is paying little attention, listening to the technical director through her headset, about to cue her in for the interview. She holds up her hand to Walter to signal him to stop talking. He swallows hard, and his heart gives an astounding convulsion. Susan comes in with her introduction: 'Listeners, I have with me in the studio Walter Gazeborough, recently retired as Commissioner of Police. I know we are in for the most fascinating of hours, as Walter Gazeborough reviews some of the more dramatic and difficult of the cases he has been associated with over the thirty or so years he has been with the police force. Walter, just how long is it that you were with the force?'

Walter opens his mouth to answer, but all he manages to say is, 'I'm afraid ... I'm not feeling ... very well' and then with a slight gurgle he pitches forward off his designer chair and falls on to the blue of the studio carpet. Susan quickly pushes her dump button, and speaks to the technician: 'Take a commercial break, will you? This is an emergency.'

While the ex-Commissioner of Police goes through the motions (literally) of death, the technician punches the commercial cartes, already waiting in the carte machine.

The audience is asked to make sure their pussies are getting what they need, if they have had their chimneys swept, not to be ashamed if they were to 'spring a little leak' because there was a product that could save them any embarrassment, and not to miss out on the bargains at the half-price menswear sale at Joe Shopkeeper's Menswear.

Susan realizes her guest is probably dead when she sees the dark stain of urine on the studio floor, and thinks of the *double entendre* of death as release. She remembers her first encounter with death, when she came home from school one day to find her dog dead under her bed, lying in a wet puddle.

The radio station plays music for the next hour while the ambulance men come, attempt to revive him and, failing, remove the body.

There is an awkward moment when the ex-Commissioner's wife, who has been listening to the station to hear her husband being interviewed, rings up to find out why the interview is not proceeding. She takes it well. 'He always had a talent for the dramatic,' she says, and decides to send a crate of beer to the radio station for their Friday 'drinkies'.

The following day the radio station records and broadcasts an obituary, which, as luck would have it, is followed directly by the monumental mason's advertisement. (Mr Burns has paid a surcharge to be first in break, thus gaining greater attention.)

Emerald's client has had a second look at last month's sales figures, and decides he must do something. Then at least he will be able to tell his board that he has initiated certain measures. He phones and agrees to take the JAMPACK, and in fact Emerald sells another five that day. At this rate she will earn around $5000 this month in commission, most of which she will donate to her latest encounter group.

Today Frances is writing a commercial for a special type of pillow, made up of foam sections of varying degrees of density, the idea being to construct a head-rest with perfect architectural qualities to accommodate each individual neck, thus ensuring total repose and perfect spinal alignment.

Julie is under a lot of pressure, due to the outstanding success of the JAMPACKS, and she has to work several hours of overtime to punch all the contracts into the system. She consoles herself by thinking of the extra money she is earning.

Susan has had her long blonde hair cut short, in a sharp street-wise number. It is partly an attempt to ameliorate the passage of time, partly a tactic to divert her from the awareness of the distressing discoloration of the carpet which, in spite of the best efforts of the cleaners, retains a puddle-shaped stain in commemoration of the passing of her distinguished guest. Looking at this gloomy stain she makes a decision: she will, this very night, cease taking the pill and hopefully she will be pregnant within a few months. Suddenly she is full of excited urgency, and certainly, at thirty-eight, she knows there is not a second to lose.

Emerald sells time. An ethereal product, but one that is supremely measurable.

David Kennedy
CHARLIE

Charlie was going purposefully along the promenade towards the gardens on a sunny afternoon. He was happy in his best raincoat (although it didn't quite fit), baggy trousers, Fifties-style hat with two peaks and a valley, grey woollen scarf and black shoes which he polished several times a day.

His head a little in front of the rest of his body, he walked under the green and brown trees where the sun shone brightly through the new leaves on to the grey pavement beneath. Between him and the municipal gardens to his left this year's cars revved impatiently at the red lights. To his right young girls enclosed in hothouse office blocks snapped at typewriters and middle-aged men sniped at board meetings. A little further on, a youth with bent shoulders slunk into an off-white cinema showing *Nothing On*. Charlie shook his head sadly. In front of the cinema a fountain welled up from an underground river into a concrete basin where Neptune sat, trident erect and eyes streaming with pigeon droppings.

Left turn into the gardens past a clinking, sagging beer tent into a landscape of painted metal chairs and tables where people sat under red and white umbrellas pretending they were in France. Eagerly Charlie shuffled across the balding grass to a smallish queue where he stood eyeing a well-built, conscious boy at the food counter.

'It's got to be ice-cold, that orangeade!' The gritty voice gave out in an adolescent squeak but his girl fluttered her velvet eye-shadow, gave him an admiring arm and off they swung to gaze at themselves in each other's eyes over the painted tables. Charlie turned his attention to the next in the queue, a grey mother in worn headsquare and tired coat harrassed by a red-faced screamer in a rusting push-chair and a curly little girl who should have been blowing her nose or holding Mummy's hand but was now wriggling away to the litter bin to pull out a collage of newspaper, lollipop and cigarette ash.

'Mummy, Oi want a lollay!' She stamped and started to lick until her mother clenched herself for another last-ditch effort and threw the mess back.

'You've got your hands full today!' said the plump, tarted-up lady behind the counter. 'Now you be a good little girl and do what your Mummy tells you!'

For a moment the whining and kicking stopped, but from the push-chair there came a sudden new burst of energetic shrieking. Charlie had started to talk to the babe and pat its little pate with a slow smile of compassion.

'Why, hello, Charlie!' The dumpling in white gave a lurid wink at the weary mother. 'Fancy seeing you again so quick! Had a good week up with the brothers, then?'

Certainly Charlie's open sunburnt face and the ring of sparse growth beneath his hat wouldn't have looked out of place in a monastery. To the mother's relief he now shifted his deliberate gaze to a fruit pie in a colourful cardboard container.

'Made up your mind then, love?' The queue was getting restless.

'Yes ... Tea ... and ...' With his food and drink Charlie received a kindly smile but he stared ahead as he wobbled his good things over to a table where he sat down with great care. He contemplated his thick white cup, lifted it with both hands, sipped, grunted with joy, rolled back his head and settled down to watch the small boys killing each other behind the flowerbeds, the married couples cross from the shops and weary with their lives, the poor old men sitting on dark wooden benches, clutching their knobbly walking sticks and wishing they were rich and young.

Enjoying the sound of finger-nails on bristly chin he looked up at the heavens and thought what a responsibility it was being Jesus. In the home for most of the day he would walk along the corridor in the heat of the white radiators repeating, 'Suffer the little children to come unto me.' Sometimes the radiator would join in but this morning it had gone off on its own and exclaimed, 'Up the Pope! I don't like kippers!' and this was confusing. In the evenings he'd sit in the lounge with his hang-dog inmates and watch television, participating in the discussions, especially the religious ones. Last night he'd been talking about his work of healing the sick and doing miracles when the men around him had suddenly stood up and begun to dance and sing.

He was strongly built. In early days he'd done some labouring, wheeling barrows and barrows of slurping cement up gangplanks. Then he'd worked in a factory sorting out the peas on a conveyor belt but somehow it had all become too much for him, he'd had a go at the foreman and they'd had to put him in the home and keep him there ever since. But he didn't mind it as there was plenty to do. In the morning he'd leap out of bed and jump around because he was the Resurrection and the Life. After breakfast, which he'd stuff in earnestly as he listened to people breathing on the radio, he'd walk along the corridor to Calvary and their terrible *treatment*, nails in hands and feet and head, but he forgave them for they knew not what they did. After lunch he'd walk until teatime and if it was fine he'd sit on the steps outside the grand red sandstone building talking to the birds and trees.

But today, special day of the week, he was out and about in the world, doing God's work with the sun all around him. Thrusting his head up and back against the metal bar of the seat he opened his mouth and snorted, for in his head was a cup of tea, a sausage and a matchstick. Yesterday he had offered one of his disciples a cup of tea and it was a matchstick. This morning he had picked up a pencil and it was a knife and it was still in his inside pocket.

Harry Smith was an insurance salesman. Brisk and efficient in his new suit he strode over the grass, briefcase in hand, his face reddish, his hair as neat as a hat and his smile as constant and white as a toothpaste advert. At the food counter he glanced at his watch, bought coffee and a couple of cakes in silver paper and made his way to the only table where there was any space. With a warm blank smile for Charlie, who had his eyes shut, he sat down, opened his briefcase, took out some papers and began to sort through them. One 'contents' at £50,000. Two 'lives' at £100,000. Not bad, though he felt he could have done even better. Last year he'd won a holiday in the South of France for his enterprise and this year he was in line for the top prize of a world cruise.

'Beautiful afternoon, isn't it! 'He grinned at the man opposite. 'Well, beautiful for Britain and Britain is beautiful, as they say.'

Charlie was wandering through a mossy wood into a meadow where the sun beamed down upon sheep, goats and little children. He opened his eyes, nodded and smiled.

God, he was good, thought Harry, and without even trying. Well, don't look a gift horse in the what-nots. 'Your afternoon off then, is it?'

Charlie nodded again and smiled over to an angry, oldish couple just arrived. The husband, small but with the obstinacy only meekness can manage, was striding to a table he had chosen with a steak and kidney pie for himself and a pair of doughnuts for his scowling wife.

'Yes it does get a little crowded, doesn't it? Nice place to come on your afternoon off, though!' Charlie was still watching the unhappy pair. 'Ah . . . what line of country are you in yourself?' Charlie turned to face him. 'I mean ... what's your occupation, if you don't mind me asking?'

'I'm a teacher,' came the earnest reply.

'Oh really!' Harry extracted an angel cake from its silver casing and the other watched, fascinated. 'How very interesting! Of course, teaching's a real vocation, especially these days when everyone's against them, the government, the public, the kids ... even each other!' Teachers weren't up to much, nothing to insure except their big mouths. Never mind, always worth a try.

'Oh yes!'

'When I was at school we didn't get the kind of thing you give them now, none of this creative stuff. It was all sitting up straight and no messing. You stepped over the line and God help you!' He checked his watch.

'God help you!' Charlie agreed, and Harry couldn't help wondering at his own marvellous knack of turning small into shop talk.

'Of course, I'm not saying that either method is right or wrong ... one man's meat and all that ...' And as if the thought had just struck him, 'I have a friend who's a teacher – correction, who *was* a teacher – at one of those big comprehensives where they pack them in like sardines, am I wrong?' Charlie licked his lips. 'Not that comprehensive education is a bad thing ... everyone at the same starting post ... but then again we can't all finish at the same time, can we! Personally I'm in favour of competition. Though if you find you're something special, mind, it's hard work,' he added modestly.

'Oh yes!' Charlie nodded, very serious.

'Anyway, this poor fellow dropped dead ... just like that! Three weeks ago, it was. Funnily enough, I was talking to him only the day before. Nice chap, something like yourself but a bit yellower round gills if you don't mind me saying so. Well, he said to me, "I don't want none of your policies, thank you, as I'm fit and healthy and haven't long to go in teaching." Too right! Poor chap collapsed as he was marking a pile of books, so I'm told. Don't know if he even got to the end of them. Tragic! Untold misery for the family and all because he wasn't covered! Well, he is now, of course, but I mustn't joke about such matters, must I! Ha ha ha!'

'Ha ha ha!' laughed Charlie.

'Terrible, though,' insisted the insurance man. 'It just shows how important it is to prepare for the future!'

'Oh yes!'

Harry Smith had met teachers more articulate but few more willing to listen to his brand of reason. He glanced with satisfaction at a neighbouring table where the battered husband was trying to lose himself in his juicy steak pie as his red-faced wife shouted.

'But I asked for *one* doughnut and a fruit pie! Can't you remember a simple thing like that!'

Charlie scraped his chin and his eyes watered in sympathy as the foxy little husband choked, then recovered himself to bite back at his wife's rock-cake face.

'Next time get it yourself!'

'Isn't it terrible that people can't seem to hit it off these days" Harry shook his smooth head at the glowering pair.

Charlie shook his head and his hat fell off. He picked it up.

'I really feel sorry for them!'

Charlie agreed, his hand went to his heart and he felt a sharp pang in his breast pocket.

'You're probably a family man yourself. Happily married, I can tell!'

Charlie looked surprised.

'Oh yes, I have a nose for that sort of thing. But there have to be worries, the mortgage, the kids, the car ... Nothing lasts, does it? And this is the point. Can you be sure that tomorrow ...'

'I don't know ...' began the man opposite with a worried frown but the salesman held up his hand with a mixture of concern and reassurance.

'Oh, I know these things aren't likely in a healthy chap like yourself. But the tragedies I see simply because people aren't properly protected. I may not know much about comprehensive education but I *do* know that a comprehensive policy can guarantee peace of mind! So there's a piece of my mind, ha ha! But then I expect I'm preaching to the converted!'

'Oh yes!' Charlie's eyes were eager and warm.

'Yes, of course.' Harry hid his disappointment. 'Perhaps you'd like to have my card, anyway.' Why hadn't the stupid so-and-so told him! What a waste of energy. But he wasn't giving up that easily. 'On the subject of property I have a couple of useful little pamphlets here ... There's one particularly good endowment policy here, very popular ... If you like to cast your eyes over it ... Did you say you owned a house?'

'In my Father's house there are many ...'

'Your father? Perhaps you'd like to give me his address if you think he'd be interested.'

Charlie watched the married couple leave at the end of their and each other's tether, the husband walking as slowly as the wife wanted him to go fast.

The boy and girl sat sipping their orangeades and admiring each other's chests, while a few tables away the exhausted mother had plenty to occupy her, what with the ranting screams of her baby and the discoveries of her curly little girl in among the dogs' dirt. Charlie sighed and placed his hands together.

'Your father's certainly a lucky man if he's got a good-sized house in this day and age! All the more important to make sure he stays that way! What I'm trying to say is, there's no way you can feel secure these days without a proper policy. I'm telling you the honest truth! *Then* you can sit back and enjoy your life!'

'I am the Way, the Truth and the Life!' Charlie's eyes flamed over the stubble of his face as he tightly gripped the salesman's arm.

'I take it, then, that this particular policy doesn't interest you!' Harry, flustered, smiled and tried in vain to wriggle away.

'Mummy! Look at that man!' The little girl trampled triumphantly on a dog's dropping before settling down to gape at the show.

'Except ye become as one of these,' Charlie smiled with divine benevolence, 'I say unto you that ye will never enter the Kingdom of Heaven!'

'I'm quite happy down here, thanks. Now would you mind letting me go!'

'Suffer the little children to come unto me!' With his free hand Charlie blessed the head of the little girl who shrieked in a toddling run back to her mother, who clutched her close. '*Are* you happy?' He stared into the insurance man's eyes.

'Not while you're holding me like this, I'm not!' joked Harry feebly, his smile beginning to desert him and the eyes of the gardens upon him. 'I'm going to report you! They'll have you taken away!'

'I am He that taketh away the sins of the world!'

Harry was pulled up and out of his seat which collapsed on to the crumpled crisp packets on the downtrodden ground.

'Whatever are you doing, Charlie? I've never seen you like this before!' The counter lady bit her red lips. 'The poor man's ever so scared! You leave him alone now, there's a good boy.' As they passed she made a grab but was handed off and fell backwards into her shelves of cardboard cartons. Harry Smith was jerked along between the tables, past the beer tent and towards the road.

'Go on, Mike! You better sort out that nutter! But don't hit him too hard, not with your full strength!' Mike's girlfriend blinked her heavy eyelashes and touched his biceps as he rose slowly and flexed his shoulders like a cowboy ready for a showdown. But by this time Jesus and his disciple were half-way across the road.

'Do you believe in me as Christ your soldier and servant?'

'If you say so!' yelled Harry above the angry surging of the traffic. A motorist rolled his window down, fumed an obscenity and rolled it back up again.

'Until your life's end?'

'How do you mean?' Weak with despair Harry Smith saw all that he had built up crumble into tomorrow's headlines.

By the fountain in front of the cinema Charlie stared into the water at the sunken treasure of copper coins and the floating sweet wrappings. He took out his knife and raised it high above his head.

'I came not to send peace but a sword!'

'Please no ... not that ... for God's sake!'

'I am the Lamb of God that taketh away ...' Charlie threw the knife into the water. It made a lovely plopping sound. Then it turned into a fish. 'I baptize you in the name of Father, Son and Holy Ghost. My yoke is easy and my burden is light!'

A shaft of sunshine was upon him as he lifted the insurance man like a child and dropped him in the water.

A flurry of pigeons flew off into the sky above.

Francis King
THE PISTOL SHOT ·

At the bus stop in Kensington High Street, darkening and empty but for an occasional passer-by huddled into overcoat or anorak, Maria tried to imagine how she would appear to the elderly couple behind her. Best of all, of course, would be if she did not appear to them at all. In London it was easy not to be seen in crowded places. But would it be so easy not to be seen in a place as deserted as this?

'We must have been here for at least twenty minutes.'

'It's really too bad.'

'And then two or three of them will arrive bunched together.'

Neither of the old people had, in fact, seen Maria except as a fur coat, a gleaming handbag and a pair of tiny, immensely high-heeled crocodile-leather shoes. Their eyes were watering from the cold, they were impatient to arrive at their eldest daughter's flat for Sunday tea and, if they were looking anywhere, it was up the street for a 49 bus.

Had either of them looked at Maria, they would probably have decided that she was foreign in origin. But whether they would have realized that she came from South America was doubtful. These days in London there were many women from the United States or Europe with just such elegance, sleekness and plumpness, and with just such expensive high-heel shoes on just such tiny feet, and just such expensive handbags held in just such prehensile fingers, their nails crimson. Such women would more often be seen hailing taxis than waiting for minutes on end for buses which never came.

Maria was tempted to look round to make sure that Carlos was still in one of the telephone boxes beside the Bank Melli and that Jaime was still hunched in the doorway of Peter Lord. But she must not do that. She must not do anything that would make the elderly couple notice her or, even more important, notice her two accomplices.

The man had a deep voice intermittently veiled with hoarseness. A glance many minutes before had revealed a pepper-sand-salt moustache, a worn black overcoat with a velvet collar on which a single white hair curled, and a stick over an arm. Of the woman Maria saw no more than that she wore a black eye-patch, and that in one of her gloved hands she was clutching her bus pass.

'Let's take a taxi.' The man cleared the hoarseness from his voice. 'No point in economizing in weather like this.'

'If we see one.' Was the woman American? Maria could not be sure.

Then the man called out in relief: 'Yes! *Yes*! There it is! At last! At long last!'

Maria did not turn to see if Carlos and Jaime were moving forward.

The all but empty bus, with its black driver-conductor, drew up. Maria stepped delicately aboard, taking care not to penetrate so far that the couple could edge round her with their passes.

'Excuse me.' Maria exaggerated her foreign accent. 'You go to Harrods?'

'*Harrods*? No point in your going to Harrods today, lady. Harrods is closed. Sunday.'

'Sunday? Harrods closed?'

'Yeah.'

By now Carlos and Jaime would surely be crowding up against the old couple. Yes, she could hear the old man's voice: 'Would you mind not pushing, please? This lady in front of us is blocking the way.'

The old woman now spoke: 'I can't see out of my left eye. It's not easy for me to climb these steps. Please! Just wait! *Wait*!' She spoke with the self-confident peremptoriness of someone used to being obeyed.

'Where do you go?' Maria asked.

'Where do you want to go?'

'Victoria and Albert Museum?'

'Yeah, you can get off at South Ken.'

'You will tell me, yes?'

Surely by now Carlos and Jaime must have finished. She gave a quick backward glance. Yes, first Carlos and then Jaime had dropped off the bus. Hurriedly she clinked down sixty pence. 'South Ken, please,' she said.

'The way those two were pushing! I thought one of them would have me over.'

'Perhaps they didn't realize this was a bus on which one has to pay as one enters.'

'But what's happened to them?' Preparatory to sitting down beside the woman, the man peered out of the window. 'Weird! All that pushing and now they're nowhere to be seen.'

'The younger one looked like an Arab.'

'Both of them did. Except that the bigger one had that blond hair. Dyed, it looked.'

Maria stared out of the window beside her, head averted. On no account must the couple think that she had anything to do with Carlos or Jaime or that she was taking in anything that they were saying.

'My God!' The exclamation came from the man, who was wriggling around in his seat, his hand tucked under his greatcoat.

'What's the matter?'

'My cheque book. Gone!'

'Oh, you probably left it on your desk.'

'I certainly did not. It's gone.'

Maria was listening intently. But, not turning her head, she never ceased to gaze out of the window at the empty, wind-swept street.

'Are you sure?'

'Of course I'm sure. It must have been one of those Arab devils. That's why they jostled us like that. Amazing! How did he get under my overcoat to my back trouser pocket? I suppose I was distracted when I heard you arguing with the other one.'

'Oughtn't we to get off?'

'What would be the use of that? Don't be a bloody fool.' Maris was shocked that someone so clearly a gentleman should speak like that to his wife (yes, she must be his wife, she had long since decided). 'They'll be miles away by now. Well, a fat lot of use a cheque book will be to them!'

'Are you sure they've taken nothing else?'

The man put a hand inside his overcoat, to the breast-pocket of his jacket, and drew out a wallet. 'No. All present and correct. Without a cheque card, a cheque book is useless.'

Maris felt a sudden exasperation, followed by despair. Carlos had clearly mistaken the cheque book for a wallet. Whatever Jaime, her son, might say, Carlos was a dolt.

The old man was now chuckling. 'Serve them bloody right! They'll have a nasty shock when they find they've got away with nothing more valuable than some unusable cheques. But the cheek of it!'

'London's become such a terrifying city. Almost as bad as New York.'

'It'll be a nuisance having to cancel all those cheques. I wrote out two — no, three — yesterday. Hell!'

'Well, it could have been worse.'

'It could have been considerably worse. But one hates to be taken for a ride. Well, you don't. But I do. I never suspected, never for a moment.'

'The way that creature shoved me! He almost had me on my knees.'

'That was a diversion. So you wouldn't notice what the other was doing to *me*.'

At South Kensington Maria left the bus. No, the couple had not noticed her, not for one moment. She had been invisible to them except as an expensive fur coat, an expensive handbag and an expensive pair of shoes with heels too high for a woman of her age.

As she made her way down on to the platform for the train which would take her to Sloane Square, her exasperation and despair both left her and she felt the exhilaration which always surged through her in the wake of these adventures, whether successful or not. She began to hum to herself, loud enough for a middle-aged man in overalls on the platform beside her to give her a surprised, appraising glance. It was for that exhilaration, as after an afternoon or a night of insatiable love-making with Jose, Jaime's father, and not for the credit cards, travellers' cheques and banknotes, that she continued with a conspiracy as exciting as any of the political conspiracies in which she and Jose had been involved back home in the now distant past. This exhilaration she shared with Jaime and the blond, shambling, lazy-eyed giant whom she knew and yet did not know to be both the lover of her son and his corrupter. That he was also, by association, her corrupter was something of which she had never thought.

The two men were waiting for her in a café in Sloane Square.

Jaime pulled down the corners of his mouth as she swayed towards their table, her high heels clicking on the marble floor and her head, with its hennaed urchin-cut, held high on a stalk-like neck. He looked as though he were blaming her for the fiasco. Carlos threw his body back in a wicker chair so flimsy that she thought that he would break it, and gave that braying laugh which so much got on her nerves.

Jaime began to say something but she cut him short: 'I know, I know! Only a cheque book.'

'I threw it over the railings of the park — into some bushes.' He concluded with a Spanish blasphemy.

Maria was reminded of the old man telling the old woman, 'Don't be such a bloody fool!' That still shocked her. Jose, in all their years of perilous vagabondage, had never spoken to her like that.

'Well, better luck next time,' Carlos said, again tipping his chair backwards and running a hand through his untidy dyed hair.

Jaime was gazing at him with an extraordinary intensity of love. Maria felt herself excluded, as so cruelly often before. 'I need some coffee,' she said crossly. Then in English she called out to a passing waitress: 'Miss! *Miss!*'

'One moment, madam. *Please!*'

The waitress hurried on.

It was from that day that Maria had felt things going amiss. The periods of exhilaration were now both far shorter and far less intense. Sometimes, although expected after some particularly dangerous and yet brilliantly successful coup, they mysteriously did not come at all, and she would feel only lassitude, depression, even despair. Then it was as though she had sniffed what she had believed to be cocaine but had proved to be merely talc.

'Look, Mama, look!' Having sensed her dark mood, Jaime would spread out the banknotes, like a conjurer inviting one of his audience to select a card, or he would riffle them through forefinger and thumb with all the negligent adroitness of a bank clerk. 'Money, money, money!'

'Money, money, money,' Maria would repeat glumly, sarcastically. Unlike Jaime and Carlos, she was not interested in money. All that interested her was that elusive exhilaration which could follow a moment of excruciating danger and suspense.

In an effort to cheer her up, Jaime bought her a ring, twin sapphires in a ring of tiny diamonds, after he had 'dipped' an American tourist for more than a thousand dollars -- how could people be so foolish as to carry such sums? he had asked -- in the washroom of Claridge's.

'Excuse me, sir - but I'm afraid that one of these London pigeons has made a - has given you a present on your coat.'

The American had erupted in jovial laughter. 'I guess that must have been in Trafalgar Square. As we left the National Gallery.'

As Jaime had removed the expensive Burberry, he had also twitched out the man's wallet from the breast-pocket of his jacket. 'It was so easy, easy!' he later crowed to Maria and Carlos.

Maria used to look at the ring thoughtfully, turning it round and round on the finger on which she also wore the thin band of the wedding-ring given to her by Jose twenty-nine years before. It was as though she were pondering on the way in which it had come to her, through more than a thousand dollars carried in the wallet of a rich, trusting gringo.

Then, mysteriously, she never knew how, her fingers went to the ring to twist it round and round and she lowered her eyes and - it was no longer there! What had happened to it?

'You must have left it in the bathroom,' Carlos said, in that hectoring tone which he so often used to her.

'Or your bedroom,' Jaime said, jumping up to look.

But they never found it.

Had she *wanted* to lose it? she later asked herself. But to the men she never put that question. She did not want them to forfeit their trust in her as their accomplice, since then she would also forfeit Jaime irretrievably to Carlos.

More bad luck followed. In Fortnum's she had contrived – yes, on that occasion she had experienced that elusive exhilaration, fizzing through her blood – to pick up and nonchalantly carry away in her own carrier-bag the bag of a woman, young and flustered, who was arguing in French with a young man about whether a cardigan would suit her or not. The bag lay discarded by a chair, far from where the two of them were standing. As so often, Maria thought with contempt of her victim: 'What a fool!'

'You'd better change these when you go out,' Carlos told her the next day, waving before her a bundle of francs from the handbag.

'Can't you do that?'

He shook his head. 'Jaime and I have some business this morning. A chick,' he added. 'A date with a chick.'

She knew it to be a lie. 'Well, go this afternoon then.' Without realizing it, she spoke to Carlos as her parents used to speak to their servants on the *estanza* when she was a child.

Jaime intervened: 'That old cow was in here asking about the rent. Due last week. We'd better settle with her. We don't want any trouble. Go this morning to Cook's. Please, Mama!'

Maria could never resist Jaime's coaxing and wheedling. It had been different when his father was alive. 'Do you mean that this is all the money we've got left?'

Jaime nodded, smiling indulgently down at her as she lay back in the sofa. 'We've been extravagant.'

'You mean – *you've* been extravagant. You and Carlos. And your chicks,' she added venomously.

Still smiling indulgently, Jaime took the notes from Carlos and held them out to her. 'Please!'

With a sigh, she accepted them.

The exchange department was at the bottom end of Cook's. As she opened her bag and took out the notes, she was aware of a young man, with a disagreeably sweet smell about him – she had always had an acute sense of smell – standing behind her, overtopping her by several inches. Then some coins cascaded round her.

'You've dropped some money. From your bag.'

She stooped, expecting him also to stoop to help her. But with extraordinary speed, he snatched at the notes which she had left on the counter, and raced from the shop, pushing aside two affronted elderly women at the entrance as he did so.

Maria now shouted out what she had so often heard others shout out. 'Stop him! Thief! Stop him!'

But no one stopped the young man. He vanished.

She lay in bed in the Bayswater flat, her eyes fixed on ceiling covered in cobwebby cracks and a hand to her forehead. Without lipstick, rouge or eyeshadow, she looked like some wizened little South American peasant.

Jaime stared down at her. 'It's not the end of the world. Carlos had some luck – for once! – in Oxford Street. Why worry? You win some, you lose some.'

'One feels – violated.'

'Well, that's what *they* feel, isn't it?'

That was precisely what she had been thinking.

'It's a filthy business,' she said.

'It's a filthy world.'

Some ten days after that, the three of them emerged from a performance of *The Phantom of the Opera* – it was Jaime who had insisted that they must go, even squandering a large sum on black-market tickets from a scalper whom he and Carlos had met in a bar – when suddenly a man strode down the Haymarket towards them. He was wearing a worn black overcoat with a velvet collar, he had a pepper-and-salt moustache, and he had a stick over his arm. Although he looked younger, bigger and stronger than on that afternoon at the bus stop in Kensington High Street, Maria at once recognized him. Jaime and Carlos did not do so.

He halted in front of Carlos, blocking his way. 'You robbed me,' he said. He had the palest of blue eyes, and there were veins, of exactly the same pale blue, on his nose and his cheekbones.

'What you saying? What this?' Carlos spoke little English.

'Come on, Carlos!' Jaime shouted to him urgently in Spanish. 'Come on! Move!'

But Carlos stood there repeating: 'What you saying? What? What?'

A crowd was gathering round them.

The man turned to the crowd. 'This man is a thief. He stole my cheque book a few days ago. Get the police!'

No one moved.

'Carlos!' Maria shrilled.

'Give me my cheque book!' Surely the man must have known that Carlos would not still have it on him? There was something absurd in the order. 'Give it to me!'

Jaime caught Carlos's arm. Simultaneously, the man grabbed Carlos by the lapels of his overcoat, pulling him towards him. 'My cheque book! I want my cheque book!'

Carlos wrenched himself free. Then he raised one of his huge fists, a chunky gold bracelet, a present from Jaime, dangling from it, and punched the old man full in the face. The man hurtled backwards, hitting the back of his head on the lowest of the steps to the theatre. There rang out what sounded exactly like a pistol shot.

To Maria it sounded exactly like the pistol shot in a South American street late at night eleven years before; and the man sprawled there, one hand and a foot twitching and his eyelids fluttering, might have been that other, far younger man, who had sprawled on a pavement, while a tricle of blood slowly accelerated from the corner of the mouth with which he was gasping for air and had then fallen, drop by drop, on to a cracked paving stone.

A woman screamed. A man said in a strangely conversational voice: 'Oughtn't someone to call the police?' Another man said commandingly: 'Ring from the theatre. Get them to ring from there.'

Carlos had already raced off. Jaime had grabbed her arm. He pushed her through the crowd, all of whom seemed to be staring down at that twitching hand and foot and that open mouth gulping for air. No one seemed to notice them. He pushed her out across the street in the face of potentially murderous traffic. He pushed her on board a bus.

On the plane, she suddenly woke with a violent start and a cry. Jaime put a hand over hers, as much to control as to comfort her. Passengers were looking round.

'What is it? What?'

'I thought ... dreamed ... A shot ... A pistol shot ...'

Jaime pressed her hand. He assumed that she had been dreaming of the death of her martyred husband, his father. But, in fact, she had been dreaming of an elderly man in a worn black overcoat with a velvet collar, sprawled out on the steps of a far-off theatre in a city which she would never now revisit.

D.F. Lewis
TOM ROSE

Tom Rose had been a magician for most of his life. Even at school, he had taken much pleasure in amusing his friends in the playground with tricks he was later to perfect under the spotlight of talent competitions, old people's home performances, birthday parties, bar mitzvahs ...

His *tour de force*, his *raison d'être*, nay, his very soulspeak, was changing from man to woman. It was not done in a flash, one moment all mouth and trousers, into a kitchen cabinet and out, the next, as a bosomy blonde with fishnet stockings, tail feathers and V-crutchpanel. No, it was more a long-drawn-out affair with the bedroom mirror. He cherished each item of clothing, ran them through his fingers, rested them upon his cheek, wet the panties with tears before tucking himself into them, oiled his calves which the silk stockings would shape, moulded breasts from prime pork into the B cups, dabbed rouge on his bristly cheeks, painted red-lips with a touch of the brush to his surly male ones, slipped a floral dress over his broad shoulders much in the padded fashion of the Thirties, fitted on the high-heels with overstrap setting off the ankles he would one day chip at with a sculptor's chisel and, the supreme finishing touch, lifted a large wig from its stand, hugged it as if it was a tame lioness, lowered it to his bald head in this crowning moment of transfiguration, groomed it lovingly with brushes of varying torques, finally, like a cherry on a cake, fixed his late mother's straw boater with a tortoiseshell hatpin.

Tonight, he was to perform tricks in this mode at an all-women's seminary. The venue was to be their massive hall, at least three centuries old, which usually served as refectory and assembly room. They probably knew God better than anyone else, but Boxing Day was a time to let down their hair.

Tom Rose was intrigued with this particular engagement which his agent (a retired schoolteacher) had booked for him at the very last moment, because there had been a late cancellation by the stand-up comedian who had a complaint, it was said, stemming from Christmas dinner. Tom had heard of the seminary as a place where most of the novices were quite young and pretty, despite their otherwise commitment to the Almighty. Furthermore, the hall, in which he was to perform, was rumoured to be haunted by ghosts that were not all that holy ...

He was allowed to go to the hall in advance, to get his bearings, prepare the conjuring equipment and more or less make peace with his Maker.

The late afternoon sun was shafting through the stained glass windows, forming shimmering pools of coloured light on the mosaic floor. The backdrop of the evening's show was already in position, a large embroidered tapestry that had been worked by many of the inmates, hanging in drapes behind the makeshift stage. It was intended to depict, Tom could see, a panoply of Biblical stories but, to his surprise, hinting at those devilish tricks that underlay, to his mind, all the acts of Christ. He went up to touch it, to see if the weave was as pure as it seemed from a distance.

'Excuse me, do not touch the quilt,' came a strong voice from the back of the hall.

He thought he saw a figure with imposing vestments floating below oil paintings that the dying afternoon light had ceased to pick out; followed by a shadowy troop of novices, evidently still in yesterday's Christmas cracker hats.

He saw a pedestal at the forefront of the stage, rather like a pulpit; guessing it was a prop for one of the other acts, he went over to look at the book that was laid out open upon it. The pages were gold-edged, and he could see the first letter of each leaf was illuminated with complex flourishes of raised ink. He tried to read on:

The Signs were twofold. They did blend one into each, forming many fabrications and manifestations of man's existence. So each could only try to peer through the Signs' dripping wild honeycombs, to see if all roofs of all towns, as was rumourmongered, were multiplied across even those lands that could not maintain life, and evil monsters did sit in the front parlours, pretending to be beings in man's likeness ...

He did not understand it. He refused to feel warm inside by basking in its mystery, as he may have done in better circumstances, for he was genuinely disturbed by the generalization of human existence as male. When referring to Man, why imply the Female? Here he was, dressed up as the most beautiful creature he had ever seen, and he closed the book's covers with a creak that broke the hall's vesperal silence.

'Do not touch my prop.' Another voice; this time a man's. He came striding forward out of the shadows. Tom thought he saw a second figure in his wake, but he could not be sure.

'Sorry, but I was sure there was nobody watching.'

Why Tom thought that was an excuse for his misdemeanour, even he could not reconcile.

'That book, my dear, is supposed to be open at a particular page. Imagine if I came on and found it shut. It would throw me and I would forget my lines.'

Tom saw that the face had age evidenced not so much as wrinkles but as knowingness in the look. The second time that day, Tom cringed, for the man was undressing him with his eyes.

'Want a game of Battleships? I've got the grids already drawn up.' The man held out two sheets of paper with squares ruled out, lettered along one side, numbered down the other. 'Four crosses make a Battleship, three a Cruiser, two a Destroyer and one a Submarine.'

Tom raised his voice to the lady level and said, 'I don't play children's games.'

'You get real crosses in the Bible.' And, without further ado, the man darted behind the embroidered tapestry and out of a side door that Tom heard slammed. The man's shadow remained only momentarily.

Later, in the corridor, Tom caught sight of some of the novices ambling two by two to evening prayers. Some were hand in hand, their faces burnished bright by recent ablutions, their dark vestments falling ankle-length, but not sufficiently loose to hide womanly shapes within. One even smiled at him, as he stood back against the wall to let them pass. He felt, unaccountably, like weeping.

All had intricately carved crucifixes at their throats, the relative size evidently denoting rank in the sisterhood. There was one woman, witch-like in her age, who was veritably bowed down by the weight of her trinket.

He followed them into the chapel, where multi-clusters of flickering candles sprouted at odd intervals between the pews like sumptuous petal-headed stems of solidified honey. The girls knelt, heads on hassocks, before the biggest, most ornate depiction of Christ he had ever seen. He put it down to the curdled light, but the blood seemed actually to move like syrup down His flanks. The face was young, too young, almost boyish in its pain. The body was sculpted from gnarled marble, veined with faint blue. The penis was fully revealed in an erection that the torture engendered.

He must leave, for he felt sick. Bodies, at the best of times, were ugly.

Not knowing where his dressing-room was situated, Tom Rose was worried about wandering into areas of the seminary that were out of bounds to visitors, but he soon found the vestry, where someone had kindly ringed the mirror above the make-up table with coloured electric bulbs. He was disturbed to see that his mascara had run, forming a scar down his cheek like a herring-bone.

After putting his face straight, he snoozed off, only to be shaken awake by the old woman with the heavy neck-piece.

'You can sit in the audience, till you're on,' she croaked.

If only the stand-up comedian had not cried off sick, Tom would be safe at home, perhaps dressed up as the man he really was.

He followed the old woman down a corridor, sniffing now and then wafts of turkey curry, and, finally, into the hall, where stage-lights had been directed upon the tapestry which, as a result, had taken on a new life: the seamless depiction of the first century would no doubt outshine any act that was performed in front of it.

He then saw the lines of novices, squatting on the mosaic floor as if they were attending a folk festival. They swayed to and fro with some faintly imperceptible music emanating from the loudspeakers either side of the stage. At first, he thought it was an organ droning but, on closer attention, found it more like a hive-ful of bees intoning an incomprehensible Sanctus.

The old novice placed him in the front between two of her number who reminded him of those who had held hands on the way to evening prayers; indeed, on looking into their wide, pale faces, he received a smile from the prettier. She placed her little end of flesh into his capacious hand ...

Tambourines were sounded from the wings, disrupting the false quiet with a percussive fanfare. On came a troop of Morris dancers, clacking large bones instead of wooden batons. And, after a series of whoops and guffaws, off they went to echoing applause.

Tom could not help thinking that his own act, timed for the end of the show, would be a let-down. There was no razzamatazz in his heart tonight.

The next were acrobats who juggled each other amid hallucinatory lighting effects. It only served to worsen Tom's headache. The girl beside him leaned gently against him, and it was this light touch that proved more erotic than anything he had previously experienced. He smoothed down the front of his dress.

Then came to the stage the man he had met earlier. Except, as Tom now noticed, the gold-edged book was still shut upon its plinth. He cursed. He would be blamed if the act went wrong.

The artist was dressed as a Roman soldier. He toted a bull-whip which he lashed like a giant rippling tongue. It cracked and cut through the buttery beams of the searchlights, as the gradually dissolving darkness at his feet revealed a number of nude girls on feral fours. Their pert breasts almost dangled ... their buttocks thrust up, as if inviting the stripe. Their skin was streaked with dirt, and their faces were sweet and gentle affairs despite the wild staring brightness of the eyes.

Tom covered his own eyes with his free hand. The sickness in his stomach that had been impending all evening was now sucking hard at his bowels. In his mind's eye, he saw himself again before the make-up mirror, as he slowly peeled off vestiges of womanhood with the tears drying out with each doffing. The pork breasts, even now, stank in his nostrils.

When he looked back at the stage, the man was standing before the book he had just reopened, peering quizzically at the text. The nude girls crouched around the pedestal (an audience within an audience) as he began to read:

'Did you ever hear of the Irishman? ...'

He coughed, turned the page desperately.

'Why did the chicken cross the road? ...'

The real audience of novices hooted fit to split their sides, despite the missing punchlines. Even the slave-girls sniggered.

Tom could see the wildness in the performer's eyes, even in the dimming spotlight. Tears streaked the man's face, with theatrical make-up running like sores. Frantic stage fright shuddered the length of his body.

Tom could do nothing but shade his eyes again, in utter embarrassment and pity.

The audience grew quieter. Tom made a slit in his hand between two fingers and saw the stage relit with beams shafting upon it from every corner, leaving the rest of the hall in relative darkness. The man and the girls had disappeared ... bringing the embroidered backdrop to the fore. And, squinting through his own tears, Tom thought he saw carnage picked out in its weave ... young grimy faces with drooling lumps of butcher's rubble slewing down their bodies, as they feasted upon barely recognizable components of the Stew of Man . . . One lithe creature, more vividly sewn into the patchwork quilt with riper breasts than the others, had a wilting worm waggling from her lips . . .

The lights were doused. The show was about to proceed.

Tom could hardly bring himself to breathe. He wished he had been buried under the ground for centuries of forgetting. But, as the footlights raised their profile, the tapestry had lost most of its virulence, dropping back into pastel shades and less obvious parables. Waddling from the wings came a creature that brought spontaneous giggles from the audience. Even Tom smiled, more in compassion than humour, for it was the most blatant drag act he had ever seen. The so-called lady was done out in an ill-fitting dress with the ragged him of the slip showing, lop-sided bosom, smudged make-up, wrinkled schoolmistress stockings, tilted wig with ludicrous boater perched upon it at a rakish angle. 'She' pulled strings of multicoloured handkerchiefs from her red-smarmed mouth, a never-ending line of regatta-day flags. Then a scrawny pigeon-chested guinea-pig with large ears was plucked from her bodice . . .

As catcalls ensued, Tom Rose felt the deepest empathy, the direst second nature dawning within the dormitory of his soul.

The shameful spectacle on the stage proceeded. In another world, perhaps another time, Tom felt out the contours of his own body: the fine seamless breasts, soft as hardened honey . . . smooth dunes of inner thigh, leading nowhere but cragless silkness . . . finely chiselled ankles . . . dewy rose-petal cheeks . . . flashing eyes, which he could not see, but knew were the windows of his ultimate being . . .

She smiled at her squatting neighbour, as she smoothed back the dark vestments the length of her limbs. And, hand in hand, they left the hall together, along with all the other novices. The show had not been worth the candle . . .

Sister Rose, many years later, sought the book she considered would throw light on her new predicament. Age did not sit well upon her. She needed a third nature to which to cling, in readiness for meeting her Maker.

She had found love in the long arcades of the seminary, feeling shadows with her hands and feeding back smiles to those who met her half-way. But love was not enough now. Upon her wrinkled neck, the crucifix weighed heavier as the evenings wore on.

Reaching the hall at the dead of night, she saw again the gold-edged volume resting like a bird of prey upon the plinth, remembered so well.

The tapestry was back in place, now threadbare and tattered at the edges. Upon its surface there only lingered abstract stitches and stains that were not needlepoint at all.

The book was already open and she could only read fragments of faded ink:

> The past is a journey into death ... man and woman lead each other to the grave ... Hope is nothing ... Sympathy, in the right hands, can outlast even Hope and Death ... moreover, ♂ and ♀ are the two Signs of Love and Hate, Hate and Love ... God has a breast or two, a long snaking whip above the entrance to Heaven ... the ultimate joke ...

Sister Rose wrote it down as she read it, as if she was the Past itself scratching with blunt quill pen *and* Hope, too, the one who would eventually read her own words and perhaps even understand them. The gaps in the text nagged at her, but before she could fill them in, she saw crouched shapes at the back of the hall, shifting in shadows. Like beached monsters trying to prime their dark flesh for easing back into the giant womb of death: as if they were foetuses of ghosts.

One shape adjusted the head of hair it bore, to ensure it was still in place, and then smoothed the wide skirt of darkness in its lap. The other was ruling lines upon paper. In fact, the white sheet was all Sister Rose could see at all clearly from the stage.

Almost imperceptibly, she eventually heard the drone of voices:

'A4.'

'Nothing – how about B8?'

'Damn, you've just hit my Destroyer!'

Sister Rose returned alone to her cell, wherein her long-term companion of the bed had passed away only the night before, leaving a gap that could never be filled ... in this life, at least.

D. Milner

MR CHERRY

Game shows that had once amused Ramdev had now begun to lose their charm. It was the contestants mainly, the variety of accents and voice patterns they brought along to the studio. Curiously, that factor made a straight entertainment show such as *Bob's Opportunity Knocks* score less well for Ramdev against, say, the more intellectual *Call My Bluff*; the accents at least were all much of a muchness in the latter even if the subject matter remained impenetrable. Then again, though, *Call My Bluff* was a bad example because the host Robert Robinson had been virtually unintelligible from the first to the last show of the autumn season. Ramdev cursed him in his frustration. He became emotional about Robert Robinson. He leant out of his seat and pointed at Robinson's chuckling face on the screen, so wide and round and high-browed, chuckling away at some pun or innuendo, and he shook his finger – crooked with impotent rage – at that chuckling face and cursed heavily under his breath, telling him to stop it, stop it. But when the camera, consolidating the joke, switched to Frank Muir's long but sanguine face, unsmiling but with that twinkle of humorous accomplishment in his eye – for the joke was his – Ramdev cried out aloud, he broke down in an agonizing seizure of incomprehension, his face crumpled and he wept and cried out openly. He really let go, lost control, and it didn't matter, he could do as he pleased, cry all he liked, as there was never anyone else in the room to see or hear him. And he broke down more and more easily these days, and talked more and more to himself, or to the television, babbling away at the screen, at the games, over the voices of the hosts and guests alike, rudely allowing his own anguish and frustration to take precedence over that of the contestants.

However, all that strong feeling, all the cursing and crying at least, was on the wane now too. He just didn't let it hurt that much any more.

He had lost his determination to understand. He had started to regress with his viewing from the evening to the late afternoon, into the linguistically undemanding and heavily pictorial world of children's television. But now even the cartoons, even *Tom and Jerry*, which nearly a year ago when he first arrived would have made him curl up in his chair with excitement, laughter and sheer admiration – all those shapes they got into, all those shapes! – even *Tom and Jerry* bored him to tears these days.

The TV room was bare and white. Besides the television itself, Ramdev's chair – an ancient club chair – was the only piece of furniture. There was a bareness about all the rooms in Ramdev's parents' house. The house was really about as empty as it had been when they'd moved into it. 'This is temporary,' his father had said, staring suspiciously around the chip-papered walls. (In Ramdev's presence he always spoke in English.) There was a little carpet in the hallway the previous tenants hadn't taken up, but otherwise all the floors were bare boards. In the kitchen there were large ugle gaps in the wall units where a fridge and a washing machine should have been. When he'd first arrived Ramdev used to hunch himself into those filthy places while his mother was cooking and he'd just talk and talk, trying to talk it all out, why he had to go back home, why he couldn't stay here. He didn't do that any more. He ate in front of the television, hardly acknowledging his mother when she gave him his food.

They were not in poverty though. The house had central heating and they kept that turned up. They had the necessities (a favourite line of Ramdev's father's) but they were not secure. His father banked all the money he made, every penny he could. Ten months ago a relative had offered Ramdev's father a place in his taxi-firm. Ramdev's father had invested seriously and had bought himself a good vehicle – a Nissan saloon with a diesel engine. But he struggled at his work and he'd been threatened with the sack more than once. Hence the hoarding, the shoring up against imminent adversity. It was his father's uncle who owned the taxi-firm, an old man now who'd come over way back in the Sixties; but the blood relationship made no difference; the old man had still threatened to sack Ramdev's dad. He'd threatened him a few times now. He swore at Ramdev's father, in English, in front of Ramdev. Ramdev's father thought his taxi-driving was improving but there were still major holes in his knowledge of Peterborough and its surrounds, and he knew that, and the holes worried him and made him frown all the time he was behind the wheel, knowing he could drive into one at any time. He was safe in the centre and around Dogsthorpe and Millfield, but if he had to take a family and their groceries from the new

Sainsbury's Superstore out to the Orton townships, for example, he straight away became anxious and confused and prone to err. The Parkways all looked the same and there were so many roundabouts; the circular sprawl of the dual-carriageways defied any sense of direction.

When in doubt he'd acquired some ways of dealing with his fares, though. Other drivers had taught him a trick or two. For example, when he didn't understand what a fare had said he'd turn in his seat and look at the fare as if he'd made some racist remark. 'Would you mind repeating that please?' he'd ask, every word perfectly enunciated, a veiled threat in the polite request. Anxious to clarify any misunderstanding the fare would usually speak up more clearly. Then if he still didn't get it second time around Ramdev's dad would nod and turn back behind the wheel again and pluck a destination out of the air: 'Near the King's Head!' was a favourite one. Reluctant to move with all those shopping bags in the boot the fare might then throw out a few names and directions, and perhaps one of these would connect with the ragged map Ramdev's father was trying to unfold right way up in his mind. By and large something did connect and everything worked out all right.

There was still that dreadful night some months ago, though, when he'd returned at 10 p.m. after driving around the Fens for several hours. It was an unlucky circumstance: a businessman was up from London to look at a house out near Wisbech, eighteen miles away. Ramdev's father would never take on anything like that again. When it had become quite undeniable that they were lost the businessman had abandoned his taxi in a village out in the wilds. It was a disaster Ramdev remembered well and didn't hesitate to use against his father. Whenever they saw each other – which wasn't more than once every couple of days, his father worked such long and irregular hours – they always exchanged sarcastic greetings. His father generally fired first, usually with some dry remark on Ramdev's choice of programme.

'You learn a lot from that programme, you know.'

Ramdev wouldn't even turn around in his club chair. 'Where you bin? You drive aroun' te fiels agen?'

And that was all. His father would then pass on into the kitchen to speak to his mother.

Another reason Ramdev's father had for saving every penny he earned and spending nothing on where they lived was that he hoped to move his family into the town soon, into Gladstone Street or somewhere around there where his uncles and cousins lived. The present house was actually out of town some three or four miles on the A47 and the sense of isolation living so far out was extreme. Ramdev's mother went into town on the first bus, before Ramdev had even caught his bus to school, and she remained in town all day after doing the shopping, visiting relatives in houses in Dogsthorpe, helping to cook a meal, helping with whatever work needed doing. She remained out all day until about five, when Ramdev had already returned from school.

Tonight, though, she wasn't home at five, nor at six either, and, fed up with the television and feeling hungry, Ramdev grumpily put on his coat and went out into the dark outdoors. He only half wanted to come out. It was the empty house: with the television off the place became nothing more than a collection of clean white cells; the sound of his footsteps on the bare boards began to follow him around like a jailer. Besides, tonight Ramdev didn't want to be at home when his father or mother returned – let them worry about him for a bit.

They were the only Pakistani family who resided in the village. A couple of young Indians ran a discount store but they lived in Dogsthorpe and commuted out here daily; they also ran another shop in the next village along towards Peterborough. Ramdev saw them go by each day in their tall white Hiace van while he waited for the bus. His father knew of their family, but hadn't been properly introduced to anyone. They had no occasion to go to the discount store; Ramdev's mother organized their meals too well for any incidental shopping of that kind. So Ramdev had no business going down into the village tonight towards that lighted shop-front. He had hardly any money to spend there anyway. Yet he felt drawn to the shop. He'd been in it many times, just hanging around the shelves, listening, watching, or looking at the pictures of himself listening, watching, on the closed-circuit TV.

It was the brothers that drew him to the shop. They seemed so pleased with their lot. And their customers liked them, liked spending their money in their shop. There was a lot of laughter and banter, especially with the women customers, because the brothers were a handsome pair, particularly the younger one who did most of the till work. And despite the hours and the routine nature of the work, the slavery to the shop, these brothers were never moody or too busy to stop and chat. Ramdev envied them their apparent contentment.

Most of all, though, Ramdev envied the way they talked amusing the customers and even laughing at their own jokes. How did they manage that, these two? While he, Ramdev, scowled all the time and simply could not shake off, even after a year, the misery of coming to England. What was the secret? That's what he hung around the shelves to find out. He'd hold back some of his dinner money so that he might have something to spend in the shop.

'You like those, don't you?' the younger brother had said last time, when Ramdev bought pastilles again. They were the cheapest thing. Ramdev had tried to smile under his scowling brows.

'Yeah. I like tem,' he said, more ashamed of the thickness of his accent than he would have been with any white. These two spoke like the whites in town just absolutely the same. They could speak Punjabi too, though; he heard them out the back of the shop sometimes. They talked about arrangements with their family in Punjabi.

Ramdev didn't like pastilles. He loathed their kind of cloying sweetness. To him they were the taste of England, sickly sweet, wrapped up in their cold foil. He kept them unopened till the next day and then tried to swap them for something at school, an apple or something, and thus recoup 50 per cent of his loss to the shop.

There was another reason Ramdev approached the shop this evening, besides his fascination with these brothers and their business.

There was a young couple who were often in the shop around this time. They were a curious pair and Ramdev couldn't work them out at all. They were either lazy and rich, or they were both so hard-working they were too tired of an evening to cook for themselves. Whenever Ramdev saw them they were buying ready-made meals from the freezer, cellophaned spicy-chicken drumsticks, deep-frozen lasagne, that kind of thing; or they were in the shop to buy treats for themselves, like mint chocolate or wine or expensive beer. They were good customers and the young brothers always had a laugh with them. When this couple were in the shop, Ramdev had noticed, the other brother, the not-quite-so-handsome one, always came in from whatever he was doing out the back, a box under his arm, his labelling machine in his hand, he always came in and joined in with the joking and fooling around. This couple were that kind of customer. The brother at the till would make some funny remark about the young woman's appearance, that's the way it would always start. She was not an especially attractive young woman, Ramdev didn't think, especially above the lights of the freezer, holding her hair back in a coarse bunch and staring indecisively into the white frost. But the curves of her body under her open coat, large smooth curves under her ribbed jumpers and tight-fitting jeans, made men look at her and quickly look away.

One evening last week they emerged from the shop just as Ramdev came to the door. They were laughing at something someone had said inside but that laughter was just dying as they left and resumed each other's company. The woman was carrying a bottle of wine and the man was eating from an opened packet of crisps. As they passed by Ramdev, he heard the woman whisper, quite distinctly, as she put her arm through her partner's, 'Let's dedicate this evening to our bodies.'

He didn't hear what the man said because of the door bell and the door closing on their conversation, shutting him in the bright shop, but that sentence lived with Ramdev now like a song he couldn't get out of his mind. Whenever someone began a sentence with that word, Let's, it finished in Ramdev's mind with what the woman had said. When his ESL teacher – a dark woman in her late twenties whom Ramdev found very attractive – when she said, 'Let's have another look at this exercise, Ramdev,' Ramdev only heard, 'Let's dedicate this evening to our bodies, Ramdev.' And the feeling it brought up in him was so strong he had to shut his eyes a moment and crush himself hard against the desk. 'Is something wrong?' she'd ask.

Tonight, though, when he pushed into the shop the bell rang out loudly in the silence of the place. There was no one in the shop, no one was at the till even when Ramdev came in. Then he heard footsteps up the further aisle and he quickly walked down into the shop.

He felt stupid and angry with himself, humiliated by the disappointment he felt. What had he come here for? What had he expected? He stood there, his hands in his anorak pockets, staring up at the boxes – he was at the breakfast cereals – staring up at the multiple pictures of combine harvesters and bowls of milk and bran.

Ramdev was perhaps the most unlikely fisherman on the Fenland waterways. His interest in the sport had grown from his desperate need to get out of doors at weekends, away from the bareness of his house, no matter what the weather. Endless walks along the dykeways and river-banks had brought him across many fishermen, and even some fisherwomen, and the thought had seized him that here was something he might do: instead of interminably criss-crossing the landscape, he too could stop and sit and stare, out of the way of any other human soul.

It wasn't quite like that, though; that sweet loneliness, that melancholy. He had problems, at first at least, with keeping himself to himself. The contemplative calm and quiet of the river-bank proved to be illusory. Ramdev quickly discovered that fishermen are a restless, gregarious lot, forever getting up and seeking each other out to share cigarettes, sandwiches and anecdotes. Singly they were OK, but when they approached in twos or threes Ramdev sometimes had to put up with some unpleasant taunting. More seriously for him, a posse of older fishermen had taken him to task about the way he treated the fish, as at first Ramdev had always killed what he caught. No matter what its species or size, he just spiked the fish through its skull with his fishing knife perch, roach, gudgeon, eels, whatever – and laid it at his side. He had seen some younger boys do this and he thought it was perfectly acceptable. This was not the way to fish, he found out from the older men.

That was all ancient history now, from right at the beginning of the fishing season. But the racism and those early reprimands concerning the etiquette of the sport had instilled in Ramdev a desire for complete isolation in his fishing. And with a little extra walking it wasn't difficult, on all the lesser waterways that netted the Fenland fields, to find a very isolated spot, particularly if it was well known to offer a poor catch. The banks of the cuts were steep and with care it was quite possible to remain secret and out of sight for as long as it pleased him to do so.

This Saturday morning, however, Ramdev was not only very conspicuous, he was also heading towards one of the most popular fishing grounds in the area – the Weir. He was dressed in a bright red anorak and a pair of white trousers and some cheap white trainers which were already very muddy and wet. He loathed this leisurewear, particularly the thin white summer trousers, the same as his father wore in the taxi all day and all night. Only poor people wore white trousers in the winter, he told his father, but it wasn't the sort of remark his father would ever take any notice of.

The Weir was a local beauty spot. There was a pub very close by with a car-park which overlooked the river and a beer garden with children's swings and games. Recently Ramdev had been on the fringes of a conversation where some boys had been discussing the pike that they caught down here. This was the fish that now concerned Ramdev: he would catch this fish they called the 'freshwater shark'; he had researched how to do so and had invested in an extra item of tackle – a shiny metal spinner that trailed behind it a cluster of vicious black hooks. From the talk he'd heard, he expected there to be a crowd of people down at the Weir this morning, all similarly kitted up to catch the pike. Fishing was not all they got up to on the river-bank by any means; there was quite a bit of drinking and general larking about and Ramdev had come prepared with something to share around should attention shift from the pike to these other pursuits.

But when he arrived at the Weir there was no one in sight. He had a good scout around both sides of the sluices and in the broad cut that ran parallel to the river at this point, but there was no one around apart from a much younger boy who looked quickly up at him and then back to his float bobbing in the choppy brown water. Ramdev returned to the other side of the sluice, putting the huge green gates between himself and the younger boy.

Too early. He was angry with himself for being so early. It was so stupid. Naturally he had arrived before anyone else because he lived within walking distance of this place — they would have to cycle from their homes in Peterborough. Besides, it wasn't even ten o'clock on Saturday morning and no English people were around yet. The pub car-park was empty and the pub's windows were dark and misty with the condensation of the night before.

The water of the river was brown and high. It ran over the top of the sluices in four smooth heavy tongues that dipped deeply into the river's surface and stirred up cross-patterns up to forty yards from the gates themselves. Ramdev frowned as he edged his way down the bank — how could any fish stay in these currents?

So sceptical was he about the prospect of catching anything at the Weir that for half an hour he didn't even rig up. He'd found himself a good spot on a curve of firm ground three or four feet from the water; he'd organized his seat and he'd had a cup of tea from his flask and a couple of cigarettes. Smoking was something which went with fishing for Ramdev; the cigarettes made him light-headed and calm. He had brought a packet of twenty with him knowing that most of the people he expected to meet here this morning were smokers. It was pleasant, this first half-hour, just watching the water and smoking and drinking his tea, though the tea chilled quickly and smelled of the flask, as it always did.

Out of boredom, really, he set up his rod. He gripped the rod upright between his knees, ready to rig up the new tackle to the line. He examined the spinner in its polythene sachet; tiny blood-red safety caps covered the black hooks and across the flank of the metal fish three strokes of blood-red paint were dashed, more to attract the fisherman's eye than any pike. Ramdev smoothed the polythene over the spinner, examining it as if it were itself some proud catch.

Once in the muddy water the spinner disappeared instantly, a slack and useless weight of trace and steel. How could any fish see this stupid thing? He cast it out and trailed it back, dipping and raising his rod as it showed on the instructions to make the spinner rise and fall in the water. Learning the skill of steering the thing about kept Ramdev amused for a while, and it was fun to bring the spinner so close to the surface he could see it flash and then to let it dive again — but the futility of this kind of fishing in these conditions soon bored and wearied him.

He reeled in and set the rod in his rod rest; the spinner hung in the air twirling on its crimped new line, a bit of reed caught in its hooks.

He left his spot and climbed back up the bank to look around again. He walked for a little, keeping clear of the place where the other boy was fishing, inspecting other possible spots, noting places he might recommend to the others when they arrived ... and all the time, as he walked about, it became more and more difficult to distract himself from this thing he had brought to share around, this gift, this treat: the smooth, concave bottle he had left in a pocket at the end of his kitbag; and in the end he couldn't stop thinking of the bottle, its thick glass and its bright red label and its unbroken seal.

He had taken it from the Indians' shop. It had been easy. A basket of assorted bottles had been left for a moment on the step up from the storeroom into the shop. The brothers were at the till with one of their regulars, bantering away. The basket was near the closed-circuit camera but well below it, so that when Ramdev stooped and slipped the quarter-bottle into his coat he was completely invisible. He had felt a powerful satisfaction, coolly opening his pastilles as he walked out of the shop, while keeping the bottle safely tucked against his midriff; it was a satisfaction more to do with taking something from the brothers than with the value or use of what he had stolen.

It was only a quarter-bottle of vodka, but Ramdev was not used to drinking anything at all. The clear empty bottle bobbed a moment, topless, then sank under the brown river.

He was all right until he tried to stand up, then he swung about, surprised, as if someone had clapped him on the shoulder from behind; throwing his right arm out for balance he knocked his rod from its stand and it slipped with a splash, reel first, into the river. More than half of it still rested on the bank and he started to bend down to retrieve it, but then, sensing that that was unwise, he straightened again.

Very slowly he climbed the bank to safety.

Once up above the bank and in view he became concerned to get away quickly from this place, from the dormant pub, from the boy the other side of the sluice gates, and from those boys from school who might arrive on their bicycles at any moment, shouting to one another, shouting out to him. He had to find somewhere he could sit and rest and be still and stop the nauseous pulsing in his head, somewhere he would be completely alone. But he didn't know this area, it was exactly the kind of place he always avoided.

He crossed at the road-bridge, on the other side of which was the turn-in to the pub car-park. He crossed the road and managed to get himself over a stile into the meadow by the river; this way seemed empty and deserted, no building in sight apart from one of those small brick pumping stations in the distance across the meadow. That seemed to Ramdev a good place to head for; the vague possibility of some kind of shelter, or at least a dry wall to lean against.

He arrived there exhausted and hot from trudging across the boggy wet grass; he had thought the labour of the walk was somehow working out the poison from his system, but it wasn't; as soon as he stopped he felt as if he were in a fever. He slumped against the wall of the pumping station feeling weak and faint, and in a couple of minutes he was asleep.

Ramdev had been in many fights and was not afraid of young men his own size and age, in fact he had seen off aggressors who were much larger than himself; yet there was a certain kind of ten- or eleven-year-old boy, no matter how puny, of whom he was afraid. On first coming to England he had often been in trouble on account of such children, for physically lashing out at them, but he had never found his way round them.

This kind of ten- or eleven-year-old boy was precocious by nurture. His appearance was naïvely sexualized: he would wear his hair gelled back from his downy face, his jeans would be tight-fitting, snug to his thin thighs and pre-pubescent crutch. Already burdened with something to prove and nothing to prove it with, he would shriek out any taunt in his shrill unbroken voice, he would call any name, even names he obviously didn't understand; he would even throw things to start something off. His undeveloped sensibilities lent him a recklessness which, were he with just a couple of friends, was enough to make Ramdev, four or five years his senior and many times stronger, turn and run away like a coward.

On waking up against the pump-house wall and seeing such a boy standing in front of him, Ramdev reflexly hunched himself and drew in his legs and clasped his hands about his knees. There was another boy, but Ramdev's eyes were drawn to the boy above him on his left, because he had that look: the gelled hair; a shiny plastic leather jacket. Ramdev's eyes were only half open; the sky was grey but the light to him was intensely bright. His drunken mind went though a quick diagnostic report, trying to re-establish control of all his faculties, but the report came back a blank and Ramdev let his eyes close and consciousness began to recede once more. Behind his eyelids there remained an after-image of a tall tree behind the boy on the left, in the branches of which was caught an old blue fertilizer bag that had been blown up into the tree, and the bag flapped there in the branches and he could hear that sound, that windy flapping sound, and in another moment, with his eyes shut, that was all he knew about, that sound of the bag in the tree, as he sank back under.

'Are you all right?'

Ramdev kept his eyes shut while he tried to sort out which boy the question had come from, and only on doing this did it fully come to mind that there was indeed more than one boy. Now there seemed to be some buoyancy in his puffy eyelids, they wanted to open and let his consciousness surface. And there above him was this second boy on the right, and he was not at all the same. This one's hair was unkempt and mousy and fell in a fringe and he was smiling at Ramdev, not a natural smile but a friendly smile nonetheless, a helpful smile, he would run and give a message to someone or he would run to the telephone and ring for a doctor if Ramdev needed him to. Ramdev shut his eyes and the tree was there again, and the bag flapping in the wind, the wind much stronger suddenly, the land so flat here there was nothing at all to stop the wind.

'You all right, mate?'

There was a hesitancy about that 'mate' which made Ramdev certain the question had come from the mousy boy on his right and he opened his eyes and looked at him again. He didn't say anything but he nodded.

Ramdev watched the mousy boy look to his friend; there was the subtlest change in his smile, so that from being open and helpful it now became mischievous and conspiring – not that he wanted to do anything mischievous, perhaps, but he had to smile this way towards his friend, boy to boy. Ramdev's brown eyes slid across under their three-quarter shut lids to find out what the boy on his left was doing. What did he want?

Nothing, apparently. He shrugged his shoulders.

They seemed to go, but Ramdev heard them stop just around the corner of the pump-house. He heard them muttering to each other and giggling, but they were intent on some other business now and any talk of Ramdev quickly subsided as they attended to it. Ramdev opened his eyes more fully. On seeing the open landscape again and the windy grey sky he realized he was cold and he pulled his red anorak together and fastened the popper buttons right up to his neck.

He eased himself off the wet tuft of grass he'd been sitting on and lay on his side to see round the corner; the wind pulled his thin white trousers from his wet buttocks.

As soon as he saw the boys busy setting up their fishing tackle he remembered his own which he had left at the Weir. He rolled back against the pump-house wall. His rod, his reel, in the water. His seat, his empty rod rest. His kitbag with his tea and cigarettes and so on. No – he patted his anorak pocket – the cigarettes were with him.

Shifting his body had brought back a queasy softness inside him, not altogether unpleasant, a kind of numbing from the inside outwards in gently subsiding, healing waves. He wasn't feeling so bad now, after his sleep. This was a more pleasant drunkenness. He took out his cigarettes and lit one to celebrate it.

He smoked and listened to the sounds of the boys that came to him between the gusts of wind around the pump-house. He heard the plop of the first cast in, and a snatch of laughter at some mistake or accident: one of them had cast clean across the dyke to the field the other side.

Ramdev was smiling to himself, sharing the humour of the incident, when suddenly the plastic-jacketed boy came round the wall. He stood a moment in front of Ramdev before declaring what he'd come for.

'Got a fag, mate?'

There was a clumsy, imitative quality about the line, and something rushed and slurred about his accent gave the boy away. Ramdev listened closely to people. He'd made a science of understanding them from how they spoke rather than from what they said. He'd turned his ear on a thousand game-show accents. This boy tried to urbanize his rural accent, cockneyfying his upbringing, and though Ramdev couldn't specify the affectation in that way he understood well enough that here was a boy who wanted to be of the streets rather than of the fields. Ramdev felt a little sorry for him, not recognizing in himself a touch of drunkenly misplaced sentiment. Lazily he took out his cigarette packet and removed a cigarette and gave it to the boy.

Ramdev held up his box of matches, though not too high, and the boy stooped and took it; still bending there he struck and cupped a match and lit his cigarette, puffing violently to get it going in the wind.

'Ta,' the boy said, straightening, and as he straightened his manner changed suddenly. 'Ta,' he said again, and he blew a stream of smoke out at the wall above Ramdev's head and with theatrical contempt he dropped the box of matches into Ramdev's lap. 'Mustaphafag sometimes, you know?'

He went back around the corner and Ramdev heard the other boy laughing furtively at the joke.

Warming to the response, the boy repeated his joke, louder, for unless Ramdev heard it again too, hidden away around the corner, it was wasted.

'I just mustaphafag, sometimes, you know?'

Ramdev closed his eyes.

How he loathed this country. The climate, the people, everything. He wanted to lean back into his weariness of it all and rest there, resigned and accepting of it all, but he knew he couldn't; that was a luxory these boys would not allow; they wanted to take all his luxuries away from him. If he didn't respond the nasty boy would get worse, he would say or do something else to provoke. And Ramdev couldn't get up and go. He felt too weak still. The waves of numbness from within took away his will-power. Yet he had to assert himself, to show the boys they could not play these games.

So, carefully, he brought himself to his feet and steadied himself a moment against the pump-house wall. He leant there, waiting for the waves to die down, to feel properly in control.

He walked around the back of the pump-house, using the extra distance to gain confidence in his step.

The mousy boy looked up first and his surprise and fear were obvious. Ramdev stood just a few inches behind him: with one kick or shove he could have either him or his friend in the water. Ramdev said nothing, letting the boy take in his position. This one couldn't be more than nine years old. Under his fringe his blue eyes were wide with protested innocence. His drawn lips exposed large crooked teeth.

His companion had glanced up a moment. In his eyes he had stayed calm, but Ramdev knew what he was really thinking: until now he had only seen Ramdev slumped in his drunken stupor against the wall; on his feet the Paki was so much bigger, and the grass of the river-bank must have felt suddenly very wet and slippery beneath his arse.

Something caught Ramdev's eye in one of the boys' knapsacks, and he knew how he was going to play it. He dropped to his knees right behind the boys, as if positioning himself to shove them both down the bank; the smaller boy visible tensed up.

Then Ramdev took from the knapsack this furled paperback book he had seen. It was a broad cartoon-strip book: *Mr Cherry and Tom Go Pike Fishing*. The book could only belong to the smaller boy. He flicked through the pages.

'Could I borrow this, please?' he said softly to the mousy boy.

The boy turned quickly. 'Sure.' He nodded eagerly and part of his fringe fell down over his eye. He swallowed hard. Ramdev took the cartoon book, rolled it tightly into a little tube, a hard little weapon, and gripped it firmly in his fist.

Then he turned his attention to the other knapsack. It was nestled close to the back of the other boy. Ramdev put his hand into the knapsack and felt around, deliberately nudging the bag so the other boy could feel his hand right there in his bag, behind him, ready to push. The boy didn't turn or move, he stayed still and silent now, this one who had made the joke just a couple of minutes ago. He hadn't so much to say for himself now.

The boy was petrified to have Ramdev's big body crouched just a foot or so behind him, and to smell the sour stench of booze coming over his shoulder from Ramdev's breath. The boy was so rigid with fear Ramdev could have just tapped him on the shoulder and he would have rolled down the bank like a rock.

'And I can have this?' Ramdev asked, bringing out a chocolate bar from the bag, a Kit-Kat.

Still the other boy didn't move in any way or say anything. Instead the mousy boy answered quickly again: 'Sure.'

'Thank you,' Ramdev said, in his softest, most English accent. He put the Kit-Kat away in his anorak pocket and zipped the pocket up.

'Thank you very much,' he repeated. He stood and then hesitated: the queasiness had returned suddenly; he'd been on his knees too long. Giving himself time to steady himself, he unfurled the cartoon book and flicked through it.

'Very interesting book,' he said. 'Very interesting indeed.' He rolled the book tightly again and slapped it decisively against his thigh. 'Thank you very much.'

He walked on round the pump-house to his wall and sat down heavily. The waves of numbness were building, the whitecaps quickening into breakers, rolling away his strength. He wanted to shut his eyes but he knew he couldn't, he mustn't. He stared intently at the tree above him, the endless bright grey sky.

There was a lull in the wind and he could hear the boys around the corner. There would have been nothing he could do if they had come back, but of course that wasn't going to happen. He could hear the sounds of tackle being hastily packed up and of short frightened giggles, accusatory whispers, the mousy boy blaming his friend, who for his part seemed to accept the blame – nothing much came from him, except the giggles, lessening now.

Then the sound of their running away.

Ramdev rolled on to his side and looked round the wall again. They were running as hard as they could, a sudden panic once they had started to flee driving them on. And the smaller one was falling behind. He carried his rod still half made up and he had to struggle to keep it from dipping in the long grass and tripping him.

Ramdev sat back against the wall. He lit another cigarette. The waves were subsiding.

He set the book in his lap and opened it.

Mr Cherry and Tom Go Pike Fishing.

Cherry was a stern, moody guy, under a low flat cap. A no-nonsense fellow. Tom crouched in the bow of the boat while Cherry rowed. Cherry puffed a short pipe.

Ramdev turned the page, having nothing better to do.

They weighed anchor right in the middle of the lake. Looks a good spot, Cherry said, slipping the oars from their rowlocks. They had the place to themselves. He frowned and puffed as he kitted up.

Never stand in the boat, not even to cast, Cherry said. Safety first.

Cherry cast, finding with his spinner a gully in the bank where a stream came into the lake.

Good place. Pike like waiting in the eddy.

Over the next page there was the pike, fanning its pectorals in the eddy. The spinner sank, its trace lifted and it swam to the pike, gliding by within an inch of its nose. The pike's large eyes crossed stupidly on the spinner: it opened its greedy jaws to accept the trailing hooks.

Back in the boat Cherry felt it and struck. Cherry sat up in the boat, his cap tilted back. He looked suddenly much younger, fighting the big fish, his pipe puffing steadily.

Tom was open-mouthed, amazed.

Amazed.

It was cold out here in the fields. Windy and bloody cold lying here.

Ramdev shut his eyes and behind his eyelids he saw again the smaller boy running away, his half disassembled rod catching in the grass. This was his book, about how to catch the pike. Ramdev had stolen it from him. As he had stolen the vodka from the shop. The brothers would know it was him. They'd watch out for him when he came to their shop next time, from the ends of their aisles, a brother at the end of each aisle, watching the Paki thief.

But this was the boy's book, open in his lap. What should he do with it? This book about Tom and Mr Cherry.

Annie Murray

KISHA

I still have the photograph taken outside the old scholar's house in Cambridge. They posed by the bay window, stiff as saints in stained glass, he looking like a blubbery version of Gandhi, and that silent wife, both still dressed loyally in homespun. Professor Devi was in a brown jacket with a high collar, Mrs Devi's sari was bordered with green. Although it was summer she had put on a western-style coat. It looked lumpish and homely on her. And Kisha, wrapped round in blue and red silk, with a shawl. I remember the shawl, what she said, finally, folding the embroidered blue back over her shoulder.

That was the one visit, the time I realized I was just beginning to understand bits of what they were saying. *Apni kothaye aghami kal jaben?* Where are you going tomorrow? But I don't like to hear Bengali spoken now.

I met the Devi family through Mr Mitra. And I came across him in the National Museum in Calcutta, which skulks opposite one end of the maidan on Chowringhee. You're not supposed to call it that nowadays apparently. It's renamed Jawaharlal Nehru Road on the street plans. Probably one of those things Kisha feels strongly about. Well, maybe.

We had a conversation, after I'd strolled through the enormous rooms, shelves bowed under the weight of fossils, outraged-looking fish and glass-eyed birds. Others full of statues, shoulder to shoulder – Buddha-Vishnu-Ganesh. He was standing under an arch of the cloistered quadrangle outside, intent on the scaffolding. One side of the square was covered by a grid-work of thick bamboo poles tied together with lengths of rope. Balancing on them with bare feet at alarming heights were men with pots of paint and brushes.

'I wonder they do not fall,' Mr Mitra said. He was smallish, dressed in a worn black suit and wearing the standard Indian black-rimmed spectacles. He asked what was my country – England? That was good; he was a teacher of music now retired and had studied at the Tagore University at Santiniketan and his speciality was wind instruments. Nearby, in the grassy square, a man squatted on hairpin legs attending to weeds. It was growing hot. Mr Mitra pulled out a pipe and sucked the end.

'You are a student?'

I was on my way to Cambridge.

'Ah,' he said. '"What does he know of England that only England knows?"' And then, 'You would be interested to meet some friends of mine.'

I had not intended to stay more than a few days in Calcutta, but it became weeks. Mr Mitra had no family and he took me round like a son or favoured nephew. He showed me things I'd never have seen on my own. We seemed to be doing each other a favour. I began to feel that at least I'd have something to talk about now when I got to Cambridge. And there was Kisha.

Kisha asked me sometime, as everyone does, what I thought ('What is your impression?' she probably said) of India. I was trying to impress her at the time and I came out with some safe, dewy-eyed stuff about how interesting, how friendly and hospitable, how much better the extended family, how spiritual – I think I even said that.

I hadn't wanted to go to Cambridge knowing nothing of anywhere much except Birmingham – there'd be all the public school lot, assured with conversation and women. And even in Birmingham I'd never really got out of where I was. I hardly knew the place. I come from 'leafy' Harborne – well-off mostly, white mostly. (People there said, Why bother going? We've got most of bloody India and Pakistan here already.) Before I left I went on foot like a tourist round Soho and Villa Roads in Handsworth – places you read about in the paper – sort of breaking myself in. And Balsall Heath. The gritty air of the Stratford Road, with skewed furniture spilling out over the pavement and display windows glittering with Asian clothes on dummies with impossible wasp waists and Sixties hairdos. People wearing floaty clothes that flapped in the wind, people driving cars that looked as if they'd been pulled off scrap heaps and given a final chance. I ate balti chicken in Ladypool Road feeling like some sort of pioneer. I began to like Birmingham, now I'd finally raised my head.

When I got to India I spent days prickly with awareness that my skin was the wrong colour. I felt obliterated, fearful that I would disappear, sink to the ground among all the relentless crowds and be trampled into dust. There was so much strangeness – Hinduism especially – bowing to painted stones draped with marigolds. So the familiarity of it was uncomfortable but a relief – the shared language, billboards advertising Nivea Creme, newspapers called *Times* and *Express,* the cenotaph in Calcutta and statues of Charlie Chaplin and Queen Victoria. (Mr Mitra talked a lot about the Independence years. He said, not unkindly, 'We just wanted you off our backs.') But then old geezers in khaki drill with bristling moustaches kept coming up to me and with a click of their heels applauding everything British, going on about how much better it was when we were 'still here', how morals were tighter and the trains ran on time. I almost began to believe it. It was all so twisted together that in the end I couldn't work out where Britishness ended and Indianness began.

Mr Mitra took me to a great many tea parties. We sat in the rooms of elderly Bengali intellectuals. The first such visit was to a house in the southern area of the city. Like most Calcutta houses it was painted in a pastel shade – in this case blue – and the paintwork was chipped and stained from all the monsoon rain. Outside, an old eucalyptus tree.

In the shadowy flat, there were a number of people arranged round the room in armchairs and on a divan. It was winter and the women were bundled up in shawls over their saris, the men in a mixture of Western suits and loose white trousers and shirts. A maid came into the room from the other side, carrying a silver teapot.

'Ah, Gora,' someone called out. 'And about time. We quite thought you had gone into hiding.'

'And from whom?' Mr Mitra said, smiling, 'Have I such a dangerous reputation?' I was introduced – Mark, a young man on his way to Cambridge. There were polite nods around the room. I felt embarrassed, as I would have at home with people from school working as clerks in the local building society. And here, I expected resentment – Cambridge seen as a symbol of the British ruling class, playing fields of Eton and all that. Gradually though, I realized the gathering was almost like a reunion for Oxbridge alumni.

The room was full of heavy chairs, dark furniture, and a musty smell, like old linen. Surfaces were crammed with incense holders, several Staffordshire figures of shepherds and maidens, silver candlesticks, three painted masks of the gods from the Jagannath Temple at Puri, old rugs on the floor, antimacassars on the backs of the chairs, and china cups and saucers on the tray.

Kisha was sitting close to her mother. She looked young – maybe fourteen. Mrs Devi gestured for me to join them.

'My husband was a student for some time in Cambridge – at Emmanuel College,' she said, nodding across the room towards a long man laid back in an armchair, his hands making curving gestures as he talked. 'I myself was a rival at Oxford. At St Hilda's College.' She seemed incapable of anything jarring, her manner smoothed by years of formality.

I nodded and smiled. How strange it all seemed. I never met people like this in England. There was laughter from the other end of the room. It seemed to centre round Mr Mitra and another middle-aged man dressed in white. Mrs Devi smiled.

'Mr Mitra is always such a joker,' she said.

'When he last came to our house, he fed some snuff to our cat,' Kisha said. 'It was so very funny.' She giggled, clapping one hand tight over her mouth. She had a soft voice, sing-song, with that high Bengali way of talking.

All around me conversations switched back and forth between English and Bengali. The gawky maid handed me a cup, delicate as eggshell and full of dark tea. She offered me sugar from small silver tongs.

'Have some sweets,' Kisha said. 'This one ...' She pressed me to eat something like a sticky brown dumpling. '*Gulab jamun* – my favourite.'

Occasionally the talk opened up to spread round the room in a wave before closing up again into distinct groups, and someone would throw a question at me. A heavy-set man seated in one corner spoke for a while in Bengali, leaning forward in his chair, until his face rearranged itself into folds of laughter. Everyone was laughing, Kisha too. I looked round wondering what the joke was. Mr Mitra was chuckling through his pipe, his cup and saucer jiggling unsteadily on one hand, and saying, 'What a fellow!' The large man, his shoulders still moving up and down, called to me across the room – 'I'm sorry, my friend. That one just does not sound the same in English!' There was more laughter.

'Don't take any notice of use,' Kisha said. 'Please tell me about your impressions of Cambridge.' She had her small hands folded in her lap, resting on blue folds of sari. 'I hope also to be a student there, when I am old enough.' Apparently that would be in two years' time. She was older than I had thought.

She wanted to take English Literature. 'My brothers are already students in Oxford,' she said. 'Nirad is studying history and Ananda is also a student of literature. But I want to go to Cambridge. I want to read Shakespeare and Dickens and Keats and T.S. Eliot – *everything*. I want to do a doctorate afterwards. Perhaps I will go to the United States. And what will you study?'

'Languages – French and German.' Looking in on other people's cultures.

'So you will study literature, too,' she said. 'Comparative literature. That is very good.' I can't say I'd ever really thought of it that way before. I thought it might give me a leg-up to a job. Cambridge was to be my passport to something. But Kisha always made academic work sound more important than anything.

Mr Mitra took me to his house where he lived alone, apart from an elderly servant. He played the flute to me. He seemed anxious to explain about Bengali culture. Maybe it was just the teacher in him. He told me about the Baul tradition of musicians and took me to hear some of them playing one-stringed instruments and drums. I decided to learn all I could about Bengal and its history. It would seem more impressive to know more about a particular area. And there was always all this talk – mixed in with someone's dying brother or pilfering servant were books, music, religion. At home no one ever seemed to have time for things like that.

And every so often, I saw Kisha. We visited the Devis' house. Its decoration was simpler and lighter – tiled floors, very upright chairs covered by embroidered cushions in Rajasthani style, and brass statues of Hindu gods. And there were books everywhere, rowed up in glass-fronted cupboards to guard against damp and insects.

The first time, Kisha was wearing a yellow *shalwar* and *kameez*, bordered with black, a red shawl and sandals. She seemed pleased to see me, I thought.

'Mark-*bhai* – so you have finally come to our house!' She laughed and took my hand. 'That is very good. Now you can look at my books.' She was very proud of her collection, mostly gifts from relatives and friends on return from Britain and the States. She'd read an impressive amount. In fact I don't think there was anything much else for her to do except read and go to all those tea parties.

'Don't you have any friends your own age?' I asked as she passed me a handful of paperbacks. She had sturdy little fingers. For a moment I thought of them moving over my skin.

'Oh yes, yes,' she said. 'Of course. At school.' But it didn't seem all that relevant. She watched me. 'These are good books, no?'

'Yes – great. You'll sail into Cambridge, I should think.'

'It is my dream.' She flicked the corner of her shawl over her left shoulder. Her plait made a gash of black across the red and yellow covering her back.

Later, teasing, she said, 'And so, Mark, when are you going to begin learning Bengali?'

I went out early the next morning, woken by crows, squawking and scrabbling along my open window frame, and walked north, towards BBD Bag in search of books. There was bright sunlight, though it was cool as yet, and the streets were packed full of people. I struggled through the mass of gangling bodies outside a cinema billing a film called *Sexy Dreams*. In BBD Bag, between the banks I found a bookshop. I bought a Bengali primer and for *Rs* 40, a Bengali-English dictionary with rough-cut pages which gradually changed colour all the way through.

So when I wasn't out walking or around with Mr Mitra or with Kisha, I sat in the corridor on the men's floor of the YWCA on Middleton Row and began on the alphabet. The corridor was open on one side and faced out over a courtyard which had been turned into a tennis court. To the thuck-thuck sound of balls being socked across the rotting net, I found out that there are more than fifty characters in the Bengali alphabet and I tried to take in a few each day. I struggled to shape my jaw around aspirated and non-aspirated consonants, using a mirror as they recommended. I tried the three ways of writing 'sh' and four ways of writing 't' and 'd'. I began on simple phrases.

'*Tomar nam Ki?*' I asked Kisha when I next saw her. She laughed with delight.

'*Amar nam Kisha!*' she said. 'Actually my real name is Shyamasree, but everyone calls me Kisha. So – soon you will be a fluent Bengali speaker.'

I wanted to touch her, make a claim in some way, but I didn't. Even though she didn't seem so young as when we'd first met there were all sorts of cultural things which put her out of reach. But I'd still be in Cambridge when she was due to arrive. I had all kinds of ideas about me and Kisha.

The Devis seemed to get used to me coming round. Before I finally decided it was time to tear myself away from Calcutta and head back to Delhi for my flight, I sat again with Kisha on the flat roof of their house where they had flowers and a few shrubs arranged in pots. It was evening. We could hear children playing and shouted conversation from the street below.

'Your mother doesn't seem to mind you being alone with me.' I kept everything at a teasing sort of level.

'My family are very modern in outlook,' Kisha said. She was sitting on a cane chair, one leg crossed over the other, and swinging a sandal from her raised foot. I noticed she had pink varnish on her toe-nails. That was new. 'And anyway, they like you. They know I'll be going to university. They let me make my own decisions.'

'What about marriage? I thought all Indian girls had to get married?'

'Oh,' she said, 'maybe later.' She was in the buttercup outfit again, and her yellow leg twitched up and down like the arm of a sewing machine. 'But that is not so very interesting, really, is it? Tell me . . .' She uncrossed her legs and leaned forwards. 'What is your opinion of Mr Mark Twain?'

When I said goodbye to Kisha, she insisted I write to her 'and tell me what you have been reading.' She said, 'It will be good to have a friend in Cambridge. And don't forget your Bengali.' She stood on tiptoe to kiss me on the cheek, and her hair smelled perfumed. I didn't have the chance to kiss her back. After I left I realized I didn't even have a photo.

They came to Cambridge about eighteen months later. I'd kept in touch with Mr Mitra, who constantly urged me to return to Calcutta. He said he was missing my company. Kisha's letters were more disappointing than I could ever have imagined. I had expected her to share her thoughts about what she was reading and to bombard me with questions about Cambridge life. Instead she wrote short notes, or just cards, containing few details. It was like reading an appointments diary. It made her distant. Sometimes she mentioned the titles of books. She said that her family had been to Orissa on holiday. Lately she had been visiting Santiniketan. She had made 'some new friends'. She didn't say where or who. She always signed off 'from your affectionate Kisha'.

There were girls at Cambridge, of course, but no one anything like Kisha. No one with her sort of passion for things which – to my surprise – had begun to motivate me. I found myself taking work more seriously for its own sake. They found me a bit heavy, I think – I had inherited it from her. They all just seemed to have got good enough grades to get in and that was it. No one pulled me like Kisha did. I wanted to be able to say I had a girlfriend in India. I thought about writing to her and telling her how I felt. The nearest I ever got was saying 'I miss you' and I had to think hard even about that. '*Bhai*', I had realized, means 'brother'. I struggled to keep up with the Bengali on my own. Now and then some image, or a letter, would bring her sharply into focus. In my mind I'd see her running up the steps of the Devis' house to the roof, the strong movement of her hips in front of me, her ear-rings thin slices of gold against the darker skin below her ears. I would undress her in my mind, very slowly, unwinding the coloured silks from round her (she would be smiling at me), imagining the lines of her body, my hands stroking her dark breasts.

In the late spring the letter arrived saying they were coming. The family were to visit England for Professor Devi to deliver a series of lectures in Oxford. They would of course see a lot of Nirad and Ananda, and would be visiting friends in Cambridge. I wondered if they were also coming to settle Kisha into this new country. She should have been due to arrive next term, but I had never got her to answer the point in her few letters.

They only stayed for a couple of days in Cambridge. I was invited to meet them at the old scholar's house.

Kisha looked older. Even the clothes she was wearing seemed more adult. She came forward with the same surprised smile and said 'Hello, Mark. It is very nice to see you again.'

I leaned forward to kiss her on the cheek. She responded, but with a formal stiffness. Her parents seemed the same – he remote, she serene. Mrs Devi asked me how my studies were going. She sat huddled in an armchair near Mrs Mukherji, as if cold.

And so we had tea again, and there was more talk in English and Bengali, to the clink of cups and plates, and Dr Mukherji said to Kisha, 'So I hear you have decided to be a rebel and go to Javadpur University? You will be taught by your father?'

Kisha said, 'Yes' rather quietly.

'Turning down Cambridge, eh?' Dr Mukherji chuckled, his chins wobbling, and slapped one chubby knee. His wife watched him, chewing cake, in silence. 'You will grow up a true Bengali!' For some reason the old man found this hugely funny.

Some sort of barrier was going up, or at least I was noticing it for the first time. Now I had begun to understand even a few strands of Bengali, all that I didn't understand was growing by the minute. This polite, formal conversation, these signs I couldn't interpret. I was growing angry and frustrated. I became certain that Professor Devi had forbidden Kisha to come to Cambridge.

'We have even bribed her, almost, to take up her place here,' the Professor said from the armchair where he was sitting, one long leg folded over the other. 'But she has become an addict of the Bengali renaissance and will have none of it. She wants to remain a Calcuttan. Actually, it is to some extent alarming. Just last month she was involved in a demonstration. She is becoming quite a little activist.' He made some more comments in Bengali. I couldn't follow it.

I had a short time alone with Kisha in the garden. Mrs Devi suggested we go. We walked, that cool afternoon, towards the orchard at the end of the garden. It had been a poor summer, and the pears on the trees looked stillborn and hard. Kisha watched the hem of her sari swish across the grass. I asked her what the hell was going on. It took time to get her to speak.

'*Why?*' I said. 'It was your dream. And I wanted it for you as well.'

Eventually she said something about how British of me – because I'd learned a few phrases of Bengali I thought I had the right to ... Then she tried to be kinder. 'Dreams change,' she said. ('We just wanted you off our backs.' Mr Mitra had been kind too.) I knew there was something she had found, and I envied it.

I said, 'I've waited for you, you know, ever since. I hoped maybe ...'

She raised one hand to make me stop. Fingering the wool of her shawl, she rearranged the end over her shoulder. 'I was just a little girl then,' she said. 'And anyway, there are so many more important things. That's all so *domestic*.'

We could see the others coming out of the house with those slow movements. Dr Mukherji waddled towards us, his white dhoti brushing against the daisies. He was holding a camera far out in front of him as if to disclaim responsibility for it. 'We wondered if you would oblige us by taking a photograph,' he said.

They all lined up in front of the window. Afterwards Mrs Devi said, 'Let us take one of you and Kisha – by the trees there.' That also deliberately kind.

'No, thanks,' I said. 'I don't like having my photograph taken.'

My Bengali dropped into the background after that. In any case, it had been a struggle because there was no one to practise with.

Very occasionally I heard from Kisha. Her brief, factual letters told me she was now studying history. She didn't tell me how much she was getting involved with politics, but I guessed. The letters were no more or less warm than they had been before, still signed 'Your affectionate ...' I struggled to write simple letters in what Bengali I could remember to Mr Mitra.

In the spring before finals I had a letter from Kisha. The usual sort of thing. She was studying hard. Nirad was back in Calcutta. The family had visited Puri to cool down at the beach. At the end of the summer, she had still not replied to my letters written in the hope that she would become disenchanted, would change her mind. I wrote again.

My exams seemed to go all right. My tutor hoped I'd get a First. Said I took my work more seriously than most students. Would I think of staying on to do research?

A letter arrived from Gora Mitra. It was, as usual, short. In it, in English, he told me that several months earlier, Kisha had joined a number of students for a march in Calcutta in support of a group campaigning for women's rights. As they had surged through the streets, the jostling had been such that Kisha was pushed into the road and hit by a truck. The lower half of her body had been crushed so that she could no longer use her legs. Now, he wrote, she mostly just sits indoors.

Manini Nayar

MOMENTS OF SIGNIFICANCE

My father was a man with an eye for detail. 'Aha!' he'd roar when an
unwary passer-by trod over our front lawn on his unsuspecting way to
the highway. 'Trespassers again!' Then he'd rush to the edge of the
garden and glare furiously at the victim, tapping the walking-stick
ominously against his good leg. I'd watch wide-eyed as the poor
unfortunate shuffled off uneasily while father thundered after him in
diabolical triumph. 'Off with you!' or 'There's no peace on God's earth
any more!' Mother comforted me. 'Now that he's retired,' she'd say
soothingly, 'the garden means a lot to him.' Father, forgetting us all,
would mutter darkly to himself, bent over a patch of crushed lilacs   a
fading magician over his broken bag of tricks.

Once he'd been magic, I remember, when he was younger and
disarmingly charming like Richard the Lionheart. I'd identify myself
with the plebeians that surrounded him as he arose handsome and
majestic, dwarfing us all. Up the garden path he'd drive his new Sedan,
trailing clouds of dusty glory, then stand against the door, laughing, his
walking-stick agleam with polish, his shoes twinkling light. Nobody
every saw his club-foot at the time. But when he retired and the sparkle
faded from his eyes, people noticed. Neighbours said it was a pity Mr
Menon's ailment was playing up after all these years. Hot and angry,
I'd cry in the coalshed, battling a nameless fear that took shape only
later when I grew up and discovered the solace of words.

But Father didn't care. Neighbours were all right as long as they
washed their windows and discouraged their poodles from saluting his
Kashmir rose-bushes. Neighbours could be tolerated with kindness.
This was a democracy. So Father would bellow, 'Good-day, Mrs
Punjabi,' even if the neighbour apprehended was Mrs Mehta who
especially loathed Mrs Punjabi for baking the richest coffee cake on the
block. Blushing with embarrassment, I'd watch Mrs Mehta fall pensive

at being incorrectly identified after nine years of neighbourly relations. But Father was never deterred by emotional trivialities. 'You should be careful,' he'd remark confidingly to her. 'With all those rascals let out from the mill at five o' clock, a beautiful lady like you could lose her front lawn to the trampling hordes.' Charmed by his own keen turn of phrase, Father would bow courteously to an ambivalent Mrs Mehta caught between annoyance and coy self-deprecation. Then unexpectedly confronting a wilting rhododendron, Father's attention would rivet immediately from women to fertilizer. His eye for detail was determined entirely by his priorities.

It often struck me that most children at this time were playing jump-rope or sharing homework. Father had no faith in communal applications of any sort. 'Useless,' he'd bark. 'Only mediocrities spend hours turning two sticks with a rope strung in between.' So I read Gibbon's *Decline and Fall* and contemplated Keatsean notions of ceasing upon the midnight while Suma Mehta brought home boys from school and wore scarlet lipstick. Whenever I chafed, Father took me for a cathartic trek over the maidan to the mill, the Inferno that disgorged every evening the hordes of lawn-trampling trespassers. At irregular intervals, Father stopped admiringly before a small surprise of honeysuckle or a pattern of sunlight on the grass to observe, 'This, Mira, is among life's significant moments.' When he hobbled past the Inferno, all the way up to the crest of the Mussorie hill, Father threw his head back, Byronic and immense. 'Our cup runneth over,' he intoned to the absent world at large. 'We can ask no more.'

Satisfied with this prophetic declamation, Father, grasping me firmly by the paw, steered me homewards. On the road back, I often caught sight of Suma playing hopscotch on the rooftop, and glimpsed another country with a twinge of loss.

These moments of regret were fleeting. Father gave us no room for sorrow. In fact, he allowed us no room for anything of which he wasn't the centre. 'An old retired bandicoot like me,' he explained to Mother, 'no longer of use to the government of India, can now concentrate on bringing up his daughter to be worthy of her ancient traditions.' Among other things like a veto on American chewing gum, this meant that I would be presented with a copy of Nehru's *Discovery of India* or the Mahatma's *My Experiments with Truth* every birthday and festival day. I eyed with alarm my growing but repetitive library collection, and mustered the courage to point out to Father the merits of unselective reading. 'Nonsense!' said father, picking up with distaste a pirated copy of Maugham's *Cakes and Ale.* 'Maugham? Choleric fellow. Not enough greens in his diet.'

But that birthday he gave me a set of the Brontës. Father was gloomy but philosophic. 'Can't impose wisdom on the child,' he explained to Mother. 'Stupidity must be self-discovered.' Delighted, I pushed my luck, since it came by so infrequently, to venture the possibility of a birthday party. 'Party?' asked Father doubtfully. 'You mean children?' The thought shook him severely. He grew gloomier, nursing visions of under-aged trampling hordes annihilating his lawn beneath small feet. A brief unworded battle raged in his eyes. Then he gave up

'Well,' he said at last, 'it's *your* birthday.' The implication was that were it *his* birthday, he wouldn't give licence to baser pleasures but might instead be profitably engaged in activities of an elevated nature. But I held fast.

And so my first birthday party was a success, with Father finally agreeing to play magician and Mother doling out cake and ices. We even hired a merry-go-round, ensuring me immediate social approval from my sticky-fingered peers. I glowed with joy, amazing Father. 'I find no point in a rumpus,' he told Mother, absolving himself of complicity. She, as always, merely smiled.

At night I snuggled under the covers, remembering that the second-form Elvis Presley, Joey Sharma, had winked at me over his ice, promising possibilities for the future. Life was good. Then Father's face loomed into my mind, awaking me. In my dream his hair was grey and he looked as if he'd just walked a hundred miles.

But the next morning at breakfast, Father seemed quite removed from wistful sorrow, having fully recovered his booming element. 'Birthday parties have a place,' he barked over buttered toast, 'but life demands that we concentrate on higher things.'

One higher thing was definitely Elvis Presley Sharma, perfect from his shiny brown shoes to his fetching sneer. At thirteen, the opposite sex were an awesome mystery, a lanky, moustache-awaiting, football-playing cabal whose notations remained obscured to feminine eyes. To break into this world I needed passwords, and these, Suma Mehta swore in a hushed whisper, were perfume, high heels and eyeshadow. Father was astounded. 'Too strong,' and 'Too high,' he snapped in succinct dismissals of the two more familiar temptations of the Devil, but it was the eyeshadow that confounded his honest soul. Being young and generous, I'd applied six coats of colour when one was sufficient to endow me with a cadaverous leer. 'Veena,' cried Father in agitation, 'the child is very ill!' I gazed at him with what I imagined was superior scorn. 'It's make-up,' I said coldly. 'Indira Gandhi and Queen Elizabeth wear it.' Father sighed in relief, then roared, 'Does your mother plaster herself? And isn't she the most beautiful woman in the world?' This question, being unanswerable, could only be countered by exaggerated tears that made final once and for all my facial experiments. With at least three colours of the rainbow streaking my face, I shouted, 'I won't listen to you!', then waited, terrified, for the skies to crash.

But Father merely sat down as if shot. He asked for his walking-stick. I handed it to him. As he tapped his way forwards on a long walk to the mill, a blind man in search of light, I noticed he hadn't invited me along.

So the slow break began. I read Lawrence and left *Lady Chatterley's Lover* open in Father's study at significant points in the narrative. I took to a close friendship with Suma Mehta, and we giggled over green nail polish and discussed menopause with sophisticated ease. In my bedroom, Gibbon gathered dust. I saw this as a natural form of poetic justice for a childhood spent in the half-understood words of others. I brought home loud rock music that shook the house, and which Father swore caused the death of his Kashmir rose-bushes, hypersensitive to primitive vibrations. Mother merely smiled through it all, helped me apply eyeshadow with a surprisingly practised hand, and soothed Father as he mowed the lawn in a murderous fury. Gossamer thin, fraying at the touch of a little warmth, there stretched a silence between Father and me.

Sometimes he'd ignore the pall, filling it up with loud admonition and advice. Often he'd succeed. 'See this ugly jimson weed?' Father would demand, while I perspired over a corner of fading lilacs. 'The enemy to civilized man. No good gardener allows jimson to ravage his handiwork. Weeds in a garden are a sign of sloth. To prove his humanity every man should be given a patch of grass ... What he does with it is a sign of character.' I'd grunt non-committally through Father's telegraphic sermon inspired by a fistful of limp plants, musing on how miserable he must have made his junior government officers. Perhaps he'd pick up an ink blotter and expound on the advantages of absorbing knowledge swiftly and silently, while the mundane world toiled beyond. Or perhaps he'd trip over an ill-placed waste-paper basket, and hold forth on the importance of discarding useless information, while filing the valuable matters in the orderly cabinets of the mind. The hidden wisdom of the everyday world is inexhaustible to a man of metaphor, but the onus of shouldering his poetic talent could be overpowering when the audience was reduced to one. I'd sigh and sit back on my heels, letting his words beat over my head, heavy flapping ravens, while Father watched the grass set forth new sprigs. His eyes would light up, his discourse on weed-killing stilled, as he saw himself a Prometheus who braved the seasonal powers to keep nature alive, a Lionheart who ruled his garden with the gracious bounty of fertilizer.

In those moments he quite forgot his limp, and would drag himself exulting from flower to flower, celebrating their colours and shapes. In those moments we held together, isolated against anger, not needing words. Sometimes Mrs Mehta peered over the hedge to be met by a loud bawl. 'Ah, Mrs Punjabi ... a bunch of lilies for the pretty lady!' Mrs Mehta would sniff and go indoors pointedly, surprising Father. 'Perhaps she's allergic to lilies,' Father mused, 'the poor dear.' Then he'd forget her at once.

He was to remember our new neighbours, though – a family from Lucknow who came to call within the week. At first Father was doubtful about extending his social circle, people being too complex for his tastes – a fact he found clearly represented by Mrs Mehta and her annoying lack of susceptibility to his charm. 'Hello, hello,' roared Father uncertainly. 'Pleased to meet you. Do sit down — mind the cushions, though. Newly washed, you know. I'm Menon ...' Here we all shook hands profusely. '... a retired government bandicoot! Ha ha!' After a period of confusion, people were restored to armchairs. Father made elaborate attempts to put them at their ease. 'And what do you do, Mr Siddiqui, if I may ask? To me, all professions are noble. I'm not like some fellows who claim the Civil Service is the only honourable calling. But ... 'He winked a roguish eye at Mrs Siddiqui, meaning to lead up to an interesting anecdote about his recent muscle graft operation. '... I can't stand doctors! Pah! Fellows make a dent in your health and your pocket.' He laughed at his little joke, slapping the walking-stick against his leg. 'I've been to doctors all my life. Greedy rascals!' Mrs Siddiqui tinkled a sympathetic laugh. 'Are you connected with the mill?' enquired Father graciously between guffaws. 'No,' said Mr Siddiqui, 'I'm a doctor.' Father immediately stopped laughing and looked thoughtful. 'On the other hand,' he said, 'my uncle was a doctor. Damned good fellow. *Damned* good.' From the corner of my eye, I saw the Siddiquis' son grin at the fireplace. He had a nice chin. And lots of wavy black hair. A contrast to father's semi-bald pate glinting saucily at

Mrs Siddiqui in the firelight. A nice smile, too. Hmm.

Father caught sight of me. 'Stop gawking at the boy,' he snapped. 'Go help your mother bring in the tea.' Mortified, I attempted to make a graceful undulating exit. But I fell over the washed cushion Mrs Siddiqui had placed discreetly by the armchair, injuring my pride temporarily and my nose for life. When I looked up from a mess of dishevelled hair and blood, the Siddiquis' son was bending over me, choking with suppressed laughter. At that moment I fell completely in love with him.

The moment, perhaps, was the beginning of the end. 'They're Muslims,' said Father bitterly. 'Do you know what your mother and I went through during Partition? Have you no heart?' I raged with equal theatrical splendour. 'You're prejudiced,' I cried, 'and out of date! It's years since Independence! I'm going to kill myself!' Father disdained to make order out of this shrapnel chaos. He muttered darkly about a serpent's tooth and thankless children, as I glared at him across a span of bitter years. At fourteen, love demands no less than at sixty-five. Only the words in which to recover it are different, changed, and slowly, I realized, going beyond us both.

It took three years before Father could bring himself to talk to Ismail. Until I was seventeen, he merely referred to 'that boy', though he tolerated the rest of the family on a professional basis. 'Doctor,' he'd say faintly to Abba, 'the pain in my side will kill me. Ulcers?' The self-diagnosis was thrown my way in a tone of noble suffering. Abba, summoned by father at midnight, replied kindly, 'Mere indigestion, Mr Menon. Nothing a few Mylantas can't cure. Ismail will bring some over.' So my knight and only hero came tumbling groggily across the lawn wielding antacids, while Father, ignoring his presence, pretended he was receiving medication from thin air. 'Allah wills all,' Abba said to Mother, cutting her apologies short, while Father enquired of his pillow what God had to do with gastric irregularities.

As soon as the Siddiquis departed, Father hopped out of bed, roaring that we had a conspiracy going against him. 'The diabolic child', he shouted, pointing a quavering finger at me like Moses against the Israelites, 'plans to bring that Muslim boy into the family. And we such aristocrats! Pure bred for a thousand years! History runs in our blood!' The diatribe continued indefinitely until the antacid overcame Father's rhetoric. Gasping and triumphant, he subsided on the bed, satisfied that he'd done his moral duty and played his part with sufficient panache. Mother and I retired to awake into another morning, sunny and peaceful, but Ismail-less, as usual.

The problem took serious root in Father's mind. Just before my eighteenth birthday, he turned to me in his study and barked, 'Are you aware of sex?' Was this retribution for having subjected father to *Lady Chatterley?* I looked around for Mother but she'd deserted me. 'Sex', explained Father, 'is not among the higher things. It does not constitute a significant moment in one's life, no matter what cheap American paperbacks may insinuate.' I made an inarticulate sound that could be interpreted as agreement or dissent, depending on the point of view of the listener. 'Definitely not,' said Father, clinching the issue. 'Now you may go.' I wafted out, thoroughly confused, especially when Mother asked if father had had his 'little talk' with me. Years later, I was to recognize that this was Father's method of not merely introducing me to the facts of life, but more specifically, warning me against the temptations of vice. Especially those committed in conjunction with the Devil next door. He little knew that my information on the subject was gratifying comprehensive, gleaned from biology texts and schoolgirl cliques. He never imagined the word mightn't conjure much mystery for me, because to him all life was a constant discovery of the everyday. That afternoon I saw him tapping his walking-stick down the path, roundly scolding the bees around the lilacs for attacking the flowers before they were in bloom. He was a most innocent man.

But I was growing up, shedding innocence like petals, seeing more closely and darkly into the world around me. At eighteen, I had come full circle to Gibbon, as his words assumed for me a depth and reality beyond mere information. The heart of things, not their surfaces, began to stir. I felt rich and chosen. Words came to me where once there had been nameless impulses and fears. With each literary effort, Father beamed proudly, showering the light of his wisdom on a recalcitrant comma or a blowzy metaphor. 'My daughter writes,' he boasted to bored visitors with the air of introducing a performing seal. 'She can't cook but she writes.' It seemed proof I wasn't a complete disappointment.

After my nineteenth birthday, Ismail and I were married. We left home for the north-east frontier where he was posted as lieutenant in the Indian Army. Father stayed close-lipped throughout the ceremony, only once engaging in a loud debate with the Udipi cook over the purging effects of asafoetida. He ignored the guests, except for Mrs Mehta who remained unaffected by his concern over her dietary preferences. After the reception, Father returned home, saying he was tired. We had scarcely spoken to each other. In the past year, words had fallen like swords between us, severing the past into ribbons, establishing silence as if it were a condition of our being, like air. Earlier that morning, Father glowered at me across breakfast while I mentally recounted my deprivations by a man who had given up on anything not in his exact image. We mulled over cheese omelettes and passed each other the salt and pepper shakers, as if they were flags calling a truce. But Father said, 'Too much pepper turns the liver blue. Creates ulcers.' Then he swept the condiments off the table.

A week later, Ismail and I left for the long future of smelly diapers and middle-aged spread, much closer than we imagined in our paperback illusions of romance.

The years passed with their usual small triumphs and forgotten sorrows. Tragedy is the stuff of Shakespeare. We lesser mortals had to be content with broken promises, easy betrayals of faith, an illicit love affair, two pregnancies, eight strands of grey hair and a stillborn child. There were moments, too, Ismail was proclaimed a war hero in the Bangladesh confusion, while I wrote a children's book that met with success. And despite Father's lack of faith, my cooking tipped the gourmet level. Ismail and I plodded on faithfully like patient mules reaching destination after destination with tired fortitude, as if this wasn't it, after all; the point of the journey lay further. And we had to go on. I knew my husband was tiring of marriage. The romance had spread thin over our everyday quarrels about smart-mouthed children and money. I had no recourse but to let him go, to play out the spool so he could wander into the welcoming arms of the commandant's wife, saddened I had failed him but glad he had relieved me of responsibility. It is so morally comforting to be sinned against.

Days passed like faint images in the twilight, a grey Bergman film of slow gestures and extended speech, as we moved and circled each other in the rituals of existence without ever a need for commitment or faith. So unlike Father who confronted life with charm and wit, even when it failed with Mrs Mehta. 'With charm,' Father once announced, 'even death can be held at bay.'

He was wrong, as usual. One December morning when Ismail was away on duty, the telegram arrived. Even before I opened it, I knew. I left at once for the Doon Valley, wondering what I must say, how I should react. Sitting stiff and erect in a third-class compartment with a kerchief knotted tight between my fingers, I remembered other losses. 'Only mediocrities cry,' Father had warned when Elvis Presley Sharma, in the fifth form, abandoned me for the girl with the unmistakably fake British vowel sounds.

He affected surprise at my arrival. 'So there you are!' he said, with the air of an unpractised magician confronting an elusive rabbit in a hat. We sat quietly. Then he said, 'Did you notice the front lawn? Aunt Seema brought us special lawn seed from America. Veena planted it all by herself ...' I glanced out of the window to a sweep of deep green velvet – majestic, vibrant, intensely warm.

I took in a breath to fill myself with its perfection. 'There's something about it so like you,' I told him. Father chuckled. 'Not me,' he said, 'The lawn's too plush – too rich. Do you remember your birthday party? We had to borrow from grandfather to pay for the merry-go-round!' I laughed, complaining that he had never told me, but Father's mind was already wandering. He pointed to a large sign on the lawn. 'Fellows from the mill still come here to cross the road. Had to put that up – can't run after them any more. Too old ...' The sign read: NO TRESPASSERS. I turned to Father, but he was fussing with his walking-stick. 'Take it away,' he said, 'I don't need it any more.'

Late that night, he died. Mother, Abba and I stood sentinel as he battled his last shallow gulps of air, lost in the twilight world of the half-conscious. I said to Mother, 'There were so many things I wanted to tell him, but we only spoke of the lawn.' She told me not to fret, that Father understood, and I believed her.

We sat together, Mother and I, dissolving memories in hot cups of tea as we spoke of funeral arrangements and policies. Mother was strangely restless, almost a child in her rejection of phone calls and visitors. I watched her now as I saw Father watching her every day across the dining-table for forty years, tracing in her face the secret life of a woman sustained by her own courage. The quiet power that had shaped Father's colour and movement, she moved alone, untouched by the flurry of our tinpot tempests. And we had never noticed. It was too late to reverse the years and begin again. Foolishly, I said, 'I'm sorry, Mother.' She looked at me tenderly as if confronting a child who regretted a spanking and wanted to make up. It's too late, she seemed to say. All this while we'd been the audience to Father's soul. Now gone, he still played to a full theatre, but we were made insubstantial, less ourselves and more the shadows on the wall. We were a ghost theatre, full of echoes, and our applause rang like sorrow in emptied hearts. Even Ismail seemed an image on a screen, my children wraiths of passing light. I stood alone in the darkness and shivered, while Mother, in her sinewed world, stacked the dishes and reset the kettle to boil.

I passed her my cup. She held it absently for a moment. Then suddenly, for no reason at all, she turned it over, upside down.

If there were a God in Heaven, Father by His side would surely have pointed out to him the significance of the moment. I could picture the Heavenly Host awestruck and admiring, as Mrs Mehta with her batting eyelashes and insufficient imagination had failed to be. Why, there might even be a new dispensation before we ourselves got there, replete with lilacs and velvet lawn from America. A Heaven ringing with Father's righteous declamations against the trampling hordes in the Inferno beneath, eternally barred entrance by the sign: NO TRESPASSERS.

I began to laugh and the pattern that had eluded me all these years jelled clear and simple. There stood Father imaged in his garden, revived in the turn of leaves, a stir of wind, all the colours and gestures of life. Time fell away, as out of the coalshed and up the garden path strode my father, magician, the Lionheart, God, whoever he was. He stood against the door, looking at us in wonder, in love, his eyes flowers, his voice a gust, his arms extended cool and gentle in morning rain. Behind him the lawn burst open in shades of purple and green, then flared and blazed with a thousand lights. Dazzled, I took the kettle off the fire, set the cup back and filled it with tea, filled it until it brimmed and ran over, overflowing all my days. Then I walked to the closet and set Father's walking-stick beside the old newspapers and moth-eaten coats. We would not need it again. And shutting the closet doors, while the world ebbed back through the open window, I felt a hand reach out and take me home.

John Rizkalla

A BREAK WITH SUNDAY

For days before, she had worried about how to break the news to her son. A narrow tea-room with steamed-up windows on a Sunday afternoon where every other parent of a boarder seemed to have crowded in was neither the place nor the time. Togetherness in fact had been made impossible the moment this obsequious Billy friend had decided at Gerald's instigation to tag along. In a mood typical of his father, experience warned, her twelve-year-old was out to thwart her.

'Well, can I?' he demanded for the umpteenth time.

'*May* I?' she corrected just as stubbornly.

'... go skiing in Austria with the school party?'

'Over Christmas!' She was outraged, though mostly hurt.

Were all the teachers bored bachelors with no family of their own? Or had they found out that for the first time Gerald's father wouldn't be spending Christmas at home, and deliberately contrived this idiotic trip to entice Gerald away from her just when she needed him most?

A young waitress was circulating, calling out about the cream cakes that no one could possibly miss, piled up as they were in gooey tiers in the middle of the room.

'That was lovely ...' Billy's stubby tongue tried to reach grains of sugar around his mouth beyond its reach. He crossed his podgy hands hopefully.

'Have another,' Gerald offered. 'I won't. I'm not hungry.'

Billy's grin was nervous. He glanced at her in case she might not second her son's generosity. How she would have enjoyed telling Billy that he'd already eaten two, that he was getting too fat to be liked. Instead she smiled.

'Please, do.'

Still he hesitated, expecting some further acknowledgement?

'Are you new at the school, Billy?'

'Just come from Cyprus, Mrs Winton. My father flies all over the Mediterranean on reconnaissance.'

He swelled still more when she attempted and even managed to sound impressed. He added, as if sure to get her approval, 'Gerald has been told to show me the ropes.'

So that was it! No wonder Billy hadn't featured in any of Gerald's skeletal letters. The two boys were in the same house, shared the same dormitory. Billy wasn't a friend at all, just a responsibility. Odd how relieved that made her feel. She said, 'Gerald's father is working in Florida at the moment.'

'Dr Winton is a botanist researching into subtropical plants in Florida.' Billy's eyes were fixed on Gerald as though to check he'd got it word perfect. 'Before that he was in Kenya ...'

'What else has he told you?' Had she sounded too alarmed?

Billy favoured her with a smile which suggested he couldn't say without breaking a confidence. He seemed quite unaware that Gerald sat sullen, refusing to support his boast. She said, 'Billy, if you don't hurry your cakes will be gone.'

The threat sent him waddling off with his plate.

'Gerald!' How did one keep one's voice low and yet forceful? 'I thought I'd made it crystal clear in my letter that I was driving down to talk to you on your own.'

'I can't read your writing.'

It was his father's voice, dismissing her efforts to elicit a response with the same arrogant impatience. Worse, he was scoring the same effect, wounding instead of angering her.

'Why are you being so unkind?' She stretched out her hand.

'Don't touch me,' he squealed, and jumped to his feet.

She felt rather than saw the bevy of heads swing round. It could only be their staring, she was quite convinced, that was pinning Gerald to the spot, at a loss what next to do.

'Sit down.' She was pricked into an unaccustomed authority.

He complied slowly, but refused to look at her. Instead his fingers studied the flower pattern of the table-cloth. He said, 'I've still got a French test to prepare for tomorrow.'

'Then why on earth didn't you do it earlier?'

'I was picked to play hooker for yesterday's game.'

'Oh, you and your rugby!'

'We won.'

'I've driven sixty miles to talk to you.'

'There's nothing to talk about. You've already made up your mind I can't go skiing.'

He had guessed she felt guilty, selfish about this. But she was hardly alone in wanting him. 'Nana has invited us up to her house. She wants to see you.'

'It's cold in Scotland. And the house is too small.'

'I'll sleep with Nana, and you can have my lovely old room.'

'I'd rather go camping like I did in Florida.'

What hadn't he and his father done together? This sudden camaraderie was a late development, a society designed to exclude and tease her.

'You wouldn't want to camp out in the garden in winter.'

'Exactly. I can't do what I like. I'm never free with you.'

His eyes blazed with resentment, dislike. It was unbearable, unfair. Did he ever say the same to his father? She daren't ask. She dug inside her handbag and came out waving a last talisman.

'This letter came from your father.'

'Fab! Give us the stamps!' Gerald's hand shot up.

'Why don't we just tear up the rest of the bloody letter? That's about all it's worth anyway.'

He sat hunched, head shaking in some kind of mock shock that she should swear. As if he never did. 'In a minute.'

She buried her gaze and hurt in that page she knew by heart. 'He's moved into the Everglades, with lots of mosquitoes. Just the way he loves it.'

'What's he sent me?' Gerald demanded.

'What makes you so sure he's sent you anything?'

'Because he promised, and *he* keeps his promises.'

He was still reproaching her for their day out at the start of the summer holidays, a week before he was due to fly out to his father. She'd promised to take him on the downmarket cross-Channel trip to Dieppe, then at the last moment had to cancel it when her mother suffered a seizure. The worst, or the best, was that it turned out to be a mild one. Instead of France they had travelled overnight sitting up in a train all the way to Oban.

She handed over a smaller sealed letter that her own had contained. The disappointment on Gerald's face gave her a twinge of satisfaction.

'Aren't you going to open it?'

His fingers were feeling the contents, much as she'd done before him. He shook his head. 'Later. Don't worry. I'll let you know what it is . . .'

'You won't!' She was behaving as if at twelve he could be as unreliable as his father.

'You can remind me.' He was bent on taunting her and tossed the unopened letter on the table.

She forced her hands and eyes away. She caught sight of Billy's figure fussing bee-like round the cake counter.

'Next tiome you bring a friend along, make sure he isn't a scrounger,' she snapped, relishing the unfair remark.

'What's a scrounger?' he asked in his best classroom voice.

Billy squeezed his way towards them, balancing several cream cakes on a plate. He stood blinking by the table, as obedient as a pet dog, quite prepared to be told to go and put them all back.

'I brought a few extra ones. Just in case ...'

'But Billy, who on earth is going to eat ...'

'I'll try one.'

Gerald grabbed a cake, bit into it. His eyes dared her to say No! His teeth squeezed most of the cream out, and it drooped down his chin in a huge blob. Too late her hand rose to stop it plopping on to the table-cloth. From somewhere inside the cake Gerald was giggling. Billy smiled with admiration, took this as his cue to sit down and do the same.

His sticky finger pointed to the letter on the table.

'What's that?'

'A present from Gerald's father.' She only answered for him because his mouth was too full.

'Is that all he's sent you?' Billy seemed to be voicing all of Gerald's earlier disappointment.

'Mind your own business!' Gerald discovered his voice all of a sudden, and flung down his half-eaten cake.

But Billy, doubtless used to similar outbursts, was not so easily silenced. 'You said he was going to send you a wrist computer.'

'Piss off!'

'Gerald!'

Billy blinked, lowered his cake, leaving his mouth clownish white. He looked more bewildered then shocked, waiting for her to vindicate the injury he'd sustained. The noise around only helped to intensify the silence that had unexpectedly built up between the two boys. There was not even a sigh of regret from Gerald.

'Billy was only making a point,' she said half-heartedly.

He wasn't, of course. Nor was her intervention going to do anything but stiffen Gerald's resolve not to retract. But then it was high time Billy was away, however messily.

Had Gerald sensed it too? He picked up his cake and started to nibble at it again. Unlike Billy, who was still hoping.

'Perhaps I ought to go ...' he suggested reluctantly.

'Suit yourself,' Gerald mumbled.

Billy licked at his powdered lips. In a last spark of resilience he fought back. 'I shan't ask my parents to invite you to spend the summer in Cyprus with me, as you wanted me to . . .'

The revelation, however startling, convinced her utterly if only because it confirmed her fears. Not only was she to be denied Christmas but Gerald had been planning his summer too without her. What had she done to deserve such treatment?

'That's OK. I couldn't have afforded the air fare anyway, not if I was going skiing . . .'

Gerald was staring at her, offering to negotiate a deal.

'Can't we discuss this later?' she found herself stammering.

Then Billy became awkward. 'What should I do, Mrs Winton?'

'Do?'

'Now.'

The stupid boy was determined to be hurt by her too.

'Well, why not go back to St Michael's?' She added before those pained eyes, 'I'll give you the bus fare.'

She ferreted inside her pocket, having no idea how much to give. Rather like a tip she slipped a pound into is sticky palm.

'Take the cakes.'

Billy left enchanted.

Mother and son confronted each other, and suddenly she ached for the shield that Billy had provided between them.

'I was rather meaner than I intended to be,' she apologized.

'Everybody is mean with him,' Gerald said. 'It's the way he sticks to people. Nobody likes him in the dormitory. That's why he keeps inviting us all to go to Cyprus. So I said why not?'

He was trying to mollify her, intensifying her guilt.

'I should have offered to drive him back to the school.'

'He'd have invited you to Cyprus then.' Gerald grinned and conquered her. 'How about driving me instead, to the airbase?'

'What airbase?'

She recalled now that his father on his few visits motored the two of them over to the American airbase to watch the huge transport planes take off and land. Each time Gerald vowed he would be a pilot when he grew up. It struck her that his wish to go to Cyprus had nothing to do with her, or even Billy, but with a fighter plane.

'It's a splendid idea. You'll be the navigator.'

She'd always thought the pastime tedious, and never gone along. Now, though, it was a godsend. The base was five miles away and furnished the conversation with enough lively directions and jokes to smooth away all tension.

They sat in monastic silence waiting for a giant plane to appear. At length Gerald burst out, 'You know last summer I shot an antelope with Dad's gun?'

'How could he teach you to kill?' She was appalled.

'Don't be stupid! It only fired anaesthetic darts.'

She resisted the urge to mention it was during one of those idyllic safaris into the Kenyan bush that they had conceived their only child.

'We went camping for a fortnight and shared the same tent.'

She could hear the nostalgia in the boy's voice, nostalgia for a bond forged in never-to-be-repeated circumstances.

'No doubt he found a complete range of his precious plants.'

'You hate Dad!' Gerald shouted. 'He can't do anything right. You know he's a great scientist, and has to work in tropical parts of the world. You've never tried to understand him.'

'Tried! I did nothing else. It was just my luck to be too big to slide under his microscope.' She stopped in horror at how brutal, too truthful she had been for once.

The stillness was broken only when a sleek aircraft began to taxi along the runway. Immediately Gerald pulled his father's letter out of his anorak pocket and threw it in her lap.

'You can open it. Day said you'd want to anyway.'

Gerald scrambled out of the car and up the embankment to the wire perimeter.

Inside were summer snapshots of a Florida landscape she'd refused to inhabit, snapshots of Gerald in Disneyland, of Gerald wading into a swamp, pointing to what at first she was certain was an alligator then realized was a tease, a crinkled tree trunk!, of father and son dripping on a Miami beach.

'He's turned Gerald against me, got him on his side. Now the boy can't bear to be with me for a day. I've lost my son.'

The pain was choking her. Clumsily she stuffed the snapshots back into the envelope, all except one which – larger, from a different spool – refused to slide in easily. She'd overlooked it but now couldn't, knowing with a part of her mind that it was as intended. Gerald on the edge of a garden swimming-pool, kneeling in front of his father and a young woman. The two adults stood wedded by their own near-naked flesh.

The jet streaked upward, scattering its thunder. She clapped her hands to her ears, yelling until Gerald rushed back and poked his head into the car.

'What's up?'

'Why didn't you tell me? Tell me you'd met her?'

'Who? Tessa?'

'You've known all along he wants to marry her? Divorce me?'

'Of course. I'm going to the wedding.'

'Bastard!'

She flung the snapshot, the envelope, into his face, intending to strike at the other two grinning at her through Gerald. She caught his cheek, lined it red. He flinched, his lips trembled, but he stood his ground, letting the snapshots flutter over and off him. There was a hint of moisture in his eyes, and she knew it was only his pride and her cruel gaze that were damming up any tears.

It was a mercy when the military jeep screeched on its brakes on the other side of the wire perimeter. A voice hollered, 'If you wish to visit the base there are special days ...'

The offer brought Gerald to life. He scrambled inside the car and slammed the door.

'Get going! Look at the time. I'm late for prep!'

Seconds later she was charging along, doubling back on unfamiliar country lanes. Where were they? He didn't know. She had rushed past every signpost. She stalled the car in a lay-by. The words came sobbing out of her.

'Gerald, I love your father. And I just don't know what's going to happen to me ... I feel so alone.'

She turned to her son for comfort, and scared him. He could not appropriate her misery, and when he was of an age to it would long have ceased to matter. His hand pressed against the door handle, threatening to escape the moment she touched him.

The possibility frightened her. She surrendered at once.

'You can go away for Christmas. You can go skiing.'

His hand relaxed but didn't come away from the door handle.

'You mean it? You won't go back on your word?'

'No, I promise. I owe you this one.'

She forgave him his joy, content to be its only victim.

'Oh dear,' she remembered suddenly, 'in the rush you never picked up your snapshots. But I'll go back for them once I've ...'

'No. I never wanted them in the first place. It was Dad who had to keep using this new camera she'd given him.'

It was the most he had time to say, the most she could expect to hear of her son's feelings. A fist began to pound on her window and an all too familiar voice was panting, 'Oh thank you, Mrs Winton! I thought you hadn't seen me, and weren't going to stop. But I ran all the same ...'

Billy opened the back door and slipped in the rear seat. He carried on chattering, dispelling the dismay he had just created.

'I couldn't find a bus. And as it was so sunny I thought I'd walk it back to school instead ...'

'You mean we're on the right road?'

'Yes, Mrs Winton.' He leant forward, thrust his hand past her face. 'Just follow it and we'll come to the back of the playing fields. Didn't you know that, Gerald?' It was Billy's turn to be dismayed, and pleased.

She started up the car engine. He seemed to have quite forgotten Gerald's boorishness, her own failure to be compassionate. Or perhaps, young as he was, he'd long since learnt to forgive, content to snatch at scraps of happiness thrown his way. It was extraordinary how warm she suddenly felt towards him.

'I've been thinking, Mrs Winton,' Billy went on, quite oblivious to the silence around him. 'Why can't you come along to Cyprus and bring Gerald? My mother said I could invite anyone.'

She couldn't help glancing at Gerald. Their eyes met and held as they shared a knowing grin. Billy noticed it and frowned.

He asked tentatively, 'Perhaps you'd like your pound back, Mrs Winton?'

Navtej Sarna

A GOLDEN TWILIGHT

Mrs Lal had to accompany her son to all the dinners that were hosted in his honour. She knew it was important for the local officials to make a good first impression on the District Collector and there was no way that they would agree to leave her out. Nevertheless she did find it repetitive. The talk would be mostly official and the ladies would let the men have a free hand so as to make the right impact. There would be almost the same menu in each house, spiced with just enough discreet gossip to make the Collector feel that he had come to an interesting place, not merely another small town.

She could feel the wives watching her, polite but unsure. They would have been more comfortable with a wife than a mother. They would have taken her to the club or vied with each other to take her on that first and most important shopping trip. Then they would have let her know, somewhat half-heartedly, what really happened to the last Collector and what awful taste his wife had. But with Mrs Lal they remained distant and polite, confining themselves to household tips.

'The fresh butter comes up by the seven o'clock bus. You should get it from the corner bakery. Or you could send the servant, of course.'

'And the vegetables, best to tell them to deliver them home. They will do it for you, they must.'

But the first week was soon over and with the pressure of the dinners behind them, the ladies delivered their verdicts on her at the club. The eleven o'clock coffee session had been resumed and was full of the new arrival.

'I mean, did she really have to come to all those dinners, at her age?', said the corpulent wife of the chief engineer, half-way through a rather oily chicken roll.

'At least sixty-five, I think,' said a twenty-five-year-old new wife, 'or maybe ... seventy.'

'What plain saris! Fine for her age, maybe.' This came from one whose sister ran a fashion boutique in Delhi, making her the last word in fashion.

'And the way she looks away when you are talking to her and begins to stare out of the window. I tell you, most irritating.'

At this point they called for a second round of coffee and carried on. Mrs Lal of course never came to the club.

The baggage arrived in huge wooden crates in a truck which had invocations to the Hill Goddess painted on its bumper. The large and sprawling bungalow quickly swallowed up the crates and Mrs Lal began slowly to bring it to life. When the books were all finally arranged in the study and the crockery was systematically set in the sideboards in the dining-room, Mrs Lal taught the servants how to clean and dust. They learnt soon what time to bring the bed tea and how much salt to add to the food. And when they came back from the daily shopping trips, they gave her an account of the expenditure on narrow strips of paper which the local shopkeepers used. One room in the front section of the bungalow was turned into an office, for the Collector inevitably brought home bundles of files and people from the villages in the interior came to see him in the evenings and on the weekends.

When she did finally find time to wander into the town she avoided the straggling bazaar that went down to the small railway station. Instead she began to frequent the town library. It was a long dusty library which seemed to be housed in a corridor rather than a hall and in which a few old men were perpetually reading newspapers. The books that she borrowed hadn't been borrowed for a long time. The last entries had been made in blank angled handwriting with an old-fashioned, thick-nibbed pen. The ink was fading and the yellowing pages seemed to smell of talcum powder. The librarian liked her because she had begun to borrow those forgotten books, and told her longingly of the days when the library had been the centre of the town.

In the evenings she took to going for long walks. Her favourite walk would take her down Circular Road where it left the vegetable shops and curved in a long languorous loop around Pine Hill. It was a quiet and lonely road. There were hardly any houses and the occasional cottage lay either far below or far above the road. For the first half of the loop she had an almost uninterrupted view of the valley and far away in it she could see the ruins of an old brewery. And just at the end of the loop, when it seemed to be stretched out in such tension that it would surely have gone off at a tangent over the twilit valleys had it not turned back just then, she would come to a cemetery. It was an old cemetery, not used since the days of the Englishmen, and there was a crumbling stone bench above it. Here Mrs Lal would sit and watch the sunset.

She loved the fresh smell that came from the pines which stood out straight on the scrambling slope and she loved the way the dusk seemed to linger till the last possible minute in the valley before settling down unobtrusively into every turn and twist. It would then become very quiet and cold and moist and remind her of the early morning walks in Delhi, forty years before. It was probably the moist feeling that touched off the memory. The grass used to be wet with the dew and she loved to walk barefoot by the twin canals in the centre of Delhi.

That fresh early morning feeling was all that she would want to remember of that horrible hot and bloody summer in which she, her husband and their two small children had formed a hopeless molecule in the terrible upheaval that had convulsed the country. It had been a summer of plunder and looting, madness and murder. They had come to Delhi, holding on to life without any real hope. Pushed on hopelessly, they had been allotted a room in the hutments which had housed wartime British offices. Each family had a room, there was a common bathroom and all the children played together in the hollow square. The children had begun to play even then and that had perhaps been the best way to rebuild life. For in any case there had been no logic to anything and there were no answers, only the compulsive need to go on.

It was in those days that she had been plagued by such a deep restlessness that it had often kept her awake at night. At sunrise, she would walk the three kilometres to the wet grass lawns at India Gate to give play to the restlessness, searching somewhere deep inside herself for strength to face the day ahead.

The same restlessness became part of her walks down Circular Road. Her mind would be in a turmoil and the years would go back and forth, cutting across tragedies and suddenly brightening up with glimpses of happiness. It all began to come back with a blazing intensity, leaving a high colour to her face by the time she returned from the walk.

The walk became an addition and she began to look forward to it with an anticipation that she hadn't felt for anything at all in years. Each day she would select for herself a phase of her life, a decade or a moment, and give herself up to it completely. And it would reward her with a flood of emotions and memories and feelings, as if in a torrent of gratitude just for being recalled again. A girl, her hair in twin braids, skipping to school in a distant town, a youthful face which seemed a musty photograph even to herself, or the empty dullness of the plateau that had come after that. It all came and went, searing her consciousness and leaving her drained and exhausted.

Sitting on the old bench over the cemetery one evening she thought a long time about her husband. She didn't think of his weak ambitions or his pathetic failures, but she thought of his gentle smile which seemed to give him strength and a kind of majesty even in his poverty. She wouldn't believe even now that he had been an ordinary man who had died a few years ago and gone into the limitless void. He still seemed to be living on like all the moments that wouldn't die within her. As she thought of him, the last light was leaving the tombstones, each with its name and date, the marks of forgotten soldiers and administrators. Halting overtures to immortality that were doomed even before they were uttered, pathetic pleadings to faithless memory. They too had gone down into the same limitless blue valley, leaving behind verses on stones which sounded momentous and ridiculous at the same time.

In the fading light, a hawk came into her vision like the spirit of life itself. It rose from the depths of the valley and circled upwards, battling the breeze. With a final burst, it rose and was silhouetted for a moment against the sun. Then it broke free of the sun and soared higher, exulting, free. With it her spirit seemed to soar too for a moment that was an eternity into the darkening blue above.

And sitting on that bench that night Mrs Lal wrote her first poem in forty years on the back of an envelope.

She wrote every day after that. The poems, according to the critic who reviewed her first book a few months later, were not the poems written by an old person. There was a freshness and yearning in them that cried youth. It was all over Mrs Lal's face, which would light up with a smile and which reminded her son of the old forgotten photographs in the family album. He saw the smile, he was a child again and he understood. When he was transferred two years later, he would not force her to go with him. She stayed back, moving into a cottage on Pine Hill.

Ken Smith

THE MAN WHO COULDN'T SPELL STRAIGHT

Where he worked, in the betting shop, they called him Chalkie, because his name was White, and because it was his job to chalk the winners up. Chalkie White. The names were interchangeable. He had another name or two, for other sorts of occasion. He was that sort of man, with that sort of name: Spider Webb, Dusty Roads. In the pub across the road where he came for liquid lunch and evening entertainment, we knew him as Sylvester.

Tall, dry, wistful, Sylvester carried about with him some far off air. He'd been a merchant seaman, many years, and wandered the world so long his origins and what he'd done before seafaring had vanished under sea mist and false dawns. Too many foggy landings, too many vague lights in vague distances, too much weather, too many drunken nights in Valparaiso, too many tumbles off the gangplank. But he had a wanderer's tales to tell, and we were ever in need of entertainment, and quickly welcomed him into our grand society of all mates together. He was like us, loners who met for company, pale drinkers gathered to affirm their good health, all gone too far from their beginnings.

It was his last trip that had done him for the sea. That and the outward journey before it, working a long slow boat down and round Africa and over the Indian Ocean to Australia. Heat on the flat sea, like hot iron; too long out of sight of land. Weary of drinking distilled aftershave and boot polish, at his last port of call along the hot coast he'd bought a large carryout of best African bush, finest marijuana heads from the Congo, and smoked it all the way to the country of the kangaroos and the duck billed platypuses. Somewhere among the steam pistons and grease guns and oily rags of the engine room he'd lost his bearings. Sometimes at dawn taking the air up on deck he saw the horizon was only the visible lip of the world, and nothing to it at all, it was an idea not a place, and when he looked down into the sea the were monsters.

I lost every marble he said. *Or was it Thursday or the Dardanelles? Did I look like myself?* All day greasing the hot thunder of the engines, all day watching the pistons heave up and down and the steam pipes hiss, and just beyond the tin plates the monstrous sea, and everywhere the heat. In Australia he left the sea and lived in Perth a year or two, got some sort of job, and lived a life there with a lady but it didn't work out. He could have stayed, and wished sometimes he had, where *by now I might have had a couple of kids and a couple of bob in the bank and a couple of suits in the wardrobe and more than a couple of pairs of shoes to my feet.*

Here's looking at you kid.

A couple of years went by, the way they do. He took another ship, his last, home. *Bad advice, that ship,* he said. *Rats as big as cats, mice, lice and bad advice.* The ventilation went, and the wildlife took over. He went crazy with the prickly heat and toothache, and somewhere south of the Red Sea some sandalmaker of a blacksmith who swore he was a dentist took out his abcessed wisdom tooth without benefit of anaesthetic.

Did I tell you about the elephants?

Sylvester was up on deck, trying to sleep in the heat. The ship was waiting for a pilot at the south end of the Suez. Dawn was up, and the mist. From the rail, half asleep and half awake, coughing into his first rollup of the morning, Sylvester saw six elephants drifting south, a slow and stately procession bobbing by on the water. Six dead elephants, some belly up, some trunk up, one arse up, all dead. No one else saw them. Sylvester called the bridge, but by the time they got to the blower and the glasses the elephants had drifted away into the mist. No one believed him. They said the hooch had finally got him. There were no elephants, the bridge said, so there were none, and none were entered in the ship's log. He insisted he had seen them, six of them, and that was entered into someone's log. Over such questions Sylvester lost his ticket at the end of the trip. He'd had enough anyway, but now he was landed without a paybook, the sailor at last home from the sea.

Time went by, as it does. The more he thought about the elephants the less sure he was he hadn't imagined them, after all, given the hour of day and his state of mind. And then one evening sitting in a seaman's club in East London he ran into a German seaman, and they got to talking. The German told a tale of carrying a cargo of animals from Africa, destined for the Hamburg zoo. In the Red Sea six elephants had died in the hold. It had been his job to dump them into the sea, just before dawn, before they went into the Canal.

Sylvester missed nothing, knew everyone, didn't mix business, kept much to himself. On the wilder shores of social intercourse when drink had been taken and he'd exceeded himself, he'd slap his wrist and tell himself to behave. He was a man whose commentary was sought, a man of many stories, a passer of opinions. *There'll be tears in the nursery*, he'd say, when the grocery money went on the wrong horse, and *It'll never happen* whenever some wild scheme to raise cash or credit was mooted. The passing parade of marriages and divorces vaguely amused him. Adultery he referred to as *moving the meat, the meat business*. Otherwise he kept his distance, seeming older then he was, bearing in his black coat the threadbare air of a rundown undertaker, his dolefulness in balance with his humour.

His business now was betting, working for Milligan who owned the bookie shop, and with whom some other bond existed, dating back into a vague space never spoken of, some debt, some old favour. Sylvester worked for Milligan, and Milligan looked out for Sylvester. Milligan himself was cocky, secretive, always busy, always right, short on words and very touch. There was something bent about Milligan, and therefore something interesting in the relationship, the claim he clearly had on Sylvester, and Sylvester on him.

And then there was Angela, Sylvester's girlfriend, whose task in life was to look darkly beautiful and heavily made-up and somewhat overblown, in order to sell makeup and beauty aids in a local department store. It was a task she clearly took very seriously. She was another life he lived, and clearly she too had a grip on his collar. Occasionally she appeared in his company, scowling, from work, and soon nudged him away. She made it clear she didn't like his mates, whom she called layabouts. She didn't approve of sitting about in bars with the cut and take, or just the gloomy afternoon for company. She didn't approve of horses in particular or of drink in general, and hoped he might be edged towards another job and another career altogether.

One evening Sylvester appeared in the bar with his suitcase and several carrier bags, bagman on the move, took but two short drinks and departed. *Moving out. Moving in*, he murmured, *with Angela. And mother.* The Kraken he called her. He took his leave, and thereafter reluctantly, ruefully, though not for long, he did his best to form the male half of a late bonding couple, with little success, though with   on her part – determination driven by desperation, and not an infrequent fury. For it was always in the cards her mission to convert him into a soul mate, a husband, was doomed from the start, given his disposition and hers. And mother's. Their honeymoon was brief, but as it ran its course Angela pursued her rights to pursue him, Chalkie, Sylvester, Alexander to her, sometimes Sandy, hounding him away to herself.

I want to talk to you, she'd say, bustling in from the weather.

She'd stay a while, tutting into her gin and tonic, crossing and recrossing with a hiss of nylon her majestic legs, delivering in Sylvester's direction frequent menacing looks, half reprimand, half sultry promise, letting him know that she'd chosen him, and he was to come back with her to her gingerbread house and mother. She seemed all darkness, and dressed fashionably in coloured scarves and skirts and heels. Her underneaths, as Sylvester called them, were as dark and exotic as the outside promised, he hinted, out of earshot. She spared no detail or accessory, her fingernails long and red and sharp, her fingers flashing rings, her face impenetrable beneath its mask. Under long batty false eyelashes she avoided eye contact, except with him, whom she'd stare at till he gave in. And then he'd drink up and go, openly parodying the whipped dog.

Away from Angela Sylvester told horror yarns about the Kraken, who had her own peculiar ways and smells and habits. Whenever Angela appeared he'd be immediately attentive, get her a drink if she would stay for one, just one, sit her down, and then withdraw, acting out the guilty man, clowning in response. They'd leave soon, following a short tug of war as to how soon. A couple of times she swept out without him, and only the first time did he follow her out. His resistance sharpened. *You're only a bloke with a hole in the middle*, he told her one night, when the relationship was growing stormy. Edward he called her. Edward and the Kraken. She'd thrown his shaving gear down the loo. The Kraken no longer spoke to him. He was becoming invisible. *But I like a big girl* he said. *Especially in winter*. It seemed she looked after him in the departments Sylvester liked to be looked after. His eyes twinkled when he spoke of her.

But for Angela working for Milligan wasn't good enough, a bookie's clerk. Horses weren't respectable, finance derived thereby too chancey. He confided there was talk of them 'making a go of it', of taking a pub together and going into the licensed trade. There was talk of marriage and mortgages. He laughed it off *It can't work*, he said, content to lurch on through the endless present while Angela hammered impatiently at the future. She wanted everything. She was a devourer. It seemed he'd have to change, and that dramatically and soon. For her he'd have to cease to be Chalkie or Sylvester or any name he chose as the occasion suited. He'd have to be Alexander, all the time.

Gradually Sylvester fell away as Angela turned on the full fifteen to try to make him into the man in her mind, *Alexander the Impecunious* he'd grin, turning out his pockets. He came in less and less. We missed him and his tales, and then the space closed behind him, and we began to speak of him in the past, and then there was a time no one had seen him, even Angela. She came looking for him, certain we knew where he'd gone. We couldn't help.

A new clerk appeared in the betting shop in Sylvester's old job. Milligan, when asked, shrugged his shoulders, his stoney Irish face saying nothing. *Up north* he said, *if you're asking me. Gone to see the bent monk.*

The bent monk?

Some monk he knows Milligan said. *Some monkery in Derbyshire.* It seems Sylvester had met the monk on a train, and the monk was from some monastery that brewed a deadly drink, ample samples of which the monk was carrying in his briefcase. The two of them got drunk together on the train. The monk told him he'd been inside for thievery, and invited Sylvester to stay at the monastery, anytime he needed to, to get away. He was the monastery's bursar. He'd gone to prison for fraud and said nothing but that he'd needed some time off from the cloister. Then he'd gone back, home to the abbey with never a word, to handle the accounts and the sales of the lubricant.

So if you ask me, that's where he's gone to. If he has any sense.

Angela came by again. He'd been gone a month and she'd heard nothing. She was throwing his gear out, what there was of it.

I'll take it Milligan said. *Till he comes out.*

Comes out where? she wanted to know. *Comes out of the monastery* he told her. She didn't believe him. She didn't believe any of us. *Monk my arse* she said, and judged it worth repeating. *Monk my arse. So what do you make of this?* she hissed, and slapped a newspaper cutting down in front of us, and waltzed out.

Sylvester was on remand awaiting trial for armed robbery. How else to get money in a large lump to secure the future Angela required but by stealing it, a make or a break, win or lose? He'd lost.

Milligan found him a brief and went to see him in the nick, came back to tell the tale: Chalkie was going to jail. With some bloke he'd met, dafter and more desperate than he, he'd gone up to Cheltenham with a gun and a sack and a note, and walked into the High St NatWest bank at noon. The note said *There is a Luger pointing striaght at you.* There was an umlaut on the Luger's u, but the word *straight* was wrong, and though they got away with a lot of high value cash, they left the note behind.

Daft amateurs Milligan said. *I'd never work with amateurs.*

It was the other bloke. They'd ditched the gun, hired a car to Bristol and flown to Jersey, there to lie low for a while. Sylvester had an uncle there, Milligan recalled, some superannuated London hood who shot up juke boxes, dead now. They'd booked into a hotel with the money stashed under the bed and stayed out of sight, planning to sit it out for a month or two in case the notes were numbered. Sylvester knew better than to perform like a punter with sudden money. The other bloke grew restless, spent some, the notes were traced, and back in Cheltenham the both of them were pretty soon helping the police with their enquiries.

It didn't take long. They sat Sylvester down in a room with a pen and paper, a chair and a desk. *Write your name* here they said. *And now we'd like you to write some more here* they said, and had him write words like *right, wrong, weight, freight, straight. Write Luger* they said, and he got it right. *Write straight* they said, and he got it wrong.

So there he was, faced with his own dyslexic evidence, the man who couldn't spell straight, and banged to rights as they like to say on TV. At the end Sylvester couldn't resist saying what he'd imagined saying all his life, so he put up his hands and said *It's a fair cop, officer*, and was charged and in due course found guilty as charged.

They gave him eight years.

Henrietta Soames

THE LOSS

All the way back she was sure she had forgotten something. Mentally she checked through her handbag: cigarettes, lighter, address book, diary, yes, she was certain they were all there. Nonetheless she pulled into the side for a moment to make sure. Her possessions were arranged in their orderly positions in her handbag, all present, all correct; but still she was sure she had left something behind. Had lost something.

She waited at the red lights in a deserted street and smiled to herself that even at three in the morning when there was no traffic, no police cars, no pedestrians, she still obeyed the rules. What was it he'd said earlier about taking risks, living dangerously, only for the moment? Well, yes, and she'd risen to the challenge then, been willing, even eager to risk her emotions then, but now, with the practical things she was still cautious, wary. He'd probably say I was a coward, she thought; I probably am.

Maybe it was her ear-rings? She shook her head to feel them brushing against her neck. Both of them? Was she sure she could feel them both? She couldn't remember when she'd taken them off, afterwards maybe, when they'd finished. She remembered him taking the combs from her hair, an action she had always wanted him to do, to take the combs from her hair and run his hands through the soft length of it. Tonight he'd done it. Tonight when it was forbidden, when it was too late. Tonight when they'd broken the rules.

What was it she'd forgotten? The feeling was still strong even when she arrived at her house; it pursued her as she quietly let herself in and went up to her room. There at last she could indulge it and go carefully through her bag again checking her jewellery, rings, bracelet, necklace, making a detailed search for the thing that was lost, the thing that would now be impossible ever to retrieve.

'We mustn't see each other again.'

'Never?'

'Not for a long time.'

But there was nothing missing. And it annoyed her that there was nothing, it made it all so vague. At least if there was something she'd know what it was she should be missing.

Still, it was comfortable to be back in her room. The relief surprised her, she'd expected to feel lonely, to miss him. But apart from the nagging irritation of forgetting something she really felt quite content, almost happy.

What was it? Maybe it was something she should have said. Yes, maybe that was it, some piece of information she'd meant to tell him, some message she'd forgotten to deliver and which now she would never be able to communicate. If I can't remember what it is, she told herself, it couldn't have been so important. But she remained unconvinced.

What had they done? A swansong or a phoenix rising from the ashes? Was it very wrong? But she didn't feel bad about it. Should she?

She really hadn't wanted to cry because her make-up, which she'd worn specially for the first time to show him, would run. And she'd kept the tears at bay for so long as they'd sat in his kitchen (once hers too), talking as he'd cooked for her, holding herself back from helping him, telling him where everything was.

They'd fallen back into their old, easy jocularity, their familiarity that she always used to complain of. 'We're too matey,' she said when they were discussing her moving out. 'You're like a brother, really. I just can't feel deeply emotional when we're such good friends.' Now that they were friends again in a way it was easier, even though the role felt odd sometimes, as if her moving out was just a pause, a new game they were playing.

Still, that evening they'd joked and talked and drank. He'd complained about his new relationship, she'd complained about hers, both aware that they were shy of sharing their good times with others with each other. They both wanted to keep something alive, a regret? a contact? Though they always agreed that they would never live together again. But too wholeheartedly maybe? Too vehemently?

And she'd only cried because in the middle of some brave speech she was making he'd leaned over, said something and touched her knee. It was his gesture that broke her, not his words. The gesture of kindness that cut through the rhetoric she was working so hard to defend herself with. He'd touched her.

Of course her make-up, so carefully applied, so nervously worn as if it was a mask he might not see through or might despise her for wearing, had run. And she had covered her ruined face with her hands, appalled and humiliated and feeling very childish.

Afterwards, later, he said that he hated to see her cry.

'But you've seen me cry hundreds of times. You know what I'm like.'

'I can't bear it.'

'Oh, I'm sorry. I'm so sorry. I didn't mean ...'

Because once she'd started crying she'd cried more, freely, abandonedly. The make-up was wiped away and with it the convention of their light friendship. But she hadn't intended it to manipulate him, not in that way. She'd just wanted his comfort.

Then they'd talked more, smoked (that was where she'd left her cigarettes and lighter but she'd collected them). Then she'd cried again and he'd kissed her.

Oh, she could say she tried to move her head, tried to offer her cheek for the kisses that were forbidden to her lips but she hardly resisted really, she didn't care. You've got to live dangerously, he'd said, and she had, she'd wanted to, nothing mattered enough to stop her. And she'd forgotten how much she used to enjoy his kisses, how perfectly his mouth blended with hers, how they thrilled her.

Upstairs he loved her with a passion she had never before admitted from him. Doing all the things, the sexual things that she had ever wanted him to do. He undressed her, caressed her, whispered to her. They looked at each other and the love was naked in his eyes, flaring like a torch.

'You're beautiful,' he said. 'You're so beautiful.'

'Am I? Really?'

'You're a very beautiful woman.'

His body was strange. So small, so compact, so forgotten. And his lovemaking so light and tender and delicate. Had it been so before? She couldn't remember, she'd spent the last year pushing it firmly out of her mind.

'The smell of you. I remember all the smells of you,' he said.

'I can't believe it's you,' she said. 'I'm happy and sad.'

And it was true, she felt incredulous, elated by his love but shocked by its still vivid intensity.

'What are we doing?' she asked suddenly.

'Playing with fire,' he replied and sucked on her breast fiercely.

But it was only afterwards, after he'd come, the cry desperate and hunted and keen. Only afterwards he woke to his conscience.

'She'll be so hurt if she finds out,' he said.

And she wanted to cry out, but don't say her name, don't bring her in here, let us have this night, this one night to remember all the things we'd forgotten, all the things we'd abused. Let us just for this one night deceive ourselves that there won't be a tomorrow.

'I'd forgotten how you smiled,' she said. 'I'd forgotten how happy you used to look when you were making love to me. You always looked so pleased. I'd forgotten that.'

And now, now as she lay in her own bed reviewing, the image of him rose over her like a wave, the sight of him rearing over her, his mouth agape and calling, calling as he plunged into her body. And now she felt how she had lost him while they were together, lost him through their friendship, through her fear of losing him, lost all the things they had aimed for and wanted and failed to achieve. Where are you, she called out to the still room, where are you? The loss cut her inside with little razor knives.

'Should I go?' she asked him.

'Is it unfair to ask you to?'

'No. I think I should go and we shouldn't see each other for a long time.'

Then he had cried, cried like a child and poured out how he still missed her, how her things were still in the house, how unexpectedly he would come across postcards she'd sent him, old messages on the phone pad, photographs he'd taken of her. All around him like the air he breathed, the ghost of her he couldn't escape. And she'd felt mortally ashamed as she'd listened, aware for the first time of the price he was paying for his fidelity.

'We mustn't see each other again,' she said.

'Never?'

'Not for a long time.'

Remember, remember, remember. One little faded photograph after another, they turned the album of their lives together, revisiting places they'd known, holding hands, going for walks. Remember, remember, friends they'd shared, conversations, adventures. The separate colours of their lives all woven together and having to be unpicked. Oh, couldn't they stay a while in this no-man's land of memory and retreat? Couldn't they just pretend?

'I'm not having an affair with you,' he said firmly.

'Oh no. I know that.'

'But I'd like you to have my children.'

Ah cruel, the games they played, the teasing they endured. A hand outstretched then withdrawn. A cuff and a caress. The promise always coaxing them in and hanging out of reach, the mystery, the hope.

'I'll go now,' she said, but made no move to leave. Instead drawing closer to him, wanting his arms again, his kisses again, begging for them.

She dressed slowly, provocatively, in the dark. He was watching her.

It would be the last time he'd see her body, maybe the last time they'd see each other.

'Why do people fall in love?' he asked.

'To lose themselves,' she answered.

She was dressed. She picked up her jewellery, replaced the combs in her hair and stood uncertainly before the bed. He put his arms around her again and she stroked him, kissed him, kissed his eyes that were still wet.

He followed her to the front door.

'Have you got everything?' he asked.

'Yes, I didn't bring much.'

'You'll be all right?'

'Yes. You?'

'I'll be busy.'

'You can always phone if it's ...' She bit her lip too late.

'I know. And you.'

But neither of them said goodbye. Lose me, find me. Leave me, return to me. Ever and ever the elastic between them pulling and releasing but not let go.

He held the door open, watching her as she walked to the car. She kissed her fingers to him, a gesture she had never before risked because she feared its sentimentality.

Just before she started the engine she heard the front door close and the bolts shot into place. She indicated to the empty street, looked behind for imaginary traffic and pulled out, driving a careful thirty through the sleeping town. She wasn't thinking of him. She was feeling calm, almost absolved, except that she had left something behind, she was sure she had. Something important, something precious, something she'd miss until she had it back. What was it? If only she could remember what it was.

Jonathan Steffen
CARPE DIEM

Emily Tremaine registered the soft hiss of her sister's BMW on the gravel of the drive below with a sinking feeling: a ton of Teutonic hi-tech, she thought to herself, scrunching its soulless way across her heart ... She clutched at the wardrobe door for support. She *had* to find a pair of clean green tights. For some reason, she knew she could only face Susan today if she was wearing green. Tights and knickers, scarves and blouses littered the floor of her attic room, hung from the backs of chairs, dangled from picture frames and lampshades. The door bell rang as Emily was in the process of ripping off a pair of black tights and pulling on a dirty green pair she had just located underneath the bed. The door bell always rang with a peculiar peremptoriness when Susan sounded it: no one else managed to imbue the old-fashioned mechanism with such a tone of command. Stepping into a pair of lace-up shoes without undoing the laces, Emily threw a scarf around her neck, exchanged it for another one, and then, with what appeared to be a single movement, swept up all the discarded clothes and shoved them in the bottom of the wardrobe. Checking her hair quickly in the mirror — on which the words CARPE DIEM were scrawled in pink lipstick — she went downstairs to let her sister in.

Susan was standing on the doorstep, her feet in their patent leather shoes planted neatly together, her hands clasped symmetrically just below her waistline. In her navy blue blazer and crisply pleated skirt, she bore an unnerving resemblance to an air hostess; even her straight and glossy blonde hair had an institutionalized look about it, as though its cut had been decided upon by a committee of PR men.

The two sisters exchanged a look of pure hatred.

'Well,' said Susan, after some moments, 'aren't you going to invite me in?'

'Oh, of course, of course,' said Emily, brushing back a lock of hair which had suddenly become tickly and bothersome. 'Come in.'

They made their way up the decrepit staircase with its chipped brown banisters and threadbare floral carpet, Susan averting her gaze as they passed half-open doors out of which emanated odours of roll-your-owns, tinned soup, babies. Dusty houseplants languished on the landings here and there; bicycles and push-chairs lingered in odd corners; and at one point they had to step over a disembowelled vacuum cleaner, its fuzzy innards trailing all over the floor.

'Geoff's been trying to get that thing to work for days,' remarked Emily.

'Who's Geoff?'

'Just someone. Someone who lives here.'

It was a long climb: both sisters were panting slightly, and trying to disguise it, when they reached the top.

'Emily, how much longer are you going to go on living in this place?' said Susan, fighting down the desire to wipe the sweat from her upper lip with the back of her hand.

'What can I offer you to drink?' was Emily's reply. 'Tea? Coffee? Coffee's only instant, I'm afraid.'

'I think tea might be safest,' said Susan, searching in her handbag for a paper tissue.

'Take a seat somewhere,' said Emily, snatching a tell-tale pair of knickers from the back of a chair and dusting off the seat with the palm of her hand for good measure. Her palm came away covered in talcum powder.

Susan chose to perch on the edge of the window-sill, crossing her legs elegantly and admiring the arches of her feet. She had to gather herself ... She had to do something to stop herself from screaming. Here was her sister, her brilliant elder sister, the one with all the intelligence, the one with all the talent, the one with all the promise, living in an Edwardian slum on the edge of the red-light district, still on the dole, still without a man, still drawing pictures of herself in coloured crayons and pinning them to the walls ... There were pictures everywhere – pictures, and photographs from magazines, and quotations from books copied out on index cards in bold felt-tip ... A hard-bound notebook lay open on the desk, covered in Emily's whirling, dense black scrawl, and beside it a brimming ashtray, a copy of the *I Ching*, and a perfect pink rose in a slender glass vase.

'Mind if I smoke?' asked Susan, to whom the combined smell of unwashed crockery and fresh talcum powder was becoming unbearable.

'Go ahead,' said Emily; 'I'll join you.'

Susan offered Emily a gold-tipped cigarette from an emerald green packet with gold lettering.

'I'd rather have one of my own, thanks,' said Emily, reaching for a crumpled pouch of rolling-tobacco. 'Filters,' she muttered, 'where did I put my filters ...?'

There ensued a search which turned up an unopened bill, a loose tampon, a postcard depicting Charlie Chaplin in *The Kid* – but not the filters.

'Have one of mine,' said Susan, through whose nostrils smoke was already contemptuously issuing.

'No thanks,' Emily replied. 'I'll just have to make do without the filter ... This is extraordinary,' she went on, scrutinizing the postcard. 'I've been looking for this for ages.'

'I suppose you think it's symbolic?'

'I do,' said Emily, her eyes flashing defensively at her sister.

'Oh, God, Emily, when are you going to grow up?'

'I would hope never,' was Emily's reply. She rolled the tobacco back and forth inside the cigarette paper so hard that the paper ripped. 'Susan, let's not have this conversation all over again,' she said, as she took out another cigarette paper.

Susan's eyebrows arched, but she said nothing. 'Well, let's at least have some tea.'

The two sisters sat in silence for a while, not looking at one another as they drank their tea and smoked their cigarettes. From time to time their eyes would stray towards one another, but then they would avert their gaze at the last second. An impartial observer might have noticed a similarity in the way they held their teacups – a mannerism they had inherited from their mother.

'Emily,' said Susan, prefacing her words with a sigh just like that of the BMW on the gravel a few minutes before, 'why do you live like this?'

'Because I want to.'

'Because you want to. Very good. And have you any idea how selfish this way of living is? Or perhaps I mean self-involved,' she added as an afterthought.

'I'm not doing anyone any harm,' said Emily, getting up with a toss of her head and going over to the tape recorder. 'Excuse me, I need to listen to a piece of music.'

Emily knelt down in front of the cassette recorder and started rummaging through a cardboard box containing cassettes. Like everything else in the room, it was falling to pieces. Like everything else in the room, it was covered in bright crayon.

'You say you're not doing anyone any harm,' Susan began – but the sound of the cassette recorder drowned out her voice.

'I've got to find the right passage,' said Emily, without looking round.

'You say you're not doing anyone any harm,' Susan started again, over the strains of a Vivaldi largo, 'but what about Mother? She's sick with worry about you.'

'She's sick, full stop,' said Emily.

'Whatever you may think about her,' said Susan, 'you have to acknowledge the fact that –'

'I don't have to acknowledge any facts!' exploded Emily, bringing her hand down on the floor with a thud. 'I've spent the whole of my life "acknowledging facts", as you call it. I've had facts rammed down my throat ever since I can remember! I'll tell you the kind of facts that interest me!' She had stood up by now and was pacing back and forth in front of the dresser. Her image stalked her in the mirror – an image obscured here and there by the postcards and scribbled notes with which the glass was covered. 'Fact one: Our parents have spent their whole lives trying to force me into a role –'

'Everyone plays a role in this life, Emily –'

'Fact two: I am not prepared to play that role –'

'You can't live without playing a role –'

'Fact three ...' But Emily seemed to have forgotten what fact three was. She sat down on the edge of the dresser and buried her face in her hands. 'Susan,' she said at last, through her half-open fingers, 'why don't you just leave me alone?'

Susan stubbed out her cigarette with a decisive gesture, got up from the window-sill and walked over to the desk. For a long time her attention appeared to be concentrated on the rose in the glass vase.

'Why don't I just leave you alone?' she said at last. 'Do you want to know why I don't just leave you alone? Because I'm fed up with doing the dirty work. I'm fed up with looking after Mother. I'm fed up with having to make excuses for you –'

'Then don't make excuses!'

'You think I should tell her the *truth*?' Susan seemed genuinely shocked by the idea.

'Why not? It can't be any worse than what she thinks about me already. God, Susan, why don't you just get off my back? You've got everything. You've got a husband who loves you and a successful career and two beautiful blue-eyed children and a great big house and a great big car –'

'You don't seem to be aware of the sacrifices I've made.'

'I am all too aware of the sacrifices you've made. You reek of sacrifice.

You carry it round with you like a miasma.'

Susan seemed troubled by the word miasma.

'Like a stench,' clarified Emily.

Susan's nostrils flared. Again she let out one of those BMW sighs. Crossing to the window-sill, she picked up her handbag, snapped it shut, then suddenly opened it again and lit another cigarette.

'I don't know why I waste my time on you,' she said in a quiet voice.

'Then don't waste it' said Emily, in a voice that was equally quiet. It could have been the same voice speaking. 'Don't waste it,' repeated Emily. 'Leave me alone. I'm happy. Just leave me alone.'

'You're happy?' echoed Susan, tossing back her head as she exhaled a cloud of smoke. 'You're living in a dump like this, with a load of dead-beats — Emily, what do you actually *do* all day?'

Emily almost laughed at this. She sat down cross-legged on the floor, hung her head, and took several deep breaths before answering. When she raised her head again, she was smiling.

'I live,' she said.

'You live.' Susan nodded. 'I see. And what else?'

'There *is* nothing else. I live. What do you do?'

Susan appeared unable to find an answer to this.

'I'll tell you what you do,' said Emily. 'You work all day in a bank and you help your children with their homework every evening and you take them out on trips every weekend and you have friends over to dinner at least twice a week and you make love every Saturday evening —'

'Emily!'

'Every Friday evening? I thought Friday was Roger's squash evening. No matter.'

'You disgust me,' said Susan, stubbing out her half-smoked cigarette. 'Really, you disgust me. Your *arrogance* disgusts me.'

'I'm right, though, aren't I? Tell me if I'm not right.'

Susan said nothing.

Emily got up and went over to the kettle. Shaking it to check how much water was left in it, she said, 'Would you like another cup of tea?'

Susan shook her head.

'You're welcome to,' said Emily. '*I'm* not in a hurry. I've got all day.'

'No,' said Susan, with a glance at her watch, 'I've got to be getting back to pick up the children.' She stood up and reached for her handbag. 'I see . . .' she started, fiddling with the catch of the bag. 'I see no point in our maintaining contact, Emily.'

'Fine by me,' said Emily. 'I've got better things to do.'

'You are a complete egotist.'

'If that's the way you look at it.'

'Well, don't come running to me for help when you need it!'

'I won't,' said Emily, very quietly.

Susan gave a shrug and made towards the door.

'What's that on the mirror?' she asked, pausing in the doorway.

'What, the photograph?'

'No, the words. *Carpe diem.*'

'It means "Seize the day" in Latin.'

'And that's what you think you're doing?'

'That's what I've just done.'

Susan shook her head and left without a word.

Emily sat down for a long time in front of the mirror after her sister had left. She heard the door of the BMW slam shut, heard the engine purr into life, heard the wheels swishing away across the gravel, faster than they had come. She took out a mauve lipstick and started tracing around the pink lettering on the mirror. Carefully she filled out every line and contour, until the phrase shone with a three-dimensional depth. Then she buried her face in her hands and burst into uncontrollable tears.

David Stephenson

WHAT WILL SURVIVE OF US?

It was the same no matter what he hunted. That last half-hour before dawn – a cup of strong black coffee on the kitchen table, the familiar array of rods and rags and little jars of oils cast about him like runes – was the most important time of all.

He selected a long narrow flue-brush and worked it down each barrel in turn, three times, methodically. Romantic superstition, Carrie used to call it; like the priest's ritual mutter over wafer and wine. She had even bought the red-and-black plaid shirt he wore for hunting because, she said, a priest should always look like a priest, else how was God to know?

She was out by several millennia, he liked to think; he preferred to trace his religious instincts back to some sort of primeval Earth-magic that no Bible-blackness could ever hope to overshadow. Whichever came under his sights – grouse, pheasant, wood pigeon, rabbit or hare – the oiled rag was the prayer he offered in advance for their forgiveness, the way North American Indians used to apologize to the silver birch that would surrender its bark for the new canoe. He caressed the walnut stock and frowned to find an invisible roughness beneath his fingertips. He reached for the wax and a clean cloth, breathing deeply of the faint honey scent that reminded him of incense.

How much keener the sense of sacrament when the target was human.

He took a photograph from his wallet and stood it against the box of cartridges, regretting its creased corners, the smudged fingerprints, the reduced colour-contrast wrought by time. It showed Carrie, not as she now was, but as she used to be: on holiday in Scotland a few years back, laughing and carefree, a thick strand of blonde hair pulled teasingly into a veil over the lower half of her face, eyes bright with invitation. She was leaning provocatively against a pine tree, wearing jeans and a T-shirt, nipples shadowy beneath the thin white cotton, all her weight on one hip. Behind her, down the hill, through the forest's ragged edge, he could just make out the fine crescent of sand where, not an hour before, they had made love. In two minutes' time they would make love again, up against that same pine tree. They had been happy then.

He checked the firing pins, then worked the mechanism a couple of times, letting his finger relearn the precise pressure of the pull.

They had been happy then. No one about except a patrol of gulls wading the waterline and, far out in the bay, a black bobbing speck that might have been the head of a seal. They walked hand in hand along the white sands, kicking them to hear them sing, becoming slowly aware of their skin's nearness, of its electric potential. They turned their backs on the sea and undressed each other behind the screen of black rocks that guarded a tiny cove. Pausing, wanting to draw it out for the rest of their lives, they saw a stag step silently from among the trees. It gazed at them for a moment's innocent curiosity, then slipped away like a missed heartbeat. Her cry, when she finally came, head thrown back, neck taut, fingers clawing at the sand, sent gulls wheeling up to catch the echo. He buried his head between her breasts, to hold her to the earth.

'If I die,' she murmured, her heart loud and rapid beneath his ear, 'then I would like it to be here, on sand, beneath blue skies, with you.'

'If,' she had said. Not 'When'. His heart contracted at the memory, forcing him to grope blindly for other, more recent pains, to keep him honest; her two lovers, for example. He got up to make a fresh cup of coffee. The two he knew about, he corrected himself; there may have been others. His right index finger tightened automatically, causing him to spill coffee grains across the work surface.

Time does funny things to a marriage, he reflected, scooping the brown specks on to the flat of his hand and dusting them into the cup; things the young swear will never happen. Love and desire, for a long time synonymous, had gradually become horses from the same stable: raised together, trained together, but destined for different riders. It was not so much that Carrie and he had ceased desiring each other as they had begun to use alternative criteria to judge the reduced frequency of their coupling.

'These days we make love; we used to fuck,' she once said, with matchless simplicity.

He wanted to agree, part of him *did* agree, but it was somehow too glib; it reduced to its component parts something he had once thought indivisible, like the atom before Hiroshima.

Besides, in his eyes, they had always made love.

He added a second spoonful of coffee, craving the kick of caffeine. He had almost lived on the stuff these past three months, becoming thinner than he'd ever been, more gaunt than he ought to be, but all the while aware that the emptiness inside was not that sort of hunger. OK, so he was no saint — he'd had a woman or two in his time – but so what? The intensity that Carrie invested in an affair was something else altogether. It was that which hurt, not the sex; that, and the sense of having missed out on something both sweeter and sourer than lust.

'I will not share you,' he remembered saying, in this very kitchen, the first time he found out.

'Share?' She seemed genuinely puzzled. 'What do you mean "share?" I'm a person, not a thing.'

He could not understand this. The world, for him, had always been a place of sharp contrasts; a place for everything and everything in its place. 'Do you love him?' he asked.

'Not the way I love you, no. It's ... it's a passion.'

It was a passion he wanted for himself. 'How, then, can you love me?' he sneered. 'How is it not the same?'

'I would die for you.'

He snorted. 'That's the difference between us, then. I would kill.'

Life had gone on. The man took a job in another town and moved away, never to be heard from again. Carrie was more discreet the second time, if indeed it was just the second time, but he still found out in the end, the bed shaking with her silent 2 a.m. sobs. He said nothing, hoarding the knowledge against the future. Against today.

He shook his head. That was not it at all. Begin to believe that, and he would be no better than a ... He switched off hurriedly, willing himself to concentrate on the practicalities, desperate to stop his hands shaking.

He went swiftly out to the garage, detached a vice from the work-bench, selected his sharpest hack-saw and a few other tools, and carried them back to the kitchen. He clamped the vice on to the edge of the table and padded the jaws with cotton waste, then laid the barrels between them, monitoring the pressure as he turned the screw. It was not steady enough. He tightened the clamps, crushing the grey formica surface. Carrie would have raged at him for days.

Cutting eight inches from the end was almost like slicing through his own flesh, but he saw no option. He had set his heart on wearing the leather jacket that Carrie thought he looked so good in; it would conceal the bulk of the gun, but never its length.

Using first a rasp then finer and finer grades of glasspaper, he carefully soothed the raw edges. The gun looked ugly now, ugly and evil, like a goblin. He had a tall man's mistrust of anything small.

But when he slipped on the jacket, and fitted the stock snugly up into his left armpit, the tip of the barrel slotted into a rip in the lining, near the hem, as if the coat had been specially adapted. He grinned sourly. Life was sometimes like that: everything coming together when you most needed it, but least wanted it.

He looked round the kitchen for the last time. It was strange how they had always felt most comfortable there, even when fighting, even when discussing her lovers. They could have been as happy or as sad in a bed-sit, he thought; all the space they needed lay inside them.

It was a shame about the vice marks on the table; but when a thing was over, it was over.

A police patrol car, doors agape, was parked at an urgent angle outside the entrance, the radio relaying tinny messages to no one.

He stood patiently on the opposite grass verge, the soft earth giving slightly beneath his feet. He waited while someone else's tragedy unfolded behind the glass and concrete façade; waited until the two officers emerged, heavy-footed, through the automatic doors, one of them wearily wiping his forehead with the back of his hand. He watched them drive away, calculating how long it would take them to get back once they got the message. Long enough, he guessed, for it not to matter.

He crossed the road and went in, nodding to the attractive girl on the reception desk, who smiled sympathetically. She was good at her job, he'd noticed, but her look of pity had a professional air that discomforted him, like an undertaker's mask of solemnity.

He rode the lift to the first floor and turned right, the shortest route, not hurrying unduly, not wanting to attract attention, but anxious now to get it over with. He never wished to revisit these grey echoing corridors as long as he lived; wanted never again to put out his hand to this swing-door, to feel its initial resistance melt away.

'Oh, hello, Mr Robson. No change, I'm afraid.'

He made to step round the woman, who stretched out an arm to bar his way.

'You can't go in just yet,' she said. 'Mr Pettigrew is due any minute.'

He tried to push past, but her wiry body contained a surprising strength. 'Come back in half an hour,' she insisted, coaxing him towards the exit. 'Go and have a cup of coffee. I'll send someone to fetch you.'

He knew too much to accuse her of not caring, but, like the receptionist's processed pity, there was a mechanical trick to her voice, as though she were reciting a formula. He stepped clear and withdrew the gun, watching the uncertainty in her eyes harden into fear. He had a sudden urge to say something, to tell her she had nothing to be afraid of, to account for this seeming madness, but his mouth was dry and he could no longer see the point of speech. He motioned her to one side. She hesitated, but only for a second, her eyes straying to the telephone on the desk. It doesn't matter, he thought. Two more minutes, five at most, and nothing will ever matter again.

He passed through the portholed doors into an inner room, a twilit sanctuary in which machinery hummed like bee-song. In the third bed, left-hand side, Carrie, flat and pale, hardly there at all, lay with a flimsy sheet drawn up to her waist, the top half of her body naked. He had complained, the first time he saw her like this, about the indignity of it, thinking how she would feel when – if – she awoke. But, as they patiently explained, trying to inject the correct note of optimism, you couldn't be always putting on and taking off clothing when a life was at risk, now could you?

Her hair was cropped short, patchy where the surgeon had cut and where electrodes adhered to her scalp. She would have hated to see herself like that, and he found himself glancing round for a mirror, thinking to cover it over, before he realized his foolishness. The dead have no need of mirrors.

A murmur of voices arose from the room next door and, in the distance, drawing nearer, a police siren. A telephone started to ring and was abruptly silenced. The machines continued to hum.

There were more electrodes attached below the shallowness of her left breast, tubes snaking away from her nose and her arm. He traced them to the machine, traced the cable from there to the wall.

'Who can say?' they had replied, in answer to his question. 'We are doing what we can.' Progress had made technicians of them all, watching one machine tend another.

'There may, of course, be some residual brain damage.' One man's engineering problem is another man's hell.

The door opened and he raised the gun to waist-height. The man in the white coat froze.

'I don't think this is a good idea, Mr Robson.'

Not trusting his voice to answer, he thumbed back both hammers, watching the other's eyes. Where he expected fear, he saw only understanding. He would have rather seen fear.

The man looked at him for what seemed like an age, then nodded and turned to go. 'Good luck,' he called over his shoulder.

And now there was only Carrie and him, the way she wanted it. He watched the slow rise and fall of her machine-timed breath, marvelling afresh at how little physical damage there was. What had been her last thoughts, he wondered, as the car bore down on her? Whose name on her lips? The only witness said he didn't even think she knew what hit her, so perhaps her mind had been focused on something totally mundane: the evening meal, the prospect of rain, the scent of wallflowers.

Not a mark on her. He couldn't get over that. They'd had to scrape the driver out of the wreckage.

Time ticked by, measured by the tyranny of a mechanical pulse. The nearby crackle of a police radio, like the indecipherable and irritating chatter of a personal stereo, reawakened him to a sense of urgency. The last thing he wanted now was to meet a hero.

The cable fed directly into the wall. He took a firm grip and pulled sharply. An alarm immediately sounded in the outer room, a single tone, loud and insistent. He levelled the gun at the door, but no one came through. The alarm clicked off, leaving a deafening silence.

He sat down on the bed and raised his wife's body, cradling her in his free arm. She was lighter than he had ever known her. She would have liked that.

'Remember the stag, Carrie? Remember the gulls when you cried out?' He wanted to believe he would see a ghost of a smile on her lips, and saw it, and smiled back.

'Blue skies, Carrie. Blue skies, and sand, and ...', he hesitated, '... and me. Not one of them would have done this for you.' He spoke softly, in case anyone overheard and laughed at him.

She continued to breathe, unaided, for about half a minute, the movement of her ribcage becoming shallower, her life ebbing gently away like the sea from the singing sands. When the pulse in her neck ceased to flutter, when the tightness in his chest eased, he laid her back on the bed and drew up the sheet, tucking it round her shoulders.

He broke open the gun and removed the cartridges, then, gun in one hand, ammunition in the other, walked slowly to the door which opened to receive him.

Love, which she had always seen as a compromise between passion and the grave, had turned out to be far stronger than either.

It was what he had always known.

D.J. Taylor
LA GRANGE

Summer '83 wasn't a good time for the repro business. Kodak had a three-month strike at their warehouse at Dyersburg, there was a run on the world silver market that sent up the price of film, and what with the expense and the flaring heat which hung over the cornfields from dawn till sunset people stopped using their cameras so much. For a time I tried to ignore the disappearing orders and the shaking heads at the roadside pharmacies – I headed north into Kentucky, went to trade fairs in Lafayette offering bargain rates, thought about going into partnership with one of the local chemists, but then the drought set in, the dust swarmed up over the bumpy Cook County backroads, the drug-store windows were full of second-hand Leicas and Hasselblads and it was suddenly cheaper to stay at home. 'When the punch comes, ride it,' Barrett the journalist used to say, so I made the call to Photomax, put the mobile lab in storage and took the job at La Grange.

It was one of those places you see very often in the south, which has outgrown its origins without ever letting go of them. The dirt farmer with a thousand acres and a contract with three flour mills who still has trouble signing his name; the small-town newscaster who makes it on to network TV and still says 'y'all' and 'I guess' when she comes home to visit her folks: such sights were common in Cook County. La Grange was the biggest track complex for a hundred miles, but they still kept on the old, slow-witted announcer who had been with them twenty years back when the site was opened and Howie Jasper, the owner, still took two days a week off to dodge the phone calls from the west-coast agents and the Ivy League track clubs and go duck shooting in Johnson City marshes. 'Just your average hillbilly with a wallet,' Barrett used to say disparagingly, but the local TV station covered two meetings a month in the summer and the results got printed in the east-coast sports papers. In the early Eighties Calvin Smith ran there at a charity meet and two reporters and a photographer arrived from Houston to write Howie Jasper up for *Track and Field*.

After that things began to take off. He had plans for La Grange, Howie Jasper told us, in that shy, puzzled way that redeems its guile with transparency. Pretty soon he had the stadium turned into a limited company with investors in Jackson loaning him money for redevelopment. He took out the old cinder track and had a sports contractor from Memphis come and lay an all-weather surface. He put a roof on the rickety grandstand and sold concessions to the local burger salesmen and the Macdonalds franchises, finessed his way into sports sponsorship schemes that would bring in the big names from UCLA and the Santa Monica track club. And, most important of all, he signed the deal that made him Clyde Hopkins' manager.

I was busy the first couple of weeks at La Grange, sending out franchise forms to the Coke and Burger King reps, dealing with the contractors who were putting in the new electronic scoreboard, but it wasn't difficult to find out about Clyde Hopkins. The bar-hall idlers and the local talent spotters who hung around the stadium of an evening taking drinks off Howie were already talking about him, this kid who still ran barefoot but could whip any college boy the west coast cared to send down. Barrett, who turned up half-way through the third week to write him up for the Cook County *Sentinel*, filled me in on the details.

'Sure, my man. All happened a month ago, down near Atalanta' Atalanta was the farming end of Cook County, seventy miles away – 'when Howie decides he'll check out some of the local talent, you know, turn up at one of the high school meets with a stop-watch and see if anything takes his fancy. And it's the usual thing – a few bullet-heads throwing the shot around, teenage high-jumpers thinking they're Dwight Stones – and Howie's on his way back to the car when up steps this kid in a windcheater and runs the hurdles in fourteen dead.'

'That's a state record.'

'You got it, my man,' Barrett said tolerantly. 'Or would have been if they hadn't been using a hand-timer. So Howie makes enquiries and finds out the kid's seventeen years old, never run outside the county before. Real country bumpkin stuff. Howie asked him where his track shoes were and he says, he'd never gotten used to them: did all his running on grass.' Barrett flicked his head towards the window, where track-suited joggers laboured through the shimmering afternoon heat. 'Lick anyone in *this* stadium, that's for sure.

'And another thing,' Barrett said. 'There's a little part-time photography job going down at the *Sentinel*. Weddings, mayoral clam-bakes –

you know the score. I put in a word.'

There was a fortnight until the *Sentinel* started interviewing. In the mean time, repairing the stadium advertising hoardings from the top of a twenty-foot ladder or sitting in the office typing up CVs, I saw quite a lot of Clyde Hopkins. He came and sat in the admin block, while the secretaries made long-distance phone calls to Miami and Tampa Bay or talked about driving to Nashville for the weekend to see the Atlanta Dance Kings, and flicked through the back numbers of *Dixie* magazine. Other times he stayed out on the track running circuits or lining up the hurdles in files of six or eight and doing stepping exercises. The other runners, the lanky PT students who reckoned on making the state championships in Jackson, the burly National Guardsmen sweating to pass army medicals, offered him handshakes, tried to buy him beers in the stadium bar, but he kept out of their reach. He seemed remote, preoccupied, embarrassed by the way people called him 'Lightnin'' after the old blues singer, by Howie's back-slapping and the posters billing him as the 'Cook County Express' which appeared in the barbers' shops and on the motel display boards. But in early July he walked away from a field that included the state champion and a sweating two-hundred-pounder who had once come seventh in the US junior trials, and Howie talked about entering him for some of the west-coast college meets or getting him a track scholarship somewhere out east.

Barrett got interested then, in his sideways-on, reporter's way. At the close of a discussion of the photographer's job, which it turned out was going on ice until the end of the summer, he said, 'Hear Howie's been talking big about the Cook County Express. Track scholarships. The west coast. Isn't that right?'

I nodded. 'A pile of forms came in the office this morning.'

'Uh huh. I heard.' Barrett smiled in that mischievous way that lifted him a thousand miles north of Cook County and put him on a TV screen opposite Paul Michael Glaser. 'Well, you can kiss your ass goodbye to that, my man. Sure, there's plenty of track scholarships going for meathead hurdlers, and nobody's going to mind an awful lot about your grade point average, but you have to be able to read and write. I talked to one of the Grange lawyers who stopped by the other day. Seems like the kid had to have that contract Howie made him sign explained to him clause by clause. You never saw anything like it.'

But there were reasons, I discovered, why it would be difficult to get Howie's prodigy up there on the national circuit with Greg Foster and Skeats Nehemiah. Two nights later at the big La Grange invitation meet he came second to a fading thirty-year-old from Mississippi who had hung around the fringes of the '76 Olympic squad, but he did it in thirteen seven zero. I skipped the post-race celebrations – there were letters I needed to write to the other big repro houses in the east – and was heading out through the empty foyer when a girl's voice pulled me up.

'You know where I can find Clyde Hopkins, mister?'

She couldn't have been more than sixteen. There was a dirt bike propped up against the foyer's glass exit gate with a Snoopy pennant fixed to its handlebars. I explained about the party.

'You want to come along? I can take you up.'

The girl twisted her fingers uncertainly for a while. She had very pale blonde hair that reminded you of Cissy Spacek. 'I guess not,' she said finally. 'Listen,' she went on. 'Next time you see him you could tell him that Terry was waiting.'

I watched her riding off through the rows of Lincolns and Pontiacs in the stadium forecourt and out on to the highway. Next day I gave the message to Clyde but I needn't have bothered. She was round at the stadium in the morning and the two of them stood there arguing while the hurdles Howie Jasper had lined up for a demonstration race in front of cable TV got taken down and the local reporters kicked their heels and drank whisky sours in the hospitality suite.

Summer dragged. The heat rose up over the parched grass and the cotton died in the fields, so that there were rumours of hardship funds and the insurance company travellers sat in the roadside diners selling fifty-dollar policies against drought. I had cool, non-committal letters from the east, from Philadelphia, Boston, Pittsburgh, from big repro houses who said they wanted college graduates or ten years' experience and told me to write again in the fall. Then a week into August Barrett wrapped his car round a fire hydrant over near the Tennessee border and broke his thigh-bone, so I took a day's holiday, borrowed Howie Jasper's pick-up and drove over to the hospital at Union City to see him.

'One of those things, my man, just one of those things,' Barrett said. He was grim and irritable because the nurses wouldn't let him smoke and there was a rumour that his mother was arriving that afternoon from Memphis. There was a copy of the *Tennessee Sports Illustrated* lying on the bed with a picture of Clyde rising up effortlessly over a hurdle, the bunch of perspiring also-rans seen dimly in the distance behind him. 'You heard the latest about Lightnin'? Looks like Howie's sending him west for a couple of months. Catching the big LA meets and the Prairie Games. Plus a five-thousand-dollar sponsorship deal from some sportswear manufacturer Howie reckons owes him a favour.'

I told him about Terry. Barrett laughed. 'Uh huh. I heard. You know he ran thirteen five eight midweek over at Lafayette? Beat Missouri Joe Constantine into third. And another thing, old man Hopkins comes up for trial at Jackson tomorrow on a repossession order. Put those two together and see what they come to.'

After that I didn't stop hearing about Clyde Hopkins. About how his pa was a dirt farmer ruined by the drought, about how his mother had to wash dishes at the diner in Degville. You couldn't stop at a gas station without some wisecracking ancient hawking his gum in the dust to tell you that he'd known Grandpa Hopkins way back in the Depression when he'd gone out west to pick oranges in California. Howie Jasper was very great around this time, bustling about in a new Fox Brothers suit, though the temperature hit 92 that week, and hosting afternoon-long lunches for the company shareholders. There were other signs, too, of this new-found confidence. Come mid-August a couple of NBC lawyers showed up for a meeting and anyone who worked full-time at the stadium had to wear a scarlet and blue uniform mocked up to look like a track-suit with the La Grange jack-rabbit logo on the back. Then, when Clyde got accepted for the September meets at UCLA and Frisco, he bought airtime on the Memphis radio stations to advertise it. And though the kid hated drinking and the air conditioning had stopped working in the heat, Howie made him put on a suit and sit in the stadium bar three nights a week talking to the fans.

I saw him there one Sunday night when it was getting late and the barman was already putting the towels over the Seven-Up dispensers and corking up the barrels of root beer which Howie bought at a discount from a supplier in Nashville and which nobody would drink. He looked a little uncertain amid the fading light, mightily uncomfortable in the suit Howie had bought for him, tie yanked up against his throat. There was a cup of coffee on the table in front of him with the surface stretched into a skin and a packet of the Bluegrass cigarettes which the farmers used to smoke.

I said, 'You don't want to let Howie see you with those things.'

He shrugged. 'Howie went off to Degville, a while back. Said he had to talk to my daddy.' When I didn't answer he went on, 'You know, I ain't ever been out of Cook County before. Never did leave it, 'cept to go to some fancy farm convention once away in Kansas, time the old man thought about buying a new seed drill. What do you reckon it's like in California?'

'Some people seem to like it.'

'Uh huh. My granddaddy went there, picking oranges in the Depression. Seems a funny thing to do in the Depression, don't it?

Picking oranges.' He shrugged again. 'You know, I don't even want to see that five thousand dollars. Don't care if Pa gets it or it goes straight to the bank. Just don't want to see it, that's all'.

And after that he disappeared: driven out to the airport first thing in Howie Jasper's pick-up, people said, off on the charter flight to San Francisco. There was a charity meet two nights later at La Grange, with a one-lap wheelchair race and a thousand-dollar invitation steeple-chase, but there was no sign of him amongst the crowd of kids in their red track-suits by the electronic scoreboard or standing with Howie's guest stars in the celebrity enclosure. Old man Hopkins came into the office a couple of times but he had that furtive, hang-dog look of the man who can't understand why people are doing him favours and he didn't want to talk. No one had seen Terry in a month.

I was keeping my head down around that time, writing letters and buying air tickets – Pictureworld in Philadelphia were finally giving me an interview – and I had to wait a few days to catch up with the sports papers. The news was mixed. He won a couple of inter-state meets in thirteen eight, thirteen nine five, then he bombed out in the West Coast games against a row of Olympic trialists and there was a story that he'd injured himself, torn a hamstring, that sort of thing. September came, but the drought lasted through: the roadside verges were white-coloured now and all along the horizon you could see the dust from the army lorries bringing water in from the big reservoirs across the state border, and Howie Jasper worried that the tarmac would crack before his big end-of-season meet. The day I got the acceptance letter from Pictureworld they let Barrett out of the hospital and he limped into the office to catch up.

'Guess what, my man? Terry got married last week. Over at Choctaw.'

'Who to?'

Barrett smiled that lazy, insouciant smile. 'Oh, just some hillbilly with a wallet. Some *farmer*.'

'How'd Clyde take it?'

'How would you take it, my man? Leastways, he's advertised in Howie's end-of-season special. The ads came in at the *Sentinel* this morning. "Local boy comes home", that sort of thing. Plus two national record-holders and an NBC camera team. They reckon Howie gets a network contract if it goes OK.'

The evening before the meet I stood on the pine-ridge two miles outside the stadium and watched the grey clouds roll in from Baton Rouge and the Gulf: the drought broke early next morning and covered the La Grange track in three inches of water. The athletes shivered and fretted but they went ahead anyhow, with Howie Jasper cursing and shouting and the NBC team filming from behind polythene shelters. By the time the hurdles came on most of the crowd had gone and there was an inevitability about the way Clyde sauntered out of the blocks with an odd, sick smile on his face, battered his way through half a dozen hurdles or so and then stopped dead to head off on to the trackside where Howie was yelling and hit him in the mouth. I watched them for a while as the rain fell and the cameramen drifted away and a couple of the La Grange investors stood around with disappointed faces, while Clyde squatted absently on his hunkers and Howie raged at him with the blood and the water gumming up the collar of his shirt. Barrett was saying something and the old announcer's voice cracked through the tannoy but I headed off thinking, of all things, about Terry, about the dirt bike propped against the foyer door and what it must have been like to pick oranges, in the Depression, in California.

James Thurlby

THE PASSPORT OFFICER

Harding said, 'I intend to tackle Bernstein about the new Detroit project right away. I shall fly to the States tonight. We shall meet in New York and I shall be there for as long as it takes to make him see sense. If he doesn't, I shall call the deal off.'

Had he detected the faintest smirk on any director's face? Trubbing, for instance. He was the joker. Did he, or anyone else, actually know that Harding had a mistress in New York? Any one of them who even suspected might find their chairman's third transatlantic trip in a month agreeable fuel for whatever mischievous sparks they were trying to encourage into flame.

But his bleak look around the table had noted nothing buy loyalty. Indeed, only admiration for the forthright and authoritative manner in which he clearly meant to discipline the errant Bernstein.

He worked throughout the day with his usual vigour. He was a baron and did not really need a board of directors. In a medieval century they would simply have been his bodyguard.

He called in the European director and set him going at Formula One speed on the new Düsseldorf plans. Lunched with Ledbury, the new Secretary of State for the Environment. A weak but obstinate man, he thought. Harding introduced him to three members of his board. Kept their egos happy if they felt they were getting a share of political exposure. And they usually obliged by supplying a fair amount of the buttering that politicians enjoy. Ledbury, as his name suggested, said very little that was uplifting. He wasn't really Green. More Eau-de-Nil. He was aware that Industry paid a lot of taxes and employed a great number of people, and that led him into interesting chameleon changes of colour.

Harding phoned his wife, Jane, at the company flat they occupied in town during the week. She was busy with preparations for a lunch for some of the board members' wives. But she had time to talk and was affectionate.

He felt ashamed, trying not to think of the flat on the park in New York. Yet he found his desire just to be with Janine almost overwhelming. How odd, that close similarity of their names. Was Janine a younger Jane? She laughed at him and teased him and he loved it. It was something Jane had done once but not in recent times. You can't tease a man who never relaxes, who has begun to live out the image that he himself has created. But in New York he did relax. Janine had not the slightest respect for his high rank. That did not enter into her view of him. In teasing him she gave him back his youth. Avidly, he grasped the philtre offered to him.

And yet, at fifty-five, his energy was legendary within the company. He had four secretaries and they had difficulty in keeping pace.

He cross-questioned the planning director with the customary asperity he used on this man, who was ex-public school. A sharp caning usually produced results. He knew exactly which mode to adopt with each executive. Planning had a soft streak. Quoted poetry at him once. But only once.

He used a much more permissive technique with the general manager responsible for Scandinavian sales. This man had a sharp mind, a head for figures. Harding let him talk. He said, 'I believe we need to be thinking about our first plant out there, Chairman. A merger? A take-over?' Harding nodded. 'Do a paper on it for next week. Let me see it first. If I like it I'll put it to the board.'

The day moved past at its usual blurred speed but he was always the rock-steady centre of the cyclone. Perceptive, appraising, critical. He made the others move. He liked to watch their flight, their efforts to come within reach of his own thought, the way they orbited him.

Every so often Janine edged her way into his consciousness. He could neither understand nor believe the reality of what was happening between them. She was the wife of a writer who had made his reputation with one good novel and followed it with several duds. He preferred to spend his time in California but she had a key role with a fashion house in New York and refused to move. The marriage was effectively finished.

Harding had met her at some lavish dinner party but he could not remember anyone else who had been a guest. Within days he knew he had fallen deeply in love. She returned his affection. That had been a year ago and they still felt the same about each other. It could not happen, of course, in his world of analysis and rational decision. But it had. And, while it was beautiful and precious beyond words, he grew fearful at the depth of his guilt and the paranoia this produced in him.

He dined with a peer and two MPs at Westminster. They fell upon him, with proper devotion to duty, about the proposed new plants in Hertfordshire. He listened attentively to their indignant questions. Smoke emissions? River pollution? Valley preservation? When they had fired their ammunition, he said, 'There will be no water pollution, no smoke emission and the buildings will be entirely hidden by trees. The company is spending nearly five million pounds to ensure this.' Within twenty minutes the discussion centred entirely on the bouquet of the Mâcon.

Frequently, he was amused by the parliamentarians, their posturings, their quick footwork. But tonight, after the first useful exchanges, he found them dull, rehearsing future speeches on matters that did not interest him. Several times a reverie took him over – about Jane and happiness long ago. He heard himself joining in the cross-table talk as if from a great distance.

His car was waiting. He loved the Rolls. Charles had collected his suitcase from the flat, and papers in his working briefcase from his personal secretary. He lay back, pulling down the central arm, and breathed deeply. 'Like ants,' he murmured to himself, 'We have to go on building for ever.' It seemed the only answer to the paradox of man on earth: bigger communities, higher demand for more sophisticated goods, yet fewer jobs because of the streamlining, and commercial survival only for those companies who were responsible but lean.

It was 10.30 p.m. when they reached the airport and he suddenly realized the uniqueness of his situation. Always before, he had flown to New York on the 6 p.m. flight, reaching that magic but tortured city at 7 p.m., their time. It was a ludicrous and punishing system to which many British businessmen were slaves. Usually wined and dined when they got there, they then found it hard to sleep.

Because of the noise factor, late-night take-offs had always previously been prohibited. By chance, earlier that day, he had been speaking on the phone to the chairman of Transoceanic. This man, whom he knew well, had told him elatedly that his airline had secured permission for a month of strictly 'trial' take-offs up to midnight using the wide-bodied 'Whispering Giants' they had bought. At once he had his secretary book him on this new 11.30 p.m. flight for New York. He would be there by 12.30 a.m., having flown for six hours, and would be able to go direct to his hotel and sleep.

He dismissed Charles, checked in, handed over his bag but kept his briefcase. He wanted to run through his Detroit papers on the plane.

The girl on the desk asked pleasantly, 'Do you wish to go straight to the hospitality suite, sir?'

He didn't. He thanked her. He usually had a pre-flight drink, but, right now, he felt he had had enough. The Mâcon had flowed generously. And then the brandy.

He made his way through the empty customs hall, virtually unmanned as the incoming flights had finished for the day. A suden flicker of alarm struck him. Without the usual medley of festooned travellers and sober-suited officials, the whole area ached with light. He was glad when he had passed through it.

He was stopped at the security gate where the sensors picked up his keys so that he had to empty his pockets. Annoyed at delay, he realized at once that he must be grateful for the efficiency of the installation. The officer was regimental, unsmiling.

And, then, almost before he had time to think of the next step in the ritual, he found himself up against the narrow defiles and the high, prim boxes of Passport Control.

Just for an instant he had a new perception of this 'gateway' to the world. He smiled cynically to himself. Unlike him to indulge in fantasy. Perhaps, with so few people about, he was being enabled to *notice* how narrow the passport 'channels' really were: each of them an alleyway scarcely wide enough to take a human body, regulating the flow, inwards and outwards, of those who leapt through the world's skies.

Before him was one of these slim ravines. On this side, he lived his life among many reassurances. His wealth, social acceptance and, above all, industrial pre-eminence, which, it was widely thought, would soon bring him his knighthood. But beyond the barrier? The great globe, its seas and continents, its thousands of cultures, its wars, risks and personal vulnerabilities. For that brief moment he stood on the edge of space. What nonsense. He stepped quickly forward to the desk.

Harding found himself face to face with the passport officer, the latter seated but at a higher level than he. He pushed the document forward. Quick flick of the pages, brief pause over the Russian and Chinese visas, then the raising of the head, the eye-to-eye stare. Always he resented that look as an intrusion into the world of the self. Impersonal yet penetrating. The bureaucrat. No smile.

But, this time, he was wrong. The man appeared to recognize him. A look of muted but civil friendliness transformed the official face. He leaned across the top of his check-point desk.

'You're taking the new 11.30 p.m. Transoceanic service, sir? I don't know if anyone has mentioned the extra flight they're putting on tonight?'

Harding, who certainly did not like not knowing all there was to know, was gruff.

'No one told *me*,' he snapped.

'To have converted one of their new aircraft to a "sleeper" in the old-fashioned sense of the word, sir. Not officially scheduled yet, but there's one leaving at midnight tonight. Why not try 5322 instead of 5321? Sleep in your own bed ... Somewhat more expensive, of course, sir.'

Harding waved aside this peccadillo and continued to look at the man aggressively.

Leaning forward himself, he said, 'You're a customs official, aren't you? How is it that you concern yourself with passenger comfort? That's the airline's job, isn't it?'

'Well, this is an exciting new development, sir. I think everybody here is keen to see it succeed providing residents are not adversely affected. But the engines *are* amazingly quiet. It will be a feather in the airport's cap if the planes can meet environmental standards ...' He talked on enthusiastically for a moment. And added, when he had finished, 'Oh, and not customs, sir. Passport Department, Home Office.'

Harding's level of suspicion declined. The words 'Home Office' had a reassuring ring, seeming to encapsulate so many of those sureties that were dear to him on this side of the barrier. New York seemed dreamlike and dangerous. How strange. He had been so pleased to have the opportunity to go there. Suddenly he felt tired. It *had* been a long day.

'I think I'll take your advice,' he said.

He so seldom took anyone's advice.

The man looked pleased: almost, Harding thought, like a preacher who had made an unexpected convert.

The official's eyes challenged him. To do what? It was at once clear.

'In that case, sir, allow me to retain your passport – and your boarding card, if you would, please. I'll send them through at once to 5322 so that your private cubicle can be made ready for you ...'

'Oh, but I don't wish to relinquish ...'

The man cut in reassuringly. 'Please don't worry, sir. I'll make sure there is no delay. I shall be with the boarding party myself. In fact, I'm taking the flight.'

'I've checked in a small suitcase for 5321 ...'

'I'll see that it's transferred.'

Harding wandered off. He felt distanced from reality. Airline and Home Office. Private enterprise and bureaucracy co-operating to sell flights. He shrugged. The world was full of unexpected associations. He thought of himself and Janine. And then he went to the duty-free area to buy some of her favourite, and wildly expensive, perfume.

He sat and dozed a little, ignoring the call for 5321. He certainly felt overwhelmingly tired. Sleep was the one thing he craved. Yet, somewhere in his mind, he was able to locate a peculiar sense of anticipation. Adventure even.

Ten minutes later 5322 was called.

'All passengers to Gate Five, please.'

He rode the moving causeway. Why was it always so slow? He hurried along it, as he usually did, impatiently.

Then, down the ramp. Plane door. Cabin crew. All smiles. So smart and welcoming. But the lights bothered him again. Why must they be so harsh? Like that wretched operating theatre he had glimpsed through the gauze of the pre-med injection. The group seemed blanched in the glare. To his blurred vision they looked remarkably like the doctors and nurses at the private hospital where he had spent some time last year.

Suddenly, terror struck.

Their smiles were all so ingratiating. Like those of his board. Were they laughing at him? My God, what had happened? Did the group, in fact, include his directors? He couldn't see. Had he been ousted in a board coup? Were they seeing him off – for ever? Did he hear Trubbing shouting? 'Go and stay with your whore in New York.'

He must get away and fight back. Phone for Charles and the car. Make for the office. Hole up there. They would never get him out of the chairman's room. That was *his* room. And they could keep their golden handshakes.

He turned and ran up the ramp to the moving stairway and stood unsteadily for a moment at the end.

Looking along the line of the advancing belt, he saw two women who seemed to float toward him. This could not be true. His wife *and* Janine? Talking to each other as if they had known each other for years.

Before he could focus his vision, the cabin crew were all around him. Airline uniforms. Concerned but reassuring smiles. So they weren't doctors and nurses after all. He had been hallucinating. His wife? Janine? He looked again. The moving walkway was empty. There was certainly no sign of his directors.

The kindly passport officer took him gently by the arm. The angelic girls soothed him.

Into 5322. Such comfort. Such luxury. Each cubicle totally private. A bunk bed that beckoned. Exuding peace. High-sided, narrow but comfortable. Silk sheets and pillow.

His fear diminished. The fear of all who hold power. Dread of the coup, the ultimate fall from power.

He undressed, donned the fresh night attire provided, and then into the bed which was absolutely the right width and length for him.

What a delight. No fear of falling here. It was almost as narrow as the passport defile. But it held him as closely and gently as if he were a child.

The passport officer appeared by his side, the public servant who controlled man's exits and his entrances.

'My passport?' Harding whispered drowsily.

'Take your rest, sir.'

'But at my destination ...'

'That's not a problem, sir. On this flight the journey itself validates your arrival.'

Jonathan Treitel

A BODY OF ONE'S OWN

The day is coming to an end: the electric light cannot be relied upon. Krishna, sprawled in his easy chair on the verandah, is studying Virginia Woolf's *A Room of One's Own*. Since he is wearing only a dhoti, the book, a small hardback in the Hogarth Press edition, stands neatly against one of his belly-corrugations. He taps a pencil on his teeth. He makes notes in the margin when he finds something to agree with, adding a grunt of, 'Very right,' and 'How true.'

A large crow jumps on to one of the electric ceiling fan's rotating blades, and journeys round on it like a child swinging on a rope. It caws. Krishna spits at the pest: it only caws the louder. He claps his broad palms together: useless. He searches for something to throw at it, but nothing suitable is at hand – apart from *A Room*, and it would be disrespectful to hurl that. What's more, his groin itches – as it always has and will; he jabs it with the pencil lead.

His long, hennaed thumb-nail presses down a corner of the current page. He lays the book on a low stool at his side. With some effort, panting, he staggers to his feet. The bird flaps away creakily. He sinks back into his chair and takes up his studies again. Straight away another disturbance arises: a Noel Coward song throbbing through the wall; he tries to ignore it. He reads: *The writer should possess both a male and female nature.* 'Yes, yes,' he hisses.

Just then the electric light ceases; the music deepens and cuts out; the fan swivels to a halt. Evidently another power cut. Well, there are too many mosquitoes at this hour to read comfortably anyway. He levers himself up, tucks Virginia Woolf under his armpit, and pads barefoot across the carpets and tiled or marbled floors into an interior chamber within the palace.

He bangs on a connecting door. He calls out in a high clear voice, 'Let me in! It is I, Krishna. I desire to complain instantly about your music-cum-racket!'

'No,' replies another, even higher voice. 'I forbid you to come in. I am exceedingly busy.'

Krishna pushes the door open notwithstanding. Arjuna – his friend and enemy of many decades – squats cross-legged on a rug, rubbing a fragrant ointment on his thighs and calves.

Krishna says, 'I wish to report my opposition to your infernal Noel Coward.'

'I like his voice,' says Arjuna. 'He sings of mad dogs and Englishmen.'

'I like his voice too,' says Krishna, 'but that is not the point. He is a disturbance whilst I am engaged in a programme of self-improvement. In days to come, please, will you play your Victrola with greater self-restraint?'

'That is not my intention.'

'Why do you not for instance follow my excellent example and read some improving food for thought in the uniform Everyman edition? For example, I will lend you Mr Robert Louis Stevenson's *Virginibus Puerisque* and Mr George Bernard Shaw's *The Thinking Woman's Guide to Socialism* and Mr Marx's *Capital*. Also fiction I do not pooh-pooh. Such as Mr E.M. Forster's *A Passage to India*.' Krishna leans over Arjuna's oiled locks and whispers, 'They say it is based on a true story.'

'No, thank you.'

Krishna sits facing Arjuna. He opens his volume at the dog-eared page.

'Mrs Virginia Woolf writes many sensible remarks. I will summarize her gist. She states that a writer must not be limited by his or her sex, but must aspire to rise above such confinement.'

'In that case, you and I are the very best writers!'

'Yes, yes!'

The two men titter and rock on their hips.

'Also, she states it is very important to have money and a room of one's own. She supplies as an example her visit to two colleges in Oxford-or-Cambridge. In the first, there are men who are rich and write good books and eat fine food with sauces. In the second, only poor women who write bad books and eat bad beef.'

Arjuna thinks for a while. Then he murmurs, 'Yes, eating a holy meat is very improper.'

Krishna whispers, 'Have you ever eaten beef, Arjuna? Is it nasty? Is it tasty? Is it not unpleasant?'

Arjuna shakes his head.

Krishna shakes his head also.

Arjuna says, 'But ... sometimes ... I wonder ...'

It is turning darker. Fireflies drift in and out past the iron window bars, glinting in the heavy warm evening air. Arjuna slaps a mosquito on Krishna's left breast – a tear-shaped stain appears below the nipple. Krishna takes a match from a Shiva Wood Products Company box, strikes it, and watches the flame jerk into brightness; he inhales the acrid fumes. He lights an oil lamp; he adjusts the wick. With the same match he ignites some floral incense in a silver lotus-shaped burner.

Arjuna lends Krishna a jar of his pungent ointment. 'You may borrow my embrocation. For keeping the skin smooth. Also rash. Also mosquitoes.'

'Why not follow my example and sprinkle baby powder on your privates and belly creases? It is most comforting.'

'Ah, nothing is comforting.'

'Very right,' says Krishna. 'How true.'

Arjuna removes the *Times of India* from under a scarlet satin-covered pillow. He waves the front page at his comrade. He recites the headlines with a mournful glee. '*Thousands dead in disturbances in Bengal. Lakhs dead in disturbances in Punjab …*'

As the sun sets and a cloud of insects seeps into the room, Arjuna swats them on his own and the other's skin with the rolled-up newspaper, following a complex rhythm, while Krishna murmurs, 'Sad,' and 'How sad,' – a kind of raga.

'Are there disturbances near here?' Krishna asks.

'I do not know. The electricity has stopped. Perhaps they killed the power station workers in the town again?'

'Sad. How sad.'

'Yes, sad … Also in the newspaper on page five, Mr Nehru says the maharajahs will have no money after Independence. Only a little pension.'

'That is very right. The maharajah is a parasite.'

'Sad.'

'He is a mosquito. He is a feudal exploiter who steals our surplus value. He must have no money only a little pension.'

'But how will he pay us?'

'He will not pay us. We will suffer.'

'Very sad.'

'Very sad, also very right,' says Krishna. 'We are parasites also.'

Silence. They stare at the pool of light around the oil lamp. The mingled odours of embrocation and sweet and incense rise and fill their heads. Thoughts spiral and swim.

Krishna says, 'I am glad the maharajah is not here. Are you glad?'

'He is in London.'

'He is in Claridge's. He has many girls and many boys. He has dance bands. He has light music on the wireless. He eats fine foods with rich sauces.'

'He eats bad beef,' says Arjuna.

'When he is here, you must make music for him, and I must recite poetry for him. Now, we do nothing.'

'Nothing.'

'Now I will show you my new secret,' says Krishna. He displays the flyleaf of *A Room of One's Own*; he cranes it close to the lamp so Arjuna can read it.

In blurry black indelible ink, in English and Hindi:

STEALING IS WICKED
O thief! you will be punished

'I have stamped it with my special new stamp,' says Krishna. 'We must stamp it on everything. There are many bad men in the palace.'

'Are we bad men?' asks Arjuna.

'We are bad,' says Krishna. 'But we are not men!'

'No, no!' says Arjuna.

'Yes, yes!' says Krishna.

They giggle on a high note. They sway from side to side. Their elbows bump.

Then they rise by leaning against each other and staggering upright. They achieve an equilibrium by pressing their palms against the other's breasts, balanced like an A-frame. They separate, breathing out heavily.

Next, Krishna takes a rubber stamp and an ink pad from the folds of his dhoti. The two men waddle around the room arm in arm, co-operating. Krishna rubs the stamp on the pad: Arjuna presses it against assorted items – transferring the inky moral on to the *Times of India*, the underside of a saffron-coloured pillow, a marble column, a stray dog, a rice pudding, the incense burner, a cream silk parasol, both their paunches, the match box ... They are tittering all the while and whistling through their gold teeth.

Afterwards, exhausted, they slump on to cushions in a shadowy alcove. They eat fried rice balls soaked in scented syrup. They clean their fingers by padding them in a bowl of rosewater. They pour each other tea from an urn.

'Ah, we are wicked,' says Arjuna.

'Yes, wicked,' says Krishna. 'But you are more wicked than I.'

'No, no,' says Arjuna. 'We are both as wicked as each other. We have been wicked in a past life. That is why we are here.'

'I do not believe in reincarnation.'

'Then you are wicked. In your next life you will be a tiny suffering creature.'

'A mosquito?' says Krishna, killing one.

'No. A worm. A worm has both sexes, I think. Or a worm has no sex. It crawls through the earth.'

'Ah, already I am a worm ... But Mrs Virginia Woolf writes that it is important to be not bitter. She states if you are bitter you will make bad art. It will destroy you.'

'Yes, sad.'

Krishna touches Arjuna's wrist. 'Sometimes, I think, if we had not been ...?'

'Many times I have seen a dog and bitch do it.'

'You throw water on them, but they are stuck and cannot separate.'

'Such exquisite suffering!'

Krishna starts singing, in his fine contralto – and Arjuna soon joins in, in his finer soprano – the opening bars of '*Pale hands I loved beside the Shalimar, where are you now, who lies beneath your spell? ...*' Then Arjuna wails the last few syllables and notes, repeating them, altering them, rearranging them in some slow, intricate song of his own. Krishna slaps his palms on his paunch, constructing a percussive accompaniment – but 'accompaniment' is not the exact word – for the two men's songs are like the dances of two dancers in one small space, each moving separately but never colliding, never mimicking one another, yet always aware of the other's presence.

Afterwards there is silence: the music continues in their heads.

And then their thoughts dance ... and eventually return to where the conversation left off.

'But if I had not been cut,' says Krishna, 'I would have died. My parents were very poor and had no money to feed me.'

'My parents also.'

'So we must be very glad.'

'Yes?'

'Yes, sad.'

'Yes.'

'Arjuna?'

'Yes?'

'I will show you my secret.'

'Which secret?'

'This is my number one secret. I have been working on it for many years.'

Krishna rises again. He makes his way, using his sense of touch and memory, through the darkened corridors and antechambers. Every inch of the way is familiar to his palms and soles: each roughness of the wall; each transition from carpet to carpet to tiled or stone floor to carpet; each shard of moonlight ... It is as if he were stepping through the labyrinth of his personal history.

He arrives in his own moonlit room.

A tiny steel key is strapped around his crotch, recessed among the loose itchy skin and the scar tissue. He detaches it. He unlocks a brass-bound sandalwood chest. He lifts a pile of yellowing papers. Holding this in both arms, tottering under the burden, he retraces his path.

He sits down again beside Arjuna. He deposits the manuscript between them.

'It is my novel,' says Krishna. 'It is entitled *Less Than the Dust Beneath Thy Chariot Wheels.*'

'Is it a good novel?'

'Of course, no. It is a bad novel. I have a room of one's own but I have bitterness in my heart so I cannot write a good novel. Mrs Virginia Woolf has explained my tragedy.'

'Is it a story of love?'

'It is a story of love. Lord George London, a British aristocrat, falls in love with Parvati, a dusky maiden. Part One is set in India. The lord meets the maiden in a rose garden. They exchange a few words and Cupid's dart pierces their twin hearts. Part Two is on a P & O liner steaming to England. Parvati almost drowns in a storm, but Lord George saves her. Passion flashes in their eyes. Part Three is on the lord's craggy estate in Scotland. I think I will read that for you?'

'It is too dark to read.'

'I know everything by heart.'

Krishna begins to recite, in a high chant:

'*Lord George's hunting dogs scampered through the heather, bringing their tribute of snipe, grouse and ptarmigan to their master. He bade them lay the feathered corpses at the feet of the fair Parvati. How noble and majestic she stood, 'midst the bracken and the howling winds. "At last," he exclaimed, "we are alone together! How many days, how many years, I have pined for this hour with thee!" "Oh," she moaned like a dove, "likewise I have felt a passion stir within my heart. Many times blessed this hour shall be!" Lord George ripped asunder her tartan blouse and laid his trembling lips upon her creamy bosom –*'

Arjuna interrupts. 'That is not right.'

'It is my novel,' says Krishna.

'If she is a dusky maiden she cannot have a creamy bosom. Cream is not dusky.'

Krishna grins triumphantly. 'She is a devotee of the sunbathing fad. She bronzes herself in a bathing costume. It is all the rage among the fashionable set. Naturally her limbs and face are dusky, while her breasts and private skin remain creamy.'

'I think it is not good.'

'Yes, it is bad!' Krishna cries. 'My novel is very very bad! The wicked Lord George stole the fair Parvati's body.'

He stamps on the front of the manuscript:

STEALING IS WICKED
O thief! you will be punished

'Also it is impossible,' says Arjuna.

'It is true.'

'Lord George must love a British lady,' says Arjuna. 'He will not like an Indian dusky maiden.'

'It is true,' says Krishna. 'It is the true story of Mr Jackson, an employee of Crowmarsh and Turnbull, Electrical Supply Contractors. He has a white moustache and thin red hair and walks with a cane. He came to the palace in '23 to install the electricity for the maharajah. He called me his juicy capon.'

'He must love Mrs Jackson.'

'Mr Jackson does not like woman or boy. He only likes us. He says we have beautiful soft skin, and smooth convexities, and no body hair, and our smell is fragrant. He has travelled across India installing electrical supply, and there are so few of us for him to adore. I was young then and he worshipped the ground I stood upon.'

'Did you like him?'

'The maharajah sent him away because he cheated his expense account. Perhaps that is why the electricity in the palace is so bad. Every time it fails, I think of Mr Jackson. It is sad.'

'We are wicked.'

Suddenly the electric light shines again; the ceiling fan spins; once more the gramophone plays Noel Coward. Soon, though, the needle sticks in a groove. Krishna and Arjuna sit side by side, listening to the repeated chord: a kind of sob. They slap mosquitoes on their skin. Eventually, after minutes or hours, the electricity ceases again. They are in the near-dark, in the near-silence. They stay there for a long stretch, while time passes and history takes place.

Krishna sighs. 'We are among the last of our kind. Soon we will perish, and poor Mr Jackson will search and search, and find no one to love in the whole of India.'

Max von der Grün

THE MEMBER OF
THE WORKS COUNCIL

People in the town knew about the accident even before the first pitmen from the night shift went home at around seven o'clock in the morning. It had occurred just on three o'clock, about four hours earlier, on the fifth floor in the fifth eastern section of the Sonnenschein seam; the pit props had collapsed at the end of the twenty-metre slope. Eight men were trapped inside. Five were rescued after three hours, injured but in good spirits. It took longer to rescue the other three, but finally towards eleven o'clock in the morning they also were found — dead.

Not much else had happened. An accident — five saved, three dead. It was not thought to be too serious. In the evening the people in the town who were involved and those who were shocked talked about it. Radio and television reported the accident. The general view was that there was no reason to upset oneself just because three men had died in an accident. So much was happening in the world every day — whole countries were shaken by earthquakes, towns collapsed, rivers overflowed their banks, mountains spat fire and sulphur; why get excited about three men who, after all, were just victims of their job?

In the Ruhr area one gets used to such things; they are part of everyday life, like the coal dust.

Twelve o'clock.

The dead men had been brought up from the pit. At the office the works management and the works council had met to discuss the urgent question of whose turn it was to inform the families concerned. That had always been a duty which neither friends nor superiors liked to undertake. It meant having to witness the first outbursts of grief and pain and stand there like a criminal unable to offer real consolation; but someone had to be the one to bring shock and terror into a home which had hitherto been blessed with happiness. There were volunteers for two of the visits, but nobody was prepared to undertake the third one because of the family's tragic history. It had already lost two sons in fatal accidents within three years, and now the last, a miner aged twenty-one, was lying in the mortuary.

The painful silence was finally broken by a member of the works council, Brinkhoff, who said: 'I shall go.'

He spoke firmly, though his voice was husky, while he looked at the mask-like faces of his colleagues, hoping that perhaps one of them might offer at the last moment to take this chore off his own back. But the other seven faces showed only relief that someone had been found, and that it would not be necessary to draw lots, as had often happened on similar occasions during the last few years.

A cowardly lot, these people, Brinkhoff thought, big-mouthed where ordinary small matters are concerned, but not when a few words of sympathy are needed. Never mind, I've agreed to go, but whatever happens I mustn't miss the football match on television this afternoon.

The Haugk family, whom Brinkhoff had to visit, lived in one of several housing estates on the outskirts of the town. Father Haugk had been an invalid for about ten years, suffering from a lung disease caused by coal dust. He was working in his front garden, and Brinkhoff noticed that he paused occasionally, lowering his rake while straightening himself up. He then shaded his eyes and looked down the street, the street along which Brinkhoff had approached the house.

The member of the works council stopped at the garden gate and said, 'Good-day, Wilhelm. Don't overdo things, leave a bit for another day. It's a nice day -- about time too.' He spoke slowly and with a certain detachment.

My God, he thought, the old man's lucky. He's his own boss and can do as he likes. Whatever happens, I mustn't miss the football match.

'Ah,' said Haugk, 'it's you, Fritz. Good-day. The weeds are growing so fast that I have to do a little bit of work every day to stop them taking over the flowers completely.'

I mustn't miss the match, Brinkhoff thought. Will Uwe be playing today?

'Are you waiting for someone?' he asked.

'Waiting? Yes, my boy hasn't arrived yet. He was on the night shift, and now it's nearly two o'clock. Perhaps he's doing a double shift again, the silly lad. You know, he's got such a sweet girlfriend, and he's set on buying himself a motor bike. You know how it is these days, young people want to get about and they're not interested in the garden. But all this overtime, he doesn't need to do it. I eke out his wages a bit with my pension.'

'Yes, yes,' said Brinkhoff, thinking that in an hour's time the match would start on television.

'But these young people always want to have things their own way,' old Haugk went on, showing his disapproval.

'What sort of bike does he want to buy?' asked Brinkhoff. A motor bike, he thought, what stupidity! Who buys a bike these days? Four wheels are four wheels, and then there's a roof over one's head. I wonder whether Uwe's playing.

'Don't ask me about that bike, Fritz, I don't know much about it. I think it may be an Italian one. I tell you, in the evenings he and his girlfriend are engrossed in catalogues and prospectuses. The shed used to be over there before he built himself a garage, a very nice one, I must admit. He even papered the walls with the bits of paper that were left over from a previous job. It looks rather bitty, but quite nice. These young people do have their own ideas.' But Haugk smiled and seemed pleased.

If we go on chatting like this I shall miss the match, Brinkhoff thought, but out loud he said, 'Yes, yes. When's he going to get this rattle-box? Is it expensive?'

'Next week,' the old man said. 'I'm looking forward to it, because he's going to take me to the pigeon show on it. But you mustn't call it a rattle-box, because he told me that the engine's quieter than any other on the market.'

My God, thought Brinkhoff, how can he go on like this, when everyone round him knows what's happened, though nobody's told him. And so it has to be me, as I volunteered to do it. What a nuisance! Will Uwe be playing today?

'What are you actually doing in this part of the town?' old Haugk suddenly asked. 'Do you want to buy some pigeons?'

Brinkhoff looked at his watch. If we go on like this I shan't be home in time to watch the match.

'Are you on leave?' the old man asked.

'No, Wilhelm, I had mine in March, so as to get some jobs done at home. That's why I took my leave then.'

'Of course, Fritz, it does help to get jobs out of the way. I did things like that myself in my younger days. But now I've got time on my hands, lots of time ...'

Yes, Brinkhoff thought, time to be an invalid.

'I tell you, there are lots of things one can do all day long. No more rushing around, no bullying, none of that "Go on, a bit quicker, come on, don't pretend you're tired." Although I'm done for now, really – my lungs are slowing down. I can tell you, I'm already frightened of the fogs starting. They always affect my throat badly. So we don't really benefit from our pensions. We've had it and are worn out once we reach a certain age. Still, what can we do about it? That's life.'

'We're all workers, after all,' said Brinkhoff, thinking to himself that those who drive others on aren't always at fault; those who are driven by them also bear a certain responsibility.

'Niggemeier's selling his entire pigeon-loft, he's moving into the centre of the town. You know, his wife's inherited her uncle's house, and that's where they're going to live. But he won't be able to keep pigeons there, so if you want to buy some at a favourable price I can recommend them. They're good flyers, he's won a lot of prizes. He's not a cut-throat either, old Niggemeier.'

'What's he asking for his pigeons?' Brinkhoff asked. If I go on like this I shall miss the match.

'If you want me to I'll talk to him about it. Or I can take you there straight away, he lives quite near here. But only if you want to come and if you've got time.'

'No, Wilhelm,' Brinkhoff said hastily. 'I've got to make one of those visits — you know what I mean.'

'For heaven's sake, Fritz, has something happened at the pit?' Old Haugk looked at Brinkhoff in alarm.

Oh, Lord, Brinkhoff thought, he knows nothing about it, though a hundred people in this neighbourhood already know that his son has been killed. How cowardly of them not to have told him!

'Yes, Wilhelm, the Sonnenschein seam, in the fifth eastern section. You must remember the place.'

'What, the Sonnenschein? The fifth eastern? Well, well. It always had some dangerous rock. In my time there was trouble every week. It was a devilish situation — however firmly you built, it came down again. And they didn't close the damned seam because it contained the best and the cheapest coal, so why worry about a few deaths or a few accidents? The main thing was that there was cheap coal and lots of it. That's always been their policy and it'll go on being like that. We can't change things. Thank God I'm not involved with that gang any longer.'

Haugk looked up at a pair of buzzards. 'That's nice,' he said. 'I've been watching them for some days now. It must be interesting to propose marriage up there.'

The papers say that it's not certain that Uwe will play, as an old injury's been giving him trouble, Brinkhoff thought.

'What did you say?' the old man suddenly shouted. 'The fifth eastern? But ... but ... my boy's been working there. You! Fritz! What's happened?'

His boy was an excellent outside left. If he'd come into the right hands, who knows, he might have been considered first-division material. I could have been sitting in front of the television now if I hadn't volunteered for all this.

'There were eight men under the breakage point, Wilhelm,' said the member of the works council, still watching the pair of buzzards. Like two wingers, he said to himself, without Haugk hearing him. 'Yes, there were eight men under the breakage point. We were able to rescue five of them, but three were trapped. You know what I mean.'

Old Haugk lit his pipe. There was no tobacco in it. He went on striking match after match until the ground was covered with them, looking like a discarded set of spillikins. Again he looked down the road along which Brinkhoff had come.

'Three were trapped, you said, three. Three! Fritz! Why three? So that's why my boy hasn't come home. Yes, that's how it is.' After a moment of oppressive silence Haugk laughed. 'So that's the story, Fritz. You wanted to tell me about it straight away, that's what you meant to do. And I, like an idiot, thought you were interested in buying some pigeons from Niggemeier, who's selling his whole loft.'

The pair of buzzards were still flying around in circles, but old Haugk looked at the matches on the ground in front of him. 'Well, well,' he said. 'Sonnenschein always had a bad lot of rocks, brittle as a shortcake.'

Has he taken it in by now? The match is just about to start. Will Uwe be playing?

'Three were trapped, you said . . . But why three? Why not two . . . or one . . . or nobody at all?' He suddenly shouted, 'Why not nobody? Why? Why, Fritz, why? Why don't these gentlemen realize that a man's life is worth more than a ton of coal? Well, isn't that true, isn't that true?'

My God, how right the old man is, Brinkhoff thought, how right! But what can be done about it? Should we do away with work altogether?

Haugk looked at the house, and saw his wife come to the door and look up and down the road without taking any notice of the two men at the garden gate. Down the road the first pitmen from the early shift could be seen hurrying along, some of them actually trotting. They want to get home in time to watch television, Brinkhoff thought.

'But Fritz, how can I tell my wife about it? How, how?' the old man asked in despair. 'I'm very grateful to you for coming here, Fritz. But how can I tell her what's happened, how?'

'I'll go and tell her,' Brinkhoff said. Am I mad? Oh, my God, what can I do? Perhaps he'll want me to inform all the relatives as well. The match has already started by now.

Old Haugk took a pair of shears and walked towards a very tall larkspur bush. Brinkhoff waited until the wife had gone into the house, then he followed her. There was a smell of baked fish in the hall, and he could hear the woman lifting and arranging saucepans. He stayed in the hall for some time, breathing heavily while he began to count the buttons on his jacket like a child: should I, shouldn't I, should I? Then he hastily opened the door, which was ajar. The woman seemed surprised to see a stranger instead of her husband or her son.

'Yes?' she said. 'Are you looking for my husband? He's in the garden ... but weren't you talking to him just now?'

Now I must tell her, he thought. Quickly, so that I shall soon have done with it. Quickly, quickly.

He said nothing. He wanted to go towards the woman, but instead he stayed in the doorway, turning his hat in his hand ... always just the hat in his hand. He saw the woman's eyes becoming larger and larger. Then she collapsed into a chair, crying, 'No! No, no, no! It isn't true!'

Brinkhoff turned and quickly ran out of the house. The old man was cutting long blue stems from the larkspur bush. He said to Brinkhoff, 'My sister-in-law's coming, she should be here by now. She wants to collect the flowers and my spade. She's got a fur coat but she hasn't got a spade.'

'You can go inside now!' Brinkhoff shouted as he ran away.

'Yes, Fritz, yes ... Such a nice girl he's got, such a ...' The pair of buzzards had disappeared.

When Brinkhoff, member of the works council, stood in the street again he was wet with perspiration. His shirt was clinging to his body, and drops of sweat were dripping from his eyebrows. He walked slowly down the street. There was nobody about. The housing estate was quite isolated, and at the end of it, which was also the end of the street, Brinkhoff sat down on the dusty grass, mopping his face.

My God, the people that exist! What kind of people are they, who sit in front of their television sets staring at a ball? What kind of people are they really, who watch and shout until they're hoarse? And I ...?

I wonder whether Uwe's been selected to play.

Translated by Helen Hobday

Per Wastberg

THE GIRL AT THE YELLOW GUEST-HOUSE

Summer arrives tentatively, rather like a visitor testing out cold water. But lakes warm up more quickly than the sea; soon July would be here, the plant life shrinking beneath the thickening foliage of the tree-tops surrounding the yellow guest-house.

Before the heather has bloomed in the crevices and the dragon-fly starts circling like a helicopter above the quaking-grass, Johan Fredrik has said to himself, but to no one else, 'I'm in love.'

But what can he do about it? He is sixteen and she is twenty-four and a student; her parents are coming later.

At meals, he watches her all the time as he eats his crunchy crispbread and honey from the National Beekeepers' Association, the way she breaks a sugar-lump in half for her tea, the way she folds her table napkin and threads it into a worn nickel ring, the way she brushes the crumbs off her dress as she gets up from the table.

She turns to him once or twice during each meal. She knows he is there and does not mind. She plays tennis with an older man. Johan Fredrik walks past and sees her white shorts and bare legs and he has learnt to catch the sound of her sandals from far away. One rainy day she hears him laugh as he stands in front of the guest-house bookcase.

'What's so funny?' she says.

He reads out aloud to her from an old handbook or manual, a piece about how to stiffen hats and soften corsets. It is a period in his life when most things seem silly if that's the way he wants to see them. They start talking to each other. He is attracted by her voice and surprised at the breadth of her knowledge.

At her suggestion, they cycle to a nearby prehistoric fort. They take jerseys rolled up on their carriers with them, then use them as pillows when drinking apple juice on a grassy slope.

She tells him about the late Iron Age, the way people had constantly to defend themselves. People were threatened then just as they are now and part of life went to collecting large stones as protection against other people. It's terrible that you aren't free, you can't go where you want to, step over boundaries. The war has been over for several years, but Europe is still in ruins.

She wants to be an archaeologist. The present and the future, events still obscure and incomplete, do not attract her. The past is definite, anchored in time. What has happened has happened and what remains to be done is to observe and interpret it.

They pick some wild strawberries, the berries of the moment, impossible to be economical with. Large white butterflies chase each other. A flycatcher takes one of them, her chick appearing and sharing a wing. The tops of the firs bend with the weight of cones.

'This is bracken,' she says. 'The kind that grows only on burnt ground. It's very hardy once it's taken root. These have probably grown in the ash left behind from camp-fires when people gathered here in the fort.'

They come across something amazing by the tumbledown wall, a roebuck fast asleep under a tree. They have approached quite soundlessly, into the wind. Its long lips move in its sleep, grazing in its dreams. They slowly turn back.

'He didn't see us,' she whispers. 'Or else he thinks we're a couple of animals.'

He meets her eyes in smiling complicity. He thinks magnetic threads are running between them. His night fantasies that leave such clear round contours on the sheet are never about her. They're nothing but the musty dripping of the body's kitchen tap. But when he looks at her for a long time, his heart thumps wildly, an impatient horse kicking in its stall.

He feels agitation and joy, emotions rushing through him like clouds. He is overflowing with sweetness and pain, his life out of control. He wants to taste her, touch her with his hunger, to let himself go, but he has nothing with which to let go. He wants to tell her everything in detail — everything, but what in particular?

He wants her to penetrate right into him and listen to every thought in his head, and at the same time, he himself wants to be someone quite different, someone she could like more easily.

He is seized with indecision. Does he love her or does he love his feeling for her? Which can he most easily do without? But he is mostly serious and definite. He wants to reach her, if only just to be hurt and bleed.

He doesn't dare say much; they sit in silence, the words in becalmed expectation.

'What shall we do now?' she says rather maternally, as if prepared to amuse him with anything.

'Undo your plaits for me,' he says.

She laughs. 'Don't be silly. Why should I do that?'

'I'd like to see you with your hair down,' he intones.

She smiles questioningly, gazing at him, then hesitantly starts undoing her brown hair, which soon falls round her shoulders like a shawl.

'There you are, nothing special about that,' she says in a matter-of-fact voice, though she does seem slightly uneasy. He examines her thoughtfully.

'Good,' he says. 'Now I know that.'

She looks changed. Something has happened which neither of them has words for. Her eyes are as light as icy water, cloud-grey, difficult to decide, though clear.

As they cycle homewards, they are both a trifle embarrassed, and at the breakfast table next morning, they simply nod to each other. He thinks that what she has done for him is indiscreet and a greater sacrifice than any girl could have made.

A few days later he gives her a badge with the local coat-of-arms on it and she pins it on to her blouse.

'Thanks,' she says. 'But you shouldn't have.'

This pleases him. She realizes he has meant more than the actual badge. He wants to be the pin which happens to scratch her breast.

They're walking under the trees in the guest-house park. It's a Saturday night. They are about the same height, he a shade shorter. She has light brown sandals and his are dark brown. He tells her about a terrible memory from the Christmas holidays.

The family had a lone goldfish in a bowl. A little pine-needle fell off the Christmas tree and the fish swallowed it. He saw it wedged sideways inside its transparent body. There was nothing he could do. In torment and horror, he tipped the fish over the edge of the bowl down to its death on the floor.

'I don't believe you,' she says. 'Why are you telling me this?'

He hardly understands himself. He is pierced right through with agonizing excitement emanating from her, and he feels he's about to explode. But he doesn't answer her question, instead putting his arm round her waist as if to comfort her and draw her closer, amazed at his own daring.

His courage is a result of his helpless devotion. Someone is trying to break out from within him, alternately jubilant and painfully strange, glimpsed like a felled branch beneath the surface of the water. He can't cope with whatever it is growing and possessing him.

They're down by the shore and he tells her they will hear the drowned young man crying, 'Find me! Find me!' from the dead, and his desolate cries will be drowned by dance music from the guest-house gramophone just as the darkness swallows his face and hair. Johan Fredrik expresses himself poetically and she shudders in the same way as Ingrid had done the summer before, but she doesn't seize his hand.

The lake water is brown and yet transparent. He looks at her strong wrists. Shall they go out in the rowing-boat with its creaking oarlocks and knobbly seat?

'The boat hasn't been bailed out,' she says. 'And there's an offshore wind.'

'The lake's full of people who've drowned. The earth's full of dead people we're trampling on. That's what it's like,' he says.

'No, I don't want to. Maybe that boy thought there was something on the bottom, a charred house, a wreck, someone caught in the alder roots by her plaits. Maybe there was something he simply had to go down and see.'

'Why do you think that?' he said in surprise.

'It doesn't sound so horrible when I say it as when you do. And you were going to say it.'

It's true. He feels a hot wave of despair and a desire for action. Perhaps he really loves her. Perhaps he will never love anyone else, and other girls will approach him with interest, with some idea of what they have missed, dreaming of competing with the unknown picture in his inner self and nevertheless knowing it was all in vain. And he would enter into nothing but friendship and trust, as was fitting for a lifelong widower.

'You don't know me at all,' she says.

'I'd like to get to know you. I want to know everything about you.'

'No,' she replies sorrowfully. 'That wouldn't be a good thing. It's best like this. I'm leaving, anyhow.'

He looks deep into her eyes to see if it is written there: you're still only a child. But it isn't. Then he's happy in all his misery over her departure. He convinces himself she is also tormented with the pain of keeping him at a distance, that she'll move close to him in divided tenderness. Then he feels a happiness as solid as hard-baked scones straight from the oven.

But when she says good-night later on and goes upstairs to her room next to her parents', she leaves him in darkness.

On her last night at the guest-house, with the help of gym shoes, a drainpipe and the trellis, Johan Fredrik climbs in through the open window of her room. He can hear his ankle joints cracking like branches in a tree. His boldness makes him feel quite dizzy.

He is shaking with excitement, quite literally beside himself, another person carrying out what a voice tells him to do. He will never see her again. She will probably never return to the yellow guest-house, and next time he won't be the same, either. He has an obscure inkling of this, so he's not responsible for what he's doing now. So everything is permitted.

This warm night is a luxury. If he doesn't make use of it, a birthmark will be scorched into his back by sunrise.

She notices nothing. She's asleep on her back, naked with the sheet half-way up her breast. He squats down by the bedside table so that his head is level with her closed eyes, and he remembers the roebuck in the woods.

Slowly, he turns back the blanket. Her nipples are pale blotches running into her skin. He holds his breath, bends down and kisses them very lightly.

A lesson from an older friend swirls round in his head: if you want a woman to give in, you must touch her erogenous zones as soon as possible.

But even deeper down there is something much more complicated, much harder to grasp: if people touch each other in earnest, do they then flare up like lighting a fire?

He doesn't want to conquer her. Lips to breast is more than enough. He breathes deeply as if he had been swimming underwater for a long time, two hammers banging behind her ears, his ribs contracting into a grid, and he feels he is about to suffocate. To his surprise, he notices her nipples have shrunk into small rough mushrooms.

She wakes up and looks absently at him for a long while.

'It's me,' he whispers, trying to smile despite the gravity of the occasion. 'Ssh, so no one hears us.'

Startled, she suddenly cries out.

'Good heavens, I thought you were Papa!'

At that moment her father knocks on the wall from the next room.

'Are you all right?' he shouts.

'I had a nightmare,' she says, looking straight into the boy's eyes.

'I only wanted to see you, nothing else,' says Johan Fredrik. 'Before you leave.'

He presses against her and kisses her on the cheek. She resists him.

'I can't understand you,' she says. 'Why couldn't you wait until tomorrow? Do you have to play at burglars? How can you behave like this? You frightened me.'

'I couldn't sleep. I couldn't stop myself,' he says.

She is not flattered, only hurt that he doesn't respect her. He wants to say, Please don't look at me with that stranger's clear gaze, sending me into exile. But the invocations which would transform what she is within him are incapable of rising to the surface.

The wind rustles the leaves in the elm trees outside the guest-house. Pity there's no thunder, he thinks. The half-moon is flying through ragged clouds like a car's headlights appearing on corners, then disappearing again. For a moment he stands with his back to her, uncertain whether he dares turn round again.

She's more awake now and, propping herself up on her elbow, smiles forgivingly. She is no longer trying to hide her breasts nor does she seem frightened.

'Johan Fredrik,' she whispers, for once actually using his name. 'Sit down here!'

She grasps his arm firmly and runs his hand rather like a shower-head over her shoulders and breasts. Then her strong slim fingers close in on the trouser material round his penis and press it down between his thighs.

He is half-lying immobile beside her, in brief ecstasy and terror of the unexpected thing that's happening. He's hardly breathing and he swallows the darkness so that it grows light around her.

'There you are,' she says, having taken over command. 'That'll have to do. We can't do anything more. 'Bye, then. And listen, that badge you gave me, please take it back, will you? I don't want any memories. I'm no good at that.'

He has the badge on as he clambers out of the window and over to the annexe where he is sleeping. She watches as his face disappears below the window-sill. He looks as if he's drowning.

It's semi-light outside, still August and a heat wave, with aromas from a stuffy kitchen. Far away the level-crossing bells sound from the main railway line; a train will be in Stockholm by the morning.

Has he made her unhappy? He has felt her skin against his tongue, like licking snow. With hindsight he doesn't know if he could have desisted. His longing was a skeleton key which opened her against her will. She has held him in that playful way which was the only way possible between them. But now he has seen her so close to, his desire seems quieted and melancholy, as if it could never reach another person.

He stands alone down by the lake, watching the light coming up between the trees in the park. Beyond the island where people go on excursions, the horizon of the forest is still black. The water along the shore is moving, bubbling below the alders, the current tearing at the roots as if on old moorings. He will bury the badge with Söderman-land's coat-of-arms on it beneath the old fort after she has gone. She's almost an archaeologist and will occupy herself with what is finished, not with what is going on. She, or someone else like her, will find it when everything is over.

He throws off his clothes and dives in, swimming through the green twilight, the water pressing against his eyeballs. He makes his way under arches of dim, blurred roots, the framework of alders and willows forming a basket, and he weaving his way through its osiers.

He rises to the surface treading water and breathing in and out to supply his lungs with oxygen, then again letting himself sink down into this bare, gnarled forest. He is stopped by a dark triangle, like a door into a low chapel. Then he senses in there the young man who had drowned – or if it is not him, just a shape representing a human being, a phantom caught in the basketwork, the water moving his hair like sea-grass from an underwater rock.

He daren't go near enough, imagining the creature holding up a hand to say, 'Ssh! Don't betray me!'

The water is grainy with rotting plants, his visibility obscured, making him unsure of what he has seen. He feels a strange mixture of terror and relief as he rises to the surface. Then he lies stretched out, spluttering like an otter among the wild chervil and foxgloves on the shore.

His head is thumping, his ears singing of water as in a shell. He peers up through the willow branches in the not yet light morning sky arching over him like a huge petticoat, and he can just make out tempting, indefinite contours.

There was something else I wanted for you, he says to the girl who is not listening. If you'd wanted to come with me down into the water, maybe you would have understood.

But she has gone, and neither will be returning.

In time, the house he had climbed into at night becomes an institution at which immigrants learn the Swedish language and how to adjust, and over the years, chalet villages, caravans, elaborate tents and Eurorail travel put an end to what had been the yellow guest-house's way of life.

Translated by Joan Tate

NOTES ON CONTRIBUTORS

HANAN AL-SHAYKH was brought up in Beirut and studied in Cairo. She worked as a journalist in the Lebanon, but now lives in London. Two of her novels have been published in English. She teaches modern Arab literature part-time at St Andrew's University.

MELVIN BURGESS lives in Lancashire with the dancer Avis von Herder and their eight-year-old son. He has had a play performed by the BBC. His first novel for children, *The cry of the wolf*, was short-listed for the Carnegie Medal in 1991.

D.A. CALLARD is a literary biographer, mainly interested in obscure or enigmatic subjects. His biography of Evelyn Scott was published by Cape in 1985; he is currently at work on a life of Rhys Davies.

FRANCIS DOWNES was born in Limerick in 1952, and educated in Liverpool and Edinburgh. After working in the West Indies for some time, he now lives in Liverpool.

CIARÁN FOLAN was born in Co. Longford. He has had stories in *New Irish Writing*, and he won RTE's Francis MacManus Short Story Award in 1987. 'The lights of a town in the distance' will be included in a forthcoming Blackstaff Press anthology.

SHAMMAI GOLAN was born in Poland in 1933, and grew up under the Nazi occupation and in Soviet Russia before reaching Palestine in 1947. He was educated at the Hebrew University in Jerusalem. A prize-winning novelist and short story-writer, he is Chairman of the Hebrew Writers' Association.

BRYN GUNNELL taught at an Indian university, and is now a lecturer at the British Institute in Paris. His books include *Calabrian summer* and *The cashew-nut girl and Other stories*.

KENNETH HARVEY describes himself as 'a twenty-seven year-old translator of sensory perception, concerned with the feel of words beneath the skin'. He lives in Newfoundland.

CLYDE HOSEIN was born in Trinidad in 1940. After a spell in London he returned to Trinidad, where he worked with Radio Trinidad and as a journalist. The author of *The killing of Sister John*, he now lives in Canada.

ALMA HROMIĆ was born in Yugoslavia, but came to Africa at the age of ten. She works at the University of Cape Town's Medical School; her stories have been published in South Africa and elsewhere, and she reviews for the Cape Town *Argus*.

MARK ILLIS's novels include *A Chinese summer* and *The alchemist*, published by Bloomsbury.

JEFF KEEFE is twenty-three, and lives in Bow.

SHERIDAN KEITH lives in New Zealand and is well-known for her writings on photography. Several of her stories have been published in the *London Magazine*.

DAVID KENNEDY lives in Cheltenham. He is married with two children.

FRANCIS KING was born and spent his childhood in India. He published his first three novels while still at Oxford; after working for the British Council in Italy, Greece, Egypt, Finland and Japan, he resigned to devote himself to writing. His most recent novel, *The ant colony*, was published in 1991. He lives in London.

D.F. LEWIS was born in 1948, and has two grown-up children. Since leaving Lancaster University he has worked for an insurance company. His work has appeared in magazines in Britain and America, and has been anthologised in both *Year's Best Horror Stories* and *Best New Horror*.

DAVID MILNES was born in 1954, and began writing in 1976. He lives in Peterborough.

ANNIE MURRAY was born in 1961. She won the 1991 *She*/Granada TV Short Story Competition, and is at work on her first novel. She has three small children, and lives in Birmingham.

MANINI NAYAR has won a prize in a short story competition organised by *Stand* magazine. She lives in South Bend, Indiana.

JOHN RIZKALLA is of Anglo-Egyptian parentage. He went to school in Cairo, and to university in Manchester. He worked in France for three years. His stories have been published in *Encounter*, *The New Review* and *Winter's Tales*; his novel, *The Jericho garden*, was published by the Bodley Head in 1988.

NAVTEJ SARNA was born in 1957. After graduating from Delhi University he joined the Indian Foreign Service, and has served in Moscow and Poland. He has written for leading Indian newpapers, and a short story by him has been broadcast on the BBC's World Service.

KEN SMITH was born in Yorkshire in 1938, and has worked as a barman, as a BBC reader and as writer-in-residence at Wormwood Scrubs. His books of poems include *The poet reclining*, *Terra* and *Wormwood*.

HENRIETTA SOAMES has had stories published in various magazines and on radio. She lives in East London.

DAVID STEPHENSON was born in 1947 and lives in Sunderland. His first collection of stories, *Independence Day*, was published by Iron Press in 1988. He is working on a novel.

JONATHAN STEFFEN teaches at Heidelberg University, and is a regular contributor to the *London Magazine*.

D.J. TAYLOR's books include the novels *Great Eastern land* and *Real life* and a critical study, *A vain conceit*. He lives in London.

JAMES THURLBY is a journalist and writer, a number of whose stories have appeared in the *London Magazine*.

JONATHAN TREITEL's novel *The Red Cabbage Café* was published by Bloomsbury. Another novel, *Emma Smart*, and a collection of stories are due in 1992. He lives in London.

MAX VON DER GRÜN was born in Bayreuth in 1926, and spent three years in America as a prisoner-of-war. He worked as a coalminer from 1951 to 1964, since when he has been a freelance writer.

PER WASTBERG is one of Sweden's leading novelists.